CAVEMAN POLITICS

CAVEMAN POLITICS

Jay Atkinson

Breakaway Books
New York City
1997

ACKNOWLEDGEMENTS

Special thanks to Garth Battista, for his unwavering enthusiasm for this project and for his sense of humor. I also want to express my appreciation to attorneys Randy Reis of Abramson, Reis & Brown in Manchester, New Hampshire, and Doug Wood of Hall, Dickler, Kent, Friedman & Wood in New York. If it wasn't for them, I'd be selling this book on some street corner. I am grateful to Ron Hutson of the Boston *Globe* and Dan Warner of the *Eagle-Tribune* for helping me break in as a journalist. Also, my thanks to Dr. William Coughlin of the University of Massachusetts Lowell, as well as Lisa Mahoney, Veronica Gadbois, Klaus Trelby, Kevin Gillis, and Dave Driscoll for bringing me out of the darkness into the age of computers. And finally, warm regards to all my rugby teammates over the years, especially the University of Florida 1982 state championship club, and Amoskeag Rugby Football Club of Manchester, New Hampshire. You are my brothers.

Caveman Politics

ISBN: 1-55821-565-4

Library of Congress Catalog Card Number: 97-70459

Published by BREAKAWAY BOOKS
P.O. Box 1109
Ansonia Station
New York, NY 10023
(212) 595-2216

Distributed by Lyons & Burford

FIRST EDITION

For Jim and Lois,
my parents

Everything begins with inhale and exhale, and never ends . . . and I remember having lived among dead moments, now deathless because of my remembrance, among people now dead, having been a part of the flux which is now only a remembrance, of myself and this earth, a street I was crossing and the people I saw walking in the opposite direction, automobiles going away from me. Saxons, Dorts, Maxwells, and the streetcars and trains, the horses and wagons, and myself, a small boy, crossing a street, alive somehow, going somewhere.

—William Saroyan, "Resurrection of a Life"

1

After playing rugby I always slept like I was dead, in the inky black void with no future and not even a dim recollection of the past. The morning after the Tampa game, NASA launched an unmanned rocket at four fifty-two. It rattled every window in the house, Loretta said later, booming over us like all hell was tearing loose. I never flinched. But when I heard the sweet *thump* of the newspaper against the front door, I was awake. A bicycle rolled across the lawn, past my window.

The clock said six fifteen. I lifted the sheet and glanced at Loretta as I got out of bed. She was very narrow, brown and freckled, with fine slender legs and long arms. In the wintertime there aren't many eligible women in Cocoa Beach—none that my roommate Surfer John and I haven't bonked, or at least tried to—and I was lucky to have her. She was a new face with no local history, an itinerant nurse in the way that I was a loosely affiliated newspaperman, in the way that almost everybody in Florida was a temporary something-or-other. "Everything is temporary," Surfer said. "Even insanity."

His bed hadn't been slept in. The last I had seen of him the night before, Surfer John was going through his peculiar mating ritual with Tina, the barmaid from Saxophone Joe's. He took his shirt off and had Loretta write TANGY across his chest with her lipstick.

"Tangy?" I asked.

Surfer nodded his blond head, smiling with huge white teeth. He thrust out his chest and strutted between the cocktail tables.

"Tonight I am tangy for Tina," he said. "You, of all people, should know that, Dolan. Keen observer of human nature that you are." Then he climbed up on the bar and performed the haka, a Maori war dance used by rugby teams in New Zealand to intimidate the opposition. Tina loved it.

The newspaper bounced onto the lawn and I looked both ways before I ventured outside in my underwear. The grass in our yard is an ingenious mix of tiny razor blades and sharpened twigs and I got three steps out there and couldn't move, it hurt my feet so much. I bent for the paper and lost my balance, grasping the rolled-up Sunday edition, toes dug in, ass hiked in the air. A car full of churchgoers drove by and I pretended to do push-ups.

I went back in and unrolled the Cocoa Beach *Post-Gazette* on my way down the hall. One of my stories was on the front page, "Group Says No to Contests," by Joe Dolan, about the chamber of commerce objection to the wet T-shirt contest at Saxophone Joe's. (They had chosen not to go with my suggested headline, "Boobs Beleaguer Businessmen," although I felt it summarized the article completely.) I had another piece inside on the citrus industry, twenty column inches on oranges and grapefruit and the local yokels who grew them, but it was the sports page I was looking for.

Loretta was lying on her face, sound asleep, and I slipped in beside her. The write-up on the rugby game was only three inches, buried at the end of the section, after the dog track and local softball results. It contained the news that the Cocoa Beach Rugby Football Club had trounced the Tampa Rugby Club, 22-9, making Cocoa Beach undefeated at the season's halfway point. John Marshall—Surfer John to his friends—had scored two tries and Steve Delong had added a try and three conversions to account for 18 of Cocoa Beach's points. *Joe Dolan* scored the other try. Seeing my name in that tiny article was better than a thousand page one bylines. American men dream of being on the sports page.

Skimming the rest of the paper, a small item on the back page caught my eye.

> MAN CHARGED IN RAPE
>
> Cocoa Beach police arrested Michael Melendez, 27, a native of Trinidad, for the sexual assault of a local woman. Police said the attack occurred early Saturday morning at Melendez's apartment.
>
> Melendez and the woman, whose name is being withheld by the *Post-Gazette,* were seen together Friday night at a local bar, according to witnesses. No other information was available.

I read the article twice and still couldn't believe it. "Holy shit," I said.

Loretta rolled over, suddenly awake. Her eyes were a bright green and her thick brown hair, streaked blond in places by the sun, cascaded over her shoulder. "What's the matter?" she asked.

"I gotta go down to the cop shop," I said, handing her the paper. "Mike's in jail."

"For what?" Loretta asked. She sat up, and read the article while I got a pair of shorts and an old rugby T-shirt out of the closet. "That's bullshit," she said, throwing the paper down on the bed. I tried to call the *Post-Gazette* but the line was busy. Reilly the night man probably had the phone off the hook to prevent late-breaking stories from disturbing his sleep. Loretta scrambled up from the bed and got dressed. "I'm going with you," she said.

Mike Melendez was the only black on the rugby team. A few guys from backwoods Florida grumbled when he came out, but Coach Van put a stop to that. "If he can play, think of him as my brother," Van said.

Mike was an art student from a prominent family. He had grown up with rugby in Port-of-Spain and made our first team easily. Once in a while his tackling was lousy and that set the good ol' boys off again, but never where Van could hear it. "Sure, he can run fast, but he's got no heart," said Steve Delong, our fullback, between spits of tobacco juice. "All them niggers can run fast."

I didn't particularly like the word but Delong had grown up in Palatka, Florida, and used it in the way that someone from Boston —like me—would say frog for the French or call an Irish guy a mick. Until I reached a certain age I thought the Polish people in my neighborhood liked to be made fun of, that continual harassment was somehow part of their heritage. None of it is very pretty, but it's the way people are. Mostly we stick to our own, in smaller and smaller groups, until it's just you, by yourself.

On the ride to the police station in Loretta's jeep we crossed the brackish water of the intracoastal, passing over three small islands that stand between Cocoa Beach proper and the mainland. Below us were some shacks and a decrepit fish camp. Black families lived in the shacks and black men, most of them skinny and stooped and gray haired, fished or sold bait at the camp. Things were quiet this early in the morning, but there were a few fishermen dangling lines in the water and one man, on a dock by himself, pissing into the channel. He looked up at us when we rumbled overhead and nodded with great solemnity.

To find most of the blacks in Cocoa Beach you have to travel about a mile inland, over the causeway that takes you off the spit. After the long stretch of open water the land starts running underneath you as marsh, scrub, then a few palm trees and the first row of unpainted shacks, fanning out toward several acres of federal tract housing and more junked cars and abandoned refrigerators than the county knows what to do with. The black neighborhood even has its own post office, and a separate business district, the black barber, lawyer, and dentist.

The police station is located on this side of town. As we drove toward it, groups of men, up early in the rising heat, stopped talking and swung their heads in our direction for a moment. They quickly dismissed us and went back to drinking beer from paper sacks and smoking their cigarettes, the butts strewn about their feet. The surgeon general wasn't making any house calls around here. The day would take its course—and a couple of white kids in an open car weren't about to disturb them and their doings.

Three Civil War cannons surrounded the police station. We drove around back to the parking lot and went inside to look for a cop I knew, Malkin, the desk sergeant, who always handled questions when I called for the paper.

The front desk was deserted when Loretta and I went in and they had the air conditioner on the meat locker setting. The two-way radio growled with static and the garbled voices of the officers on patrol. In the back room, through an open door, I saw a uniformed man seated at a table, his feet up, reading a magazine. Someone radioed in with a loud squawk but the man didn't budge. The call came in again and the man strode to the console, still carrying his magazine and trailing the smell of cigarettes and coffee. It was Malkin.

"Sergeant, can you tell me—"

Malkin stopped me with a wave of his hand and picked up the microphone. He was a squat, stocky man, with a pockmarked face and thick black hair on his forearms and sprouting from beneath his collar. He wore a gold signet ring on the hand that held the microphone and a gold rope chain around his neck. He disgorged a jumble of code words and numbers into the microphone and after listening for a response, abruptly signed off.

"What can I do for the press this morning?" he asked, smiling at me from behind his narrowed black eyes. "I don't imagine you're here for my life story."

"Fascinating as that may be, no, I wanna see Mike Melendez—arrested yesterday afternoon."

Malkin picked up a clipboard and glanced at it. "I got seventeen prisoners. What's he in for?"

"Some kind of assault charge, I think."

He flipped the page, and then ran his fingers along a receding hairline. "Okay, the rapist. Yeah, I got him, but nobody can go in except his lawyer. And he don't want a lawyer at this point because he says he didn't do it."

"I'm not here to interview him or anything, it's just a visit."

"It doesn't matter. His mother couldn't get in," Malkin said. "The arraignment is tomorrow and he's not on the bail and bond list because of the charges. You can't go in."

The speed with which Mike Melendez had been tried and convicted of a sex crime amazed me. For the police, it was obvious the equation went black guy + white girl = forced sexual intercourse. It didn't matter that this girl had picked Mike up in a barroom in front of forty or fifty witnesses. Already he was *Mike Melendez, rapist*. Another cop, a muscular, red-headed guy, entered the squad room and reached in a box on the counter for a doughnut. He fished one out and began squeezing it, the jelly oozing between his fingers.

"Nothing happens on Sunday," Malkin continued. "No bail. No appearances. Nothing. Even the niggers know that."

He used the term very casually, in front of me, the other cop and Loretta, and our silence lent respect to his ignorance and somehow formed a covenant between us. I should have corrected him on the spot but in those few indecisive seconds I had, by default, joined the posse out chasing the nigger rapist, riding hard through the sagebrush with the rest of the vigilantes. Something turned cold in the pit of my stomach.

"Mike Melendez is no rapist," I said, arguing half of the point.

"That girl took him home last night. I saw it. I was right there."

"Then your friend needs a lawyer as much as anything," said Malkin, already tired of the conversation. He rustled his magazine and tapped his signet ring against the edge of the counter. "There's a list on the wall there." He walked off from us to the back room.

Loretta turned to look at the list of lawyers and the other cop, who had squeezed the doughnut into a shapeless blob, leaned on the counter for a moment admiring her ass. The nickel-plated badge over his pocket identified him as Phillips. He was a young cop, the bodybuilder type, his red hair cropped very short and his uniform sleeves rolled up tightly over his biceps. Officer Phillips had small, almost girlish bones in his hands and wrists, stretch marks on his arms, and a blotched, puffy face from taking too many steroids. He read the faded slogan on my T-shirt—SOLVE IT WITH VIOLENCE, PLAY RUGBY—and grinned at me. It happens all the time. The muscleheads at my gym see a rugby shirt and say, "Yeah, rugby. I wanna play. I'd kill people out there," but they never show up. Hand them a rugby ball and they would piss their little bikini pants. All they want to do is stand around with their musclehead buddies and look at themselves in the mirror.

"You play rugby, huh?" asked Phillips. "That's a rough game." He shook his head. "You're kind of a little guy. You should try some bodybuilding first. Now that's a sport."

Bodybuilding isn't a sport, it's a show. And bodybuilders are a bunch of drug addicts. I didn't say anything, only wished Officer Phillips another ten years of steroid use and an eventual devastating bout with liver, heart or brain damage. That would knock him down a few pegs. He'd wind up in a hospital bed somewhere, a mass of tubes plugged in his withered arms, saying, "I'm small now, and I'm afraid."

But today he was in the mood for trouble and he tried something else to get me going. "I went out to pick up your pal Melendez yesterday after we got the complaint," he said, nodding his head. "The girl came in with her white trash boyfriend and filed it. So we get out to the perp's address and he's wearing a silk robe. One of those short ones that barely covered his balls, and he's playing some jungle music on the stereo. A regular stud."

I didn't say anything, and he kept on.

"He wasn't expecting us, that's for sure," Phillips said. "We took him in like that, too. Gave him a screen test on the way when he wouldn't shut up. It was hilarious, you wanna know the truth."

No response from me.

"You ever seen Melendez's place? He has beads hanging in the doorway and a zebra skin on the wall. Like some kind of fucking witch doctor. But you shoulda seen his face when we read him his rights. His chin just about hit the ground."

Loretta came up behind me and put her hand against my back. When she did, she brushed the notebook I always carry in my pocket.

"Yup, Melendez really thought he was hot shit," continued Phillips. "Now he's just another spook we got in the tank, crying he didn't do it."

I took the notebook out of my pocket and began writing, in my own shorthand, turning the pages over. Phillips went pale, arching his neck to see what I was putting down. I knew he couldn't make sense out of it.

"You said 'spook,' didn't you?" I asked, scribbling away.

"Wait a second. Hey! What are you doing?" Phillips said, the veins standing out in his neck. "I didn't mean it like that."

I scribbled for a few more moments and put the notebook away. "You should be careful what you say to a reporter."

"I never said any of that," exclaimed the policeman.

"Any of what?"

"Any of what you got in your notebook."

"How do you know what I have in there?"

Phillips shook his head. "Whatever you got, I didn't say it."

It was gratifying to be a journalist, loved by the people. I slipped my arm around Loretta's waist and steered her toward the exit. "You won't really know until tomorrow, when the paper comes out." Loretta pushed on the heavy glass door, the air outside like a furnace. We turned the corner and I glimpsed Phillips still standing there at the front desk, a constipated look on his face.

Loretta gunned the jeep through the parking lot. It's true what they say about the pen being mightier than the sword. I just take one out and pretty soon I'm waving it around like the Three Musketeers.

"Where we headed?" Loretta yelled, keeping to the center line on Orange Boulevard, the warehouses and discount tire stores blurring on either side.

"To see a guy over on Fourth Street." I gave her some directions.

Loretta glanced at her watch. "Now? It's barely eight o'clock."

"Those rednecks will torture Mike half to death if we don't get him out of there." I explained what a screen test was.

Once when I was arrested after a bar fight, they loaded all four participants into the same cruiser, our hands cuffed behind our backs. As soon as we got rolling some genius started spitting at the cops through the wire mesh that separated the front and back seats. There was lot of yelling and commotion and the cops couldn't tell which one of us was doing it and didn't care.

"You a movie star, pal?" the driver shouted. "You a bunch of movie stars back there?"

He slammed on the brakes and the four of us crashed into the heavy wire grille—"There's your screen test"—bloodying noses, cracking one guy's front teeth. Nobody spit after that.

One of the cops thought I did it. Even though Surfer followed us to the station and posted my bail right away, they decided to have a little fun with me. The county jail was upstairs, guys serving a few weeks for neglect or drunk driving, and they sent me for a strip search and assigned me a bunk in the dormitory. Two guys started hassling me as soon as the big metal door clicked shut.

"Fresh meat, Jerry," the tall crazy-looking guy said to his companion.

Jerry sat down on the bunk across from me, playing with an unlit cigarette between his fingers. He had massive tattooed arms and a bulbous nose and one of those squashed-down prison faces that meant he got arrested whenever he showed up on a street corner.

"Gimme what you got," he said, raising a finger.

"Huh?"

"Gimme whatever you got, cigarettes, money, like that, and things will go smooth," said Jerry. "Isn't that right, Baxter?"

His associate smiled with all eight teeth. "That's right."

"Don't worry about him," Jerry said, watching my eyes. "I just say go and Baxter goes. He follows instructions very well." He made a brief gesture in the direction of the other, mostly black men residing in the dormitory. "It's these niggers that don't behave. But they don't stick together. Goddamned nigger just as soon cut his own mother's throat as one of us. It don't make no difference."

Over in the corner a knot of blacks was gathered around, taunting an Elvis impersonator who had also just arrived in the dormitory. He had the thick blue-black hair, the trademark sideburns and sunglasses, and the fringed leather jumpsuit of the young Elvis. Holding one of the striped jailhouse pillows across his lap, his eyes shifted back and forth among his tormentors. They jeered at him, grabbing for his sunglasses and crucifix, shouting out requests and roughing the kid up just a little bit.

"Lookee there," Jerry said. "Even ol' Elvis ain't safe no more. It's a fucking shame."

He was right about that. Elvis was made to stand on top of a bunk, the sweat pouring down his face like it did in his old shows, giving us the pelvic flutter and shaky right leg. He tried to sing, but he was so scared nothing would come out. His audience howled, pelting him with disposable lighters and bits of soap.

"Give us them ly-rics, boy," one of his fans insisted, between fits of laughter. "Put a damn voice on it."

The greatest lounge singer who ever lived tried again. He wet his lips and worked his jaw, sweat flying from his brow and the rattail ends of his hair. Jutting out his hip, he struck a characteristic pose. The lump in his throat slid up and down and he raised his fists in the air, his mouth twisted in that familiar sneer. Loose and expectant, his audience swayed at his feet.

"Do'em all those wild-loving things," called a man in a knit cap.

A crackling tuneless shriek escaped Elvis, and that was it. The men around him erupted with laughter. They threw him to the floor and commenced kicking him and beating him with their fists, in a light special way that wouldn't break anything or even bruise him. It was just for fun, but nobody told Elvis. He tried to scream and two of them held a pillow over his face. His leather fringe slapped the concrete floor as he thrashed about.

"You don't do any singing now, do you?" Jerry asked me.

We heard a key in the lock and the heavy bolt was drawn back. In a flurry everyone returned to his bunk, except Elvis, lying in a heap on the floor. A cop stuck his head through the open door, checked his clipboard to be accurate, and called my name. I shrugged at Jerry and his sidekick and went out. My incarceration was over.

Driving down the boulevard, the early sun tangled in the ends of Loretta's flying hair, I went through that memory the way a magician passes a hatpin through his forearm—in a blink, presto! it was done. And although I was talking about my screen test, I wound up thinking about Elvis. What stayed in my head was the idol of millions beat up on the jailhouse floor and those convicts laughing in their bunks. It didn't matter that the real Elvis was dead and the guy they had was probably arrested for child abuse or something—that was no way to treat the King.

Loretta swung the jeep onto Fourth Street and downshifted, bringing us by a few stores and then a row of well-kept cottages set back from the pavement. A little farther on, one of the cottages was squared off by a picket fence and displayed a small sign that read ALOYSIUS P. TIMMONS, ATTORNEY-AT-LAW. He was a black lawyer with a reputation for being tenacious, thorough, and affordable. When Loretta pulled over and cut the engine the neighborhood fell silent and the doors to the jeep creaked in the still air. The palm trees lining the road were blighted by something, split brown at the center and ravaged, as if by lightning.

We walked up onto the porch and Loretta pulled the bell. I peered through a curtained window at the interior of the house, the furnishings gray in the early-morning dimness. Nobody was stirring. Loretta tried the bell again and I shifted for another look, up the hallway toward the back of the house.

Suddenly there was a woman's face behind the glass, the color of tea with milk, floating there like an apparition. I ducked back near Loretta and the door opened.

"Hi," Loretta said to the woman, who stood in the doorway wearing a gray cotton suit and high heels. "Is Attorney Timmons here?"

The woman nodded and showed us in. She was in her fifties, tall and fierce looking with a model's cheekbones and full purple lips. The house had a strange, slightly unpleasant odor. It reminded me of grammar school.

The tea-colored woman looked at us for a moment and pointed her long arm toward an office across the hall from the living room. "Go on in and I'll get Mr. Timmons. He's right now having his breakfast."

She disappeared up the hallway and Loretta and I crossed the carpet, which was damp from a washing, and went into the tiny cramped office. Morning light came through the blinds and glinted off the glass fronts of the diplomas and other certificates hanging on the wall. There was no telephone in sight. A blotter, an ink-stand, and a ceramic egg were all that was on the desk. Behind it was a rolling chair—the only chair in the room—giving the impression Lawyer Timmons did business quickly, acting more like a judge in his own house. A worn spot on the carpet in front of his desk marked the place where I was required to stand.

I reached out and closed my hand on the smooth polished egg. One end was sliced off to make it stand up, and when I turned it over, I saw that it wasn't an egg after all but a miniature ceramic watermelon, dark green with wavy black stripes, and little gem-stones instead of seeds. Footsteps came down the hall and I replaced it on the desk.

Lawyer Timmons filled the door frame, his bathrobe reaching almost to the floor over a pair of old cotton pajamas, frayed at the cuffs. His face was lined and judicious, drooping a little at the jowls, and his eyes, above a pencil mustache and broad flat nose, looked out somewhat bloodshot from the sides of his head with great calmness and rectitude.

He cleared his throat, summarizing the situation, and went behind his desk. Upon sitting, he picked up the ceramic watermel-on and placed it exactly where I had taken it from. I looked down at my feet and noticed I was standing dead center on the worn place in the carpet.

"All right, now. What could be wrong with you people?" Lawyer

Timmons asked. It was a curious choice of words. His voice was quiet, befitting the early hour, but it had a deep resonance and easily filled the room.

"I have a friend in jail on a rape charge and he needs a lawyer."

Mr. Timmons had already guessed that Mike was black and cut to the heart of things. "Was the complainant a white girl?"

"Yes. But she took him home from the bar and everybody saw it."

"Everybody white saw it, you mean. What they did, in fact, see might very well change when it gets to a courtroom." The wheels squeaked on the bottom of the chair and Lawyer Timmons rolled a little way from the desk onto the wood floor. "I'm not interested in this sort of case."

The woman came to the door wearing a jaunty pillbox hat and attached veil, white gloves to her elbows. "I don't suppose you'll come to church and pray this boy out of jail," she said to Mr. Timmons. "Why don't you try practicing law on him?"

Lawyer Timmons made a barely perceptible noise, something like a sigh, through his nostrils. He rolled back to the desk and picked up the little watermelon, using the rough end to abrade the calluses on his other palm, which was white compared to the blackness of his hands. The gemstones must have been sharp because shavings of skin fell onto the desk blotter.

"I knew a good lawyer once—white man from Georgia," he said. "His advice was never take a case you can't win and never represent a client who can't pay."

"You don't live by that," the woman in the doorway said, pulling up her gloves.

Mr. Timmons put the watermelon in its place and smoothed the lapels of his bathrobe. "I have kept to the second half of his advice," he said. "I take only those clients who can afford my services."

"You'll be paid," I said.

The woman cocked her hat over one eye and left the room. The screen door slammed, then a car engine turned over, caught and drove away. I recited the facts of Mike's case and Lawyer Timmons sanded his calluses without a word. His was either an encompassing intellect or an abiding indifference, I couldn't tell which. When I had finished—including the bit about Officer Phillips and the screen test—the tall pajama-clad lawyer said, "I charge fifty dollars an hour for criminal work and there's no telling how long this will take."

Lawyers always look down at their hands when they mention fees, no doubt smiling to themselves about how mechanics and carpenters make a living. Mr. Timmons was no exception. A cat entered the room on silent feet, tiger-striped gray and black, tail in the air. It went between my legs, then under the desk and out the other side.

"Mike won't mind paying, so long as he wins," I said.

Lawyer Timmons stood up, clearing his robe. "Mike Melendez is already a loser," he said. "It only remains to be seen how badly and at what final result."

We were shepherded to the front door. Lawyer Timmons opened it, illuminating the dark moist carpet of the hall. "How can you tell he's gonna lose?" I asked. "You haven't even talked to anyone yet."

"I've talked to you. And I know your friend is in for a certain kind of hell," Lawyer Timmons replied, squinting into the sun that rested just above the shattered palm trees across the street. The cat avoided the wet carpet and came to sit beside his leg, in a patch of sunlight. "It didn't take any school or book learning to teach me that."

"There must be something you can do—seeing Mike didn't rape her."

"If I ever have to stand up in open court with this case, I'll use every bit of lawyering I ever knew or heard about," said Mr. Timmons. He stooped a long way to scratch the cat between the ears. "If Mr. Melendez is asked to leave the country and never come back, it'll be cause for celebration."

"Won't it come down to her word against his?" I asked.

"Yes, except only our side will be restricted by the truth. People will swear on the Good Book they have seen and heard things they could not possibly have seen or heard." He looked straight at Loretta. "She wouldn't want any nice folks to think she'd slept with a nigger and liked it."

Loretta didn't blink. "What can we do?" she asked.

"Nothing much, Mizz," said Lawyer Timmons. "Except maybe find out who filed the complaint and get her to drop the charges, although I'm not holding out much hope for that."

We went onto the porch, the cat following behind us. "Thanks a lot," I said. Lawyer Timmons nodded and stuck out an impressive hand for me to shake, huge and bony. He scratched the screen, calling the cat back inside. "President Lincoln," he said. The cat shot back into the hall just ahead of the closing door.

It wasn't until we were on the causeway heading back to the beach, racing over the flat shining water—it was still only nine o'clock in the morning—that Loretta said what was on her mind.

"Are you sure he didn't do it?"

I looked over and saw her jaw was tight and her hand shook a little holding the wheel. "Sure I'm sure. Mike wouldn't do something like that."

Loretta was grim. "I hope not." There was an old rock 'n' roll song blaring over the radio. Below us, graceful white birds lifted off the intracoastal, tearing at refuse, and Jimi Hendrix went on about shooting his old lady.

2

Near the courthouse, almost everything took on significance and a pronounced air of ceremony. The gardener made perfect military turns with his electric lawn mower and people on the sidewalk straightened their shoulders and spoke in hushed voices when they passed by. Looming magnificently above the street, four stories of pink Georgia marble, was the home of the county superior court—the Hall of Sorrow they called it, polished like a mirror and topped with a statue of Blind Justice holding her scales.

I ran the jeep to the curbstone out front and turned off the engine. At quarter past nine on Monday morning the long stairway leading to the courthouse doors was empty, then two sheriffs came outside, escorting a black man in chains and leg irons whose bald head was as smooth as the courthouse walls. The prisoner was reduced to an awkward shuffle by his impediments and they half-carried him down the stairs.

"Now tell me, what was I gonna do?" implored the prisoner in an agitated voice. "That little jitterbug up and shot me. It was two months I felt good enough to hit him with that tire iron."

The sheriffs remained impassive and signaled for the county van that was parked a short way down on the other side of the street. The van swooped across and a third sheriff got out and unlocked the rear door for the prisoner. "The judge say the computer don't be liking my numbers. Man, things go so fast in that room, I'm on roller skates. And that was never me in Palm Bay. I don't rob no Jiffy Marts. There ain't nothing in them."

The prisoner stooped down, gathering his chains, and allowed himself to be hoisted by two of the sheriffs into the van. He dropped onto a metal bench and the chains slithered between his legs and pooled on the floor at his feet. Some of them spilled over the edge and prevented the sheriffs from closing the door for a moment. "Shee-it, you been on me so long now you think to do it right," the prisoner said, retrieving his chains. "My lawyer say I can get me an ed-u-cation in there but I say listen, man, I'm going to jail, not Yale. I been *indicted*, not invited." They closed the door on him and he went on talking to himself, muffled inside the van.

All the sheriffs were white. The driver, the smallest of the three, said, "I swear, if there were only two of them left, they'd kill each other."

"We lock 'em up," said one of the guards, his face like pie dough, chewing on a toothpick, "for that very reason."

The sheriffs chuckled, and drew out their nightsticks and then walked around front to get in the van. "He got ten years?" the driver asked, shaking his head.

The sheriff with the toothpick snapped his fingers. "Just like that."

I used to cover the court beat for the *Post-Gazette* and when the first arraignments let out at ten o'clock, I recognized a lot of the characters descending the stairs. Ahead of everyone were thin-faced lawyers, sweating in their tailored suits, anxious to escape from one client to get the meter running on another. They swung briefcases to clear the way and sprinted to their car phones. Petty thieves, wife-beaters, and other degenerates came next, released on low bail or recognizance, some humbled for the first time since childhood, but most confident of being lost in the system, unprosecuted, or dismissed. A few of the victims trailed behind them, clutched by family members, bewildered and angry. Then stenographers and bailiffs on recess, fumbling for their cigarettes. Law students and messengers and gallery haunts. The whole sorry lot.

At last Michael Melendez came through the ornate doors of the courthouse and trudged down the steps. He was tall and broad-shouldered, almost symmetrical, with an angular, high-cheek-boned face. Eyes downcast, his hands in the pockets of the same jeans he had been wearing Friday night, Mike stood frowning when I headed him off.

"Oh, good morning, Joe," he said. "Nice to see you."

"Where's Mr. Timmons?" I asked, looking over his shoulder.

"He's inside arguing with the district attorney for a charge of simple assault," Mike said, as if he was discussing someone else's case besides his own. He looked tired, his large, almond-shaped eyes low in their sockets. "However, I'm afraid Mr. Rasterree has already decided that a rape conviction would be more politically advantageous."

He managed a weak laugh. Michael Melendez had a funny way of speaking sometimes—the Queen's English to be sure, measured and precise, but like it was being spoken in translation, by an interpreter perhaps, somehow devoid of idiom and colloquial reference.

"So what happened the other night?" I asked.

Mike looked hurt for a second, then his eyes narrowed. "Are you covering this for the paper?"

I put up my hands like he was pointing a gun at me. "Nothing like that. I'm trying to help, that's all."

"Sorry. I'm a little shook up," Mike said. We turned and walked down the rest of the courthouse steps. "Friday night, when we were all at Saxophone Joe's, I met a girl and bought her a few drinks."

"I saw that much."

"Her name is Sherri Hogg. We danced, talked, and went out for something to eat afterward," Mike said, shifting his eyes around. He had a nice deep cut on his nose. "Then I asked her back to my place. In the morning, we went out to breakfast and everything was fine."

"Did you run into anyone?"

Mike shook his head. "No."

He glanced up and down the sidewalk. "I expected to see some of the other guys this morning. All for one, one for all."

"They must be working," I said, a little too quickly. "Surfer wanted to come, but there's a launch this week and he's putting a lot of hours in."

We were both glum. I didn't tell Mike that news of the charges against him had spread through the team and they were calling him "therapist"—the rapist. For some it was their usual gallows humor but for others there was a streak of real nastiness in it. I felt myself standing straight at that moment, stiff and uncomfortable, and it occurred to me that Mike Melendez and I weren't friends. I had gone out of my way to be *friendly,* maybe too far. But I didn't really know him. It was strange. I had never in my life known any black people.

"Thanks for coming to the police station," Mike said, breaking the silence. "And for hiring Mr. Timmons. God, he's expensive, though. I don't have the money."

"Can't your family give you some?"

"I'm not going to tell them," Mike said. He was already thin and haggard, spent by his weekend in jail.

"It's gonna do a job on you if you don't get it cleared up quick," I said.

"They won't let me talk to her. And if I can't talk to her, she won't drop the charges," said Mike. He looked panic-stricken for a moment. A black workman passing by on the sidewalk acknowledged him, gave him the nod, but he didn't seem to notice. "I'm guilty of nothing. I don't know why she'd do this to me. She wanted it."

"I'll go talk to her. Where does she live?"

"I don't know. Off Orange Boulevard somewhere. She said a trailer park."

We shook hands. "I'll take Loretta and check it out. You should just go home."

Mike indicated the courthouse. "That's a scary place." He licked the edge of his trimmed black mustache. "They talk about you like you're not even there. I didn't get to say a thing."

A slightly built man in an expensive suit came outside, accompanied by a young woman carrying some files, her eyeglasses low on her nose. The man had a full head of wavy yellow hair and thick yellow eyebrows drawn close together over a sharp pair of hunter's blue eyes. "That's the man," Mike said. "Hulic Rasterree."

The D.A. conferred with his girl on the landing, checked his watch and sent her back into the courthouse for something. While she flew up the stairs, Rasterree took out a microcassette recorder and began dictating into it. "I'm going to tell him," said Mike. "This whole thing is crazy."

I held his arm. "You better talk to Mr. Timmons first."

He didn't have to wait long. Lawyer Timmons was already at the landing and had joined Mr. Rasterree in conversation. He towered over the district attorney, brown-faced and serene, even more impressive without his bathrobe and pajamas and I remembered being impressed then. It was hot and Lawyer Timmons handed Mr. Rasterree an attaché while he struggled for an instant to remove his jacket. Mike, amazed at this familiarity between them, shook off my grip and bounded up the stairs to the landing.

"I want to say something now," Mike announced, startling the two lawyers. "Sherri Hogg is a complete liar." His voice rose with excitement. "She insisted we make love all over the apartment. It was her idea."

Lawyer Timmons recovered from his surprise and stood between his client and Mr. Rasterree. "Enough," he said in that low resonant voice. "You'll only get in more trouble. Go home."

"How can I get in more trouble? She's actually saying I raped her, the little tramp," said Mike. He sidestepped Lawyer Timmons and got close to the district attorney. "Mr. Rasterree, this is madness. I forced nothing on Sherri Hogg. If I can't defend myself—"

Lawyer Timmons grabbed Mike by the shoulders and spun him around. Mike lost his balance on the lower stair and I caught him by the waist and steadied him. "I'll defend you in court, if you give me the chance," said Lawyer Timmons. He straightened his tie and descended to us. "Are you looking for new assault charges?" he asked. Then he addressed me for the first time. "Get him out of here."

It unfolded like a car wreck, something you watched without comment from the midst of an enormous calm. I led Mike down the stairs. Hulic Rasterree, for his part, witnessed the episode with one eyebrow cocked in amusement, a faint smile across his fleshy lips. He had just seen heedlessness and a compulsion to anger. And although he must have been dancing a jig inside, he was careful to betray nothing in those predatory blue eyes. It looked like an easy conviction.

"They're crucifying me," Mike said. "I can't believe that little bitch is ruining my life."

He broke away from me again when we reached the sidewalk. "Let me give you a ride," I called after him.

"No," he said, waving his fist. "Leave me the fuck alone."

Hunching over, Mike strode away, his hands shoved in his pockets. I had always imagined he walked to a calypso beat, a talented man, artist and athlete, with the buoyancy that comes with that. But now he merely shuffled, his head bent, casting sly distrustful looks as he passed along the storefronts. There were plenty of other black men downtown who walked the same way.

A burst of laughter from the courthouse steps drew my attention. Mr. Rasterree and Lawyer Timmons, an almost comic difference in size between them, still conferred on the landing, hovered over by Mr. Rasterree's assistant, who in the radiant light surrounding the two men hardly seemed there. I climbed into the jeep. Lawyer Timmons had just said something witty and the district attorney clutched the arm of his colleague in a patronizing gesture and brayed, revealing his shiny gold bridgework. Except for looking at their watches repeatedly, they could have been a pair of old friends meeting anywhere, on vacation perhaps, chatting about restaurants and the local hospitality. The innocence or guilt of Michael Melendez was as obtuse a concern as gravity or what they might be having for dinner the next night. Things would work themselves out either way. It nearly made me ill. Just then a gap occurred, and I eased into the traffic.

Being a reporter for the *Post-Gazette* is not backbreaking work. There's barely any supervision and a lot of funky hours, and I drove on to the office in no particular hurry. The newspaper occupied three large rooms above a surf shop and an adjoining garage that housed the presses, the photo lab, the loading dock for our "fleet" of four trucks, and the circulation office. Retired folks in shorts and golf sweaters and old beachcomber types haggled at the counter over their subscription price, tracking in sand. Surfers leaned their boards in the corner and bent like wild-haired monks over the classified ad forms, trying to sell their cassette players or VWs in order to make it through another winter.

This time of year, the sea is glassy and flat to the horizon with a series of translucent waves about a hundred yards out, kicking up like blue-gray porcelain tipped with white froth. When they weren't in the water or on the beach, or plying some get-rich-quick scheme to squeeze a week's pay from half a day's work, the surfers were hanging around the circulation office. They would sell everything they owned down to their last pair of baggies (their T-shirts said SURF NAKED), mortgage their souls to the devil himself (if he promised a nice break in hell), before they would part with a surfboard.

Ah, Florida. On the map of the U.S., it looks like some old geezer who couldn't reel in his tool. Where the bars are filled on Saturday night and all the Baptist churches first thing Sunday morning. Nobody seems to work very hard, which sets the perfect tone for life at the *Post-Gazette*.

I left the jeep in a yellow zone, stuck an old parking ticket on the windshield, and went up to the office. At the top of the stairs I met the sports editor, Ross Donleavey, carrying a set of golf clubs. They jangled against the wall and Donleavey reached for his toupee and made a light-fingered adjustment.

"If it isn't Joe Dolan, legend," he said, swinging his golf clubs to the other shoulder. "Feel like a round of golf this morning?"

"I just cannot wear lime green shirts and yellow pants, sorry," I said, indicating Donleavey's outfit.

Someone behind him in the newsroom snickered and Donleavey's face got red, contrasted to the unnatural brown of his hair. "Your rugby boys are getting out of control," he said. "I see on page thirty-two that one of your pals was charged in a sexual assault. There must be a lot of pent-up aggression there."

He spoke as if his mind was a complex, mysterious place, but there wasn't much unusual going on there. "You know, Ross, you're working here because of analysis like that," I said, pumping his fleshy hand. The temptation to push him down the stairs, golf clubs and all, was overwhelming. "I don't blame you for taking the rest of the day off. You must be tired."

Donleavey pulled his hand away and left without another word, bumping down the stairs. From above, his hairpiece was off center. He raised his shoulder to balance the golf bag and swatted at his toupee, trying to shoo it into place.

I detected the slight smell of lilacs and my boss, Maxine Olnecki-Smyth, the day editor, came and stood by my side. "There goes a great writer," she said as Ross struggled with the door below. "What that man can do with a tractor-pulling contest moves me to tears. He's a poet."

"But he's no me," I said.

Maxine smiled with well-kept teeth and swept a mass of thick auburn hair from her neck. "The world is starving for ordinary Joes," she said. We laughed, and Maxine dug an elbow into my ribs. Then she swung around to face the newsroom. I was her favorite, but she tried to be discreet.

"For Donleavey, the paper is like a giant high school that never ends," I said.

"Except he was eighteen in high school and now he's sixteen in life," said Maxine.

My repartee with Maxine was one of the best parts of the job. She was a fine editor, and as such, overqualified for the *Post-Gazette*. Graduated from Columbia and straight out of the New York literary scene, the former Maxine Olnecki of West Islip was in her midforties now, still slim and dark, the possessor of great table manners, a wardrobe of flat shoes and seersucker and an inestimable wit. She also played a fair game of tennis.

Maxine was on the fast track when a detour landed her in Cocoa Beach. At twenty-four, she was an editor at *Cosmopolitan*. By the age of thirty, Maxine had earned the position of senior editor with a big publishing house but left New York to accompany her husband, an architect, to Florida. He had been offered a job conjuring an entire town from a hundred thousand acres of swamp west of Orlando and Maxine had plans for starting her own literary magazine. Within five years, her husband's vision of utopia had collapsed under tax and zoning laws and their marriage quickly followed suit. Now her ex-husband was designing strip malls in San Diego and Maxine, divorced and childless, had exchanged all her talented young writers for Ross Donleavey and me.

I had a couple of messages at the desk, one to call Surfer and the other reminding me to pick Loretta up at two. "I'm glad you can fit working here into your schedule," Maxine said, reading over my shoulder.

"So far," I said.

Jimmy Pitochelli, the cartoonist, strolled up with his pad and showed us his latest creation. It was a gigantic rocket being launched from Cape Canaveral, blasting a hole in the sky, with the words HOPE FOR THE ENVIRONMENT written on the fuselage. Surfboards and porpoises and beach umbrellas were being tossed in its wake.

"With all the NASA junk that's been washing up on the beach," said Jimmy, "I thought this would work with the pollution editorial running on Wednesday."

Maxine took the drawing in her hands. "I like it," she said, but held it away, chewing on the inside of her lip. She did the same thing with my stories. "Give me two scientists in the foreground, two real goofballs. They're happy, congratulating each other. One's saying 'Wheee!' and the other says 'Up in smoke.' "

She handed the drawing back. Jimmy stared at it for a moment and then began sketching. The scientists appeared, a couple of nerds with black-framed glasses and protruding features, one of them waving his slide rule. Money was spilling out of their pockets and they leaned back as though drunk, cheering the spectacle.

"Now that's exactly right," Maxine said. "That's how big business and government feel about the environment. Jimmy, you captured it." She clapped the cartoonist on the back. "You're brilliant."

"Wait until you see the ideas I've got for Sunday's feature on the judicial scandal," said Jimmy. "They'll blow you away."

Maxine stood with her legs apart, feet pointed outward, like the schoolteachers I had known, her hands jammed in the shallow pockets of her toreador's coat. "Get those pencils out," she said to the cartoonist, waving him off.

Jimmy hustled to his desk and we went past a row of computer terminals where some of the reporters were composing and on to Maxine's office. She took off her coat and hung it up, revealing the network of straps and filmy undergarments she wore beneath her blouse. Then, in semiprivacy, after reaching up and tilting the blinds shut, Maxine untangled a strap or two and pulled up her pantyhose in an unladylike gesture that I loved.

"You really know how to push the buttons, Maxine," I said, referring to Jimmy's antic behavior.

"It doesn't take much to get these guys going," she said. "It's like something shiny to a crow."

I sat down and Maxine adjusted the tiny fan on her desk so it oscillated between us and then she dropped into a chair, kicked off her shoes and put her feet up. I put mine up, too.

"What's this judicial scandal all about?" I asked.

"Jimmy's not supposed to pop off about that," said Maxine, removing her earrings. She dropped them on the desk. "That's something Shirley and Walter are working on."

Shirley Kimball and Walter Dzioba were the *Post-Gazette* heavyweights, two old hands who took on most of the good stuff. That included local mayhem of a considerable measure: murder, kidnapping, bank robberies, drug-dealing clergy who abused children, and any other lurid tale that promised to sell a lot of newspapers. Shirley, with her red hair, garish makeup, and black lingerie, was the expert there. Walter favored the more technical web of deceit, an occasional three-, four-, or five-part investigative series on smelly contracts at NASA, or the corrupt politics, racketeering, usury, and systematic arson that plagued the beachfront just as they plagued every town in America. Anything that required Jimmy to come up with a colored chart or bar graph was Walter's baby. And if Shirley and Walter were working on something together, it had to be sleazy and complex, and it had to be big.

"Sure, Walter and Shirl get judicial scandals and what do you give me—orange juice features," I said. "They have editorial cartoons drawn to order and my story's lucky if you run an old Polaroid somebody found lying around. I'm telling you, it stinks."

Maxine looked at me shrewdly, the delicate lines around her mouth and opaque gray eyes showing themselves for a moment under fine taut skin. She knew I was angling for something and had to make sure I got what she wanted me to have.

"You're the one who insisted he come off hard news and go into features," said Maxine. "So don't give me that crap." She shot an elastic at me that whizzed over my head. "Just remember, everything needs work, but you can't work on everything."

"If I have to cover one more dog show, I'll kill myself. I'll put a schnauzer to my head and blow it right off."

Maxine giggled. "You should take some sleeping poodles or jump in front of a Saint Bernard."

"Tell me about this judicial scandal and I'll tell you something about the Melendez rape case," I said.

"I never heard of it."

"The Melendez case. It's been in all the papers. A black man accused of raping a white girl, a local."

"Oh, that," Maxine said, with a wave. "Shirley's on it, although she hasn't gotten very far yet. What do you know about it?"

Shirley again. She was probably in her black bra under a cloud of perfume, letting Sergeant Malkin play a game of connect-the-freckles on her chest while she read through the evidence files. What Shirley had, she put to good use.

"I know plenty. I was at the courthouse this morning for the arraignment. What's the scandal about?"

Maxine frowned and put her feet on the floor. "I'm not running the editorial desk on the barter system, Joe," she said. "Tell me what you know and Thursday you'll collect the paycheck you've no doubt become accustomed to."

It was then that I put strategy aside and sang like a canary. I went into great detail on Michael Melendez and my association with him, what I had witnessed Friday night at the bar, and my visit to Lawyer Timmons and the jailhouse. Everything except the name of the girl Mike was with. I was saving Sherri Hogg for myself.

"What's the victim's name?" asked Maxine.

"I don't know."

"Find out," Maxine said. She wrote something down on a notepad. "And give it to Shirley. I want her story even if we can't identify her."

"Why can't we?"

"Victim's rights."

"That's bullshit," I said. "What about Mike Melendez's rights? We've already published his name and he hasn't been convicted of a thing. It'll be his mug shot next. Just because he's black doesn't mean he—"

A knock came at the door. Walter Dzioba swung it wide and entered the office, a short ready man with dark skin and bloodshot eyes who walked with a limp. He was well dressed for a reporter, white duck trousers and an oxford shirt, his hair slicked back, and he was chomping on a pencil instead of his usual cigar, which he was trying to lay off. "Pardon me—," he said, interrupting. He spoke with a faint drawl, wrapped around that peculiar southern mannerliness that bordered on impertinence. "I'll come back a little later."

"No, no, Walter. Come in," said Maxine. "What is it?"

Walter shifted his eyes over to my side of the room and Maxine said, "It's all right."

"I found someone at the courthouse who'll talk to me," Walter said, in a cool professional tone, limping over to the desk. "A clerk in the judge's pool. She's saying funny business goes on with some of the criminal cases—assaults and robberies, mostly. In these rigged cases there's a pretrial review of the facts and decisions are made outside the realm of ordinary plea bargains. The source told me it's done to speed up the docket. A kind of summary justice."

"It sounds more like lynching to me," said Maxine.

Walter fished a crumpled piece of paper from his trouser pocket and scanned it. Maxine was all ears. She sat on the edge of her chair, her knees pressed together, and leaned forward like a child, hands folded in her lap. Her tiny wrinkles smoothed by her expression, she looked altogether pretty, her head cocked to one side, damp with tiny beads of perspiration on her forehead and upper lip.

"These deals that are made—which include the judge and lawyers from both sides—are actually verdicts negotiated in advance, without prior consent or knowledge of the defendants," he went on, referring to his paper. "There's been at least five such cases in the past several weeks, and four guilty verdicts, according to the source. I have some of the names. The verdicts are never announced. The trials go on as scheduled, but they go quick—charges, arguments, verdict—just like that."

"Wow," said Maxine, her gray eyes widened with interest.

"Wow, indeed," replied Walter. "But I have to tell you, Maxine, there's no hard evidence so far and there won't ever be much. These are smart people who're doing end runs on the Constitution and are well aware of it. It was just a rumor but now it's a confirmed one."

"Who's the source?" asked Maxine.

Walter looked at me again. "I want to hold off on that right now," he said. "And do some more digging first."

"Are Aloysius Timmons or Hulic Rasterree in on it?" I asked.

"Defense lawyer and assistant district attorney."

My question caught Dzioba off guard. There was a pecking order in the newsroom and I'm sure he felt himself above the sharp little beaks of junior reporters like me. On the other hand, I was in Maxine's office with my feet up on the desk, acting like I was her nephew or something. I pressed the advantage.

"Odd names," I said. "You couldn't miss them."

Maxine was silent. Dzioba stared at me—we didn't like each other much, for no particular reason—then he looked down, and said, "Rasterree is on the list, Timmons is not."

"Rasterree is prosecuting Mike's case," I said to Maxine. "He was in the courtroom this morning."

With the long slow fires of regret she felt burning inside her, Maxine had learned not to grasp at easy solutions or accept things at face value. It was what made her a good editor. "A connection between what Walter is saying and what we were talking about won't necessarily solve your friend's problem," she said, leaving the other reporter in the dark. "These wheels turn so steadily that some people get caught up in the grinder whether they deserve it or not."

Walter drew his eyebrows together and cleared his throat. "I want to get started on this," he said. "What I'm missing is someone who knows about a deal being made and doesn't like it. Someone who'll talk."

"There was a guy this morning on his way to Raifort for assaulting another guy with a tire iron," I said. "He was complaining up and down how about fast things went. I didn't catch his name, but he was convicted in the first session and it sounded like he had a long sheet."

A pause ensued. Dzioba spread the crumpled piece of paper on Maxine's desk and wrote something on it, revealing dark stains under his arms. He said thanks without looking at me.

"Will you have something for Sunday?" Maxine asked.

"I'll have a draft for you by Wednesday's deadline, somewhere around fifty inches, I think," Walter said. Then his eyes narrowed and he held his lips straight across in a tight line. "Shirley's going to have her hands full with the rape story. I'd like to handle this one alone—if you don't mind."

Dzioba had once been nominated for a Pulitzer Prize when he was in Atlanta, smelled a sure thing this time and wanted Shirley dropped before the story took off. What a prick. But that pretty much defined *journalist*. Walter Dzioba was a veteran newswriter with a fine reputation, respected in the community, polite to a fault—and he was a notorious cutthroat. In such a competitive business, where your name was on the product and that product was sold from bins on the street every day, you couldn't blame the guy for looking out for himself. We were all free lances in the harshest sense of the word, and most reporters went around with several knife hilts protruding from their backs.

An odd little noise entered the room. Maxine had this habit of hyperventilating when faced with a difficult decision. Beneath the hum of her desk fan, and the soft rattling of the presses beyond the newsroom, I could hear a chuffing sound as her breath went in and out. It reminded me of my mother and the year she spent tethered to a plastic cord that fed oxygen into her lungs and restricted her movement. Some days that summer she had to remain in bed, a basket of pharmaceuticals and inhalants by her side. Lilacs flourished outside her window and the heavy smell permeated the sickroom.

"I need to think about those assignments some more," Maxine said, with a tiny gasp before she spoke. "Keep on working. I'll let you know."

Walter stood with the doorknob in his hand. "Very well. If y'all will excuse me then, I'll be getting back to it."

"Try to handle it delicately, Walt," I said, unable to resist a wisecrack.

The older man looked at me out his veiny eyes and said, "What would a Yankee ever know about delicacy?"

Walter closed the door behind him and after he was gone, padding away on his crepe-soled shoes, I threw him the finger, but down low where Maxine couldn't see it. "Don't let him bullshit you," I said. Maxine got up from the desk to clear her skirt and I went on. "Or Shirley either. I wouldn't trust them as far as I could throw them."

"They have my confidence, as you do," said Maxine, resting half of her slim little behind on the edge of the desk. "You're all good reporters, all professionals."

"Then let me work with Shirley on the Melendez story."

"We'll see," said Maxine.

"That's what my father used to say when he meant no."

The day editor, her eyes now a dark solid gray, gazed at me with a look of concern. "Forget about the news, Joe, and concentrate on your writing. Try to write one good, true thing. The news is like cheap wine—it gets you drunk, and that's it. But nothing quenches the thirst like good writing, writing that goes down like cold clear water. Believe me, I know what I'm talking about. Being an editor is like being constantly hungover." This rare piece of gospel finished, Maxine waved her hand twice in front of my face, stirring up the scent of lilacs again. "Now get to work."

3

Outside the *Post-Gazette,* on my way to the jeep, a crazy man on a bicycle almost ran me down. He came wobbling along the side-walk dressed in several torn shirts and jackets despite the after-noon's oppressive heat, a gangling bearded man with a knapsack on his back and two saddlebags jammed with empty soda bottles and other junk. "Hello, Joe," he sang out to me, doffing his greasy hat. I had no idea who he was, but he knew me. Apparently I was his close associate.

As usual, I was late meeting Loretta and roared between the traffic lights, running all the yellows. Loretta worked at one of those doctors' collectives out near the highway and hated being there an extra minute. She called it one-stop shopping for hypo-chondriacs and the elderly, the kind of place that had its hand so deep in the government's pocket fishing for Medicare payments that Uncle Sam thought he was on a date.

People too old to stand up were being treated and third-party billed for athlete's foot and tennis elbow, or else undergoing expensive therapy for ringing in the ears, sleep apnea, and other disorders that were impossible to disprove or cure. Cocoa Beach was fast becoming the Elective Surgery Capital of the World. One particularly unpleasant doctor at the collective played those no-money-down real estate tapes while he operated and had a computer modem in his office that put him online to Wall Street.

His name was Dr. Jackson. He drove a Stutz-Bearcat made from a replica kit and he had the hots for Loretta. In many cases, doctors are matched in their arrogance only by the dictators of small undeveloped countries who parade around in their showy uniforms demanding to be worshiped. But this sawbones really took the prize. He financed his elaborate lifestyle with other people's misery and every time he stared down a case of rheumatoid arthritis he saw a new condominium. He was one of those guys who, when they handed him his medical degree, they must have taken away his personality.

Loretta was sitting on the curbstone out front when I pulled up, in her little nurse's cap and snug white dress. Two elderly patients stood on the corner nearby, a woman with a cane and a jaundiced man leaning on an aluminum walker. "My husband died, you know," the woman said to her companion. Her voice was bright and gay.

"I didn't see it in the newspaper," the man replied. He swiveled his head on a loose wrinkled neck, casting his gaze up and down the street. "Why didn't my wife see it?" he asked, a note of criticism in his voice.

They gazed at the jeep and tried to remember what it was. Leaping to the curb, I pulled Loretta to her feet and kissed her. "Get me the hell out of here," she whispered.

The jaundiced man frowned at me for a moment and continued his monologue, nearly shouting at us. "The doctor told me I had a cancer. I said 'Oh thank God.' I thought he said canker."

Loretta pressed her lips against my ear. "I've had enough of these people for today."

"My daughter lives in Toledo," the woman added, smiling at thin air. Her flesh was spotted and pale, like the skin of poultry.

The man went on about his doctor. "'I'm gonna get a second opinion,' I told him. 'Okay, here's one,' he said. 'You're a little deaf, too.' "

"This guy should be a comedian," I said to Loretta. We scrambled into the jeep. "Uh-oh. Here comes my old pal, Dr. Jackson. Let's go."

Waving his arms, Dr. Jackson hurried toward us, his stethoscope flapping against his chest. "Too late," Loretta said. "I better find out what he wants." When Dr. Jackson realized we were waiting for him, the impeccable young surgeon slowed to a walk and tugged at the lapels of his suit jacket to adjust the fit. He ran his fingers through his fifty-dollar haircut and screwed on a condescending Ivy League smile, just the top teeth showing.

"Loretta, dear. I'm glad I found you," said Dr. Jackson, hovering near her. He resembled a mannequin with his smooth skin and blue contact lenses, wearing clothes that belonged in a store window. "Will you work for me Saturday morning? Diane can't come in and I have to see several patients and do a procedure on someone before noon. I'm really stuck."

"Saturday is my day off, Dr. Jackson," Loretta reminded him.

"Call me Rob," said the surgeon, drilling Loretta with his plastic eyes. "I promise we'll be through at twelve. And I'll pay you double time."

During his blabbering, Dr. Jackson had taken Loretta by the hand and was poised with one foot on the running board of the jeep. Shifting into gear might have incurred a serious groin injury, but the moment passed.

"I guess I can make it, Dr. Jackson," said Loretta. "I can use the extra money."

"If you're free afterward, I'll treat you to lunch," said the conniving doctor. Then the bastard had the nerve to wink at me. "And since we're going to be working together, call me Rob. I insist."

The jaundiced man and his companion inched closer to the jeep. "Rob, do you have a minute?" the man asked. "You remind me of Dr. Dube, the hairstyle, the accent, everything. He dropped dead, you know."

"I've got to run. See you Saturday," said Dr. Jackson to Loretta, disappearing up the sidewalk and into the clinic.

Like all the other athletes in high school, I had a brief annual physical that consisted of a seedy doctor holding my jewels in his hand and saying "cough" in a thick foreign accent. Apparently these doctors traveled around from school to school performing this strangely limited examination, demonstrating little interest in other anatomical regions. Dr. Jackson was part of the new breed. I could see him leering at my girlfriend behind those phony lenses of his, cloaking his lascivious desires in obscure medical terminology. His proposition was simple, but had nothing to do with healing the sick. The clinic was quiet on Saturday mornings and he would be alone with a pretty nurse and his collection of real estate tapes. A whiff of laughing gas, some anesthesia, anything was possible.

"I'm feeling rather poorly," the jaundiced man said to us, holding out his thin yellow hand. "They tell me to just go home and take my medication, but at my age, I don't buy any green bananas."

The woman leaned on her cane, nodding. "I'm from Texas originally," she said. "Everything is big in Texas."

Loretta and I smiled politely and sped away from the curb. "What a place," I said. "All the optimism of Hitler's bunker. I don't know how you can stand being around sick people all the time. Yecch." I felt for my pulse. "Five minutes and I think *I'm* developing symptoms."

"The girls call it God's Waiting Room," Loretta said.

I looked back in the rearview mirror at the jumpy diminishing image of the two old people. "They won't have to wait very long."

Loretta kicked off her shoes. "I hate to admit it," she said, "but sometimes you just want to tell them to shut up."

"And that doctor. What a weasel he is."

"I'm sure he loves his mother," said Loretta.

"There's no guaranteed place in heaven for that. Even ax murderers love their mothers."

Loretta's skin was smooth and brown against the white cotton of her dress. Her little gold earrings caught the sun and she loosened the hair at the nape of her neck and let it fly out behind her. She crossed her slender legs, hugged herself with her long tanned arms, and grinned at me, sticking out her narrow pink tongue. I tried to grab it, feeling its slick pliancy for an instant between my fingers, but she pulled it back, snapping her teeth shut.

"I'll tear it out by the roots," I said, both of us laughing, the jeep careering across the road.

Loretta scratched at my crotch with her nails. "Let me see that nasty little thing," she said. "I'll bite it right off." A postal truck approached in the other lane and I wrestled with the wheel and heaved the jeep back to our side.

"Wheee-doggie!" said Loretta. Her eyes were a sparkling natural green. "Where the hell are we going?"

"Top secret newspaper business," I said, running my hand along the inside of her thigh. "I could tell you, but then I'd have to kill you."

I drove onto Orange Boulevard and stopped at a convenience store to look up Sherri Hogg in the phone book. There was an Albert Hogg on Merritt Island and a listing for S. Hogg and T. Batem on Launch Lane in Cocoa Beach. Before I started searching the trailer parks, I put a coin in and dialed the number to make sure Sherri was home. The phone rang four times; someone picked up the receiver, there was a brief expectant silence, and then a female voice answered, vexed and defensive, maybe even a little drunk.

"Sherri?"

"Who is this?"

"A friend. I want to talk to you."

Her voice rose. "Bullshit. You're a reporter or a fucking cop. Leave me alone. I got nothing to say." The line went dead.

When I got back to the jeep, Loretta said, "Don't tell me—you rented a cloak and dagger and you're investigating the Mike Melendez thing on your own."

I didn't answer and Loretta twitched her shapely behind against the upholstery. "Joe, this really doesn't have anything to do with you. You don't know what went on. Besides, I'm hungry. Let's have lunch."

"I promised Mike we'd go talk to the girl."

"Oh, fantastic," groaned Loretta. "I'm not asking you to slay dragons for me, I'm just asking for a cream cheese bagel." Her fidgeting increased. "I don't think I'm ready for this."

Two rednecks going into the store whistled at Loretta and made speculative comments about their chances of scoring with her. "I suppose you could catch a ride with those fine gentlemen," I said.

"Never mind," Loretta said. "Let's go." We drove to the first trailer park and went up and down the narrow streets between the units, past the oversize mailboxes shaped like barns and space shuttles and the giant plastic sunflowers and other lawn ornaments. The complex had no such street as Launch Lane and we got back on Orange Boulevard in search of the next park. They were plentiful.

"Maybe Mike did it, and maybe he didn't," said Loretta, testing my resolve. We were usually on the beach by this time in the afternoon. "Nobody's ever going to know what really happened except Mike and this Sherri Hogg person. Which is pretty much what Lawyer Timmons had to say."

"I just have to see for myself, that's all." We turned into the second park. "In another life I was the recreation director on the Titanic."

I had never set out to become a spokesman for racial equality, but this phenomenon had occurred once before. During the winter of my prep school year the Deerfield wrestling team traveled to a godforsaken place called Moncton, New Brunswick, for a meet with some of the tiny colleges up there. Even under several feet of snow the city and its outskirts were drab, a depressed pocket of French-speaking Canada in the hinterlands; the gym where we wrestled was a dark, moldy cavern on the grounds of an agricultural school.

Two of my teammates were also from greater Boston, the heavyweight Skip Mulligan, a big, mean street kid from Dorchester, and Danny Dubinski, who survived childhood in the Mission Hill projects. Dubby was 178 pounds with the build of a Marine Corps drill instructor. The three of us roomed together on this particular trip, in a dingy motel about a mile from the gym. We wrestled Friday, lost, and then wrestled twice more on Saturday, with Skip losing his first match but drawing his second to remain preeminent among us, and the rest of the team losing dismally to the older, more experienced Canadians.

Saturday night at the motel, in a relentless snowstorm, Skip trooped out and bought a case of beer and some potato chips and we sat in the room in our underwear gorging ourselves and making fun of the French programs on the television. The beer was stronger than what we were used to, and soon we were drunk, rampaging around the room while the snow piled up outside.

For sport, we lured Willie Fusco, the team's smallest wrestler at 109 pounds, into our room with promises of beer. Dubinski stripped him naked and threw him out in the snow and we watched with glee as our lightweight ran up and down banging on doors. That entertainment ended when Willie, red-skinned and shivering, got the manager, who let him back into his room with the passkey.

Skip and Dubby then turned their wrath on me, the smallest guy in *our* room, overturning lamps and a chair and tearing up the bedclothes in pursuit. They finally captured me between the bed and the wall, Dubinski scissoring my legs and Skip, his huge knee pressed like a millstone against my back, manuevering until he had both my arms twisted behind me. "Get the fuck off me, you stupid mick," I screamed, claustrophobic under all that weight. "Let me up, you fucking polack."

I was scared; Mulligan and Dubinski, with their strength and perverted senses of humor, and nothing else to do, could have held me in such an untenable position for a long time, all night if it suited them. I thrashed from side to side, and they shifted for more pressure, laughing in sinister little bursts.

"Fucken Dolan, you don't like our nationalities, huh," said Mulligan, slobbering on my back. "That's because you pussies from Brookline love the niggers. You love the fucking niggers and have them over to dinner in their nigger suits and laugh when they tittie-squeeze your sister."

This idea came to him out of the blue and he persisted with it, keeping my arms pinned behind my back and my legs motionless beneath me. "Tell me you hate niggers and I'll let you up," he kept saying.

"Fuck you," I said, and he jacked my arms up even higher, to the point of dislocation. I'd been getting my ass beat all weekend, I was dehydrated, and the nauseating taste of beer and potato chips filled my sinuses. Not a soul could hear me and I knew it. I closed my eyes, went limp, and said nothing more. My mother had died that year, orphaning me, and I was on the brink of some dark empty pit. "Tell me you hate niggers," Mulligan said, this time from a great shaded distance, or like I was hearing it underwater.

They could easily have suffocated me or broken my neck. And I resigned myself to whatever would happen. I felt my heart pounding, moving in a crazy rhythm beneath my skin, beating at all the pulse points: in my neck, my groin, behind my knees. But I kept silent. You're in that situation and all you've got left in the world are your principles, some renunciation you won't make, a last bad idea you just will not surrender to.

Loretta and I were working on our fifth trailer park, in the scruffy back lots, when we found Sherri's street. All the satellite dishes, some as big as the ones at NASA, made me realize we were in the land of industrialized white trash. Launch Lane ran beyond the last of the double-wide trailers, in the place where roads crossed empty squares like the undeveloped parts of a cemetery. On either side, concrete slabs veined with cracks, and unused hookups that extended from the tufted saw grass, gave the place a stark, spooky look. At the next intersection, we encountered a headless doll in the center of the roadway and I drove carefully around it; a little farther on, perhaps as a warning to trespassers, the doll's blond head was mounted on a stake, her eyes fixed in a stare, blue and unblinking.

Loretta shuddered. "Uggh. *Joe.*"

"Nice day," I observed, as a black thunderhead of clouds moved in, "for a murder."

The first slow drops fell as we entered a stand of moss-laden trees at the end of the park and pulled up beside the only trailer in sight. It was an old humpbacked model, resting on two wheels and a cinder block in the middle of a clearing. The yard was packed dirt, littered with motorcycle parts, dog dishes, and an assortment of broken power tools and other wreckage. A line of laundry hung motionless between the trees and the sudden darkness of the rain clouds and clumps of Spanish moss cast an ominous tint over the scene.

Sherri Hogg, as I remembered her from the bar at Saxophone Joe's, was a somewhat tall, moderately attractive girl of about twenty-five, overdressed for the beach strip, in a clinging black dress, sequined high heels, and too much purple eye makeup. The woman who came to the slatted door of the trailer was closer to thirty, barefoot in shorts and a stained tank top, cellulite dappling her thighs. She was wan and mousy haired, no taller than my chin, and she had an abundance of crow's-feet around her smallish violet eyes. But the resemblance was unmistakable. It was her.

"Hello, Sherri," I said.

"Who the fuck are you?"

"We talked on the telephone a little while ago. My name is—" She began closing the door and I stuck my arm out and caught it, startling her. It was raining harder now and Loretta and I hunched under the tiny eave above the door, drawing the three of us together in the stale smell from the trailer. "Just a minute. Some people saw you dancing with a guy Friday night and now the police are saying he assaulted you. I was just wondering what you say."

The wrinkles around her eyes deepened into tiny layered ridges, creating a hooded effect. "My boyfriend's coming back any minute and he's not gonna like this." She shook her head. "T-bone don't want me talking to nobody about what happened. Not if there might be money in it."

"What money?"

"Could be money from the paper for my story. One of them grocery store papers. Or the tee vee news. Maybe even a movie." She was really out in fantasyland, a goofy dreaming look on her face. "They pay a whole ton of money in Hollywood for this kind of thing, T-bone says."

That explained volumes. T-bone was the T. Batem listed in the phone book, proud owner of the all the greasy widgets lying around; he was Sherri's boyfriend and from the general look of the place, inside and out, he was not particularly fond of working. My thinking was, either he put Sherri up to the charges because he thought there might be some easy money in it, or else she concocted the whole story to preserve their relationship and her standing in the redneck community. It sure smelled like a frame-up.

"I just might be interested in your story," I said. "I'm Joe Dolan and this is my assistant, Loretta Sweet. From *Florida Times* magazine. It sure is raining hard out here. May we come in?'

Sherri opened the door a little wider. "I never heard of the *Florida Times.*"

"We're a glossy," I said. "Oversize format."

"Oh." Sherri let us in. It was a lame answer and she never questioned it for an instant. Loretta poked me in the ribs. She hated to be included in my little charades.

The inside of the trailer was dank and smelly. Half a glass of wine and a stubbed-out menthol cigarette were in front of a chair drawn out from the table. A televison set flashed its blue soundless light in one corner and some inexplicable presence made itself known. I turned around and faced it, staying in front of Loretta.

"Nice fella," I said. It was a huge, gleaming-eyed brown and black mutt, the thick collar of fur about his neck standing out in an alert bristling ring. Teeth bared, sitting with his chest inflated, those watchful eyes followed each small movement I made, measuring the distance between us.

"What a well-behaved dog," I said, straining to be casual. "He didn't make a sound when we came in."

"Toby don't bark at all. He used to have a tumor in his throat but they cut it out," said Sherri, herself avoiding the dog. "Now he hates loud noises."

"Is that so?" I whispered.

Sherri nodded. "Wow—he's looking right at you, like he knows you or something."

"We've never met," I said quietly, but with confidence, since Toby was an unlikely dog show contestant. "We won't be staying long. If you'll just give us a sense of the story, we'll talk it over at the magazine."

"I think I should wait until T-bone gets back," said Sherri. "He said not to tell no one about the case without him being here."

"We'll be happy to sit down with you and Mr. T-bone at your convenience and go through all the facts," I said. "But we're in a hurry today. I just need to know: what happened at Michael Melendez's apartment last Friday night?"

In the ensuing silence, the rain beat against the tin roof overhead. Sherri knotted her hands, picking at her chipped broken nails. She stared at the floor, then I noticed her gaze run up Loretta's lean brown legs, her narrow hips, over the tanned skin of her neck to the thick sun-streaked hair. Sherri dropped her eyes and once again her own stringy hair obscured her face. It was an unmistakable gesture, one of inferiority and embarassment.

"He was rough, rougher than I expected," she said after a time, her shoulders quivering. Something like a strangled cough escaped her throat and she said, "My God—everyone's gonna know about this."

Loretta squeezed Sherri's elbow in silent reassurance.

"T-bone drives truck on weekends and sometimes I go out dancing," continued Sherri, with an air of recital. "I go to Saxophone Joe's to dance and get drunk and if someone wants to buy my drinks or take me out for tacos or something afterward, that's fine with me. But I'm T-bone's girl and everybody knows it."

My conviction that Mike was being framed grew stronger. "The flirting, the drinks, the late supper—you're not denying that," I said.

"Look, I danced with the guy. I helped him spend some money. I never said I'd sleep with him."

"What about going back to Mike's place," I said. "Whose idea was that?"

"His."

"And you went along with it."

She gave me a cold glance. "He said he needed his glasses or something. We were only stopping for a minute, then he was supposed to take me home."

"But you stayed all night and went for breakfast together in the morning."

This was where Sherri's story broke down and she knew it. Her voice rose, sending Toby to his feet, scrabbling on the linoleum, his throat convulsing in great silent barks. "If I tried to leave, he said he'd hurt me." Toby leapt against her, his tongue lolling. "Get off me." She snapped the dog across the nose with an open hand and he sank back into his cubbyhole beside the door.

I was unrelenting. "A woman dances and has drinks with a man and goes back to his place—that usually adds up to something. But you talk like you were kidnapped. I don't know if I believe that."

"Believe whatever the fuck you wanna believe," said Sherri, slamming her hands against the kitchen counter. "I have to live with it."

At that moment, I understood Sherri Hogg's dilemma. Rape or no rape, she had to somehow justify being with Mike Melendez in the first place. A spray of upper-class manners, his tropical elegance and poise were certainly strong enough lures at the time, but now Sherri was facing the charge of consorting with a black man and getting desperate. Stuffed inside this crackerbox with T-bone, I imagined Sherri made up a fabulous tale to protect herself. And now Mike Melendez was going to burn for it.

Toby continued to x-ray me from his corner. The air was thick and slow, dense with layered moldy smells. I wanted to get out of that dark little trailer in the worst way. Loretta was beside me, fidgeting like mad.

"Are you all right?" she asked Sherri.

"T-bone's gonna be coming," Sherri said, her eyes drawn back into their hooded sockets. "I don't wanna talk no more."

She turned her back on us and for the first time I saw the thick ropy abrasions running across her shoulder blades, a few days old, flaked with papery brown scabs; and the deep, five-fingered gouge mark on the fleshy part of her upper arm. Loretta gasped and I almost vomited, dizzy for a moment. The abrasions were friction burns of some sort, the other like the impression of a meat hook. There was nothing fabulous or imaginary about them. They were the handiwork of a beast, someone who was hateful and probably afraid of women, a garden variety sadist.

"Sweet mother of God," I said under my breath.

A rumble overtook the little trailer, more thunder perhaps, but quickly localizing in the distinct gravelly approach of a motorcycle, its mufflers roaring, up through the gears in a rising crescendo until the engine cut out altogether and it glided into the clearing with only a slight rattle of the tailpipe. I looked out the small fogged window as T-bone pulled up beside the jeep. He gave it a suspicious once-over and slowly eased the bike onto its centerstand and dismounted.

"Get out of here," ordered Sherri. "This fucking minute."

"You got it," I said.

Toby was leaping, writhing, and cavorting in silent agony on the kitchen floor and I stepped over him and went outside, the women and then the mute dog following behind me. The dark clouds had swept across the sky leaving huge patches of blue and the rain had lessened to an occasional patter of drops, slipping from the leaves like jewels in the columns of light that slanted between the trees. All through the clearing steam rose from the ground in little plumes, silvery puddles reflected the open sky, and hubcaps and dog dishes glittered with rainwater.

T-bone leaned against the grille of Loretta's jeep, his arms flung out across its hood, studded boots dug in at the heels. He derived his nickname from the extremely broad, rawboned shoulders that protruded from his sleeveless denim shirt, jutting up from a skinny waist and long spidery legs. T-bone was about thirty-five, taller than six feet, one eyebrow creased in half by a thin white scar shaped like a crescent. He had a grizzled hound dog look to his face and he turned it briefly in my direction before dropping his head to examine his dirty wrist and flat damaged knuckles.

"State your business," he said when I was quite close to him. His shrewd watery eyes flashed at me, then moved away. "This here is Mr. Dolan," answered Sherri. "From the *Florida Times* magazine."

"Was I talking to you?" asked T-bone. "I don't think I was."

Sherri cringed. "You said you wanted to make a deal."

T-bone laughed at her. *"You said you wanted to make a deal,"* he mimicked. "Yeah, a deal where the niggers can have any white girl they want and there's not a fucking thing anybody can do about it. Give me a fucking break. You just stay in the trailer where you belong and I'll take care of this."

Sherri reached for the wet laundry on the line, wringing a sodden towel until it bled rainwater down her arms. "Go ahead, Mr. Dolan," she begged me. "Tell him about the magazine."

For a brief moment T-bone seemed capable of reason and he gazed at my canvas shorts and polo shirt with the tail hanging out. "Lemme see a business card," he said.

"We were just leaving," I said.

He moved sideways, blocking my path to the jeep. Looking at him, it was at best problematic that some innocent people were in jail and T-bone was not. "Are you *Joe* Dolan?" he said.

"That's right."

"You stupid shit," he said to Sherri, his eyebrow separating into two pieces about a half inch apart. "This guy's from the *Post-Gazette*. He's a fucking reporter. What did I fucking tell you? Don't talk to the cops and don't talk to no fucking reporters without me."

"Whoops," said Loretta into my ear.

"I didn't say nothing," Sherri said, giving me a look of betrayal. "They asked me questions and I told them they hadda wait until you got back."

"The paper wants Sherri's version of what happened," I said. "And she should be able to tell it on her own."

"I'm already talking to the paper," T-bone replied. "A broad named Kimball offered me fifty bucks for an interview, but that ain't even close to what it's gonna take."

The *Post-Gazette* had a rule against paying for stories, not based on ethics, only because it was cheap. If Shirley was putting money out, it was from her own pocket. Handing out money corrupted the source and made the facts harder to obtain. But Shirley didn't care about the facts in the Melendez case. She had the scent of the judicial scandal and was trying to keep Walter from shaking her loose.

"Maybe you made a mistake. The news gets old and smelly real fast," I said, quoting Maxine. "What's worth fifty bucks to someone today might not be worth anything tomorrow."

"I'll decide what it's worth," said T-bone, anger coming into his voice. The left side of his face contorted again, splitting his eyebrow in two. "Not you. Not the fucking newspaper. Me. I call the fucking shots here."

"So it doesn't matter what Sherri thinks," I said. "And what really happened at Mike Melendez's house probably doesn't even matter. You're the one calling the shots. That makes perfect sense to me."

Toby thumped his rear paws against the ground and shook his blocky head from side to side, following the conversation. Sherri dropped an armful of laundry into a puddle and started to cry. "Don't you fucking start," T-bone shrieked, pointing his finger at her. "I told you to go in the fucking trailer, now get in there. If you'd kept your mouth shut from the beginning, like I told you, I'd have everything taken care of."

The dog flung himself twice in the air at this new excitement, landing on his back, the air escaping from his jaws in hoarse little whispers. On the third leap, he brushed against his master and was driven back by the heel of T-bone's boot. "You fucking dumb dog," he cried in a rage. "I'm about to kill you."

Sherri ran to the trailer, slamming herself inside. "You fucking people at the newspaper better get this straight," said T-bone, whirling toward me. He indicated Loretta by pointing but kept his eyes fixed on mine. "Or the niggers downtown will be having a field day." I got behind the wheel of the jeep and Loretta went around to the passenger side, stopped by T-bone, who drew himself up before her, the left side of his face in convulsions. He took out a bent wrinkled cigarette, fished unsuccessfully for a match, then stuck it, unlit and drooping, between his lips.

"Where do you think you're going?" he asked Loretta, controlling her movements for a few seconds.

Loretta looked him in the eye and said in a low steady voice, "Get out of my way, you degenerate."

I had to laugh. Suddenly T-bone became indecisive, stammering for a moment as he put one hand on the jeep, his shoulder bulging out from under the ragged edge of his shirt. "All right," he said, letting her pass. "This time."

Loretta got in beside me and I ran the jeep in a tight circle around T-bone, splashing him with mud. Beyond the mossy trees, the sun was already scorching the pavement and a rainbow was beginning to emerge across the faint blue sky in the east.

"Did you see Sherri's back?" Loretta exclaimed. "It looks like she'd been horsewhipped. I don't know why women stay with ass-holes like that."

Neither did I. But the abrasions on Sherri's back probably had little to do with her domestic situation. The way the skin was flak-ing and the length and rawness of them meant they were rug burns of some sort, not bruises from being hit. "Those marks couldn't have been made by T-bone unless he took her someplace carpeted and ground her into the floor," I said.

"They didn't happen by themselves," said Loretta, glancing sideways at me.

Along the neat avenues of the trailer park, wet Confederate flags hung from several poles. In front of one gaudy bedizened unit, standing two feet high, was the famous ceramic figure of a black stable boy holding a lantern. He was dressed in yellow trousers, an orange vest and bandanna and a short-billed cap, eyes wide with fear, his mouth curved into a vaudevillian O.

"I bet he's nervous in this neighborhood," I said.

We turned onto Orange Boulevard and spread in front of us was an iridescent double rainbow, stretching from the beach across the intracoastal, brilliant pulsating bands of lime green, yellow, and red.

"It looks like a prism," Loretta said with awe.

"I was in prism once," I said, fumbling under her blouse. "Me and Elvis."

"I bet you were," said Loretta. She was a self-proclaimed member of the Itty-bitty Tittie Committee, which was too bad, because I like big ones, the bigger the better. "Did you know that breast implants cost over five thousand dollars?" she asked.

"You could get a nice used pair," I said. "Or just run down to Jiffy Boob for some temporary ones."

Loretta slapped my hand away. "Sure I could. Now watch the road and stop playing with my tits."

4

The Stutz-Bearcat was alone in front of the clinic when I dropped Loretta off at work Saturday morning. The coupe, which was an amazing facsimile of the original, sat chromed and sleek, upholstered in brown leather. Its deep burgundy color was polished to a reflective sheen and the intials RPJ had been etched into the windshield with a diamond-tipped instrument.

"*That,*" said Surfer in the backseat of the jeep with the rugby gear, "is the car of an asshole."

"So you know Dr. Jackson," I said. "Perhaps he corrected your double hernia or sold you some time-share in Fort Walton Beach."

Surfer shook his head. "I just know an asshole when I see one."

"Stop it, you two," said Loretta, pinching me.

I slipped sideways and sparred with her, tapping on her chin with my fingers. "Keep your left in his face," I advised. "Jab. Jab. Jab. Get on your bicycle. Stay out of the clinches."

Loretta tried to kiss me and then gave up, laughing, and climbed out of the jeep. "You're nuts," she said. "Don't worry about me. I'll be fine."

Surfer John jumped into the front seat, his shirt already off, and began fumbling with the radio, fragments of song cleaving the quiet sunny street. Loretta stood on the curb and regarded us for a moment, a look of worry crossing her face. She wore a fuzzy yellow sweater over her nursing uniform and in the morning light, it transformed her pleasing woman's body into the figure of a little girl.

"You guys be careful today," she said, unimpressed by our antics.

"Don't do anything foolish."

"We're going to smash into huge lantern-jawed men while wearing absolutely no protective equipment," I replied. "We wouldn't dream of doing anything foolish."

Surfer beamed his million-dollar smile and repeated happily, "Wouldn't dream of anything foolish."

Loretta frowned and turned to go and I ran after her like a forsaken child, my shoelaces untied and flapping against the sidewalk. I caught her near the glass doors and took her in my arms. "We won't get hurt or anything," I said. Loretta kissed me and rested her head for an instant on my shoulder, sighing, "Just be careful."

"That was touching," Surfer said when I came back to the jeep. He squared himself to the dashboard and flung his arm forward, signaling a cavalry charge. "Now: on with the road trip."

We lurched into the empty street and I had the feeling you get when school ends in June and you go flying down the street empty handed, screaming with your pals at the prospect of all those unfettered summer days. Except now we were consenting adults and had money and a vehicle. I looked over at Surfer and he had tied a length of bungee cord around his head and was smearing suntan lotion on arms that were already burnished gold. Nobody ever believed he was an engineer. His technical manuals were a jumble of letters and numbers and symbols, as indecipherable as any hieroglyphic from ancient times, and he would flip through them in front of the television like they were comic books.

Bagpipe music came over the radio. "I love that sound," I said as skirling filled the air.

Surfer screwed the top onto the suntan lotion. After about ten seconds he changed the station. "Me too, but I can only take so much of it," he said.

We met the rest of the team at Fat Bob's Hotcake and Bar-B-Q a few miles outside town. Surfer and I liked to get there early, share the team gossip, and, after an hour dawdling over our soggy pancakes, set out down the highway like a band of marauding pirates.

Sean and Iain Caffrey, the giant twins, were just inside the door gobbling mints and flirting with the little blond who worked the register. Both Caffreys married very young, a gang of kids and dogs between them, and they began flirting with any women they could find the moment they stepped outside for a road trip, communicating with brotherly winks and sly lecherous grins, two lumbering ham-fisted Romeos. Sean was bent over the counter engaged in deep conversation, and his shorts hung down in a disgusting half moon.

"Let's go eat," said Iain to his brother. He pulled a small wad of bills from his pocket. "I'm starving."

Sean waved behind his back like he was swatting flies. Then one of the managers called to the cashier and she left her post. "Ooh, that dog'll hunt," said Sean, clutching his groin for emphasis. "I think she wants me."

"I think she wants you to drop dead," Iain said. "C'mon. Let's eat."

"Stop telling me what to do," hissed Sean. "If I wanted my wife on this trip, I would have brought her along."

The cashier returned, a plain-faced kid about seventeen with dyed hair and cherry lipstick, and Sean began talking to her again in a low suggestive voice while she filed her nails, oblivious to whatever advances were being made. Iain tugged his brother's shorts down to his knees and when that brought no reaction except an absent-minded attempt to pull them up, he said, "It's a lost cause." He turned to me. "You and I both know he doesn't have a chance, but he thinks he's wearing her down. Me, I'd rather eat."

"Watching you guys is like watching a documentary," I said.

They were serving food beneath the spot where some workmen were installing a new ceiling. "I've got a hankering for some asbestos pancakes and insulation bacon," I said.

I followed Iain through the cattle chute and we both picked up blue plates for the special. Martin Campesi was sitting at a table beside the chow line with Duke Ritter and Todd Baker, and Martin poked Surfer in the leg and asked him for a loan.

"I never carry cash," Surfer said.

"Why not?" asked Martin.

Surfer pulled out the lining of his pockets. "Because I don't have any." A pretty waitress walked by. "Ever kiss a rabbit between the ears?" he asked.

"Do us a favor, then, and nick us a bit more grub," Martin said, getting back to the point. "I'm famished."

Surfer loitered at the rail, bantering with Todd and surreptitiously passing fruit squares and bananas and shaky plates of Jell-O to Martin, who hoarded the goodies under the table. Surfer kept the items of food coming beyond all reasonable limits, until the floor around Martin's chair was stacked three deep with stolen victuals. The good-natured New Zealander took them in hand, his eyes darting in every direction for a sign of the manager.

"All right. All right, Sur-fer, that's enough, damn it," he said. "I don't have a bloody tapeworm, you know."

Iain and I skittered away, beneath the oil portrait of "Fat Bob" Soriano, who surveyed this hilarity from a place far up on the wall above the barbecue pit. His meaty red forearms folded across his midsection, dressed in his cooking whites, spatula in hand, Fat Bob gazed out at his establishment with a look of satisfaction on his fleshy parboiled face. After all, what did he care about the profit margin—he was dead. A massive embolism killed him, right there at the pit during the evening rush, and after the ambulance took him away, the hired help continued dishing out the greasy red-stained pork, beef, and chicken parts he was famous for. Fat Bob would have wanted it that way.

Iain took four pints of chocolate milk and several yogurt cartons for himself. Yawning ferociously, the slight bulge of his hairy stomach drooping beneath his T-shirt, he stacked hotcakes a foot high on his plate. "It's hard to decide what to get in the buffet of life," he said.

"How can you eat all that?" I asked.

"We Caffreys have to travel like those old wagon trains," the big man said, towering over me. "Store up the provisions, send out the scouts, and leave several months before kickoff."

"You and Sean must have eaten your poor mother out of house and home."

Iain laughed, and picked up two oranges with his outspread hand. "Me and Sean? I have five brothers. It was a battle royal every night. There was always a whole lot, but never enough." He looked at me for a moment. "Now that I have my own family, I can give them all they want."

A little farther along the line, Iain and I met up with David Edelstein, resplendent in his black and silver warm-up suit, pointing a thick finger at the trays where the breakfast meats were piled. On the other side of the glass divider, a white-jacketed attendant used a pair of pincers to fill his order.

"Don't be stingy with that bacon," Edelstein said. "And give me plenty of sausage, too."

"Is everything kosher this morning, Dave?" I asked, clapping him on the shoulder as we passed by.

We carried our trays into the dining room. More than half the team was already there, a few still eating and the others reading the morning paper, talking, or milling in the aisles. Avoiding Steve Delong and Whizzer and that bunch, I took a seat across from Duke Ritter, who slid his chair over to make room for Iain. His face inflamed, Duke sagged at the table, bleary-eyed and smelling of beer. Surfer joined us and I separated my hotcakes into two stacks and gave him half.

"Duke: congratulations," he said, digging in. "You look like hell."

"Don't worry about me," said Duke. "I always play better with a hangover."

He was telling the truth—the Duke in any condition was murder on the rugby field. His father, King Ritter, had reportedly been the best football player ever to come out of Erie, Pennsylvania. Booze finally got the King and booze was going to get the Duke, too. Until then it was a pleasure just to see him play: limping onto the field with his rotten nose, terribly out of shape and balding at 26, but never missing a tackle, claiming every dangerous ball that was kicked to us, very low to the ground and like a stampede when he ran through the defense.

Sporadic Violence Bob and Gaston were at the next table drinking iced tea and watching big Josh eat with the horrified expression of spectators at a bullfight. And Josh handled what was on his plate with the grim confidence of a matador, sighting down his fork, ready for the kill.

"Don't get too close," I warned his tablemates.

Sporadic Violence Bob held up his hand with one finger bent down. "This close?" he asked.

A dozen conversations went on around me and I heard Mike Melendez and the rape charge mentioned several times. "I bet he did it," said Whizzer. "He's always sniffing after the white girls." Steve Delong's drawl surfaced for a moment in the din. "I don't mind niggers until they all get in a group and start acting like niggers," he said. "They're the worst, them and the fancy ones like Melendez." He caught me staring at him and looked away.

At our table, David Edelstein was telling Duke and Iain about his trip to the Middle East over the winter holidays. He met Israeli farmers in the Gaza who bought lands "semicleared" of mines at bargain prices and grazed cattle on them for a few years as a way of activating the undetected explosives. Interrupting, Surfer mentioned how he had once seen Colonel Sanders himself, of fried chicken fame, dressed in his trademark white suit and hat, ordering servants around on the front lawn of his mansion in Kentucky.

"If you bring me another box of that fucking chicken, I'm gonna shoot someone," he supposedly heard the Colonel saying. "Now put another cow out to the minefield and let's have some hamburgers."

Everybody laughed, but it wasn't quite as much fun without Mike there. He never ate much, usually half a grapefruit and several cups of black coffee, and then he'd wander around in his rubber flip-flops and shorts, muscled like an anatomy chart under his shining ebony skin, until finally settling at my table. Rolling his coffee cup in his hands, that quick smile bursting across his face, he'd lower his chin to his chest and stare at me for a long moment. "J-oo-e, what can you tell me, mun?" he'd ask in that soft musical voice, eager for the news.

Mike could talk rings around such notable rugby club intellectuals as David Edelstein, the New Zealander Martin Campesi, and myself. He knew so much about so many things, it was hard for him not to show off when he contributed to a discussion. But Mike was comfortable with us and a certain easygoing segment of the club; not so with Steve Delong and the other crackers, who wanted little to do with him off the field. They loved his rugby the way prairie settlers loved a hired gun—after the shooting a coolness always set in.

Conversation at our table shifted to Todd and his new girlfriend. He was going out with the daughter of the man who invented resealable plastic bags and was said to be instantly, madly in love.

"With him or her?" Iain wanted to know.

"It sounds like a bag job to me," said Surfer.

"The girl at the bank this morning caught me looking at her tits," Duke mentioned. "I just smiled and kept looking. What the hell. There's not going to be a surcharge or anything."

It was time to leave and the various groups drifted from the tables. "Hey, wait!" Sean Caffrey exclaimed, as his teammates streamed past. "I didn't eat yet." One player after another jeered him. Noting Sean's habit of boring us with his sexual and rugby exploits, Surfer jerked his head in the big man's direction and said, "If I didn't have such great affection for him, I'd find him insufferable."

"How do you think I feel?" asked Iain. "He tortures me with all his old memories."

Todd snatched up a lit cigarette from an ashtray in the foyer and, placing it between his lips, affected a relaxed Continental pose, his arm draped around an invisible companion. "Who am I? Who am I?" he asked. "I'm that couple you used to see in the cigarette ads, except I'm alone because my wife died of lung cancer."

Walking to the cars, we were startled by angry shouts from one of our new players, an air force test pilot and the fullback on our second team. He flew advanced fighter planes and other highly classified aircraft, but couldn't walk and chew gum at the same time, and on the rugby field he made every easy play an adventure. His name was Captain Edward O'Hara and we called him Special Ed.

"Thieves," he roared. "Undisciplined civilian trash."

Special Ed was standing beside an old primer-spotted roadster, hands on hips, staring at the hole in the dashboard where his stereo had been. Torn wires hung out of the dark little space, something most conspicuous, like a dentist with a missing tooth.

"Call the MPs. Secure the perimeter," said Special Ed, shaking his fist. "The no-good little bastards."

"Forget it," advised Surfer. "It's long gone."

Special Ed opened the door and fumbled in the glove compartment and in the space between the seats. "They stole my box of tapes, too. I always listen to Verdi on the way to the games. It gets me psyched."

This statement baffled Sean and Iain and they stood there speechless, blinking in the sunlight. For rugby players, confessing a love of opera or ballet was like passing a lingerie shop and yearning for a new bra and panties. Moving quickly to cover the silence, I said, "At home, we glue razor blades underneath the dashboard. Just about every time you see a Puerto Rican downtown, he's carrying a bagful of car radios."

Duke Ritter looked at me funny when I said that. Even Surfer's jaw dropped a little bit and I felt the blood rush to my face. Behind us Steve Delong had come up with Whizzer and, overhearing my remark, Delong said, "The Yankees always love the niggers for some reason, but they never have anything good to say about the spics."

The Caffreys and Duke and Surfer laughed, and Delong gave me a playful little shove and then walked away. "I don't think the Puerto Ricans took Ed's radio," he said. "Call Mike Melendez. Maybe he has it."

Special Ed was oblivious. In addition to abysmal hand-eye coordination, he possessed that upbeat military attitude that could be sickening—one of those bottle-shaped guys with a high-and-tight haircut. "I said this morning I was going to listen to *La Traviata* on the way to Orlando, and damn it, I am," he vowed. Then he cleared his throat and started singing. "*Sempre Libera degg'io follegiare di gioja. . . .*"

He zoomed off. "What the fuck was that?" asked David Edelstein, wandering up.

"That was Special Ed practicing his opera," Surfer said.

"It sounded like someone strangling a cat," observed Edelstein.

"If he's going to practice anything, he should practice catching a rugby ball."

Special Ed crossed the parking lot and entered traffic, yodeling in Italian. I kicked at a few stones on the way to the jeep, trudging along with my head down. "Forget about it," advised Surfer. "Look at the Israelis and the Palestinians. The Democrats and the Republicans. Everybody hates somebody. That's just the way it is."

I remembered my father meeting one of my prep school instructors, and when he thought no one would notice, glancing at my mother and soundlessly forming the word *Jew*. It was graduation day and Mr. Green, a delightful eccentric, was leading us across campus, his academic gown billowing in his wake like a sail. I had always thought of Mr. Green not as Jewish or anything else, but as a teacher, and a particularly fine one. Now my father—who never did anything to suggest he might be anti-Semitic—with a word raised the specter of something foreign, a usurious money lender or swindler, the cardboard figure we imagined when somebody cheated. This vision seized me and I slackened my pace, Mr. Green continuing on ahead, his chin jutting out. A huge distance began to separate all of us, and the surrounding green lawn of the campus stretched and lengthened in every direction like the sea.

At the first stoplight, a battered Cadillac pulled up beside us, driven by a slim shirtless black man. His companion was an unattractive white woman. A young white girl played with an electronic game in the backseat and across from her was a black youth about fourteen years old. He watched the girl playing through slitted eyes.

I found myself somehow disliking them, sure of something unnatural in their presence. It was instinct, an old embarassing reflex, like putting your hands up to protect your face.

The woman turned her head and caught me staring; our eyes met in a short hateful embrace, and she turned away. The child poked her hand between the seats and the woman reached over and slapped the girl on her bare upper arm. The man refused to look and I wondered what was going through his mind. Another slap and the girl began crying, then the light changed, the Cadillac shot forward, and the last thing I saw before we turned onto the highway was the youth in the backseat giving me the finger.

"Fuck you, pal," said Surfer, throwing it back. "See what I mean? There's no reason for that."

The driver of the Cadillac and his companion might have been in love, married, members of a church, or just friends running an errand together. What was distasteful and subversive about them was a mystery. It all came from me, out of the depths of some nasty false lesson I had assumed from earlier life. My prejudices were leaking all over the place. Steve Delong had made a small surgical cut and now I was bleeding profusely.

Surfer and I killed most of the trip talking about our game against Orlando. We expected trouble from their best player, known only as Mitch, a gorilla who covered a lot of ground and really enjoyed thumping the opposition. But the rest of Orlando was terrible and we were good and getting better. *Rugby* magazine up in New York favored us to win our division and considered Cocoa Beach the dark horse of the entire Southeast.

Reading about ourselves in *Rugby* was a matter of pride when it was circulated at the American Legion hall. But now the thought of all the extra stomps and punches we would receive from our many admirers in the league had my heart booming out of control.

"Do you think Mitch reads *Rugby* magazine?" I asked Surfer, clutching my chest.

"I don't think Mitch can read."

An elderly couple abruptly switched lanes in front of us and Surfer braked hard and cut the wheel to avoid hitting them. "Jesus Christ! Look out," he yelled, passing them on the right. He waved his fist. "You're gonna die soon and it's gonna hurt. A lot."

"Apply the horn liberally," I said.

Surfer was angry. His scientific background showed in his precise driving more than anything else, and he had little patience for erratic behavior on the highway. "They're the worst fucking drivers on the road," he said. "As soon as you turn sixty-five, the state should mail you a bus pass."

"Old women wearing hats are the worst," I said. "And disabled American veterans."

"No, I have it," replied Surfer with enthusiasm. "The absolute worst driver in the world is an elderly nearsighted woman who is a disabled veteran—"

"Wearing a hat," I said.

Surfer looked in the mirror. "I've never met such a person on the open road and I hope I never do," he said.

Orlando begins as a Jiffy Mart and a Burger World about ten miles out and grows into a thousand Jiffy Marts and Burger Worlds surrounding the Disney enclave and other parasitic theme parks. The landscape is dry and flat, studded with skin bars, fast-food joints, tiny junkyards, and mile after mile of razor-tipped chain-link fence.

I knew the rugby field by the location of a giant pink asphalt whale beached on a vacant lot, its tail rotted off and lying on the ground. We turned onto an access road and passed in front of the whale's massive head, the steel skeleton beginning to show beneath the falling pink flesh, weeds growing from its jaw. The dead whale was just some promoter's dream gone awry, but as we went past, it gave me a sense of foreboding. Half-sunken ships, abandoned storefronts, empty warehouses, and other defunct man-made things had haunted my childhood. Every angle of the whale seemed to have a distinct visual memory attached to it, an imprint of sorts, and there was no escaping the torrent of preternatural dreams and images that nearly overwhelmed me. Dread mingled with the trickle of adrenaline in my bloodstream, almost levitating me out of the jeep.

This feeling carried over to the rugby game. At the park we put on our stuff and immediately began warming up. Coach Van was there, somehow materializing just before kickoff as he always did, and he called us together before we took the field.

"You played hard for twenty minutes last week and that was enough," Van said. "When are you going to play rugby for a full eighty minutes? You're not dominating these games the way you should." He drew us in tighter. "We all want to fool around, enjoy ourselves, and socialize, but the trick is to win," he said. "I love to win."

Once the game begins, particularly if I take a hard shot early and adrenaline takes over, I can play like a demon. Before that I'm very nervous. Already time was accelerating and my mind was taking quick frozen snapshots of certain things while the rest of the world blurred. I ran up and down to get loose, feeling the capacity for violence rising in me like water to the top of a glass. Sean Caffrey walked by in a trance, his eyes fixed like a zombie's, a great bandage wrapped around his head to protect his ears. I heard a tiny sound and Steve Delong was kicking at a single blade of grass, hitting it in the same place every time, his leg whirring from high behind his head. Stretching my calf, I bent and smelled urine in the dry turf. Moments later, the referee blew his whistle and Delong sent the ball high and deep.

I try to remember the games, slow them down and make sense of them, but the thing just comes and everything ends in one second. I launched myself into the first pile-up and felt wonderful from that point on. Someone passed me the ball, I gave it to someone else, and we careened into a jumble of players, grinding forward until the ball was flicked away and I was in the open field, chasing it again. Mitch was trouble, making a lot of tackles, holding our advance with an almost superhuman effort. But we started punching through, tiring him out, and Edelstein scored on a fine zigzagging run. Delong made the conversion.

Before halftime we got two more tries. Coach Van met us under the goalposts, in the blinding sun. Special Ed and Josh ran out from the sidelines with jugs of water and we clustered around them, waiting for a drink.

"I hope you're not satisfied," said Van, an imposing figure with his great mane of white hair and faded USA jacket. "The Indians at Little Big Horn didn't surround Custer and then shake his hand and let him go home." His voice rose quickly. "They rode in a swirling rage of death until there wasn't one fucking cavalryman left. Then the job was done." Van blocked a water jug from being passed in front of him and added, "Just make sure we're the fucking Indians today."

"That's the coach for you," Surfer said, as Van stalked away. "Always kidding around."

"He can't believe nobody has punched out old Mitch," said Edelstein.

Surfer picked the grass and twigs out of his hair. "Don't look at me," he said. "I'm a lover, not a fighter."

"Give me a pen and I'll fire off a stern letter," I said.

"Van is about ready to do it himself," Edelstein said. "If looks could kill, fucking Mitch would be lying there dead right now."

"I'm starting to feel like a decisive Hamlet," I said. "Fuck him. I'll kick his Laertes ass."

"I'll do it," said Duke Ritter, listening over my shoulder. "I'd rather fight for two minutes than run for two minutes, anyway."

Duke was true to his word. Early in the second half, he and Mitch went at it, hammering each other like two dinosaurs. The referee ejected them and the game settled down. Then we piled on twenty more points for an easy win. Afterward, during the second game, Sean went to Burger World for some food and a keg was tapped beside the field. We set up some lawn chairs and howled with laughter as Josh stumbled around out there, players sat down and rested in the middle of the field, and Special Ed let several kicks sail over his head or dribble between his legs.

"Put a tent over that circus," Todd called out, amid calliope sounds from some of the other spectators.

"Special Ed is running around out there like a wild boar," said Edelstein.

"Yeah, look at him," I said. "He's a crashing bore."

We stayed late and Surfer drank beer until the sun went down and the keg was empty, lingering by the cars, with David Edelstein, Delong, Martin Campesi in a pair of ridiculous-looking surf pants, and the Duke. A few Orlando players were across the lot, fading in the dusk, and as evening came on, their voices carried on the motionless humid air. One of them left the group and walked toward us, clacking over the pavement in his rugby boots, his jersey torn and bloody. Mitch held a pitcher of beer in his fist, using it to signal a truce, the foam lapping onto the ground.

"Have a drink," said Mitch, pouring Duke a beer while the others stared into their empty cups.

"Sure," the Duke said, smiling beneath his battered nose. "I was getting a little dry."

"You got a good punch," admitted Mitch. He was built like an old-time strongman, a massive rib cage, thick in the shoulders and hips and not very tall, his head carved out of monument stone. "The last time I got hit like that it was a Golden Gloves nigger. Quickest right hand I never saw."

"That's too bad," Duke said. He motioned with his cup and Mitch filled it up again.

"If anyone of 'em has a hard punch, I give him that much,"

Mitch said.

The strongman drank a great deal of beer from the pitcher and topped off Duke's cup with the last of it. He glanced first at Martin and his baggy fluorescent pants, then at each of us in turn, with vacancy or mild contempt, finally resting his eyes, the newly blackened one half shut, on the lumpy face of Duke Ritter. A mighty belch escaped him, and he wiped his mouth with his sleeve and spat on the pavement.

"I think you're all a bunch of fairies," said Mitch. "Excepting you." He shook Duke's hand. "Somebody has to stand up and take the shit for everyone else."

Mitch turned and made for his truck on bowed legs, his stomach distended, the clack of his boots echoing in the dimness. "You see the gut on him?" asked Edelstein when Mitch was walking away. "He's going to make some cardiologist rich in a few years."

"He liked your pants, though," I said, nudging Martin.

Martin stumbled, then caught himself. "The man knows style when he sees it," slurred the New Zealander. "I am making a definite fashion statement here."

"Oh, there's something definite about it, all right," Surfer said. "No wonder he called us a bunch of fairies."

"What do you mean?" asked Martin, with his bent-up rugby nose and pageboy haircut. He fanned out his trousers and looked down on them. "These are the most comfortablest pants in—in the known hemisphere!"

We all hooted. "What the fuck is the known hemisphere?" Delong asked.

"That kind of vacant statement is what advertising is all about," I said.

Edelstein dug out his car keys and jangled them in the air. "I'd like to stay and bullshit with you all in the known hemisphere but it's getting late."

"Uhh, I don't feel so good," groaned Martin, holding his head in both hands. "I better sober up, before tomorrow morning comes crashing down on me like a thermonuclear warhead."

"Go ahead, go home, you quitters," I said. "We were funny for ten or fifteen minutes after the Tampa game, but we couldn't sustain it. Tonight, sure, we've been funny for twenty or thirty minutes, but until we can maintain a high level of being funny for eighty minutes, we'll never be a first class comedy team."

Yawning ensued, a few pompous belches, and some handshakes. Martin lurched over to the fence and vomited. I passed in front of Duke, who still leaned against Delong's truck, staring into space. The cup was empty at his feet and he massaged a growing lump on the side of his head that I hadn't noticed before.

"You okay, Duke?" I asked.

"Yeah. I was just thinking about what my buddy Mitch said."

Cars and trucks departed around us. "Well, you stood up to him, all right."

"I did," said the Duke in a low voice. "And he broke my jaw."

Surfer climbed into the jeep with a paper bag and reached in and peeled the wrapper away from a cold greasy hamburger.

"You're not possibly going to eat that," I said, starting the engine.

"I'm like a pigeon," he said. "I'll eat anything."

Surfer flourished the hamburger, brushed an imaginary speck of dust from it, and took a gigantic bite. He chewed vigorously, smiling at the sour look I must have been giving him. Suddenly his jaw slackened, the smile dropped from his face and Surfer's throat convulsed in a deep, involuntary swallow. "Not even a pigeon would eat that," he said, heaving the burger into the darkness.

Surfer wrapped himself in a beach towel and fastened a T-shirt around his head like a turban. "Examine carefully anything you put in your mouth," he said, citing another rule of his.

I turned past the rotting pink whale without a second thought, my old comrade beside me, nodding in his homemade burnoose. The moon clarified the strip of highway running out ahead of the jeep, and above us was a benign sky that had so often threatened storms. Patterned by a high thin layer of clouds, the night moved easily around us, limning the open countryside with moonlight and softening the day's heat with unexpected streams of cool air. These were the nights that made me wonder what was out there, in the known and the unknown hemispheres, and whether I was speeding toward insight or damnation.

Surfer was reading my mind like some silent companion on the long midnight trek across the desert. And with that clairvoyance he was famous for, he turned toward me, his turban flapping over his shoulders, and brought all my questions to a point of summary. "I hope there's a fistfight at my wake," he said. "And the headline: 'Local Eccentric Dies Owing Millions.' "

"You got a good shot," I said.

5

Two weeks after Mike Melendez's arraignment, I spotted a disheveled Elvis at a taco stand down the street from the courthouse, next to a yellow plastic container marked HOT SAUCE. It was early in the morning and he was wearing the same leather jumpsuit he'd had on in jail, covered by an old dungaree jacket, his hair slicked back except for an unruly lock falling across his forehead. Eyes covered by a pair of mauve-tinted sunglasses, he hunched over the sidewalk counter, alternating pulls at a longneck bottle of beer with huge wolfish bites from a tired-looking burrito that dripped red grease down his arm.

When I approached, Elvis dropped the burrito on to the dampened counter and turned his back on it. A violent little breeze came up the alley, blowing shrouds of waxed paper and broken cigarette ends about his sockless ankles.

"That you, Elvis?" I asked.

He looked at me with suspicion, his hand tightening on the bottle he had slipped into his pocket, nervous and ready to run or fly at me. "Who wants to know?" he asked, in that unmistakable Memphis voice that was both husky and warbling. This was the Elvis of 1959 or so, slender and almost delicate, but still unpredictable, a little dangerous somehow, like his cork was in too tight.

"We were in jail together."

Elvis seemed relieved. He leaned against the counter and flipped the lock of hair back into place with an expert toss of his head. "I thought you were a cop or something, man. When were you in the joint?"

"The time all the brothers made you stand up on the bunk and sing. Remember?"

"Yessir," said Elvis. He drank from the bottle and replaced it in his pocket. "I just wasn't up for the gig."

"They beat you up pretty bad."

He laughed. "Aww, they were all right. They didn't hurt me none. I grew up with a lot of colored guys in Tupelo and they know I'm just like they are. My mama used to say we're all like Baby Jesus—musicians, that is, and colored folk. Playing with the world like it was a big old ball."

He almost had me believing, as he went on about living in shotgun shacks and playing roadhouses for small change and his jam sessions with the old bluesmen from Sun Records. Even though the real Elvis was deader than stone in his crypt at Graceland, there was the undeniable eerie feeling of a visit from the young Elvis, before the drugs and paranoia and fame all crushed him. It was American history sprung to life, no different than Thomas Jefferson or Henry Ford materializing at the taco stand.

"What are you doing in Cocoa Beach?" I asked.

"Taking me a little vacation," said Elvis. "Figured I'd play a few clubs, shimmy shake on the beach and chase the señoritas." A cloud passed overhead, and he looked sad for a moment. "Tell you the truth, I had a fight with the Colonel and said I could make it on my own. Caught a bus down here, and ain't worked a day since." He tipped the bottle to his mouth. "A few weeks back, I was in a fight, got picked up, and then I got arrested again for stealing a bag of cookies from the Jiffy Mart. I've had nothing but trouble for six months. I'm supposed to be in court this morning, only I'm figuring maybe I should run."

"You have to go, or you'll really be in deep shit. But we'll have to get you cleaned up first."

I took the beer away from him and deposited it in a trash can.

Up close he was pretty ripe and it crossed my mind that I was dealing with a street person, another homeless crazy. He was filthy and the burrito he had been eating, from the looks of it, had originally belonged to someone else.

"I'll probably never make it to Vegas now," he said, as I led him away.

He had a guitar and some clothes in a locker at the bus station. I took out a pair of blue jeans and a clean shirt and bought him a razor and a toothbrush from one of the vending machines. While I rushed around the empty station, checking my watch, Elvis drew out his guitar and sat on a bench in front of his locker and began playing it. Strumming along, he whistled the first verse of an old spiritual and then sang the next two in a hushed mellifluous tone, drawing the attention of a passing dog who trotted in and the sleepy ticket clerk, behind bars in his tiny office.

Elvis tapped his foot and let his voice rise and fall among the contours of the song. With sharply inhaled breath, exact pauses, and the rasp of his fingertips over the frets of the guitar, he made a low clear ringing against the tiled walls of the bus station. Something childlike in him evoked the old-timey slaves and their raspy chant of hope. He hadn't written it, but he *knew* it and somehow it came over him. It was like he had a secret and was letting it out a little at a time.

The song ended. The bus station resounded with its echo and then a rich silence descended on the room. Sitting at Elvis's feet, his head cocked to one side, the little stray dog waited for an encore. I cleared my throat to mention the lateness of the hour and the dog ran off. Then Elvis got up and went into the john to wash up and change his clothes.

Even the ticket clerk seemed aware he had witnessed something unusual. "We don't allow no singin' in here," he said. "But that boy can play anytime he wants."

When Elvis finally emerged, clean shaven, looking a lot younger in his blue jeans and western shirt, he stuffed his jumpsuit and guitar into the locker and we hustled over to the courthouse for his hearing. The sun was rising above the clouds and the chill of early morning had disappeared. On the street, people rushing to work stopped for a moment and stared at Elvis as he loped past.

"Damn," he said, feeling in his pockets after being recognized a few times. "I think I left my sunglasses in the damned bathroom."

But he really didn't mind the attention. Elvis seemed euphoric, where only thirty minutes earlier he had been ragged and depressed. Apparently the music had cheered him up, stirred his personality. A deliveryman called to him and Elvis made the hang loose sign with his hand and waved. Women whistled and honked their horns. "Hello, sweet young thing," he said. "Sorry I'm in such a hurry this morning." Then he whispered to me, "I could eat three puddings just like that one and still want more. I got me an appetite for the ladies."

Crossing the street to the courthouse, the bearded guy with the knapsack and soda bottles rode up on his bicycle, cursing at me and trying to cut us off with his front tire. In the middle of the intersection Elvis stopped and placed his hand on the man's shoulder.

"Do you need something, friend?" he asked.

The man's eyes rolled downward, his rage expiring, and he sank his chin deeper into his beard and showed us the greasy crown of his hat. "I'm hungry," he said.

Elvis fished in his pocket and handed over two wrinkled bills. "Here, friend. Go have yourself something to eat."

The man tipped his hat, riding off without a word. "You don't look like you can spare the two bucks," I said to Elvis. "You should've let me give it to him."

"It was me called upon to touch the Jesus in him," Elvis said, guiding us to the curb.

"Huh?"

Elvis laughed, blinking in the small winter sun above the courthouse. "That's good ol' southern revival talk," he said. "When I was a young'un, Mama used to listen to the gospel shows on the radio and in between the preachers would come on. I remember one time this feller talking about his visit to a leper colony. How he preached and handed out Bibles, careful not to let any of the lepers touch him. He kept the Bible up between them like it was a shield. Then it was revealed to him and he hugged that ol' leper and put the Bible directly into his hands. 'Until I let the Jesus in me touch the Jesus in him,' the preacher said, 'I wasn't truly doing God's work.' "

"You just let the Jesus in him touch the last two George Washingtons in your wallet," I said. "How are *you* going to eat?"

"At the table He prepares for me," Elvis said, "I will eat and drink my fill."

Elvis had more than a little preacher in him and kept me spellbound going up the courthouse steps. But I hadn't forgotten that his act of faith immediately followed his vulgarity toward women. He would swagger and boast and then turn shy, open doors for you one minute and then expect you to wait on him, fawn over him, praise him the next. His humility followed his pride in rapid succession, the mark of a man on shaky ground and more than vaguely familiar. Everything about him, from the way he flipped his hair into place to that marvelous untrained voice, all the contradictions added up to the late, great King of Rock 'n' Roll. It was uncanny.

Court was not yet in session and a word with the bailiff informed us that Elvis's hearing was several cases down the docket. "A lot of these things get pleaded out," he explained. "If it's not too serious, they might give him a suspended sentence."

I knew the bailiff from my time covering the courthouse beat, a nice enough guy, but brisk and very professional, never one for volunteering information like that.

"Thanks for the tip," I said.

"Don't mention it."

He gazed at my companion, who was occupied by the carnival atmosphere in the room, the comings and goings of the various prostitutes and lawyers and housebreakers, some huddling in little conferences, some standing together in silence, and the bailiff leaned forward in his chair and said, "I loved ol' Elvis. I really did."

We moved off and found space in the rear of the courtroom. Elvis began amusing himself with little feats of optical illusion, like touching his two index fingers together a few inches from his face and staring until a disembodied baby finger appeared between them. His sleight of hand left something to be desired as he made a coin disappear and then gasped in mock surprise when he found it again. A magician he was not.

A pretty young whore sat down on the bench next to Elvis and he flourished a tiny paper bouquet under her nose, her face lit by a brief weary smile, Elvis in profile, grinning at the whore's tiny pleasure and his own skill in prestidigitation.

Hulic Rasterree came in, hauling an armful of file folders. With his arrival the murmuring decreased, the crowd parted, and he made his way unmolested to the prosecutor's table. Despite being a small man he was conspicuous with his wavy yellow hair, the fine tropical suit he wore, and the superior air about him. It kept everyone away except the bailiff, who delivered the docket sheet into his hand and withdrew.

"That's the feller who sent me to jail the last time," Elvis said. "He sure don't like me none."

"Don't worry," I said. "Rasterree's okay. He'll give you a break."

It was hard to be convincing when some of the shiftiest defense lawyers in the room wore sudden looks of concern and paced up and down with lined foreheads. Hardened criminals were panicking, whispered conversations had resumed in earnest all over the courtroom, and I watched as two lawyers slunk over to the bailiff and changed pleas to guilty. Elvis was ready to bolt. His hands trembled and one leg began shaking and he practically vibrated himself off the bench.

"I'm going to jail, ain't I?" he asked.

"For stealing a bag of cookies? No way." I tried to sound confident, even though the D.A. looked like he'd send his own mother to jail for double parking. "I'll speak to Rasterree," I said. "You better go see about your lawyer."

Elvis gripped my arm. "If they send me away, I want you to take care of my guitar. It's the only thing I got in this world."

"You're not going anywhere," I told him. "Go see about your lawyer."

A few people stared as he walked across the room, nudging each other, amazed at the resemblance. He was graceful, thin hipped, the lock of hair dangling across his forehead. One of the whores said something to him and he shook his head and smiled and went on. She must have felt a pang because her face softened and she looked after him fondly for a moment.

"I'm gonna have to report what I'm thinking right now to my parole officer," another whore said, and the first whore pulled her hair and stomped on her toes with a spiked heel. "That beautiful boy is all mine, so forget it," she said.

Hulic Rasterree was alone at the prosecutor's table making notes on an elongated yellow pad, his bushy eyebrows drawn together above those predatory eyes, absorbed in his work. He was racing through the files, but in a precise manner that indicated he was actually reading them—with the benefit of an astounding memory. No one besides the bailiff had dared disturb Rasterree and, as it became clear I meant to speak to him, some of the court officers shook their heads and made signs for me to turn back. It was too late. I leaned against the heavy oak table and had that tight feeling in my throat I'd get in school when I had to see the principal.

The district attorney knew I was there. His head inclined a little to one side and he continued his note taking. No doubt he was used to making people wait. A clerk approached with some papers to sign and was refused. It was like a panhandler asking the Sultan of Brunei for a nickel.

"There's a case I'd like to speak to you about," I said. "A friend of mine—"

The district attorney lifted his head and startled me into silence with the cold blue penetration of his eyes. A face so pale and smooth was intimidating, an educated haughty face, marred only by tiny crow's-feet in the corners of his eyes; and that color blue like the color of arctic ice.

"Well, what is it?" he asked.

I started to explain myself, referring to the young man signing autographs for the whores in the back of the room, where Rasterree glanced without comment. Thin streams of perspiration ran down my sides and my voice rose in pitch and accelerated as Rasterree's silence lengthened. He listened impatiently and when I was through he recognized me and subtracted that from what I had said.

"What are you, sir, some kind of roving advocate for habitual criminals?" Rasterree asked in an unexpectedly nasal voice. He indicated Elvis by moving his eyes in that direction and then coming back to meet mine. "This man is a paranoid schizophrenic with a long history of disorderly conduct and petty theft. I'm going to ask that he be turned over to the county psychiatric hospital for evaluation and treatment. He's a menace."

"No, he's not," I insisted. "He walks and talks and sings just like Elvis."

The bailiff stood to call the courtroom to order and Rasterree closed his files and waved me back from the table. "His claim that he is a deceased hillbilly singer only reinforces my belief that you certainly could find a better way to spend your time."

"What's he gonna do?" Elvis asked when I returned to the back benches and sat down. "Will he give me a break on this thing?" He rubbed his hands together until he saw the look on my face and slumped forward, cradling his head. "Doggone, he ain't," said Elvis. "Man, I'm going to jail."

The judge entered the courtroom, a bald dour-looking man in a long black vestment, and we got to our feet as the bailiff called out the *oyez.*

"It's worse than that," I said. "What he really wants to do is put you in the fun house and let them make your head smaller."

Elvis stared at me.

"They want to put you in the hospital," I whispered.

He looked relieved. "Don't scare me like that, man. For a minute there, I thought they were saying I was crazy or something."

The courtroom grew still and the first case was heard, a Cuban man who set off an uproar when the police department failed to supply a witness on a gambling charge. The judge dismissed the case. Confused at first, this Mr. Morales, dressed in a rumpled leisure suit, kept turning to his wife and three children sitting behind him. All of them were crying except one, the oldest boy, slender and dark haired, the interpreter for his father, who spoke little English. A torrent of words passed between them. When at last he understood, Mr. Morales, provoked and appreciative, reached into a paper sack on the floor beside him and removed a dead unplucked chicken, waved it about while making joyful exclamations in Spanish, and then tried to give it to the judge. The bailiff lunged from his seat and, joined by another court officer, restrained poor Mr. Morales.

He was knocked sideways and the chicken flew from his hand in a lifeless arc and landed in a small feathered heap on the floor. The limp chicken produced an intensely comic effect and the gallery screamed with laughter.

The judge banged his gavel for order. A last snicker floated out from the back of the room and then there was silence. One of the court officers picked up the chicken and I noticed that the defense lawyer was squeezing the bridge of his nose to keep from laughing out loud at the droopy neck and stiff yellow feet of the dead bird.

"There's something damned funny about that chicken," Elvis said.

The accused shook himself free from the officers and suffered a long baleful glare from the judge. A moment passed. The judge looked down at some documents spread before him, hid a brief smile with his hand, and said, "This case is dismissed. And Mr. Morales, please leave your poultry at home if you ever have the misfortune of appearing before this court again."

The accused gambler did not retire. "No play cards for money," he stammered in his best English. "I tell about cards."

"That's all right, Mr. Morales," said the judge. "The charges have been dropped. You can go now."

The bailiff took Mr. Morales by the arm but he stood his ground. His wife and children came to his side and he remained before the bench, encircled by his family. "The police no like *mi familia*. No like smell, no like music, no like eat. Okay. I am strong for work. Strong for America. No want police come."

The judge looked at the Moraleses' eldest son and indicated he wanted what he said translated. "It may be the police made a mistake, Mr. Morales. But that doesn't matter now, since there won't be a hearing. You're free to go."

"No free," said Morales. "Ashamed."

Since his case would not be heard before the morning recess, I left Elvis sitting there among the thieves and whores and went out to the lobby to call the newspaper. Maxine was busy and for a few minutes I held the line for her, aimless music tootling in my ear. Lawyer Timmons entered the courthouse. His face was composed and serious and he was carrying an old-fashioned leather briefcase. I waved him over.

"Good morning, Mr. Dolan," he said. "What can I do for you?"

"I was just wondering—"

"About Mike Melendez," he interrupted. "I'm on my way to the pretrial this minute." He glanced at his watch. "I'm going to ask the judge to drop the charges for lack of evidence."

"What's he going to say?"

"He'll say no, of course. This is where they got the expression 'Going through the motions.'"

"So nothing's changed," I said.

"Unless the skin color of the parties involved has miraculously changed, no, nothing has. That's what this case is all about. I thought you understood that."

This last remark was delivered in a chiding tone, and I ignored it. "Sherri Hogg's story is full of holes," I said. "The boyfriend put her up to it."

"You've met him?"

"I met him, all right. He said the newspaper better get the story straight or the 'niggers downtown' would have a field day."

Lawyer Timmons remained looking at me through large bloodshot eyes. This sort of vulgarity did not shock him. His feeling toward what T-bone had said was probably like the one a scientist had while examining bacteria through a microscope. It was all flagellating scum and the tiny variations in it produced only a mild professional interest.

"Sherri and this T-bone think they're going to make a bundle of money somehow," I said.

"Selling their story?" asked Lawyer Timmons, with an arched eyebrow.

"I think he's already decided who's going to play him in the movie."

Lawyer Timmons made an unpleasant face. "Not only a racist but a man of ambition, too." He glanced once more at his watch. "And Sherri—what does she say about it?"

"She says whatever T-bone wants her to say. Apparently he beats her. He's nothing but a bully."

Lawyer Timmons lifted one of his long weathered hands into the air, palm turned outward, making a biblical gesture for emphasis. "Some men have this little voice in their hearts: 'Nobody's going to remember me,'" he said. "And that makes them do unspeakable things."

He hurried away to his meeting before I could respond, one stride to everyone else's two across the polished marble floor, commanding attention until he passed beneath an archway and disappeared from view. The phone continued pouring vapid instrumental favorites into my ear. And as I considered the great tyrannies of history and the small ones I had suffered or seen pressed on others, the truth of what Lawyer Timmons had said emerged from the dull landscape of the music. Hitler certainly wanted to be remembered, and he sent his storm troopers marching to see that it was done. The blitzkrieg was merely his autograph in the sky over Europe. Hitler killed a lot of nice people. So did Stalin. Some killed only one, but were real picky about it. Sirhan Sirhan. John Wilkes Booth. Judas Iscariot. Singular, frightening names. Everyone remembered the killers.

Villains throughout history retain immense popularity while a hundred thousand good deeds fade into thin air. Even the beloved crooner Elvis was remembered more for the harm he had done to himself and those he loved than for his marvelous silken voice. My own parents were getting hazy in my recollection. Long stretches of my memory were scorched white, and passing over them was like traveling through the blank open spaces of a desert. It was all very pleasant, but indistinct, uncharted and unremarkable ground. Something nobody would remember.

The phone buzzed in my ear. "Joe who?" asked Maxine. "Do I have a Joe Dolan working for me?"

"Working around the clock to bring glory to my editor and honor to the Cocoa Beach *Post-Gazette,*" I said.

"Where the hell are you?"

"At the courthouse. There's a lot going on down here. I want you to send a photographer."

"Shirley just went down there with a camera. And Walter's there, too," Maxine said, gasping a little. "But that's great. I've got six news reporters covering fifty square miles and three of them are at the courthouse. What am I worrying about?"

"Please don't hyperventilate, Maxine. I just need somebody to take a picture of Elvis for me and then I'll be in."

Her voice remained calm. "If you can get a picture of a three-headed baby goat or a woman kidnapped by aliens bring that in, too. I always thought we should sell the paper in the grocery checkout." She muffled the receiver and spoke to someone else. "I think Joe Dolan's lost his mind."

"Maxine, listen to me. Don't worry. There's a guy down here and I want his picture, that's all."

"Joe—an *Elvis* sighting? I've got wire stories piling up on my desk and you're calling in dead celebrities. There must be a good—"

Someone rubbed a hand over my behind. It was Shirley Kimball, and immediately I was thrust into her dense cloud of perfume. Never taking her eyes away, she leered at me in a way I found flattering but a little scary, like being invited to hit major league pitching.

"Your hand is on my ass," I said, without covering the phone.

"What?" asked Maxine.

"Oh," cooed Shirley. She batted her long false eyelashes. "I didn't even realize."

Maxine began hyperventilating again. "Joe—what the hell is going on? Who's that?"

"It's me," Shirley said, taking the phone. She leaned forward to accommodate the brief cord, shoving her breasts at me, their freckled tops bulging up from her trademark black bra. "Sure I'll send the boy wonder straight home. He's been very naughty today."

Maxine said something to Shirley that I couldn't hear. The red-headed senior reporter shifted her hips inside her leather skirt and rubbed the outside of her thigh against mine, smiling with flecks of lipstick dabbed across her upper teeth. The smell of perfume hung in the air like rotting vegetation.

"No, I haven't interviewed Sherri yet," said Shirley. She listened to Maxine a moment, frowning. "I know she's important. I'm still working on the crazy boyfriend. He won't let me see her."

Maxine's tinny agitated voice seeped into the marble chamber, captured by the incredible acoustics that made Lawyer Timmons's footfalls seem like thunder. "—get one from Sherri now, or you'll be covering church fairs again."

Shirley hung up the phone. "Bitch." Ignoring me for the moment, she chewed her lip and stared at a spot on the floor. "Have you seen Walter?" she asked.

"Not yet. But he's here." I rubbed it in. "He's working on a big story, I guess." Shirley let out a string of curses and I dangled the bait. "If I took you over to where Sherri lives, you'd be back here before Walter could say 'Pulitzer Prize.' "

Shirley's eyes darted this way and that and she agonized for a long moment, I knew, over beating Walter without my help. "What do you want?" she asked.

"I want you to tell me what's going on at the courthouse. And I want you to take a picture for me. Then I'll show you where Sherri Hogg lives."

"Great. No problem." Shirley swung her camera up and snapped three quick shots of me shaking my head. "Not pictures of *me*. Somebody in there," I said, pointing to the courtroom. She giggled. "Oh. Okay. Great."

I led the way. "You really do have a nice butt, Joe," she said.

I swung open the door and a court officer frowned and made us sit down. Court was already in session. Hulic Rasterree was standing before the bench conferring with the judge and Elvis was behind the defense table, looking sad and hollow eyed. The judge cleared his throat.

"All right. I'm going to agree that the accused complete a two-week psychiatric evaluation at the Cape County Hospital," he said. He looked at Elvis. "Then, sir, I want to see you back here in my courtroom to answer this charge."

"Man, that was fast," I whispered to Shirley.

"Now you know what's going on," she said.

Elvis's lawyer, a seedy hook-nosed man with sunken cheeks and dandruff, patted his client on the arm and nodded to the judge. "Thank you, Your Honor. You'll like it in there," he said to Elvis. "They'll treat you real fine, son, real fine."

"In where?" asked a dazed Elvis.

Two sheriffs came and took him out through the prisoner's exit. Rasterree paused to let Elvis walk by and then returned to his seat, a smirk playing across his face. Just as Elvis disappeared into a stairwell he smiled ruefully at me and made the hang loose sign with his hand. Shirley raised her camera and snapped his picture. A few of the whores grumbled and sighed and attention turned to the next case.

"Elvis has left the building," the bailiff said under his breath.

I approached the dandruff-flecked lawyer. "What happened?"

The man looked at me like I was speaking a foreign language. "He's my friend. What happened?" I asked again.

"They're taking him to County. Three hots and a cot," the lawyer said, closing his briefcase. He yawned. "It'll get him off the streets."

"If those head doctors start poking around, they might never let him out of there," I said, a fountain of guilt rising in me.

The lawyer shrugged. "Unless he's really who he says he is, that's not such a bad idea," he replied. His lips flapped open and he shook his soft red nose at me. "Hmmph—*you* don't think he's Elvis, do you, son?"

I didn't answer him. Shirley gestured from the doorway and we left the courtroom and went outside. The stairs to the street were empty. Grumbling to myself, I followed Shirley to her car.

"What's bugging you?" she asked, donning a pair of cat's-eye sunglasses. "I got his picture okay."

"They're taking him to the funny farm, and it's my fault. If it wasn't for me, he'd be halfway to Las Vegas by now."

Shirley waited beside her car with one leg thrust out, a high heel stabbing the pavement. In the sunlight the gilt frames of her eyeglasses sparkled and her breasts were pale on top with a dark appealing shadow between them. "If you weren't such a goddamned Boy Scout, Joe, you wouldn't get yourself in these predicaments," she said, half kindly. "Just write your stories, kid, and the hell with everything else."

I stared at the shadowy courthouse looming over us. "It was me called upon to touch the Jesus in him," I said, shading my eyes. "Ain't that something?"

Shirley didn't hear what I said or chose to ignore it, and got in the car and snapped her key into the ignition. "Are you coming, or what?" she called to me. "Let's go. Walter is screwing me on this thing."

I gave Shirley directions to the trailer park and we screamed away from the curb. "There's a lot of sneaky shit going on," she said over the disco music blasting from the radio. "Walter's sneaking around like a goddamned fox. I can't trust him." She jerked her thumb over her shoulder, back toward the courthouse. "Every mother's son in that place was wearing crepe-soled shoes, or didn't you notice? Sneaking up on each other to beat the devil, the whole lot of them."

Shirley was in a lather. When she got herself going, her Alabama roots began to show and her sophistication disappeared. She used a lot of country expressions and old-fashioned cuss-words. "You better be talking straight, Joe," she said, wagging a finger at me. "Or I'll take your balls off with a pair of rusty snips."

I crossed my legs. "Sherri will be there, don't worry," I insisted. "But her boyfriend might be there, too. He's a real Christian. Attends Saint Xenophobia church, right here in Cocoa Beach."

"I'll handle him," Shirley said, clenching the wheel of her plushly upholstered Buick. "He ain't nothing except poorhouse trash."

Since he was already down, it seemed like a good time to give T-bone a kick or two. "When I met him, he said some broad offered him fifty bucks for Sherri's story and that wasn't near enough. He said he was calling the shots."

"Try to bleed money out of me, that jackleg son of a bitch," Shirley said in a compressed voice. "We'll see who does most of the bleeding when we get there."

We breezed down Orange Boulevard in the sparse late-morning traffic, the big car humming with power and the air conditioner blowing a glacial stream of air against Shirley's tightly packed breasts. In spite of the current, her gaudy red hair remained motionless under its glaze of hair spray. Shirley was a warrior. I felt safer approaching T-bone with Shirley Kimball than I would have under armed guard.

"You talked to T-bone," I said. "Do you think Melendez raped Sherri Hogg?"

Shirley looked at me sideways, her small green eyes sliding

between the thick rails of eyeliner she wore. "I'm a reporter, not a fortune teller." After a moment she added, "I wouldn't give him a nickel's chance in that courthouse either way, not from what I've been seeing."

We turned off and rode alongside the row of flat metal trailers, shiny in the heat. Shirley cruised the Buick through the empty weeded section and went into the mossy trees at the far end of the park. I showed her where the old humpbacked trailer had stood. It was nowhere in sight.

"This was the place," I said, as we got out of the car. The air in the clearing was heavy with moisture. "They were right here, I swear."

Shirley paced the length of the clearing in a silent rage. She knew I was telling the truth: there were tire tracks indicating something heavy had been dragged away. The tracks made two deep furrows that ended at the pavement. Her hands balled into fists, breasts heaving at their restraints, Shirley dug into the clay with her spike heels and the flesh quivered for an instant along her jawline. The frames of her sunglasses glittered in the noon light falling directly overhead.

"I've just about had it with those two," she said in a voice that was soft and menacing. "This here rape, so-called, is starting to disappear behind the crime of making a profit from it."

I leaned against the Buick in that smoldering damp heat I'd never gotten used to, scratched my bean and thought of Elvis, who hadn't hurt anyone, trussed up in a straitjacket on his way to the nuthouse. "The whole thing is sure getting blurry," I said.

Shirley produced a cigarette from God knows where, lit it with a slim gold lighter, and, her face obscured by smoke, said, "Everything in this business is fucking blurry. You get your byline and your paycheck. The rest is all bullshit."

6

When rugby practice was over I lay down on a soft patch of grass, dizzy and sick, my head pounding from the effort. Everyone drifted away, their voices fading on air that smelled like rain. The county fairgrounds, where we practiced and played our home games, were a vast green plantation dotted with horse barns and vacant candy-striped concession booths. Evening dew was on the infield, wetting the back of my jersey, and a bank of fog gathered between the giant live oaks on the other side of the paddock.

Sulkies were clip-clopping around the track, chewing its smooth red surface, and the stables and silent glass-fronted grandstand were dark and full of shadows. Beyond me, some players were lying in the grass, talking and stretching, or just staring up at the faded purple sky, chewing on sticks of hay. Insects buzzed low over the ground and the late sun slanted in, striking a set of goalposts in a way that fastened them together with a rope of light.

I dozed for a moment, woke up, and raised myself on my elbows. It was sunset and the moon had appeared, looking like a giant coin above the wall of oak trees. The other players congregated in the parking lot, pulling off their sweaty jerseys, toweling down, and putting on their sneakers for the ride home. So long, Iain. See you Thursday. See ya, Martin, they said in those soft strong voices.

"I got a joke for you. I got a joke for you—" Todd Baker was saying. "Why won't cannibals eat clowns?" Everyone paused in their conversation and he hit us with the punchline. "Because they taste funny!"

His face had this marionette quality to it, his eyes bright with mirth, and when he delivered the line, and then repeated it, trotting off to his bicycle in that thoroughbred canter of his, we laughed and our laughter rang out against the darkened trees surrounding the track.

It was a rugby player's joke. Most people I knew had no idea what rugby was. They thought we beat the hell out of each other with sticks, but that's lacrosse, an Indian game. If all sports are really about war, then rugby is an eighteenth-century epic of bayonet charges and hand-to-hand fighting. On an expanded football field without yard lines, the teams line up facing each other like infantrymen wearing cleated boots. Every few moments, the combatants steel themselves for a fresh assault into the teeth of the enemy. From the sidelines it's chaos, bodies thumping each other, the ball squirting into the air. But we understand it perfectly. To us, it's poetry: violence and creativity under the rules.

"Are you coming to the bar?" Todd asked me.

"I drink no more forever—it's like an atheist going to church."

Then Todd, fastening his soggy uniform to the back of his bicycle, winked and said, "Even atheists go to church sometimes."

Surfer swung his leg over the seat of his dirt bike and put up the kickstand. "Let's go, Geronimo," he said to me. "I wanna make beer call." My leg cramped and I sat down in the dust to stretch it, my eyes going up to the tall spreading trees overhead.

"You could build a nice house out of that," I said, admiring the thick sturdy branches.

"Not me," Surfer said, starting the bike with a rumble. "I know very little about wood."

Everyone was beat-tired except for Surfer John. He was hardly even damp with perspiration, his bronzed face untroubled, not a sun-bleached hair out of place. It was unlikely that Surfer had ever sweated much over anything in his life.

When I made his acquaintance the Marine Corps had just discharged him—"premature ejaculation" he called it. His hair was short and he was filed down from all the PT but he still had the surfer's mischief in his eyes and he looked like he'd just walked off the set of *The Endless Summer*. I named him Surfer John and it was only later I found out he really did own a board and hailed from Daytona Beach.

He grinned at me now from behind a pair of silver goggles, his legs straddling the bike. He looked like an astronaut except for the long hair, one of the mad technological cowboys he helped launch into space.

A flash storm hit on our way to the Legion hall, two or three minutes of dense pelting rain, lightning in flat-bladed swaths to our left and right and multiple thunder exploding in the distance. Surfer laughed with each strike, bending low over the handlebars as he accelerated. Other cars and a few light trucks pulled to the shoulder of Orange Boulevard to sit out the deluge but Surfer roared past them, sending up a long rooster tail of water behind us. "Can do," he shouted.

As the rain subsided, we found the American Legion hall, a strange gothic building in the middle of some palm trees, and coasted into the gravel lot. It was one of those dimly lit, cavernous function rooms, a piano at one end, exposed beams overhead, and the pervading smell of old cigar smoke. The bar was just a window cut out of the wall that afforded a view into the members' bar on the other side—fat, middle-aged women and pouch-eyed men sipping their drinks in silence, watched over by the impassive portraits of dead soldiers from World War II, Korea, and Vietnam.

My teammates were gathered in the light of the bar window ordering up beers and Cokes. Some were in stocking feet and others clattered over the hardwood floor in their cleats. The jukebox was blasting, drinks were being spilled, and conversations and fragments of conversations went swirling around me. Rugby practices are little pockets of socializing interspersed with lung-searing pain and the foreboding of full contact minus the adrenaline. The payoff comes in the bar.

Big Josh came up to me wearing a stethoscope around his neck and pressed the business end of it against the wrong side of my chest. "I'm your party doctor," he said, moving on to Surfer. "Welcome to the Center for Health Prevention."

"You can never be too rich or too thin," I said to Surfer as we watched Josh fumble for change at the bar, his belly shaking like a huge pudding.

We got something to drink and a while later Todd rolled in, bicycle and all, circling the empty dance floor with his hands behind his head. Iain Caffrey jumped up on stage and accompanied Todd's stunt on the piano, a tinkling off-key ragtime, looking comic on the tiny stool with his huge bare legs and oversize hands. Todd spun around and rode backward, the other players stomping their feet and clapping with the music.

Roger the bartender stuck his bald head through the window and observed this vaudeville for a few moments. "Okay, boys," he said good naturedly. "Let's calm it down a little bit."

Circling again, Todd made a nimble leap from the bicycle without stopping and it sailed through the open door, crashing out in the foyer. The sound of the front wheel, clicking as it went, filtered back into the bar.

"And don't you ever come back here again," Todd said over his shoulder. He shrugged at the bartender. "Troublemakers," he whispered.

Roger laughed and shook his head and handed two more fistfuls of beer through the window. Voices rose as collective exhaustion gave way to the energy of the cocktail hour. The pain of wind sprints and tackling practice and the monotony of all those drills miraculously disappeared after the first fifteen minutes. "I had a dream last night that it snowed at the beach and we made snowmen and went ice skating, then Loretta showed up dressed in a fur bikini and I drank a beer," I said.

"I'm happy to hear that your Byzantine dreams have not lost their enduring narrative quality," said Surfer. "Heck, if it's just a dream," he added, "you might as well have a shot, too."

I had been dry for over a year. After about three gallons of rum-and-Coke one night at Saxophone Joe's, I cried over the phone to Maxine, telling her how much I missed my dead mother and father. She was very nice about it, even though it was three in the morning. Then I went home and smashed half the pickets on our fence with a baseball bat. Too much liquor makes me lose my inhibitions, and I'm uninhibited enough already.

The door to the Legion hall opened again and, picking his way around the mud-spattered bicycle, in walked Mike Melendez. A pall descended over the room. In three weeks Mike had lost a lot of weight. His clothes hung on him and his wrists and ankles were thin. Every face in the room was turned in Mike's direction, but for the moment no one spoke to him. He paused halfway to the bar, surveying us. A long moment passed.

Steve Delong stood against the wall, his face sullen and dark under a battered red baseball cap. "Well look who's here," he said and spat on the sawdusted floor.

"If you're gonna do that, go outside," said Roger.

"Don't worry, he's strong. He'll pick it up," Edelstein said amid a few chuckles.

Duke Ritter passed in front of me and shook Mike Melendez's hand, guiding him to the bar. I shook Mike's hand and so did Surfer and Iain and Edelstein. One or two at a time they all came over—except Delong and Whizzer—and said something, or poked Mike in the shoulder and bought him a beer. The countertop was soon crowded with bottles of Guinness. Mike's eyes were shining and his lips set in a grim line. Tall and straight, he still looked royal, but worn out, a king under siege.

"I'm gonna have to help you drink these beers," said the Duke through his wired jaw. "Somebody's got to do it."

Coach Van came over. All we really knew about Van Valkenburg was that his first name was Tom and he did infrequent fix-it work to scratch out a living. He was big and rangy without being muscular, very pale skinned, and the proprietor of two misshapen banged-up knees. He squinted at Mike through small, pale blue eyes, hands on his hips, the longish uncombed white hair falling to his shoulders. "Lost some weight," he said.

Melendez nodded.

"Well, put it back on," growled Van. "You look like a fucking anorexic. And get your ass out to practice."

Mike scuffed his feet against the parquet floor and looked down. "Uh, Coach, I'm having some trouble right now and I don't—"

Van had already started walking away and he jerked his head around in Mike's direction. "That's got nothing to do with rugby. Who you are or what you do in the world doesn't matter to me one goddamned bit." He took in those of us standing by the bar with a single stabbing glance. "You have your humdrum little jobs, your families, your girlfriends—and nobody gives a shit. But when you're on that field, you're rugby players. Why play if you're not going to win? And if we get there together—"he stared straight at Delong "—believe me, none of you will care how we did it."

Coach Van shook his head at what dummies we were and left us standing there in silence. He returned for the last word. "Rugby's not a game, it's a bloody religion. That's why we play—because this is a tribe. After the game, after we pound the piss out of the other team, over a few beers we can look each other in the eye and know we're unique."

Josh was stunned. Edelstein likewise. Sean and Iain Caffrey, side by side in their dirty rugby togs, were as silent and motionless as a pair of cigar store Indians. Tousled and sunburnt, they were so wholesome they looked like giant pieces of wheat. Roger, his bald head shining, rested his elbows on the bar and looked out at us with a fatherly expression on his face.

Coach Van had struck a chord. It came as a sudden, startling jolt and I felt a warm sensation spreading across the back of my neck. Van had just said out loud what athletes never, or at least rarely, discuss among themselves. And he had done it for a reason. There had been a lot of negative talk about Mike Melendez and Van didn't appreciate it. Mike was one of the horses that pulled the wagon. We needed him to win. Van put in long hours at the fairgrounds, for nothing, working us into some hard clean image of a rugby team he had in his head. You could see it in his eyes sometimes when he ran us out to the far fences in a tight bunch and called for our return. He was a man with a vision and that vision was running toward him over grass that stank sweetly of manure.

Even Duke Ritter, laconic and artless, with his bulbous alcoholic nose and cauliflowered ears, was on the same wavelength. "Joe," he said, handing me one of the blue-tipped matches he liked to chew on. "It's my last one, buddy."

A few guys wandered away and Roger left the window to serve one of the members who'd called for another drink. Cigar smoke billowed in the arc of light over the bar, and the dusty smell of it mingled with the odor of hay and sweat that clung to us. Edelstein coughed. He was a health fanatic in just about every respect except his fondness for bacon and sausage. His coughing persisted and Todd smacked him on the back several times, making a distinct percussive sound.

"Don't fucking die on us," said Todd.

Duke chipped in. "You're unique," he said.

Grinning over his beer bottle Surfer said, "Me too. I want to be just as unique as everybody else."

Mike Melendez no doubt felt as good as he had been feeling lately. He stood with Todd and Surfer and drank some beer. Then I handed him a bag of potato chips from the wire rack on the bar and said, "Here. Eat. You look like a goddamned anorexic."

"I'm not sure these will help me," Mike said in a soft voice. He tore the bag open and Surfer and Todd plunged their hands in and began crunching on the chips. Mike ate one or two and the bag was empty.

"Hey, we get hungry, too," Todd said, shrugging at the look I gave him.

"No wonder he's so fucking skinny," I said. "Give the man some room." Opening a bag of cheese popcorn this time, I steered it to Mike's chin. "Go ahead, Mike. Bulk up on this."

Iain and Sean Caffrey descended on the popcorn like two giant yellow buzzards. "Nice to see ya, Mike. Gee whiz. Popcorn. Arggh," they said, tearing the bag to shreds. Kernels scattered everywhere and Iain bent down and ate some of them off the floor. The rest of us shied away and watched the Caffreys fight over the stray popcorn like the scavengers they were. Sean even licked the inside of the bag. Mike stood there amazed, a tiny scrap of plastic held between his thumb and forefinger.

"Can I get you something else?" I asked him.

"I couldn't eat another bite," said Mike.

Edelstein put one of his heavily muscled arms around Mike's shoulder, lifting a face into the light so freckled and broad it might have come straight out of County Cork. And he ran and hit as hard as any stony boy who ever talked with a lilt. Except that he was from Miami, of the polo-playing Edelsteins, and as Jewish as matzos.

"What makes us different from you?" he asked.

"You're standing over there and we're standing over here," said Todd.

"That's not it," said Edelstein. "Look a little closer." He gripped Mike's shoulder and straightened himself, like they were posing for a photograph. It was dramatic: the muscular Irish-looking Jew and the tall regal islander. "Come on. It's obvious."

Surfer took a step toward them. He started to speak and then checked himself, wagging his head. "I just can't quite put my finger on it," he said.

Edelstein looked at me and I shrugged. "I'm a reporter. What do I know?"

Mike wore a dreamy, almost bored expression, staring over our heads. Several feet away, Delong scowled and fretted himself, his face shaded by the baseball hat. He certainly had an opinion, one that worked at him like a virus. He wanted to say something but Duke Ritter preempted him.

"You're both lefties," he said.

Edelstein was pleased. "Duke, you're a genius. Mike and I are lefties," he said.

"That's fascinating, Dave," I said. "But—so what?"

"It's simple," he answered, coming away from Mike toward us. "It means the whole world is right-handed. Think about it for a minute. Doorknobs, light switches, the shift for your car. Turn around and try everything lefty for a change. It ain't easy."

"What bullshit," said Delong. The greasy hat threw a shadow across his eyes when he stepped into the light. "You want people to feel sorry for you because you're a lefty?"

There was silence for a moment, then Todd said, "People feel sorry for *you* because you're an asshole." Delong glared at him.

"Yeah, turn around and try something lefty, Steve. Like jerking off," said Surfer.

We all laughed. Delong flung a hateful wordless glance at Mike Melendez and stalked off, his cleats rattling over the dented parquet floor.

"What a fucking pinhead," Todd said.

I looked over at Mike standing back against the bar. He was unsmiling, drawn about the face, almost sickly. His rugby-playing days were over, no matter what anybody said. The clatter of bottles and glasses filled the Legion hall, the dusty smell of cigars, and nobody seemed to notice the gloom that had settled on Mike Melendez. He was finished with us and was starting to thin out and fade, like a spirit that children don't believe in anymore.

The jukebox played a song about driving through Nebraska while the beer flowed and loud voices competed with the music. In the midst of this uproar Iain Caffrey's wife appeared, towing one of their reedy blond-haired kids. Lila was a petite woman, milky blue eyes set in a snub-nosed cherub's face, but when she moved through the crowd of rugby players they ducked their heads and shrank back from her. The effect was like a game warden surprising a group of hunters. Spotting Iain at one of the tables, Lila called his name in a shrill voice. Immediately he went to her.

"What are you doing?" Lila asked.

Everyone was watching, although most pretended not to. "Just having a beer," said Iain, towering above his wife.

"Having a beer at—" she glanced at her wristwatch "—nine-thirty on Tuesday night." Lila placed her hands on her hips and scanned the room. "I guess no one reminded you tonight was Bobby's science fair, or that Michelle has been waiting outside dance class *in the rain* since quarter to nine."

Iain stood there blinking at his wife, orange stains from the cheese popcorn on his mouth and a fine orange powder dusted across his rugby jersey. "I forgot," he said.

"She's gonna kill him dead," Surfer whispered to me, covering his eyes.

Lila smiled coldly. "It's a good thing one of us remembered," she said. "I'll go pick up Michelle now."

"Okey-dokey," said Iain.

For a moment he probably thought he was getting off easy until Lila said, "We'll talk about this at home. Tonight," and, holding her husband's gaze, nodding with the certain knowledge he would be punished in some tacit or obscure way, Lila left him standing there with little Bobby. Her blue eyes were glittering as she turned to go, the rugby players parting before her like the sea.

Iain should have kept his mouth shut and gone home as instructed. But all the testosterone collected in the Legion hall had a strange effect on him. Coming forward along the lane that had been cleared for his wife, Iain made a noise on the floor with his cleats. For the entertainment of the boys, he threw his shoulders back and stiffened his long thick body in a military posture. At the fatal moment when Lila heard the sharp click against the parquetry and looked back, Iain raised his arm toward the ceiling in a Nazi salute. It was painful to watch.

"Oh boy. That's always a crowd pleaser," said Edelstein.

"She's gonna kill the whole worthless lot of us," Surfer said, his hands over his face.

Lila shook her head, smiling faintly, and spoke to Special Ed, who was standing near the door. "Thank God you're not him," she said, and went out.

Sean Caffrey sprang from the corner where he had been hiding and punched Iain on the shoulder. His hands in a machine gun position, he aimed at his brother and made an *ack-ack-ack* noise, laughing until the tears came.

His little nephew gazed up at him. "Uncle Sean," said Bobby, waving his hand. "Mom said Auntie Linda's gonna git you, too."

Sean's face trembled. "I should go," he said, glancing toward the door. "It *is* getting late."

Bobby ran among the players collecting sticks of gum and having his hair tousled while the Caffrey brothers looked at each other like someone was sawing a limb beneath them.

"I say we have another beer," Iain declared.

From out of his taupe-colored eyes Sean agreed. "Yeah. Why should we jump when they say jump?"

It was the fastest beer in history, largely symbolic, gulped without ceremony by the huge Caffrey twins, but the significance of it was not lost on those gathered around the bar. Admiring them, we hung about in a loose knot, as if they were the last authentic cowboys or the practitioners of some dangerous fading art, steeplejacks or harpooners, who tempted fate and thought little of it. They were married men. They were heroes.

"Okay," said Iain, wiping the froth from his lips. "Let's go."

He handed the two empty bottles over the bar to Roger, who saluted him with a nod. Iain and Sean shook a few hands on the way out. "Wherever you go, we go with you," big Josh said, as two or three guys hummed "America the Beautiful."

"I wish you were going instead of me," replied Iain. At the door he turned and regarded us, making a small forlorn wave, then he called out to his son who was kneeling on a stool in front of the pinball machine.

"Come on, Bobby," he said.

The boy glanced at him over the whirring pounding machine, ensconced in cigar smoke, his happy blazing face reflected in the glass as the beery onlookers coached him, clapping him on the back, the silver ball dropping as swiftly as his own youth through the blinking lighted maze. He made an unmistakable plea with his eyes: *I don't want to leave. Let's stay. Let's stay all night.* His father, grim now, shook his head no and the boy slipped off the stool and passed, waist high, between the men palming damp bottles of beer and chewing their tobacco, absorbed in conversation.

"Go home—are you kidding, Dad? This place is great," exclaimed

Bobby, his blond head falling beneath Iain's giant hand as he was directed out the door.

"I used to say that to my father," recalled the Duke. "Only we never went home." He stood beside me, his belly sagging at the heavy cotton of his practice jersey, the teeth wired together behind thin brown lips, and then he slowly blinked his eyes at the memory of the great King Ritter, gone out of bars and vanished from the earth: father, drunkard, athlete. Sighing, Duke said, "Guess I should get a move on myself," and shifted his weight, the last of the beer in the bottle he held disappearing down his throat with a soft gurgle.

That began a general exodus. Everyone with a shadow of domestic commitment went home in the next fifteen minutes, leaving me, Mike Melendez, Surfer, and Josh hunkered over the bar on our elbows, riding the downslope of the evening. Mike stared at his hands. Bones protruded from his wrists and he looked old and tired. Josh gabbled at the liquor bottles fitted with gleaming metal spouts. Always industrious, Surfer spun a quarter on the smooth polished bartop, like a planet glittering in orbit until it lost momentum, wobbled, and clattered to a halt. On the other side of the bar sat the regulars, the gray-faced men and their implacable wives, and two men alone, several stools apart, drinking with precise mechanical finality and looking across at us, expressionless, with eyes that did not see. Roger was in the middle, wiping glasses with his bar towel.

"It's no different to me if I stay here or go home," said Mike.

"Stay here then," I said, "and pass the time."

"Passing the time gets to be a real chore," Mike replied. The men across the bar sniffed the air as if they smelled something. "After a while you can hardly stand it."

I went over to drop a coin in the jukebox and then, stretching my legs, continued on to the bathroom. The music started. The men's room, with its long trench-style urinal, was bright and clean and the tiles picked up the music and amplified it. Coming back out, to my right I saw an empty table in the members' bar, the face of a young marine, long dead, hovering over it—a few steps along the corridor, another phrase of the song, I glanced into the ladies' room, where a heavy woman in a green dress leaned against the mirror, applying makeup—and then into the main hall, dark after the brightness of the men's room, the music blaring, sending an unexpected burst of adrenaline through my veins. A series of dim figures, one of them familiar in outline, passed in front of the muted glow from the jukebox.

Surfer and Josh were on their feet, facing a group of new arrivals, six men in tattered jeans and biker jackets, damp from the road and smelling faintly of gasoline. Mike remained on his stool, arms crossed, looking at them. Standing in front of the others was T-bone. A cigarette dangled from his lips. He had a smirk on his face, a look of surprised good fortune, and it was obvious he had discovered Mike Melendez quite by accident. The song on the jukebox ended.

"Well, if it ain't the boy I was just talking about," T-bone said, his eyebrow split in two by the white crescent of scar. "The one that raped Sherri and thinks he's gonna get away with it."

Mike said nothing. He looked straight at T-bone and a strip of muscle twitched along his jaw.

"The son of a bitch—" T-bone raised a finger. It twitched and he lowered it "—nigger who thinks he can mock *me* and get away with it. You don't know how close you are, so fucking close to being dead . . ." his voice trailing off in soundless rage, knocked out of him like he had been struck.

Beside T-bone was my old cellmate Jerry, squashed face and huge tattooed arms, his narrow slitted eyes moving over the faces opposite him. He stopped on mine. "He-ey there, buddy," he said.

His tone was light, almost personal. "Seen ol' Elvis lately?"

I nodded "Last week. He's gone in the hospital."

"Too bad," sympathized the convict. "He should be more careful with his singin'."

T-bone swung his eyes to me. After a moment, he registered. "You're like a fucking rash." He glanced at Jerry. "You know him?"

"Sure. We was in the joint together."

For the time being my prison record appeared to be an asset. Jerry was relaxed, slouched to one side, his lips curled up in a gesture that was like a dog smiling. He looked peaceful enough, but T-bone and one or two of the others had hell in their eyes, itching for someone to say the wrong word, any word. Josh was like a kid at a scary movie. His hands were limp, touching his face, and he looked at the bikers with a startled expression. A loud noise and he would be hugging the rafters. Surfer was his usual tranquil self. He was pretty good with his dukes—the Marine Corps saw to that —and had so much Zen confidence he never felt threatened in any kind of weather.

"Peace," he said to T-bone, making a V with his fingers.

The tall biker turned and said, "Fuck off, beach boy. This is between me and him. It don't concern you."

Mike rose to his feet. His aspect was large, looming, a hardened expression on his face, blankness in his eyes. In spite of a real effort not to, T-bone leaned away from him, retreating an inch without moving the heels of his jackboots.

"I forced nothing on Sherri Hogg," Mike said.

T-bone's eyebrow began fluttering. He reached out with his hand toward Mike's chest like he meant to brush lint from his collar, the arm long and sinewy, his shoulder knotted with muscle. Before he got there, Mike's hand shot up and caught him, their fingers interlocking, shaking in a single fist.

"Don't touch me," said T-bone, enraged. "Get your fucking

hand away from me."

The other bikers lunged forward, then suddenly veered off, like horses after a gunshot. Roger the bartender had appeared beside me, gripping a varnished, bone white ax handle. He was flanked by three of the regulars from the other side of the bar, hair thinning, bags under their eyes, in nylon sport shirts and seedy black pants, still staring at nothing. They were grim faced, these men who had witnessed long odds before, at Anzio perhaps, Chosin Reservoir or the Ardennes, and there was something in their death-seeing eyes that prevented the bikers from swarming us.

"Clear out," Roger said to the leather jackets. "The bar is closed."

T-bone swore at him. Snarling, the ratty ends of his hair whipping against his neck, he wrenched his hand free from Melendez and drew back, surprised at Mike's grip strength and unnerved by the ax handle and solid presence of the old veterans. He threw a single wild punch and Mike slipped it, pushing T-bone off balance with an open hand, graceful and quick.

"Like I said: get out," repeated the bartender, lifting the ax handle from his shoulder. The regulars stood beside him in their black trousers and pressed white shirts. They looked like umpires and had that same authority and disinterest in the proceedings.

"We'll go when I'm fucking ready to go," T-bone said. He looked at Melendez. "Sometime you're gonna be alone. Or asleep. And you don't have eyes in the back of your head." Again Mike crossed his arms and said nothing. "Around here, no nigger can do what you did and get away with it. I'm gonna make sure of that," said T-bone.

"What you've done so far is mighty impressive," Jerry interrupted, laughing at T-bone. "You're mopping up the floor with this guy, just like you said."

T-bone whirled on him, amazed at the challenge—Jerry still slouching, in a black leather vest over an old T-shirt, his arms like two bruised cantaloupes. Jerry's face was squashed around a narrow crooked nose, but lightened, almost softened with amusement. He shook his head at T-bone, laughing with a snort. Then he winked at me. "This has been as exciting as going downtown to watch the late haircuts," he said.

The other bikers were uneasy. Evidently they had expected a brawl, the usual smash 'em up, and now they were facing down some seedy old baseball umpires who didn't seem the least bit afraid and a tall well-muscled black man with hands quick as two snakes. They moved toward the door, one man harmlessly kicking over a chair.

"Where y'all going?" T-bone asked, cutting his eyes in that direction.

Jerry laughed once more. "Down to a barbershop for some real entertainment," he said, trailing after them. "We've had enough of this." When he passed in front of me, he made a little sound with his tongue against his teeth and said, "Dodged another bullet."

The first of the motorcycles rumbled to life outside. T-bone cocked his head, turning an eye up to the rafters, the other motorcycles joining in the chorus until the sound grew deafening and the acrid smell of spent gasoline filled the room. T-bone worked his jaw up and down, his curses lost in the prolonged roar of the motorcycles.

Raising his voice above the racket outside, Josh sent T-bone toward the door by saying, "I think you should go."

In the doorway T-bone stopped and pointed a long arm at Mike Melendez, the motorcycles obscuring some of what he said as they faded down Orange Boulevard, "—coming for you, because I am. There's not a man walking can do that to me twice." He glanced once more at me and disappeared through the foyer into the damp close night, moving in a peculiar sideways gait to fit his shoulders through the exit.

One last motorcycle screamed away from the Legion hall, and Mike sat back down on his stool. It was getting late. The veterans turned and filed down the corridor to the other side of the bar.

"He better think twice next time," Josh said, taking a few steps toward the door. He raised a soft pink fist, holding part of his stomach in, the rest of it shaking when he shook the fist. "I might have to get rough."

Surfer took the stethoscope from him and administered it. "You better sit down, Josh," he said. "I think there's some chipmunks running around in there."

Exhaust fumes hung in the air, mixing with the cigars and stale beer and traces of oil soap. Roger had lowered the ax handle and was leaning on it like a cane, the sweat pebbled across his shiny forehead. He reached in his pocket for a wrinkled handkerchief and swabbed his brow.

"I'm too old for this shit," he said.

Beyond the streaming light from the bar, in the dim corners of the other room, the veterans had returned to their tepid whiskeys. Beside wives who sat as still as marble they had once again lapsed into deliberate, sightless reverie.

"It was nice of those guys to come over," I said, pointing my chin at them.

Roger nodded. He put his free hand on the bar and I noticed he had SEMPER FIDELIS tattooed in faint blue letters on his forearm. "Y'all are in here every Tuesday and Thursday night," he explained. "And they understand the word *team*." The bartender raised the ax handle into the air, and leaning across the bar, deposited it on the other side. "We all understand that here."

"I can't expect any of you to fix my problems for me," Mike said. He stood to go. "But I appreciate it, anyway."

"Any trouble is a man's own," said Roger. "No denying that."

He went around and got behind the bar and began clearing off the bottles, his bald head shining in the light. Mike looked at the bartender when Roger's back was turned, like he was memorizing something about him, and then walked past me and Surfer and the heroic Josh, over the scarred wooden floor, silent, erect, not slowing down on account of the darkness, his eyes ahead, staring at nothing.

7

Loretta was waiting for me when we got back to the house. She was sitting with her legs folded beneath her on the sofa, in a pair of tight cotton shorts, sandals, and a white tank top jersey, snug across small taut breasts and the flat plane of her stomach. The jersey rode up, exposing rich smooth skin, tanned like her arms and legs and very dark in contrast to the outfit she wore and the light-colored fabric of the sofa.

"Joe—it's nearly midnight. Where the hell have you been?" she asked, her tongue darting out between small white teeth. Loretta swung herself at the hips and placed her feet on the floor, red toenails to match her fingernails and lipstick. "You were supposed to take me to a movie. Instead, I'm watching tee vee all night."

Surfer gave me the brief open-palmed salute that Nazi generals used on each other and ducked into the bathroom like the coward that he was.

"Sorry," I said. Then I sat down at the far end of the sofa, picked up the remote control and began grazing through the channels, settling for a moment on a track meet.

"That's the second time in a week you've pulled this shit," she said. "I don't have to put up with it."

Loretta rarely swore. I looked sideways at her and then back at the television, to a javelin that arched across a blue sky and landed quivering in the turf. "I said I'm sorry. You can spank me if you want to."

"Not on your life," said Loretta. She yanked my hand out of my lap, pulling it toward her. "I'm not kidding, Joe. You have to stop being so selfish." Her eyes were wet and shining. "You never do anything that doesn't suit you."

"And I never ask you to do anything you don't want to do. That's fair, isn't it?"

Loretta squeezed my hand, which held the remote control, shutting off the television. "Yeah that's fair, but it's not a relationship. We laugh, we have fun, but half the time you're not around. I don't know where you are or what you're doing."

This made me nervous. Loretta slept at my house two or three nights a week, and I drove her car, but we never had any deep conversations. We never talked about the future. She was funny and intelligent and loved to rumble between the sheets. It was casual. I never asked her if cancer ran in her family or how many men she had slept with.

"At this point do you consider me your girlfriend?" asked Loretta.

"Companion," I stammered, eyes flickering away before I trained them again on Loretta and attempted to redeem myself. "Sidekick. Female associate."

Loretta nodded. "See? I know you don't mean anything by it. It's a reflex, that's all. But Joe—" she scooted closer and grabbed both my wrists "—Joe, it's got to be deeper than that." She dropped my hands and turned her head away. "Or else forget it."

"Of course it's more than that. You're the sugar in my coffee." I slipped my hand around her waist, stroking the cool brown skin between her shorts and the jersey. "You're the lead in my pencil."

"Right now I'm the ants at your picnic," Loretta said, peeling my hand away. "And if you think I'm going to sleep with you tonight, you've got bats in your belfry."

I reached over and turned a dial on the wall behind us, dimming the lights. I whispered and cajoled. In five minutes, Loretta was naked against the sofa, and when she came up on her elbows, the pressure had left an Indian pattern across her breasts, a delicate intaglio of what appeared to be tiny marching figures.

Slipping off my T-shirt I said, "I'll give kisses to you like I was Rockefeller and they were dimes."

"Dollars," Loretta responded, laughing like a small clear bell. She stared with her luminous green eyes into mine for a long while, glittering and warm, and then she lowered her head, her hair soft against my cheek. A soundless roar filled my ears. Loretta said something I couldn't hear and I felt her whimper in the abyss—life—and it echoed through my heart and intangible self. Percussion, dream, loss.

Afterwards as indifference set in and I played with the strands of Loretta's sun-streaked hair, her eyes grew large and round and she said, "I can't believe my only competition is a big field, fourteen other guys, and a funny-looking football."

"So how did you find me?" I asked, remembering the night we met. While leading a conga line through Saxophone Joe's this lovely brunette floated across the room into my arms. "There were a lot of guys in there. You could have had your pick."

"Like who?"

"I don't know. Like Surfer. He gets a lot of women."

Loretta frowned, then shook her head. "Surfer came up to me and smiled like he thought he was a real stud and I was going to melt at the sight of him." She giggled. "I told him he looked like a big yellow monkey."

"And nobody else appealed to you? Thirty or forty guys in the bar and I was your first choice."

A pink tongue darted out to moisten her lips, the redness gone from them, rubbed off. "You looked tough and smart but you had kind eyes and a nice smile—" I rolled on my back and Loretta traced her finger lightly across my chest "—and you had, I don't know, a look, the kind of look I like. I can't explain it."

It was still a warm night, no sounds in the neighborhood, only a feeling of impending summer, stopped time, and peace. I was elated, a strong light sensation in my chest, and Loretta drew back and looked at me in wonder. There were tears in her eyes, then she settled her head on my shoulder, and said, "I love you, Joe. Just be nice to me. That's all I'm asking."

I didn't say anything.

The door to the bathroom opened slightly, emitting a bar of light, and Surfer peered out at me from his tiled prison. His head and shoulders emerged and he played an imaginary violin. I waved him back inside.

"We should get up," I said.

"Not yet," Loretta said, stretching against the furze of the rug. "I want to enjoy this." She climbed on to my chest and tapped my teeth with her fingernail. "Everything disappeared there for a while. No walls, no house, just us."

Surfer poked his head out again and I motioned him back.

"Let's go. Chop-chop," I said, jerking on my T-shirt and shorts. "Big day tomorrow." Loretta sat up, open mouthed, and I tossed her shorts and jersey underhanded and they clung to her face and one shoulder for an instant before falling to the floor.

Blushing and speechless, Loretta fumbled into her clothes, stunned by the quick chill that had descended on the room. Twice she paused for an explanation, while I avoided her eyes and straightened up the sofa cushions. Her clothing askew, hands tightened into fists, Loretta glared at me for a long awful moment, freezing me dead inside. Under a prolonged silence, she left the house.

"Beautiful," I said, dropping onto the sofa, my head in my hands.

Surfer eased the door open and tiptoed out of the bathroom, turning his head in every direction. "Is she gone?"

"She's gone, all right. Probably for good."

"Sorry, man. But my legs were cramping up in there. Big time." He pressed a button on the remote and the track meet reappeared. "I love television. It's a window to the world," he said, flipping the channel to a bowling tournament. "If they ever make bowling an Olympic sport, I'll kill myself," he said. Again the screen filled with female shotputters grunting and screaming with effort. "I see these Russians on tee vee and I know there's women out there who can kick my ass."

"There's one in Cocoa Beach who's going to kick mine," I said, looking at the massive heavy-thighed women on screen.

Surfer thrust his legs out, slouching on the sofa. "Forget about it, man. Treat a whore like a queen and a queen like a whore."

"I can't get away with that when it comes to Loretta," I said. "She's no dummy." Indifference maddened the opposite sex, stirred them to desire, conjuring up all their subdued predatory instincts. Wait long enough and they would pursue, eyes and teeth glittering. But if I ignored Loretta for any length of time, she would just disappear like smoke and I knew it.

"It's impossible, genetically, for a man to be truly monogamous," said Surfer, drifting on to his favorite subject. "There's scientific studies that prove it. Women produce one egg a month and here we are with ten million sperm. Out looking for eggs." He flipped through the channels. "In the caveman days, every woman wanted the strongest caveman for her protector. She kept the cave clean and he kept the other cavemen away. When he wasn't doing that, he was busy breaking into the other caves."

"Whenever I go down to the beach, the girls are all targets and every guy I see is the enemy."

"That's it, man. Caveman politics," said Surfer, intent on the television. "The only difference is, now the cavegirls get breast implants and wax their legs and the caves are all air-conditioned with cable tee vee." He grazed several more channels, staring at the spectacle of late-night evangelists, tractor pulls, idiotic game shows, and old movies. "Ten thousand years of civilization and there's still nothing on the fucking thing."

For a moment he switched on some men in baggy clothes and baseball hats, chanting to a syncopated beat. "Memo from the right: pull up your pants, turn your hats around, and get a fucking job," he said. Surfer continued changing channels with the imperceptible movement of one finger, the colors from the screen playing over his serene tanned face. He was an accomplished caveman. No one could count the number of caves he had broken into.

"Leave that on," I said, from my position on the floor, indicating the television with an outstretched bare foot. It was one of those hidden camera programs and we watched in silence as a man proposed marriage by having a plane tow a banner past that read SUSAN—WILL YOU MARRY ME? and the woman, bucktoothed and wearing glasses, screamed in anguished delight when presented with an engagement ring.

"What is it with that?" I asked. "They see that ring and they go fucking bananas."

"That's because it represents your soul," said Surfer.

The woman throttled the man by the neck, jumping up and down. "Represents?" I said. "It *is* your soul."

Surfer rolled up the sleeve of his T-shirt and pointed to a raised pink circle on his upper arm. "It's not going to happen to me. I've been vaccinated," he said.

"Me too," I said, feeling my own arm. "I think." Suddenly I pictured myself married to Loretta and was startled by the grim clarity of the image—owning a house, getting serious about my job, going to watch rugby games in bermuda shorts and long black socks. Then a pregnancy and diapers and little tax deductions waddling over the kitchen tiles. The thought of babies being zipped up in those little suits made my heart beat erratically.

"What does the vaccine do?" I asked.

"You get restless," said Surfer. He flipped back to the track meet where a marvelous black girl in a formfitting suit did a series of limber exercises. "It's very hard to hit a moving target."

The girl stood up, tall and muscular and beautiful, shook her long straight hair, and began running with incredible ease. Her lips were red and moist, like summer fruit. "Every time I get a girlfriend it starts out great," I said, "and then I feel like I'm being measured for a tuxedo."

"Just like meeting a funeral director and being sized up for a coffin," said Surfer.

He drew his feet up on the sofa, sat cross-legged like an Indian and looked at me, ignoring the black girl and her graceful warm-up. "There's only one way to do it. Stay with a girl until you meet someone more interesting or she gives you the brush-off, whichever comes first." Surfer exhaled through his nose. "When my parents got divorced, they couldn't even stand the smell of each other. I was only twelve, but I decided that was never going to happen to me. Not a fucking chance."

My own father died on the golf course—"Took an extra stroke," I said to my prep school friends, acting tough—and my mother lapsed into near catatonia, like half of her body had been cleaved away. She remained that way for two years, smoking herself into final, fatal emphysema. Then in the hospital I took my mother's frail bony hand in mine while she breathed hoarsely behind the oxygen mask, tense in her suffering and conscious for the last time. Her world was pain. Staring at the wall, she whispered, "Your father."

A gun sounded on the television and the black girl jumped into the lead, devouring the orange track with her huge strides, arms swinging high in the air, her tresses unfurled like a long black pennant. She hugged the rail on the turn and then went furiously down the back straight, six, seven, eight lengths in front, a brilliant smile appearing on her face, the rich red lips stretching back, releasing a burst of unexpected triumphant laughter. She broke the tape, gasping for air.

"You know, when I'm playing rugby, I don't think of anything else," remarked Surfer. "In that sense, rugby is the absence of time, the absence of any other desire."

The next morning Maxine was waiting for me with an oversize photo of Elvis glistening between her fingertips. Her shoes were off and the papers on her desk, usually stacked in neat little piles, fluttered in disarray when the fan oscillated toward them. Maxine had a flushed look on her face and was more animated than even three cups of coffee were able to make her.

"This just came up from the lab," she said, waving the picture at me. Her gray eyes were shiny and dark. "You were right. It's Elvis." Maxine turned her wrist to study the picture. "What a hunk, a hunk-a burning love."

Something odd attended Maxine. It was as though some tropical disease had brought out a raving bloom in her. Perched on the edge of the chair, her face rosy even without makeup and her hair loose and fluttering with the papers on the desk, Maxine ogled the photo of Elvis with an expression of unchained interest that would have made Shirley Kimball blush. Finally she tossed the photo back on the pile.

"Get me this story and I'll run it on page one," she said. "Piggy Uno."

I felt Maxine's forehead. It was cool.

"What are you doing?" she asked.

"Making sure you're okay. First you said I was right about something and now you're talking Elvis features. That's not like you."

Maxine leveled her gaze at me. "I am fine, thanks for asking," she said. "And it may come as a shock, but I want you to write me a news story. Who is this guy? What's his name? Where does he come from? All in the style they call the inverted pyramid. You may remember it. It's been in all the papers."

I drew back. My boss loved irony and double entendre, polemics were her specialty, and to the music of argument she danced the dialectic, as fast and as hard as you wanted to go. Sarcasm was a blunt instrument, something for the dolts at the *Post-Gazette* who planted whoopee cushions and talked in pig latin and sailed paper airplanes across the newsroom and out the open windows. It was lightweight, and much too crude for a tactician like Maxine Olnecki-Smyth.

"There's something funny going on here," I said.

The door opened and Walter Dzioba entered without knocking, which was unusual. He wore pressed chinos and a monogrammed shirt, doused with cologne, his hair combed straight back and oiled like a dirt road. Limping past me, his silent compact figure closed on Maxine and she appeared ready to kiss him.

"Good morning, Wally," she said.

I blinked hard. *"Wally?"*

"Here's my follow-up on the judicial scandal," Dzioba said, dropping a computer disk on top of the unkempt papers. "I think we should run it tomorrow. I'll have another big one for Sunday."

"I bet you will," Maxine said, covering her mouth in horror. Her eyes were illuminated from within and her hair, loose and waving, crackled with static electricity. She looked great. Dzioba brushed against her leg and they stayed that way a moment, silhouetted against the window blinds. My heart fell. The two were lovers.

"Associated Press is sending someone up from Miami," continued Dzioba in a flat tone. The veteran reporter was concealing his excitement very well. "The *New York Times* called. The *Washington Post*. They all want it. And we're way out ahead of them." He raised his dark rough face to Maxine's. "This one has Pulitzer Prize written all over it."

There was a reverent pause. "You worked for it," said Maxine, "and you deserve it."

"We both do," corrected Dzioba. "Writer and editor. We win it, we'll go up there and accept it together."

I felt sick. Dzioba was ready to claim the two biggest prizes in journalism, the Pulitzer and Maxine Olnecki-Smyth. Maxine, Maxine, smelling of lilacs, with her fine intellect and a life separate from all of us and above the grubby paws of a cutthroat like Dzioba. He wheeled toward the door on his bad leg, looking at me with the upward bloodshot glance he used on Ross Donleavey and the other nobodies. "Oh, hello," he said. "I didn't see you there."

When he was gone, behind the click of the doorknob and a thin shaking of frosted glass, Maxine brushed her hair away from her face and said in a soft voice, "Don't you dare judge me, Joseph Dolan. If you can't deal with it, why then it's better to leave everything else unsaid."

I headed for the door without a word and Maxine got up and intercepted me. She clutched my arm, her voice barely rising above a whisper. "Work isn't everything, you know. Not even for me. I was just so tired of that empty house."

"But—Walter Dzioba?" I said. "The guy drinks gin, for crissakes. He goes out with strippers. And he must be fifty years old."

"Fifty-two," said Maxine. A tear glittered in her eye. "And I'm forty-one. When you're alone at that age, Joe, some of your dreams get modified. A few get canceled altogether. Walter's okay. He's read a few books and seen some of the world. He's a pretty fair writer. And he has good manners. I could do a lot worse."

A shadow loomed outside the door. "Maxine—can I come in?" said Jimmy Pitochelli. "I've got some great drawings to show you."

"Just a minute," she called out.

"Walter's pretty slick," I warned. "Sleep with you, win the Pulitzer, and it's so long *Post-Gazette,* hello *Miami Herald*. I wouldn't put it past him."

Maxine took an elastic from her pocket and in a deft manuever gathered her hair and snapped the rubber band around her short thick ponytail. Her eyes were dry and her face composed and businesslike. "Sharp analysis from a guy who ten months ago couldn't tell the man in the street from the man in the moon," she said.

"Bullshit. Ask me anything."

"Define *irony,*" said Maxine, fixing me with her editor's look.

"A raccoon dies of natural causes in the middle of the highway."

She laughed. "All right: *oxymoron.*"

"Australian prison."

Maxine swung the door open and pushed me out. "Go talk to Elvis." The eager cartoonist rushed in. "Hi, Jimmy," she said. "Let's see what you've got."

The county hospital was an hour away, in Christmas Springs. Three low brick buildings in a grove of sassafras trees, and a huge well-tended garden in the rear surrounded by chain-link fence, where I found Elvis after parking my car and getting a visitor's pass from the front desk. The blazing sun turned the lawn white with glare and sent a low shimmering haze over the ground that undulated like a liquid and rose in places to knee height. Down in the dirt between the leafy rows of okra, Elvis looked up when I called to him and made a gesture of recognition. He came walking toward me, the swoop of jet black hair falling across his forehead, barechested in the heat, with those 1950s abdominal muscles creased in the middle like a washboard bent almost in half. Elvis pulled up short, wiped his hands on his filthy dungarees, and stuck one through the fence for me to shake.

"Hey, Elvis," I said, glad to see him. "How you doing?"

"Fine. Just fine. Working in the dirt reminds a man where he comes from." He dropped my hand. "And where he's going." His grin faded completely. "But the name's not Elvis. It's Edgar Tylus Lindenberg. From Chalybeate, Tennessee."

My mouth hung open and my hand dangled from the aperture in the fence.

"The doctors have been helping me," he explained with a shrug.

"You seemed so . . . so real," I said. "There's just this uncanny resemblance, the singing, the walk, everything."

"A lot of people ain't what they seem," he replied. "Truth is, I never even been near Memphis. I'm a car salesman. Never once played a song for money. It was what they call a de-lusion."

"You've got talent," I said. "Like it or not, it's in there. You can't deny that."

The lock of hair fell across his brow and he twisted his chin sharply, flipping it back into place. "I was sick," he said. "My singing and playing was all part of a lie and doctors here are helping me see that."

"They're helping you become Edgar Lindenberg, car salesman?"

He nodded yes, but reluctantly, as though behind the shining windows of the hospital someone was watching him. "I reckon so," he said.

We talked a while longer and I offered to pick him up when he was released and drive him to Cocoa Beach so he could catch the bus back to Chalybeate. He spoke without enthusiasm about the Pontiac dealership and his room in town and a girl named Charlene Buttles. Then he handed me the small brass key to his locker at the bus station.

"Get rid of that stuff," he said.

"What should I do with it?"

"Throw it away, burn it—I don't care. I don't need any of it no more."

I shook his hand again, the sharp edges of the key cutting into my palm as I crossed the white shimmering lawn, passing for a moment into a deep pool of shade beneath the sassafras trees. A man wearing a starched lab coat over his suit emerged from a car parked near mine and strode with authority up the wide graveled walk toward the front entrance of the hospital. He was tall and stern and Germanic. His eyes, unblinking as I settled in his field of vision, seemed to categorize my various neuroses and psychoses before swerving ahead to take in the undulating lawn and white blazing sky. No doubt I was assigned a case number, diagnosed as oedipal, obtuse or self-aggrandizing. For most headshrinkers, a glance at the slogan on your T-shirt was like looking at an X ray. These guys analyzed your dreams, made you stare at ink blots, and, if you were lucky, transformed you into something ordinary. They were emptying the world of craziness and leaving it void of personality. A process that left you cured, certainly, but somehow interested in gardening.

The bus station was deserted when I went in, except for the ticket clerk, sitting behind bars in his office. He didn't recognize me. Inside the locker were the stiff leather jumpsuit, dingy and smelling of perspiration, an ornate crucifix on a heavy silver chain, the guitar with its mother of pearl finish and the mauve-tinted sunglasses. Relics of history, pretty much dead without Elvis to inhabit them.

I folded the jumpsuit in the bottom of the locker and drew out the guitar, tense and fragile, the long bony neck tilted forward. It was light in my hands, and foreign; I couldn't make it play. I tapped one string and a tiny swelling sound came out of the body. My voice an off-key whisper, I strummed an old Elvis ballad, hearing it in my head, tremulous and rich.

"We don't allow none of that in here," growled the clerk.

I replaced the guitar and draped the heavy tarnished chain of the crucifix around my neck. Dropping fifty cents in the slot, I turned the sharp little key and pocketed it, against the wishes of Edgar Tylus Lindenberg and his esteemed doctors, but in keeping with a wordless pact between me and the historical Elvis, made long ago in front of a scratchy black and white television set.

8

The sea was pale green, wrinkled like a piece of foil in the late afternoon sun that glinted off its innumerable facets, stretching ahead of us to the horizon. Surfer carved a white trail, jockeying the catamaran up and over the rising green swells under a steady northward breeze. In harness, I leaned out from the hull, the water in its diamond brilliance shining just beneath me.

"Coming about," Surfer said, changing course, the boom swinging across at me.

"Aye, aye, Captain." I unclipped myself from the trapeze and scrambled under the boom, resuming on the other side.

We sailed for another hour and then found the beach, hauling the cat to the edge of the froth, the sun gone but the sky incandescent, no one on the flats; just an old sea turtle, its innards torn away by sharks. Surfer undressed the sail and gathered it in.

"I drank enough piña coladas last night to float the Spanish fleet," he said.

"How you feeling?"

He yawned. "Like someone put out a thousand cigarettes on my soul." Stretching himself on the taut canvas, a life jacket for a pillow, he quickly fell asleep.

I sat motionless, dangling my legs over the stern, and listened to the silky hypnotic rustle of waves on the beach. It was high tide and some of the waves reached the boat, expiring in white foam beneath my feet, leaving a gossamer imprint that faded completely as the next one arrived.

The surf lulled me, brought back childhood: salt smells, suntan lotion, the sand that stuck to your calves mixed with flecks of mica and then followed you home, in your sneakers, in the car, turning up the next morning in the bathtub like gold in the bottom of a pan. I half-expected to see myself, skinny and freckled, running tirelessly up the beach, watched over by my mother and father who talked in low murmuring tones under a huge umbrella, white as fish bellies and hidden from the sun in a narrow wedge of shade. They seemed like lovers then, away from the house. And I gave them time to be alone, because there seemed to be so much time, all the time in the world.

In the distance, staggering on the incline, a man approached, coming slowly in my direction. He weaved as though drunk, but after studying him a moment I realized he was avoiding the waves as they broke and flattened themselves on the sand. Something familiar about him, the arrogant set of his head, his shoulders thrust forward, nagged at me until he got close enough to delineate his features, the smooth face and thick yellow hair, ruffled by the onshore breeze; then the expensive clothes, loafers and white trousers and a striped polo shirt, the heavy gold watch on his wrist.

Hulic Rasterree stopped near the catamaran without a word and without any gesture of greeting. The only sound besides the gentle purling of the waves was a soft comic snoring from Surfer, behind me on the canvas. Rasterree took a tightly folded newspaper from under his arm and unfurled it.

"What the hell is this?" he asked.

"It's called a newspaper."

"You people are crucifying me," said Rasterree, stabbing the front page of the *Post-Gazette* with a manicured finger. In a box that ran the length of the paper was the third installment of Walter Dzioba's story on judicial tampering. I hadn't read it.

"Not my department," I told him. "Crucifixion is two sailboats down. I'm in feel-good."

Rasterree grunted. "Don't play cute with me," he continued. "I don't know who you people think you are or where you get your information, but this is unadulterated bullshit. My reputation is impeccable. My integrity is beyond reproach." His mien turned threatening. "And the reach of my influence is considerable."

"Listen, I don't care if your fucking golf scores are low—I don't write hard news. If you want to make a statement, call Walter Dzioba. I'm sure he'd be very interested in what you have to say."

Rasterree started to speak and checked himself, his face clouded with frustration—humility was not his strong suit—and snapped the newspaper in half, again in quarters, and tucked it back under his arm. He stared at me with those blue ice cubes for another moment.

Then the district attorney with the expensive watch tried a different tack. He rhapsodized about growing up poor in Ohatchee, Alabama, mountain country, where he and his kin had nothing except long mortgages and short tempers. His unusual first name grew out of a southern tradition from earlier times when a man might name his son with the surname of a close friend. Hulic, he explained, was Slavic, and his grandfather was first given the name. Later a childless uncle was called Hulic and in deference to that uncle, his own father named him Hulic. He drew a mysterious portrait of a thick-jawed man, speaking in a strange accent for turn-of-the-century Alabama, his name given, perhaps, in exchange for a goat or a pig or a doctor fetched in a gale.

And he carried that name out of the Alabama hills to the state college and later to Harvard Law School and before the bench of the highest courts in the land. He was the first college graduate and the first lawyer and the only elected official in the family. The pride and joy of the bucolic Rasterree clan. What the newspaper was doing to him was criminal and despicable, violated his civil rights, and cast him down among thieves. It was quite a tale. Enough to make me want to stretch out on the canvas next to Surfer and start counting Uncle Hulic's sheep. I stifled a yawn.

Newspaper reporters, like cops and priests, have heard every story under the sun. After a while you barely listen. Except for inheriting the name of a Slavic sodbuster, what Rasterree was saying was nothing new. It only made me glad my father had not been a tobacco farmer and named me Feinburg or Hoss Dolan. Growing up was bad enough as plain old Joe. The playgrounds and ball fields in my neighborhood would have been hell on earth for a small boy named Horovitz.

"Walter Dzioba—not me, Dzioba—is writing stories about deals being made at the courthouse," I said. "That may or may not be true. I don't know. And I really don't care. It has nothing to do with me."

"Yes, it does," said Rasterree. He leveled his gaze, the thick yellow eyebrows coming together. "If I'm indicted, or even if I slip and fall in the shower, then I won't be in a position to help your friend, Mike Melendez. Will I?"

So that's how it was. The district attorney was trying to swing a trade. It was enough to make me laugh out loud, his weak understanding of how things worked, as if I could change things for him at the *Post-Gazette*. His publicity goose was already cooked. If we ever printed a retraction, which occurred rarely, it was a tiny item buried among the advertisements and legal notices in the back of the paper. And Maxine and Walter were not about to withdraw their entry for the Pulitzer Prize they hoped to win. They were making hash of Hulic Rasterree and no one was losing any sleep over it, myself included.

"What can you do for Melendez?"

"Hypothetically? I can drop the charges for lack of evidence. What I can do in that courtroom is fairly long, broad, and deep," he said, with a cocky lift of one eyebrow.

"Yeah. I think I read that somewhere."

Rasterree scrambled to recover his modesty. "Your other friend who thinks he's Elvis," said the yellow-haired man, raising a finger into the air. He looked at me steadily. "Consider the Lindenberg case already lost and forgotten about."

"He doesn't think he's Elvis anymore," I said, with an unintended note of sadness in my voice.

"Even better. It will be a token of my good faith. Certainly a small matter, in any event."

Edgar Lindenberg rode a bus out of Tennessee believing he was Elvis. And Hulic Rasterree descended from the Alabama hills on the wings of his own arrogance thinking he was God. Apparently the South was full of such inspirational tales.

"This is what I have in mind," the district attorney said, still measuring me with his chilly blue stare. "I have some documents, memoranda, that prove I never went along with any tampering. They were sent to Judge Tate and to my boss in Tallahassee. They're on computer disk. I'll copy the disk and give it to you. All you have to do is make sure this information gets in the paper."

I couldn't help smiling. "You could put anything you want on a disk and that doesn't mean my editor is going to believe it."

"With the software we use in my office, dates cannot be faked," said Rasterree, keeping his depthless eyes on mine. "Everything is chronological and these memoranda appear in an irrefutable time sequence between other certified documents. They're legitimate."

An alibi as shiny and complex as this one didn't come along every day. "Who's to say you ever sent those memos?"

"Oh, of course Judge Tate and Bob Rosenthal will say they never received them. What would you say? The memos go a long way toward impugning them and exonerating me. They were sent by registered mail. I have the signed receipts."

I was impressed. "You have signed receipts for registered mail on the dates that appear on the memos?"

"That's correct," said the district attorney. "The day after, actually."

There was no way of proving what was signed for, but that didn't really matter. It all added up in Rasterree's favor, and together with a passionate speech of some kind, he was going to be looking pretty good. "You are one smart fella," I said.

"And quite innocent."

"So why me? Why not go right to Walter Dzioba with this? It's his story."

Rasterree cut his eyes away from mine, shifting them out to sea. The side of his face was like a smooth plaster mask. "I need something. You need something. Quid pro quo," he said.

During the course of our conversation we had drifted forty or fifty yards down the beach. The sliding waves were warm as bathwater, lapping at my ankles. Most of my footprints were already washed away but Rasterree's loafers made sharp cutouts in the sand, trowel shaped like hooves, arched over a single rolling dune. They hovered close to mine, stalking me. Surfer was watching us from the sailboat. He sat up on the canvas and raised his arm and held it there. I signaled that everything was all right.

"There is an unhappy truth beneath this scandal that most people just will not face," Rasterree began. "It is this: a great percentage of the country's minority population—and here in Cocoa Beach that means African Americans—are poor and undereducated, which makes their situation desperate. So, driven by forces beyond them, they steal. Or rape. Or murder. Racist or not, that is a fact." His face was composed and serious. "Blacks are deprived. Deprivation breeds criminality, ergo blacks are criminals. The logic is inescapable."

A knot in my throat wouldn't allow me to speak and Rasterree handed me his newspaper. "I won't keep you," he said. "You'll be soon hearing from me." He started down the beach, which remained empty, littered with shells.

"Michael Melendez," I reminded him.

"That will be taken care of when the times comes," he said. "I'll talk to some people."

I walked back to Surfer. "That's one stiff-looking paperboy," he said. He took the newspaper from me and bent it open to the funnies. Surfer spread the pages on the canvas deck and studied the comics while I explained who Rasterree was and what he wanted.

"Making deals to prove he never made any deals, huh? Interesting strategy," observed Surfer. "And let's face it, Joe, you're no brain surgeon. He probably thinks he's gonna tap dance all over you."

"I'm not even a urologist. But the district attorney is forgetting one thing," I said. "Not giving a shit is my biggest asset."

Surfer groaned and held his head and collapsed onto the deck, pressing the crinkled newspaper beneath him so that when he sat back up a few moments later, his chest and half of his stomach were imprinted with stubbled clowns and Vikings and frazzled cats who walked upright. "Never trust a man who wears loafers to the beach," he said.

The sun fell through the windows of Lawyer Timmons's office onto Michael Melendez. It was a brilliant February day, and as hot as August in New England. The Timmonses' cat, President Lincoln, lay stretched at Melendez's feet in a pool of light, his tail flickering over the wooden floor. Long powerful sunbeams dropped against the wall behind Lawyer Timmons, illuminating every crease in his jowled face.

"*A-hem,*" said Timmons, clearing his throat for the third time. He wet his lips and rubbed his eyes beneath his spectacles, blinking rapidly. It was a deliberate moment, a moment of decision, and like many older men Lawyer Timmons was unable to quiet himself or remain still. "*Uh-uh-um-um,*" he said, deep in his chest. He took off his spectacles and put them in his pocket.

Mrs. Timmons came into the room carrying three glasses of iced tea on a tray and Melendez took his without looking up. Then he sat with his thumbs pressed into his eye sockets while he turned my version of Rasterree's offer in his mind. Receiving the frigid sweating glass of tea, I thanked Mrs. Timmons and said again to Melendez, "Do you want to get out of this mess, or not?"

He didn't answer. Mrs. Timmons, tall and attractive and made up with glowing purple lipstick and purple eyeshadow, stood with one hip thrust against the door frame, the round metal tray dangling at her side. Her hair streamed back from her face in spiraling highlighted points and the bone earrings and interlocking ivory necklace gave her a tribal appearance. She was the color of burnt sienna and the makeup against her coloring was as stark and definitive as the markings on the face of a warrior.

"If Rasterree gives us those memos, we'll print them," I continued. "We have to. End of story. The rape charge goes away."

Melendez set down his iced tea without drinking from it and picked up the day-old newspaper and read some more of Walter Dzioba's article. His skin, stretched over his facial bones, was like kid leather. Lawyer Timmons and his wife and Melendez were all close by in the small airless room and there was the pungent odor of body oils and pomade.

"If Rasterree finds any other way of ducking the scandal, there goes our leverage," I said. "So now is the time."

Melendez looked across at Lawyer Timmons. The attorney hemmed into his closed fist, rubbed his left eye with it, and remained silent. "What do you think, Mr. Timmons?" asked Melendez.

"It's not a point of law," the attorney said.

Mike raised his eyes and inclined his head, gesturing for an explanation.

"I'm here to advise you on legal matters," Timmons said. "I can tell you what to file if and when the charges are about to be dropped. I cannot tell you—or Mr. Dolan for that matter—how to influence the district attorney to refuse prosecution of the case.

That's in another realm."

"What about telling Mike what you told me the first time I came here," I said. "That this case would be hell and you'd use every trick you ever learned to get him out from under it."

Timmons glared at me and picked up the miniature ceramic watermelon from the desk and weighed it in his hand. He kept his eyes on mine, nostrils flared above the pencil mustache, then his gaze shifted away when President Lincoln leapt silently to his feet, stretched himself to one and a half times his normal length, shrank back to his true size, and left the room by a path that took him between Mrs. Timmons's legs.

"A-hem," said Lawyer Timmons.

His wife started. "Go easy now, Aloysius," she said.

The attorney nodded. "When you're a black lawyer, you have to be better prepared than other lawyers, more polite in court, your arguments have to be seamless, you must be well read in every precedent, your shoes must be shined, and never, under any circumstances, can you touch a female clerk or be seen drinking at lunch," he said. "Because they are just waiting, some of them praying for you to make a mistake, and when you do, they'll be there with the rope looking for a tall, tall tree.

"So you can understand," he went on. "I want to help Mr. Melendez, but even more than that I want to continue practicing law."

Mike Melendez stared at the carpet. I remembered that there was also a strangeness between him and Timmons, something that separated them despite the color of their skin. Melendez was from a wealthy family within a predominantly black culture, Trinidadian, and Aloysius Timmons was an American, born and raised in the Deep South, a man of ability who nevertheless had been treated as inferior his whole life. In the courtroom, his intelligence and skill as a lawyer may have produced a grudging respect. In the supermarket checkout, on downtown streets, it was a different story. Another realm, as he called it. Out there, he was treated no better than a well-dressed circus animal. Housewives and store clerks and dental hygienists looked down their noses at him when he walked by, excruciating for such a proud man, for any man.

Surrounding him was more than just this tiny office with its diplomas reflecting the afternoon sunlight, and the worn carpet and furniture, and somewhere in some other room the frayed pajamas and bathrobe. And it wasn't only the modest house and the seven-year-old car in the driveway. In Lawyer Timmons's face there was evidence that things had turned out too small for him and his talent and the disappointment over it was as palpable as the strange sour odor that filled the air. He sagged with fatigue. Aloysius Timmons was panting at the heels of all his small dreams, with no strength to overtake them.

Mrs. Timmons shifted her weight from one rounded hip to the other and beat the metal tray against her shank like a tambourine. "There must be some way you can help," she said to her husband.

"I will say that, in terms of this arrangement Hulic Rasterree is proposing, linking Mike's case to these documents he wants to see published, *res ipsa loquiter*—the thing speaks for itself," said Mr. Timmons after a long moment's consideration. "It begs the larger question of Rasterree's guilt. He's probably no longer in a position to offer any deals."

"Did he offer you a deal on this case?" I asked.

"Yes. Right after the arraignment—" Timmons gestured in Mike's direction "—Rasterree called me into his office and said that if I could persuade Mr. Melendez to plead guilty, he'd arrange a sentence of two years in the state prison and two years probation. Another case I was on would turn out the way I wanted it to."

"Prison," said Melendez, shaking his head at the carpet. He covered his eyes with one hand.

"Lose a jury trial, and you could serve eight years," Timmons pointed out.

"But you didn't take the offer," I said, swiveling Lawyer Timmons back toward me. "And you never said a word about it."

"Plea bargains are one thing. But when you're tying cases together and speculating on future litigation, you're into collusion and tampering. I knew deals went on. Other lawyers were taking them. I simply chose not to."

"You didn't expose them, either," I mused out loud. "You didn't go to the Bar Association or the newspaper."

Mr. Timmons turned his face toward his wife, and the light through the windows seemed to enter the dark pupils of his eyes and illuminate them. He and his wife regarded each other for a brief moment, her expression not overly fond but considerate, and admitting of whatever differences existed between them. She might have been a woman gazing at a portrait, something that could not be altered. After a short while, his eyes came back to mine and the light shifted and they were dark and solid again.

"I stretch just as far as my reach allows me," Timmons said. He hemmed in his throat once more, moving a small measure sideways in the chair, and it creaked under him. "As I lawyer, I have a grip on my integrity. My ethics are always my own. As a darky, a porch monkey, a spook, a nigger, Uncle Tom, a pickaninny, Mr. Charlie's boy, a coconut or nappyhead, all known to me, I've learned to keep my mouth closed and a lot of my ideas to myself."

Mrs. Timmons looked greatly pained. Her husband had uttered those foul names as if they had been state capitals or a list of obscure legal terms, like the tedious lessons of children that only lend themselves to tedious recitation. He was expressionless, but he kept his eyes away from his wife. Who Aloysius Timmons really was and what he thought about it—a fact unknowable in even the simplest instance—was a complicated matter and one that devoured huge chunks of time in their life together.

"Please don't use language like that in my house," Mrs. Timmons said in an odd quiet voice. "You might just as well spit on the floor."

"I am sorry, Diva," he said, and his face indicated he truly was, "but I want Mr. Melendez and Mr. Dolan to understand things exactly as they are."

Whenever I worked nights at the paper I read the wire reports as they came in and therefore collected warehouses full of information amazing and absolutely useless and so startling as to be more extraordinary than anything I could have invented on my own. One week a well-known scientist published a research paper that said diamonds from outer space killed the dinosaurs. A giant meteor collided with a second meteor, his theory went, and pieces of carbon entered the atmosphere, mixed with certain gases, producing a voluminous glittering hail of precious stones that pierced every natural shelter on earth and sliced through the thickest hide and plate, dropping every last prehistoric beast in his tracks. An art expert at the Louvre in Paris the same week announced that the paint on some of Van Gogh's later work was so thick that the deepest layers were still wet, more than a hundred years after having been painted.

Strange things came over the wire every day. A lot of them never made it into the *Post-Gazette*. There was plenty of local news, high school sports, politics, and crime to fill the columns. The people of Cocoa Beach were worried about their bank accounts and taxes and often dwelt on their receding hairlines and the odds of getting skin cancer. They seldom cared to *understand things exactly as they are*. But I did. Why a man like Lawyer Timmons would use such vulgarities in describing himself was just as interesting to me as the fate of the dinosaurs or why the paint on Van Gogh's *Starry Night* wasn't as dry and dead as he was. Maxine said I was a born reporter: dumb enough to ask a lot of questions and smart enough to remember the answers.

With a slight movement of my head I took in all three faces. I could ask questions until doomsday and some things I was never going to understand.

But if you try, you can reach something in just about everyone. Lawyer Timmons, sitting in that brilliant square of light from the windows, his long face ravaged and his eyes sad and bloodshot and tired, was a man like my father: unsatisifed being a hacker and still as dedicated and principled as he would have been if elected president of the United States. They were two men who knew disappointment and how to live with it. Tall and bosomy Mrs. Timmons, round in the flank, pressing everywhere against her silky undergarments, was something different from any other woman I had met: strong she was, and fertile, even though she and her husband were apparently childless. Yet there was a warmth behind her sternest gaze that was maternal and meant she was listening, considering especially those opinions she did not agree with.

Mike Melendez I knew from the rugby field. He was unpredictable and talented out there, near perfect in his technique. Mike could kick the ball over the heads of onrushing defenders and catch it cleanly on the other side, running flat out most of the time like the Fijians did and always ready to pass you the ball from a funny angle, behind his back, anywhere. Rugby was certifiably dangerous and every player had that glazed going-to-war look, something that softball and tennis didn't offer. Once, against Winter Park, I was lying near the ball, pinned there, and this huge cracker was churning through the welter of players, his cleats pounding the turf like a tilling machine, bearing down—when Mike Melendez, with a quick-as-death change of direction, came knifing in, low and blurred as he passed over me and knocked the cracker on his ass, illegal as hell, drawing a penalty and an ejection. That tilling machine had been about two feet from my head and coming. Mike yanked me up from the ground and I said, "Right on," into his ear.

"Next time," he said.

This was next time. But I wasn't as much help to him as he had been to me. "Thanks anyway, Joe," said Melendez, appearing shrunken inside the gray linen shirt he was wearing. "But I don't want any deals." He looked away, studying the brocaded wallpaper. "I never did anything wrong and I'm not going to say or encourage anyone to think I did."

He pushed up from his chair to leave, almost upsetting the untouched glass of tea by his feet. Lawyer Timmons rose to meet him and said, "I'm afraid, then, this thing will drag out. There are several depositions I need to take and the discovery hasn't even been scheduled yet. Then jury selection and challenges. That will take months."

Melendez didn't say anything more and began to leave and Mr. Timmons came around the desk and followed after him. "I'll walk you out," he said. Mrs. Timmons yielded to the two men and reappeared in the doorway a moment later, like an apple surfacing in a pail of water.

"It's at least something that you're trying to help," she said.

Through the window I could see Mr. Timmons and Melendez pausing by the front gate in earnest discussion. "It's not doing him much good," I said.

"I don't see none of his other friends," replied Mrs. Timmons, turning her solemn high-cheekboned face to every corner of the room. "You're the only one."

Outside Mr. Timmons was patting Mike Melendez on the elbow and then the accused rapist turned and walked off along the gutter toward his car. Remembering something, Timmons swung open the gate and called after him. Melendez started back and then placed one foot on the curbstone and waited for Timmons to come out. The lawyer drew close and again began to speak.

"Mr. Timmons can do more for him than I can," I said.

"In a professional sense. And as a black man," she agreed, glancing out the front window at her husband. "But you're standing up with Michael Melendez and you're not a black man or a lawyer. You're not winning any popularity contest, either. Compared to that, well, Aloysius is doing no more good than a mouse at a fire."

I wandered over to Lawyer Timmons's desk and picked up the ceramic watermelon. "I have to ask you—where did Mr. Timmons get this?" Mrs. Timmons let out a *harumph* and crossed the little room to take it from me. Her fingernails were long and unpainted and the pink half moons beneath them were the same color as mine when our hands touched.

"That's the Watermelon Award," she said. "Another lawyer gave it to him when he was in the district attorney's office up in Atlanta, a long time ago. His name was Hatfield, this other lawyer, Lucien Hatfield, and he was white, an old man. Aloysius always said Hatfield taught him more by beating him in just one case than he learned in ten years before the bench."

"Mr. Timmons mentioned him the first time I was here. He said there was a white lawyer from Georgia who told him never take a case you can't win or a client who can't pay."

Mrs. Timmons nodded her head. She replaced the trinket on the desk. "That's Lucien Hatfield. He practiced law for a long, long time. He's dead now. When he gave Aloysius that watermelon—those are real diamond chips in there—he told him it was a pleasure facing him in court because he was a tough prosecutor but one who could always be beaten because he didn't use every advantage to the fullest." Her eyes had become focused on the doorway as if she expected the old white lawyer to materialize there. "Once in a while in court when things weren't going well Hatfield would set himself to explode, ranting and raving at some poor witness who wasn't getting things out the way he'd been coached, and the judge would bang the gavel, calling for order and threatening Hatfield with contempt. Then after the recess Hatfield would come in like a whipped dog and apologize to the jury and then practically cry when he asked them not to blame his client for his own misbehavior. Hatfield would have his fingers in his vest, looking down at the floor or the railing of the jury box, and he'd say something like 'My failings are my own and I trust you will not allow me to taint my client with this undignified outburst.' Of course it's a new jury each time so it was a great tactic and he won a lot of cases that way."

I sat on the edge of the desk, and she continued: "Hatfield knew Aloysius was going into private practice and moving here to Florida and said it was okay to let him in on a secret. 'Guess what—you're a Negro,' he said. 'And those white juries are going to look up and see a nigger and in their minds they're going to recoil from that prejudice and try to be fair to your client by overcompensating. So let them know you're a negro. Bring a goddamned watermelon and fried chicken to court if that's what it takes to win. Because winning is what it's all about, son, winning and nothing else.' "

President Lincoln appeared and with an agile bound leapt into Mrs. Timmons's arms. She looked out the window again as Lawyer Timmons passed through the front gate, swinging up the walk like a statue that had animated itself, imperturbable as bronze, weathered and slightly cool to the touch. "He never saw it right to take that particular advantage," Mrs. Timmons said.

When the door opened Lawyer Timmons came into a silent room. "I know how doctors must feel when they tell a patient he has cancer," said Timmons. "The agony will last many months and if the cancer doesn't kill you, the cure will."

9

Loretta stopped calling me and she stopped coming by the newspaper and rugby practice to pick me up in the jeep. At first there were no side effects except a slight tendency to talk to myself as if Loretta was there, answering phantom questions and making short speeches to the chair or the dresser. Then the vague hallucinations—hearing her call my name in the shower or expecting a satisfied murmur or caress at night in the darkness under the sheets. Loretta's perfume remained on some of my T-shirts and the pillowcases. I would wake up and the familiar odor would be there, comforting me, and then it would penetrate my sleepiness that I was alone and I would thrash about in the bedclothes like a fish caught in a net.

"So call her," Surfer said, surprising me near the telephone. I had been hovering around it all afternoon, and when I said call who?, no way was I calling anyone, he laughed. "Why not?"

"I dunno. Pride, I guess."

Surfer shook his head. "Fuck that," he said. "That's like wearing your pants in a swimming pool."

He flapped past me into the living room and I went out and took a bicycle from the garage and set off toward the beach, riding aimlessly until I found myself circling Loretta's neighborhood. Twice I went by the end of her street before I got the bicycle moving in the right direction. Her jeep was in the driveway of the tiny cinder-block house she was renting. I jumped the curb and rode over the lawn to the backyard.

The windows were all open and I could hear classical music

coming from the radio in the kitchen, and an occasional high-pitched remark from Bernie, the parrot she kept in a cage above the sink. I glimpsed Loretta passing from one room to another in her nurse's uniform and leaned the bicycle against a palm tree and approached the back door. The sun was bright in the yard and I squinted into the gray interior of the house while Loretta ran water from the tap, humming to herself. She filled a little device that attached to the side of Bernie's cage. Looking at her through the screen door, as she moved about in the dim recesses of the kitchen, was like looking at a satellite photo, grainy and indistinct. Places where I had so casually laid my hands were as remote as the deserts of Africa.

Loretta fitted the device to the bars of the cage and Bernie drank from it. "Love you, too," he said, stretching his blue head toward her.

I was gripped by the feeling that I didn't want to be there. That I shouldn't be there. Then Loretta turned from the sink and cried, "Oh," startled by my shadow across the doorway.

"It's only me," I said.

"Oh!" said the parrot. "Only me. Only me."

"Joseph!" Loretta came halfway to the door. "You scared me."

"Sorry. I didn't mean to."

Loretta dropped her gaze, staring at the tiles beneath her feet. "I'm just on my way to work right now," she said, without looking up.

"That's all right. I only came by to say hello." There was weakness in my voice and it quavered a little bit. "And to see how you were."

"Love you, too," said Bernie. He turned his head unnaturally. "Love you, too. Oooo-ooo."

"I'm okay. How are you doing?"

"Pretty good." I couldn't think of anything witty and stood there empty-headed and smiling. Where a moment before I hadn't wanted to be discovered, and would have retreated if I could have done it quietly enough, now my legs felt mired in cement and I couldn't tear myself away, although Loretta gave every sign that's what she preferred.

"Maybe we should talk," I said after a short silence. "We haven't done that for a while."

Loretta glanced at me with a hard look in her eyes and came closer to the door. "I don't think we ever talked, Joe. Not really. That was your problem."

I had this feeling that was like the blood draining out of my heart. There was a hole at the bottom of it and the blood just all ran out. Suddenly, everything Loretta and I had ever done together, watching the late show on tee vee, the jeep rides, even just sharing an orange or the newspaper, took on a terrible finality and was too painful to even think about. I guess nostalgia is the only emotion that can be paid for with a mortgage, amortized over the years. But in an instant the past had become a liability. I was wearing a T-shirt Loretta had given me and it was like wearing something from a museum.

"We have a lot of fun together," I said.

"Life isn't always fun," said Loretta. "Sometimes it's just being able to communicate with someone. The last time we were together you practically threw me out of the house." She looked up and there were tears in her eyes. "That's a funny way of communicating."

My voice broke. "I'm sorry."

"Too late," said Loretta. She was close to the screen now, one hand on the doorknob and her head cast down to one side, so that through the pattern of the screen she looked like a pointillist Madonna. "Our relationship wasn't going anywhere. I'm twenty-six years old. No hard feelings, but I want to move in a definite direction."

"Love you, too," Bernie said.

"Like what?" I asked. "Getting married?"

"Yeah. Someday I want to have a house and kids and a husband who loves me. There's nothing wrong with that."

Bernie's head moved erratically, his eyes spinning in his little blue skull, and he kept silent. "No, there's nothing wrong with that, Loretta," I said, staring into an enormous flaw in my character. "Lots of guys would love to give you that."

Loretta met my eyes. "I know they would. But I was waiting for you to come around. Eight months. You weren't coming." She continued to look at me, her eyes glossy and wet. "Women want mystery, but they also want potential," she said. "They like a tough guy, an independent. A guy that doesn't take any shit. I was head over heels when I found out you played rugby. It was almost like being a lady at court and going to watch the jousts. You were so handsome out there, Joe, muddy and bruised, you looked like a little boy. At night you'd be tired, and always so happy. Nothing ever bothered you on Saturday nights." For a moment it looked like she was going to open the door. "I know you love your teammates, and the best thing about you, Joseph Dolan, is you never fly anyone's flag but your own."

Bernie gave a long clear whistle and said, "Only me! Only me!"

"But a woman needs to think she's going somewhere," said Loretta. Her eyes lost their romantic sheen and became philosophical. "That the relationship has potential. It's a fine line. With some women it takes six years to see a dead end, others see it in six weeks."

"What's your rule of thumb?" I asked.

"I don't know." She grinned. "I guess it's eight months."

I tapped my foot on the concrete slab outside the door and crossed my arms, rocking away from her with my head tilted back. "Uggh. You'll probably marry that asshole Dr. Jackson with the tinted contact lenses. Be rich. Have a lot of perfect kids with all As on their report cards. It's depressing."

Loretta giggled, and for the first time she was present to me, we connected. "I don't know who I'm going to marry, Joe. But we both know it's not going to be you."

"I'm not even sure I believe in marriage. It's certainly not foolproof."

"No, it's not. It's a gamble," said Loretta, zeroing in. "Your parents died and you don't have to tell me—I know that really hurt you. But you can't spend the rest of your life trying to avoid falling in love with someone. Everything ends sometime. That's no reason not to start."

Bitter thoughts crossed my mind. "Why not? I mean, why go through all that?"

"You'll just be old and lonely if you don't."

"You want to see old and lonely," I said, a terrible edge in my voice, "you should have seen my mother. After that, anything would be better than dying of a broken heart. I'd rather be alone in a room without a friend in the world."

"Your mother had you, though," said Loretta. "Don't forget, children come from marriages."

One day I came into my mother's sickroom, heavy with the scent of lilacs from the trellis outside the window. When I switched off the television she woke from her nap and I sat on the bed. Her strength was fading, she said. And she was tired of it. It was the only time I broke down and admitted failure, that by not saving my mother I was somehow a bad son.

"You're the best son anyone could ask for," she said, taking my hand. "But you're a man, too, and you have your own life. You're going to be the hardest hit when I go. You'll have to survive without me. Just remember, Joe, that I'm your friend, that I've always been your friend and always will be."

Loretta moved behind the screen and it reminded me of going to confession at the church in my old neighborhood. She made a fist with her right hand and thrust it against the screen. "You're like this—" she relaxed her fingers, spreading them wide "—when you should be like this."

It was the sort of advice you received on piers and gangplanks when you were embarking on a journey to someplace you weren't coming back from. I didn't say anything, just swallowed it the way you did with good advice you knew you weren't going to take, nodding my head that it was true. Around me, I felt phantom handkerchiefs waving and faint loving cries of *bon voyage* and *farewell*.

"Maybe you should go out and get drunk," suggested Loretta. She fingered the nameplate attached to her snug white uniform. "That's not the kind of thing I say to most people, but a little fun wouldn't hurt you. You haven't had a single beer as long as I've known you."

"And I haven't been single as long as I've had you, either."

She laughed and said, "I gotta go."

"All right. Don't worry about me. I'll be fine. Just another broken-hearted derelict going through garbage cans down on the beach strip."

"Good-bye, Joe," Loretta said. She closed the inner door and locked it, abandoning me on the stoop. A moment later, I heard her go out the front door, start the jeep, and drive off.

In the hot silence of the backyard my joke grew in size and got personal with me. It was not a long drop to the bottom, to a bar stool next to all the other tattooed and shaggy losers, the crippled and lame, their mustaches drooping over mouths badly in need of dental work. They were the refuse of the beach district—like Elvis that morning at the taco stand—mostly addicts and transients and a few working stiffs, the hard souls who couldn't accept things unless they were getting behind seven or eight drinks.

I retrieved my bicycle and walked it over the lawn to the street. Looking up and down at the quiet houses, the little plots of flowers, the crooked mailboxes, I pushed off from the curb, my left foot on the pedal, balanced for a moment on one side of the moving bicyle; then swung my right leg over the saddle and headed for the Legion hall.

The parking lot was nearly deserted, just a mint-condition Cadillac and a couple of rusty pickups, and when I passed through the swinging doors of the Legion hall and my eyes had adjusted to the sudden moist darkness, a man in a rumpled gray suit approached and steered me toward the glowing window of the bar like a tugboat nudging an ocean liner into its berth. "Friend—you need a drink," he said.

He was a small pudgy man with a round head, balding on top, and childlike blue eyes that relieved the pallor and fatigue of his complexion. A complete stranger. But he kept his hand on my elbow, pinning me to the rail as he signaled to the hefty middle-aged barmaid. She stubbed out her cigarette and came over.

"Unspeakable goddess that you are, another whiskey and soda for me, and for my young friend here, a—"

"Beer," I said.

"Beer," repeated the man, satisfied. He placed his money on the bar and the barmaid brought the drinks and made change for his twenty-dollar bill, returning to her seat by the television. The man handed me the glass of beer and took up his drink, gesturing at the bright array of decanters and bottles forming a pyramid across from us. "There it is," he said, clinking his glass against mine. "The party without food."

He drank half the whiskey and soda in one mouthful. "Go ahead," he said, encouraging me. The beer was sweet and appetizing. I had never suffered with a drinking problem of any sort. Only the fear of remembering, of feeling sorry for myself, kept me away from it, even during rugby season when beer after the games was part of the experience.

"I'm airborne," the man said, looking up at me. "82nd. I used to be six foot five until I jumped out of all those goddamned planes. My name's Sanchez. Pedro Sanchez. I don't look like no Cuban, but that's what I am. I run thirty minutes every morning and drink like a fish. It's okay to drink like a fish so long as you drink what a fish drinks! I read that on a tea bag once. I had six bypasses. Look. You wanna see the scars?" Sanchez undid the top buttons of his shirt and showed me a long raised blue trail that ran the length of his torso. "My old man died at thirty-seven. It's hereditary. They said: get it done or you're gonna die. And you might just die anyway. Fuck it, I said. I'm gonna live. It's all bullshit. Nothing means nothing. Just live. Can I buy you another drink? I love you like a brother. I'm airborne."

All I could do was stick out my hand and say, "Joe Dolan. Nice to meet ya."

"No it's not. It's never nice to meet me," replied Sanchez, laughing. "I'm a real son of a bitch. My own kids can't stand me. Because I see through them. I see through everybody, Joe. They're all afraid of life. Any guy walking down the street—run up to him and say *Boo! Life!*—and he'll shit his pants. You know why? I do. Because he's walking with his eyes rolling on the ground, he's so fucking scared. He's got the house, the kids, the car, some deadly nine-to-five, and he's wrapped so tight in that straitjacket he thinks he's safe. Anything new or out of control comes along and he's fucking *petrified.* Back when I was so damned stupid I was playing a lot of golf I used to play with this brain surgeon up at Orsino. Know what he said to me once? He said brain surgery was like a two-foot putt. But if you miss it, the patient dies. I didn't know what he meant until the day I woke up in the recovery room with a fucking piano on my chest and my balls in a vise. What I wanted to tell that son of a bitch was that life was like a forty-foot wedge out of the deep sand for par and there wasn't a fucking guy walking who had the *cojones* to take the shot. To me that's a gimme. I'll swing *that* fucking club one-handed and blindfolded with a drink in the other hand and a brass band on the fairway behind me playing 'Hail to the Chief.' I could be dead inside a minute. So I'm A-1 fucking airborne. That hand—" he straightened his arm, his stubby white hand an inch from my nose, running lengthwise "—is steady as a rock."

My glass was empty and I started on the second one, already at my elbow. Pedro Sanchez was sweating wildly. The armpits of his suit jacket were damp and his face was turning gray, hovering near me, the eyes wide and urgent and staring into my eyes so hard the blue seemed to be bleeding from them. He was not right in his mind, but he struck a raw nerve when he said, "That's goddamned right, Joe. Life is time, and time is all you have."

We had the public half of the bar to ourselves. It was strange to be there in the middle of the afternoon, the dusty light falling through the unpainted top halves of the windows to reveal every dent and dimple in the worn parquet floor. A bowl of cocktail onions gleamed like pearls. Without the rugby players the place seemed drowsy and lifeless until Pedro Sanchez pulled the rip cord, charging the room with impressive manic energy. The barmaid was probably used to being left alone and, despite the fact Sanchez was a prodigious tipper, she looked annoyed when he called for another round. The Cuban flung the money on the bar and swept up the drinks and pressed on with his monologue.

"—is the funniest goddamned thing you ever heard? I sell life insurance! Ha-ha-hee-hee-hee. Life insurance! As if there was such a thing. Let me tell you a little secret, Joe: it's death insurance. Nobody takes a damned penny with them when they die, and still people buy it from me like it's going out of style. Look at the suit I'm wearing. These shoes. I make a bundle. I tell most people my story, show them the scars, and they buy even more. They double their premiums. I'm making money in spite of myself. It's fucking crazy. They should cash in their policies and go to the racetrack. Fly to the Antilles or some damned thing. Do you have any life insurance, Joe? None? Maybe we should sit down here and talk about that. Get your checkbook. Ha-ha-ha-ha. I'm only kidding. Fuck that. You're better off pissing in the wind. Insurance is probably the only thing you can't get in this life. How old are you—twenty-six, twenty-seven? According to the actuarial tables you'll live to be seventy-five or seventy-six years old. But the tables don't take into consideration plane crashes and car accidents and jealous husbands, or a great deal on a condominium that just happens to be built on top of an old chemical dump. All you own is the breath going in and out of your body. That's the secret. Inhale-exhale. I'm forty-five years old. Every second I'm standing here, I'm cheating the hangman. That I'm even talking to you right now is a fucking miracle."

Sanchez covered his mouth with his hand. His cough was like the single report of a gun in the distance, dull and dry and then followed by a sharp echo. He leaned past me for his drink. "Make way for the walking dead," he said.

I drank my beer and ate a bag of peanuts. The alcohol made my arms and legs heavy and my head extremely light. Listening to Sanchez inspired me. He had channeled his madness into an extraordinary effort to stay alive, but not for any length of time, that wasn't the point. An hour spent on something meaningless was an eternity to him. No, it was more like *depth* of time he was aiming for. In just one of his crazy minutes Pedro Sanchez found everything he needed.

Excusing myself, I went into the hallway to make a telephone call. It was long distance and after reaching the switchboard I waited several moments for the party to be summoned. While I was holding, a vapid numbing music oozed from the receiver. Electronic, seamless, and indefatigable, it was the same tripe we used to drive people off the line at the newspaper when they called to complain. Synthesized music could try the patience of even the most obnoxious do-gooders, politicians, activists, advertisers, and touts. I imagined that Pedro Sanchez tore telephones out by the roots when he heard it, cursing a blue streak. You could not be expected to live through six bypasses and put up with crap like this. Somewhere lurking in the recesses of corporate America was a silent behemoth of a company that made untold millions building golf courses and selling life insurance, all to the endless, tuneless, debilitating sound of Muzak.

Finally my party came on the line. Some details were arranged and I hung up. Sanchez was leaning over the rail talking to the barmaid when I returned. Lights behind the bar threw an eerie greenish cast over his skin. His banter was nonstop. She moved like a dancer. Had she ever been a dancer? He knew a dancer once who had the singular talent of cracking walnuts with her thighs. The barmaid ran a hand through dyed blond hair the texture of cotton candy and moved her significant bulk a step closer to the charming Cuban, yielding to his relentlessly profane flirtation. Winking at me, Sanchez continued, rhapsodizing on the possibilities of an assault on such a desirable mountain of flesh. "I like a big girl," he said.

The barmaid paused to refresh the drink of a gas company employee on the other side of the bar.

Sanchez asked if I wanted another beer. Yes, I said, but it was definitely my round. He protested, flashing his diamond pinkie ring, but I insisted. Reluctantly, he agreed, and I ordered a whiskey and soda and a draft. Waiting for them, our backs to the bar, I told Sanchez I needed a favor. Anything, he said. Goddamnit, ask me anything. Well, I was supposed to pick up a friend of mine and I didn't have a car.

"I'm your man," Sanchez said. "A ride, a loan, a drink—you name it. You're like a brother to me."

I really appreciated it. But it was an hour each way. That was no problem whatsoever, he said. We would buy a bottle at the drive-through and go in his Cadillac. It was a nice car, comfortable and roomy, and he loved cruising in it.

The barmaid brought the drinks over and Sanchez compared her breasts to sculpted pails of vanilla ice cream. She shook her fist and said he shouldn't talk to her like that, her boyfriend would be coming in soon. He was a beer salesman and he got real jealous when guys came in and talked dirty to her. Just then the pay phone rang in the hallway and she came around to answer it.

"Let's get outta here," I said. "A woman that size is bound to have a very large boyfriend."

"The bigger they are, the harder they fucking fall," said Sanchez. "I'm airborne."

"That was him," said the frowsy barmaid, returning. She stood before us, top-heavy, wobbling on her high heels. "He's right down the street at Little Jake's making a delivery. He'll be here in five minutes."

Sanchez let his gaze wander over her enormous legs and haunches, the size of an NFL lineman's, to the roll of fat around her middle and breasts that swelled impossibly outward, stretching the fabric of her tank top to the limit. Her lipstick had been applied like a child's crayon, making her mouth a round red hole. And the roots of her hair were comically dark.

"Why go out for a hamburger when you have steak at home?" Sanchez asked, posing the question to himself.

The barmaid teetered on a single heel, grinning at him. "You're cute," she said. She opened the trapdoor on the bar.

Tracking her massive rump as she brushed past him, Sanchez said, "Of course, I *could* go for a burger right now." He reached out and grabbed a rich handful of her flank. "A big juicy one."

The barmaid turned, and with startling grace, sank her hand

into Sanchez's groin. "A hot dog will suit me," she said. "Even a small one."

Sanchez rose on his tiptoes. "Vigaro-vigaro-vigaro!" he sang in his best soprano. The barmaid gave his package a final twist and then released him. Sanchez jumped back in delighted horror, clutching himself. Satisfied and smiling, like she had just demonstrated a mathematical theorem on the blackboard, some painful lesson, the barmaid said, "I move fast."

"*Goddamn,* she's all woman," exclaimed Sanchez.

A truck pulled into the parking lot. It clattered over the stones and broken asphalt, grinding its gears, and then I heard a mechanical beeping sound as it backed up toward the doors of the Legion hall. "Pedro," I said. "Let's go."

He came toward me, his tie askew, sweating profusely, and then flung his arm back toward the bar for emphasis. "That's some woman, Joe," he shouted. "That's some goddamn woman right there."

"Be careful," laughed the barmaid, hands on hips, thrusting out her gargantuan breasts. "Next time I'll tear that thing right off."

"My dear, my darling, I'm looking forward to it," said Sanchez. He glanced at me. "Even though every step is taking me closer to death, I love this joint."

The clang of metal came through to us from outside. I pictured someone bigger than Van Valkenburg, with a keg under each arm. Holding my palms out toward him, I implored Sanchez to retreat.

"Let's take a ride, Joe," he said, then gestured to the barmaid. "I'm coming back. Wild horses couldn't keep me away. I'm airborne."

A tired-looking man in dirty blue work clothes entered the hall as we went out, dragging a keg of beer on a two-wheeler, the veins standing out on his narrow forearms. Sanchez hustled to open the second door for him, nodding as the salesman struggled past with his load. The top of the salesman's head barely reached my earlobe, and the weight of the keg, fixed by a single rubber strap, threatened to roll the man under.

"Thanks," he grunted. Vexation formed a series of ridged parallel lines on his forehead. "These fucking things get bigger and heavier every day."

Going out to the car, there was a short silence as we absorbed the salesman's remark, until Sanchez erupted with laughter, dancing over the shattered pavement in his alligator shoes. "Nine-to-five, Joe, nine-to-five," he said. "Now what was I just telling you? He's never gonna take the shot. Line that putt up an inch from the hole and he's not gonna take it. Never in a million years. His hands are shaking. He can't work up a good spit. I could sell that poor bastard a whole briefcase full of insurance. But if I die, I die. I'd rather be me dead than *him* alive. Who gives a fuck, really? That keg was like an anchor around his neck and it's dragging him straight to the bottom." He threw me the keys and went around to the passenger side, pausing by the great wing of the Cadillac. "Joe, when that barmaid grabbed me by the nuts I was in heaven. That was living, boy. It felt good, and it hurt—just like life. A night jump at two thousand feet was nothing next to that. It's a goddamned good thing I'm airborne, Joe. A ground humper couldn't take this shit. I'm so full I'm spilling over. Let's go get your pal. What's his name? I don't care. I'll buy him a drink. Already I love him like a brother."

The late-afternoon sky was streaked yellow with sunbeams and the breeze off the intracoastal rattled the stiff brown fingers of a palm tree overhead. Sanchez was squinty in the horizontal light, his suit coat in a wrinkled mass over his shoulder, and the shirt he wore, drenched with sweat, was flattened against his chunky torso. He stripped off his tie and I could make out the darkened ridge of his scar beneath the shirt. It was a stigma he didn't really deserve.

"Edgar," I said. "My friend's name is Edgar."

10

Rack 'n' Ride was a drive-through liquor store at the end of the beach strip, empty at that hour of the day, with music pouring from the tunnel entrance and the refrigerated glass cases shiny in the light. The original Rack 'n' Ride had been a car wash and guiding the Cadillac into it was like squeezing an elephant in there, my jaw tight, goosing the brake.

"Don't worry about scratching it, Joe. I'm insured," said Sanchez, flopped in the passenger seat. "I got this buddy that owns a funeral home and I was in his showroom last week turning over the price tags and I said, 'Shit, Rollo, do they drive these things to heaven? This is outrageous,' and he just shrugged and told me, 'We got basic transportation and we got luxury. You're looking at a two-door sedan,' and I flipped the tag back over and said, 'I own a nice Caddy now, but when I die, you can bury me in the cheapest thing you got on the lot.' So plan in advance, Rollo said. Buy it all now. You must be on drugs, I told him. I'd flush it all down the toilet before I'd spend a single red cent on my funeral. My money goes for booze, broads, the track, and any other damn thing I feel like. I haven't paid my taxes for five fucking years. They can't tax me where I'm going, Joe, where we're all going. And anyone who can die owing the federal government a hundred and sixty-nine thousand dollars is all right in my book."

The attendant ducked in the window. "What can I get for you fellas?" he asked. He was a lean-faced young man with a ponytail and several earrings in each ear.

"How about two six-packs of that Canadian beer over there, a bottle of champagne if you got it, a quart of single malt Scotch, four cigars, a bag of corn chips, a bag of them pretzels, beef jerky, and two packages of chewing gum," said Sanchez, handing the kid a hundred-dollar bill. "Put the booze in one of those foam coolers and pack it in ice and put the other stuff in a box—not a bag. Throw it all in the backseat."

The attendant stared into Sanchez's fiery blue eyes for a moment and understood he meant every word of it. Straightening up, taking in the larger portrait of the gleaming Cadillac and the well-dressed, well-fed man in it, he busied himself with the order, running to various cases and racks, stowing the items in the containers requested. Occasionally he asked for a clarification on brand name or size, his voice echoing in the tunnel, and Sanchez answered. Whatever else could be said about him, Pedro Sanchez was a man who knew what he wanted, down to a particular lightly salted corn chip.

The back door swung open and the ponytailed attendant placed the cooler and the loaded cardboard box together on the seat. "Anything else, sir?" he asked.

"An air freshener," said Sanchez. The attendant added it to the total on the register and when he tried to hand over ten dollars in change, Sanchez waved him off. "Keep it," he said.

The attendant nodded thanks, and then glanced at the contents of the backseat like there were two boxes of dynamite back there. "Have a good one," he said. "Be careful with that stuff."

"Hey, it's a gamble," said Sanchez, as the electric window went up. "Life's a fucking crapshoot." He was talking to me now. "If you stayed in your house all the time, a meteor would probably hit it and you'd get blown to kingdom come. When it's over for me, I want you to pour a quart of good Scotch whiskey on my grave and I don't care if it goes through your kidneys first."

Easing the Cadillac through the rest of the tunnel, over the concrete lip at the edge and down to the smooth apron outside, I looked both ways to measure the traffic and stopped for a car that was coming out of a laundromat across the street. It was Sherri Hogg. The car passed in front of us, her moon face flashing behind the blurred windshield like a goldfish in a bowl. I was working on the Elvis problem, so I didn't say anything, only noted the make and color of the car and the direction Sherri was heading. One delusional paranoid at a time was my limit.

Sanchez unwrapped the cellophane on the air freshener, which was shaped like a little Christmas tree. The pungent smell of evergreen filled the car. "How long has your pal been in the hospital?" he asked.

"Two weeks. It was a psychiatric evaluation. He's not sure who he is."

"That's an easy one: whoever he thinks he is," said Sanchez, reaching over the seat for two bottles of beer. He opened them and handed one to me. "We'll get that straightened out right away. A couple of shots of whiskey and he'll know who he is, for better or worse. Hell, when I set to drinking, I think I'm Thomas Edison, for crissakes, I'm inventing so many kinds of bullshit." He patted his bulging stomach. "If I didn't drink, though, I'd be on the cover of one of those men's magazines wearing a pair of pants two inches too short. This morning I'm out running on the beach and I see this gorgeous broad in a bikini. First I'm the biggest stud in central Florida and then I start cramping up and it's back to reality—I'm a forty-five-year-old fat slob with a blue zipper on his chest. My mating song ended right there. Anytime you see a nice broad you go into a song and dance. You're like the praying mantis, do-si-doing around each other, moving your hands like this and that—" he made insect motions "—then you both buckle on and ride until you're through and one bites the other one's head off. You either get on top and drive or you take the bottom and get ridden into limpdicity." I laughed at that, and he said, "If people start saying it, then *limpdicity* is a word. Webster's dead, but the language keeps on growing, Joe. The dictionary keeps getting bigger. That's what I'm telling you. If you think you're Joan of Arc or Abraham Lincoln, then fuck it, that's good enough for me. I don't need to see your feet on fire or a stovepipe hat to know who you are."

We rode along with the windows down, taking in the cool tidal air, through the last set of lights and onto the coast road.

"You're fucking crazy," I said, feeling reckless, the beer working on me and all that latent horsepower responding to the slightest touch of my fingers.

"Of course I am. Crazy as a loon," said Sanchez. "And so are you. Every manjack walking is crazy. They're just afraid to let it out. Afraid to love the world, Joe, and what's in it. Go into a supermarket one day and look at the people pushing carriages up and down past the pyramids of tomato puree, I say—*the pyramids of tomato puree*—then they're waiting in line and handing over their little coupons and asking the clerk to double-bag their order. What they really *want* is to smash watermelons with a hammer, run their carts into each other, trash the pyramids, and tear open every bag and box and jar in sight. Empty canisters of whipped cream all over the floor and slide naked in it, guzzling wine coolers. Think of the last time you were in there, Joe. Didn't you see a girl you wanted to bend over the cucumber rack with mist coming down from those little nozzles, watching her close her eyes in the angled mirrors they got in there, her skirt up around her neck, her tiny underwear coming loose, and in your ear, nothing but lies, lies, lies?"

I paused for a beat, and said, "Well, I'm only human," and we both laughed, Sanchez leaning over the seat toward me, his eyes blue and bulging, a stick of beef jerky in his hand, pointed at the roof. "Exactly," he said. "And you have to be crazy to take that gamble."

"Loretta used to say that," I replied, and as I spoke her name, dread flashed through me like a sword. "She said that anyone who would play rugby in the mud and rain must be crazy, and shouldn't be let indoors with civilized people."

"Who's Loretta? Your wife?"

I shook my head. "It was like trying to keep a smoke ring in my wallet, hanging onto that girl. I just couldn't do it."

"You can't hang onto anything in this life, Joe," Sanchez said, after a mouthful of beer. "That's why I'm airborne. Up there it's you and you alone, screaming into the big blue empty." I glanced sideways into the screaming blue void of his eyes and he continued. "Nothing except a patch of silk between you and certain death. And you're lucky to have that. Because the thing, Joe, the thing that most people try to forget when they're going by the pyramids of tomato puree is there's absolutely nothing between you and certain death. Not a blessed thing. It's around every corner, under every bedsheet, always just one heartbeat away. You're better off heading right into it, because if you're not flying toward it, believe me, it's flying toward you."

We were moving inland, the afternoon shadows stretched across the road, dissolving into twilight, and in that soft violet hour we finished the first six-pack of beer and nipped at the whiskey. Route 20 was newly paved and straight, two lanes bordered by the perfect white fences of horse farms and citrus groves, and it was hardly any effort to keep the car running in the exact center of the road. For a while bottles were passed back and forth across the front seat and we drove on in silence. The beer made a cold streak inside my chest and the whiskey ran a trail of fire down the middle of it.

"There sure is a lot of pain out there," I said, thinking, in quick succession, of Maxine and Lawyer Timmons and Sherri Hogg and the frail seedy umpires from the Legion hall. They would never slide naked on the glossy tiled floors of the supermarket.

"A lot of pain," agreed Sanchez, gazing at the countryside rushing by. His face was tired and pale. "Most of it self-inflicted."

Pressing down on the accelerator, I felt the car rise and strain forward; then I switched on the headlights, throwing a feeble light ahead of us on the pavement. "You just can't let it turn you into a stone," I said.

Sanchez opened two more bottles of beer. "For a lot of people, death is like a mugger waiting in the alley, and the absolute fucking boredom of their lives is like the police station. They feel safe there."

In the fresh-fallen darkness, the county hospital, lurking among the sassafras trees, had the appearance of a Spanish villa, and the lone figure descending the stairs did nothing to dispel that illusion, lank and agile, one hand pocketed, coming toward us like a man dressed in evening clothes. His gait was distinctive, even in the gloom, where spotlights embedded in the great dark lawn projected white crescents onto the stucco walls. Other hidden sources illuminated the gravel walk curving toward the spot upon which Sanchez and I stood, car doors flung open, watering the shrubs.

"Here he is," I said, zipping up.

Edgar Lindenberg came in range of the powerful headlights of the Cadillac, moving as though on a cushion of air and dressed, not in a tuxedo, but in his soiled dungarees and a short canvas jacket he wore over a black T-shirt. His hair swooped down on his forehead and in the concentrated shaft of light, his face was shiny and smooth like the blade of a hatchet. A slight odor of disinfectant clung to him. We exchanged greetings, shook hands, and then waited for Sanchez to finish what was becoming a monumental piss. He grinned proudly, sending out a glistening arch of water, steam rising from it in the glare of the headlights. Edgar shifted his feet and the popping sound of the gravel was amplified beneath his boot soles.

"For me the simple pleasures are what matter most. I don't trust a man who doesn't piss outside once in a while," Sanchez said as the stream of water petered out and he turned toward us with his fly open.

"Pedro Sanchez: this is Edgar Lindenberg," I said. "From Chalybeate, Tennessee."

Sanchez stuck out his hand and Lindenberg hesitated for a moment and then shook it. "Damned if you don't look like Elvis," said the Cuban. His eyes cerulean in the tunnel of light that surrounded us, Sanchez nodded toward the hospital and in a moment shifted his gaze back to Lindenberg. "You look fit as a fiddle," he said, surveying the young guitar player. "You coming out of the hospital puts most people to shame. I came out on a platter like a rib roast."

Lindenberg's thin girlish mouth twitched in a nervous half smile and he lowered his head, the lock of black hair falling over one eye. He flipped it back into place and when he spoke, out came the husky warbling drawl they had not been able to cure him of. "The sickness was in my mind," he said. "A paranoid de-lusion."

"Hell, you're every bit as sane as I am. Or Joe here," roared Sanchez. "Of course you are. Those head doctors are a bunch of phonies. The only profession that earns more for doing less are the meteorologists. Wave your dick around and you're collecting more data than a hundred of their fucking satellites." The Cuban darted back to the car and grabbed the bottle of whiskey. "Hell—have a drink. You know what they say, *in vino veritas,* baby. In vermouth there is truth. We get to the bottom of this bottle and we'll know who everybody is."

Lindenberg eyed the bottle. At first he gave no answer. Held toward him at the end of a short ham-fisted arm, the whiskey bottle hovered within reach. Sanchez's pale and perspiring face was just to one side of it, above the wrinkled suit with dark wet spots on the trousers and a shirttail protruding from the open fly. The bottle swayed for an instant, half filled with a golden liquid as thick as oil, sloshing back and forth. He was being tempted with his old life.

I said nothing. Drunk as I was, I knew with great clarity that I wanted Elvis back and was waiting to see what Lindenberg would do to resurrect him, scuffing the gravel with nervous feet, his mind racing behind those hooded eyes. He followed the involuntary palsied movement of Sanchez's hand and said, "Guess I'll take a rain check," mesmerized by the liquor stirring in the bottle.

"Suit yourself," said the Cuban. Unscrewing the cap on the whiskey, he took a generous swallow and then shoved the bottle against my chest. "Joe?" he said.

I shook my head. "Beer for me," I replied, heading for the car. Lindenberg went around to the other side, admiring the Cadillac with a keen professional eye, and when he was lost in contemplation, Sanchez passed close by my ear and whispered, "Don't worry. We'll take him out for a little shock therapy."

Lindenberg stared at himself in the burnished sheen of the Cadillac. Only by touching the car could you tell it was running, the engine so sophisticated as to be virtually silent in an idle.

"She's a beaut," said Lindenberg. "The Sedan Deville, the last eight-cylinder they ever made."

Sanchez joined him on that side of the car. "They make little tin go-carts now, loaded down with all that air pollution crap. You might as well take the bus as drive one of those damned things. The whole industry's gone fairy." He tapped the shining metal with his fingertips and it gave out a sound like a kettledrum. "But this roaring gas hog is the real McCoy. A real piece of America. When this baby rolled off the old assembly line, grown men cried. It was like the last buffalo making dust on the prairie."

"Three hundred sixty-eight cubic inches generating a hundred fifty-eight horsepower at a maximum ninety-eight hundred rpms,"

Lindenberg said in his salesman patter. He ducked his head in the open window. "Leather upholstery. Mahogany dash. Fully loaded. Very, very nice."

Sanchez pointed to the vacant driver's seat. "Go ahead," he insisted. Before Lindenberg could protest, he climbed in the backseat and said, "You drive. Joe and I are seeing the world much too clearly to get behind the wheel now."

"Are you sure?" asked Lindenberg.

"I can't drive from back here," said Sanchez. He fell over on the seat and, bending his knees, tucked his legs in after him when I closed the door. Through the window I saw him lose his balance and roll off the seat. "Look out!" he cried. "I'm airborne."

Lindenberg glanced at the pudgy round-faced figure sprawling on the floor of the backseat and then looked at me over the roof as we each paused on one leg, about to get in. "Is he okay?" asked Lindenberg.

"Define *okay,*" I said.

Sanchez managed to right himself after a brief struggle and threw an arm over the cooler, the other buried to the elbow in his box of provisions. "The only design flaw in these babies is the slippery rear seats," he said. "So fuck it, let's get going."

Our new driver wheeled the Cadillac in an arc, the headlights sweeping across the empty parking lot like the beacon of a great naval vessel. Lindenberg's eyes shot upward one last time to the rearview mirror and a glimpse of the hospital, its walls scalloped with light, looming in the dark tangled branches of the sassafras trees. He seemed relieved to be going.

"Say good-bye to that place," said Sanchez, draped over the seat between us, his head poised there like a pale fuzzy melon. "The school for weathermen. If you come out of there and can find your ass with both hands you're a regular fucking Magellan. No offense, but that place is for nuts. I've been there. Talk about the inmates running the goddamned asylum. Fuck those guys. They'll never be jump-qualified." The Cuban pressed a button that lit the tiny red light on the stereo and Chuck Berry started singing "Maybelline" like he was in the shadows back there with him. "We're airborne," he declared over the music. "I love you guys like brothers."

Lindenberg turned onto Route 20 and smiled for the first time since he had been in our company. He let out a single note of satisfaction, flipping his hair back into place. "Well, brother," he said. "I can't say I'm sorry to be out of there. Or sorry to be at the wheel of this fine machine." I drank my beer, and Sanchez turned his head and winked at me. Somehow he knew what my plan was.

More beer came up from the backseat, and pretzels, and then a cigar, but that made me light headed after just a few puffs. I tossed it out the window and watched it scatter a ring of sparks on the pavement behind us, swirling in a miniature cyclone until they were caught in our wake and disappeared. "Like a man's soul," said Sanchez, looking back.

I opened a package of chewing gum to clear the foul taste of the cigar from my mouth and offered some to my traveling companions. "Not when I'm drinking," said Sanchez. "It'll confuse my taste buds."

Lindenberg took a piece and I asked, "Are you going back to Tennessee?"

He nodded. "There's a bus leaves for Chalybeate at midnight. Charlene's meeting me when it comes in. She talked to Mr. Beckel and he's gonna give me my job back selling cars."

"You certainly have to sell something," agreed Sanchez, wagging his head between us.

"What kind of place is Chalybeate?" I asked.

"It's just a town, you know," answered Lindenberg. He gave a little shudder and hunched over the wheel. "People leave you alone. I've been living there my whole life up to now and nobody ever bothered with me."

Sanchez spoke up. "I can find people who are indifferent to me anywhere. I only want friends who are passionately for me and enemies who are violently against. Just black and white. There's an old saying and I live by it: If you don't know who the asshole is within two weeks, it's probably you. Then just come out swinging. Things are so much easier that way."

"Maybe," said Lindenberg, considering this. "But there's something to be said for peace and quiet."

"It'll be plenty peaceful and quiet when they finally get me under the ground," said Sanchez. "I'm sure we'll all have our fill of it and then some."

"True," said Lindenberg.

"Something to think about," I said.

We drove on, past a solitary gas station and into wide flat open country. Huge draughts of night air entered through the windows and rolling bluesy music filled the car, trailing out behind us in the darkness. "Too bad this isn't a convertible," I said.

"You could always sit outside," offered Sanchez.

"Hey—that's a good idea."

Lindenberg glanced over at me but said nothing. The speedometer registered ninety-five and the car seemed to be barely moving, only a whisper from the engine, the road ahead of us flat and straight and no other cars in sight. Sanchez was silent and his eyes burned like two pilot flames in the dimness. Reaching out to grip the roof, I pulled my head and shoulders and then my entire upper body out of the window. Up from the upholstery in a single movement, I balanced my feet on the windowsill, crouching hard against the line of the roof. With my T-shirt billowing outward like a sail, I duckwalked forward onto the hood.

The countryside was passing at a tremendous rate. I remained in a crouch, my back to the windshield, the hood gleaming before me like a pool of oil in the inconstant light of the stars. I turned my head to either side and could hear the music falling onto the darkened road behind us; otherwise, it was quiet; the wind stopped my ears. When I looked briefly inside Sanchez was like a wax figure, his round head outlined against the back window, and Lindenberg, the hair falling across his forehead, stared out at the long silver path formed by the headlights on the pavement in front of us.

I crept forward over the gleaming sheet of metal, staying to the right, out of his line of vision. The front bumper was a long way off. I was drunk and yet sure footed, tuned to the pitch of the engine, light and flexible and in total sync with the other players. Lindenberg was the one driving, but I could feel Pedro Sanchez balancing the open country, my space walk, and the Cadillac in some crazy airborne section of his mind.

The hood was warm beneath my hands. Once or twice I flexed my knees upward like a sprinter raising himself in the blocks, and the onrushing current of air supported me, almost lifting me into the moist black night. Above was the glittering cloak of the sky and no more than two and a half feet below me, rushing beneath the tires, was certain death. I was airborne.

We approached a single crooked tree on the horizon and seconds later, as we hurtled past, something winged and black, a large nocturnal bird, animated itself and took flight from the upper branches, a blot against the stars. A shadow fell over my heart and I remembered the terrible vigil I had kept during my mother's final illness. Holding her bony little hand, nodding at her bedside, I saw, or rather felt, something insubstantial, a hovering presence outside her doorway. It passed by like smoke. In a moment I got up and looked either way along the dimly lit corridor. Nothing.

I went back to my chair and sometime later, half asleep, I looked up and our visitor was back: the Angel of Death, a huge ferocious being in a buckler and carrying a sword, with black-feathered wings crawling with mites and other hard-backed insects. He was looming in the doorway, tall and silent. When I was fully awake, I walked to the door and made the sign of the cross, hoping to keep the room clear. For the next few hours the prayer remained in force, but what transpired in the little room seemed perhaps worse than death, and toward morning I let my prayer lapse to bring relief.

The Cadillac surged ahead, cleaving the narrow road, between low stippled fields and with a slight whistling sound that was like a sailboat on the sea. The car was going over a hundred miles an hour. Into the moist rushing darkness I spoke a single word:

"Loretta."

Far in the distance there was a speck of light, another car coming toward us, and I turned from it and crept back over the hood. Through the windshield I saw Sanchez uncorking the champagne. He beckoned to me, laughing like he had inhaled nitrous oxide and making comic gestures. Lindenberg was staring at the road, like a child intent upon some marvelous game. He looked happy. Indeed, he looked changed, his old self again.

Getting back inside was tricky—I extended my left leg along the side of the car as far as it would go, held the edge of the molding with both hands, and describing a small arc, dropped sideways through the window in a difficult free-fall manuever. Huddie Ledbetter was on the radio, old Leadbelly himself, strumming his guitar and singing as he had not done for many years.

Lindenberg sang the choruses along with him, deep and melodious compared to the bluesman's high-pitched rasp, one hand on the wheel now, his other arm out the window, beating time against the door panel. The scratchy old delta blues reverberated inside the Cadillac, and my two companions grinned like idiots, poking and pulling me in several directions and yodeling out the windows. Waves of adrenaline broke over me and I felt Leadbelly's harmonica and guitar rattle in my lungs and pound along with my heart, almost as if the music was coming from inside me, my own personal blues, filling the space among us until it unfolded out the windows and scattered itself across the night.

"If that isn't being young in America, I don't know what is," shouted Sanchez over the radio. He thrust the bottle of champagne into my hand. "I haven't had this much fun since my old jumping buddy Monte Watkins skied Aspen naked. Down the whole mountain in a tuck and *whiz* through a church group, his blue ass blazing. Frostbit his knob but he strapped on a hot water bottle and we went out to the bars and nobody stopped laughing till the next day." The Cuban shook his head. "But that was nothing compared to what you just did. Joe Dolan, you're the most goddamned crazy son of a bitch I ever saw or heard about and I love you like my own brother. *Zing. Zang.* You walked out on that hood at a hundred miles per hour like it was the only thing left on earth to do. To the *extreme,* brother, to the absolute fucking limit. Save the wild stuff for last because that is always your fucking best."

"It seemed like a good idea," I said. I drank from the champagne bottle and with an automatic gesture handed it to Lindenberg. "No big deal."

"No big deal? You must be joking," said the Cuban. "Yalta was a lemonade stand and Winston Churchill was a soda jerk compared to that. Everest was an anthill. You know why? I never been there." He made vigorous conjuring motions with his hands. "That was a religious act or my name's not Pedro Aurelio Garnera Sanchez. You just put your complete trust in another living, breathing human being. An act of pure faith. There is no gray area between you two now. Or any of us. We are all three connected as brothers. And that's not gonna end, Joe, when other things end. Everything is perfectly clear in my mind. Look at the sky! Look at the stars! We're right here under them and it feels like a miracle.

You, Joe Dolan, are a new kind of American hero—" he placed a cold white hand on my forehead "—and I'll follow you anywhere you want to go, on my hands and knees if I have to, because you, my friend, you shoot from the fucking hip."

"Amen, brother, amen. You're not just whistling Dixie," said Lindenberg. Sanchez and I turned to look at him in the same instant. He took a long graceful pull on the champagne bottle and then rested it between his legs, one finger of his left hand guiding the wheel. His body was slack against the upholstery and the lock of blue-black hair dangled on his forehead. With a loose grin, he leaned out of a passing shadow and said, "As soon as Leadbelly came on the radio the car just about drove itself and I knew everything was going to be all right again. You gotta dig this cat. Some of the sessions players I jammed with told me they never saw a feller could drink so much, make so much music, and bedevil the ladies so much as he could. Went to prison twice for killing somebody and sang his way out both times. He sure had the wildness and so do y'all—but no offense. It's a good thing come to a good man."

My mouth dropped open in amazement. It was Elvis all right. The Elvis of the early television shows, the early movies, slim as the bottle he was drinking out of. Every line he spoke warbled and ran like music and he was so full of nervous energy, brimming over with melody and rhythm, that he appeared to be in motion when he was sitting still. Beside me, Sanchez was also shocked into silence, mystified by the transformation.

"You fellers look like you mighta caught you the vapors," said Elvis. "Here. Have a drink."

I took the champagne back. "How you feeling?" I asked, looking closely at him.

"Sound as a dollar," Elvis said. He pointed to his head. "Oh—that. They had me turned six ways from Sunday in that hospital there for a while. They're aimed at making you doubt yourself. But you never doubted me when you got out on that hood. Like Mr. Sanchez was just saying, it felt like a miracle. There's nothing back in Chalybeate, Tennessee, that's gonna answer to that. No sir. There ain't many things certain in life, but I won't ever sell another car, new or used, and that's for sure."

I had read that in wartime men made daring single-handed attacks against the enemy that saved lives among their comrades and afterward they could not begin to explain what had moved them to action, and in fact often could not remember much at all of what had occurred. I looked out at the darkened landscape unfurling on either side at an incredible rate. The hood ornament, gleaming like a jewel, seemed a long way off. It was true that many things were uncertain in life but I was quite sure I would never again ride on the hood of a Cadillac at a hundred miles per hour. In the future, wild ideas might occur to me, midnight swims and wiseass remarks and any number of pranks and other impulsive hilarity, but it was a sure bet I would never duplicate that particular feat under any circumstances.

"Where do you want to go?" I asked Elvis.

He indicated the empty black stretch of road ahead. "There," he said, and, after a moment, "to get a gig."

"We'll find you one at the beach," I said. "Your guitar and sunglasses and the jumpsuit are all there. Thought I'd hang onto 'em, just in case." I hoisted the crucifix up from under my T-shirt. "This, too."

Elvis smiled at me. "You keep that, Joe. It'll remind you of how the Lord works. And someday, I make it big, I'll think of you duckwalking under those stars, man."

I replaced the crucifix and felt the warm metal rocking against my chest. Elvis reached for the champagne again and said, "Wish me luck."

"In spades," I replied.

Sanchez wasn't quite following all this. He looked back and forth between Elvis and me, his eyes glinting in the pale oval of his face as we drove closer to town and streetlights appeared at shorter intervals along the side of the road. The Cadillac flew like an arrow toward the glowing arch of the horizon.

"Well, fellow shoppers," said Sanchez, distracted for a moment as he fished the last three bottles of beer from the icy water of the cooler. "I see that you have discarded all your coupons. Said fuck the pyramids of tomato puree. Good then. Put on your silk because you're officially airborne. Airborne and flying right toward it."

11

I was waiting for Maxine in her office, after being summoned and finding it empty, gazing out through a tall vertical window that overlooked some treetops and a broad expanse of darkening blue sky. Silhouetted at dusk birds swooped across, in varying but small numbers—and then one who flew solo—to the soft but detectable accompaniment of Mozart's "Requiem," from the cassette player on the corner of the desk. This air ballet continued until the music was over and, as if on cue, Maxine thrust open the door. She made a tiny noise of recognition in her throat and, bringing the smell of lilacs with her, circled to the far side of the room, glancing mischievously at me.

Maxine wore her thick shiny hair down past her shoulders, and in a white silk blouse and black stretch pants and matching gambler's vest with pearl buttons, she had the bounce of a teenager. "I must be a great editor," she said. "And a great boss."

"You must be," I said.

She came and sat on the edge of the desk, legs slightly apart, her palms hinged and dangling between her knees. "I mean—look at the material I have to work with. Very raw."

"Like sushi," I agreed, nodding at her. I had no idea where this was going.

"But once in a while, once in a great while—" began Maxine, her gray eyes dancing between narrowed eyelids "—something happens to make me think I chose the right profession. That's when I read something I like. Or better yet, I read something I know a *lot* of people will like. Joe—those are my best days."

Bracing myself for what promised to be another lecture on Walter Dzioba and his considerable talent, I continued nodding. It seemed like everything he ever wrote was turning into Holy Scripture. Maybe for a treat after work he would show the rest of us how he walked across the intracoastal without using the bridge. But Maxine was still Maxine, and I liked her so much I was ready to sit there and take it.

"I've been getting lots of calls lately from editors in New York and Miami and Washington. They've been reading the *Post-Gazette* and are interested in some of the stories we're following and the reporters who are covering them. I've even received calls from prize committees," she said. "On the one hand, I'm thrilled—our work is being noticed—but on the other hand, I don't like to see my good reporters becoming famous and leaving me for the big papers—although they will, and they should, and helping them as much as I can before pushing them along is really part of an editor's job." She stopped there for a moment and smiled, revealing most of her neat well-kept teeth and the fine lines around her mouth. Above the smile her eyes were glittering and sad. "It's just that you get attached to certain people and letting go of them is hard, even though you know it's right."

I was already looking forward to Walter Dzioba's farewell dinner, where I planned to give a rambling long-winded speech. "Good riddance," I said, charitable as always.

Passing over my remark, Maxine sorted through the pile of newspapers and newspaper remnants on her desk, folding open a *Post-Gazette* that was more than two weeks old. She found the column she was looking for and, glancing up at me, donned her reading glasses. "Effective newspaper writing—the kind that sells papers—has to do more than just explain something. As a fine editor once told me, a good piece of reporting must 'enlist our sympathies,'" said Maxine, sitting primly on the desk and looking at me over her spectacles. "Listen to this." She cleared her throat with a tiny cough, lifting the newspaper up.

> Lindenberg waved to the gallery and, flanked by two deputies, disappeared into a legal system that, according to several of those present, often appears hopelessly entangled and corrupt. "That boy never saw no justice," said Eudora Jackson, 59, a spectator. "Looking the way he does and making people smile ain't no crime I ever heard of." Echoed her friend, Wembley Tyne, 66, from Dunwoody, Georgia: "They always pick on the weak. The weak go down a whole lot easier." Tyne, who said he frequently attended trials because they were "better than anything they got on the tee vee," noted that the very next hearing, a man charged with embezzlement who was well dressed and known in the community, ended in a dismissal. "Nobody in a tailored suit ever cared much about Elvis," he said. "Elvis was for the folks who got nothing. I know it, and you know it."

It was my story. The picture of Elvis taken by Shirley Kimball was across the top of the page. In it, Elvis was looking over his shoulder, his hand up in a loose wave, smiling as he was being steered toward the yawning black doorway in the background. Half of one deputy was in the frame, the starched white shirt and bull neck and his close-cropped head, urging the prisoner forward. Injustice, comic despair, and the surreal were pressed into that instant—a sliver of time where you recognized Elvis and wondered where the hell they were taking him. When you read the story, maybe you laughed, maybe you drew a mustache on Elvis or crumpled the page in disgust, but you at least acknowledged the truth in what Wembley Tyne had said. Picking on the weak was easy and the guys in the pin-striped suits never thought twice about it.

Maxine took an envelope from her desk and handed it to me. "That's a check for five hundred dollars. Your story won the Florida Press Association prize this month." She smiled at me. "It's a wonderful piece of writing, Joe. The award is nice, too. Other editors notice who wins."

A little embarrassed, I said, "What's the big deal? Dzioba has a closet full of these things."

"But that's Walter Dzioba's work. That's his life," Maxine said. "This is yours."

The sky outside had closed to a glowing purple lined in red at the horizon. "Now seems like a good time to ask for a raise," I said.

Maxine laughed. "Well, it isn't." Then she did a strange thing. She brushed the hair from my forehead and, leaning forward, kissed me on the side of the mouth. "Just don't go too far, too fast," she said.

We both stood up, avoiding eye contact, and Maxine straightened the pile of newspapers on her desk and then ushered me out of the office. "Whatever happened to Edgar Lindenberg?" she asked, the lilac smell roused by the opening of the door.

"I went to the hospital with this nutty Cuban guy and we all got drunk and now he thinks he's Elvis again."

Maxine rolled her eyes. "So much for objectivity. You know, it might be news to you, Joe, but most journalists do not become characters in their own stories."

"My methods may be unorthodox, but no one can argue with the results," I said.

Things were slow in the newsroom. A secretary was bundling up the outgoing mail and two of the drivers were using her desk to fill out their time cards. Bob Reilly the night man came in—wrinkled Hawaiian shirt, his eyes red with too little sleep, and his hair mashed flat on one side of his head. Maxine watched him aim for the coffeepot and said, "Joe, I want you to hunt around and see if you can dig up something new and interesting on the Sherri Hogg rape case. For Thursday. I moved Shirley over to the judicial scandal, after all."

"Walter's not liking that," I said.

Maxine's soft gray eyes were steady on mine. "What's good for Walter isn't always what's best for the paper," she said. "Editorial decisions are separate from all other decisions." She pointed the way to my desk. "A rule that works just as well on that side of the newsroom as it does on this side."

Reilly was pouring himself a cup of coffee, in conversation with a secretary standing beside him with her arms full of mail. As I crossed the newsroom they turned in my direction and Reilly called out, "*You* won a Florida Press award?"

"Yes, Virginia, there is a Santa Claus," I replied.

I sat down at my desk to finish something I was writing for the next day's paper and, after a short while, Ross Donleavey approached and stood in front of my desk. The sportswriter was dressed in a plaid blazer and a new toupee that was much too dark for his eyebrows and the fringe of dusty brown hair above his collar.

"I just heard about your award," he said. "Very impressive, Joe."

Donleavey could hold forth for hours on his favorite subject—Ross Donleavey—and consequently I had never once heard him compliment another reporter on his or her work. "It was the luck of the Irish," I said. "A little leprechaun dust on the typewriter."

"No," said Donleavey, shaking his head. "I saw that story when it came out, I remember, and—" he held out a small damp hand for me to shake "—it was good. You deserve it."

I mumbled thanks and went back to what I was doing. He started off, but with my peripheral vision I saw him turn his gaunt, slack-eyed face to me again. While Donleavey hovered for a moment longer, twirling the Rotary pin on his lapel, in walked

Shirley Kimball, her sheer blouse and tight white jeans defining every inch of her. "I . . . I—how do you write like that?" Donleavey blurted out. "I mean, how do you learn—where the heck did you learn that?"

Looking down at his battered old shoes I said, "I guess I read alot. I read Walter's stuff. Shirley's. Yours, too. And the Miami papers. The *New York Times*. Everything."

Donleavey seemed disappointed in my answer. "I read myself blind. Write and write and write. But not as well as that." The Rotary pin fell to the floor and rolled away under the desk. "Eighteen years and I haven't even been nominated for an award."

"It doesn't mean anything," I said, hoping this wouldn't go on a moment longer. "You do a good job, Ross, covering your beat."

"Oh, I don't begrudge what you've got—your talent, I mean," said the sportswriter, his colorless eyes fixed on mine. "I'm only saying don't take it lightly, son. It's uncommon."

Half an hour later, Shirley Kimball emerged from Maxine's office. The newsroom was quiet. Ross Donleavey had gone to cover a high school basketball game and Reilly's figure was motionless behind the frosted glass of the layout room, slumped over a light table. In curvy profile, Shirley gave me a long look and then waltzed over, passing close enough to brush against me, the scent of her perfume more tropical and alluring than Maxine's lilacs. She perched on the edge of my desk, legs crossed, submerging me in her sweet lingering haze. Under her blouse she sported a black bra that was seamless and capable of hoisting her good-size breasts to an appealing position and maintaining them there indefinitely.

Shirley directed a look straight into my eyes and I blushed. "Joe, I think you're incredibly handsome."

I was skeptical. "You think all the guys are incredibly handsome."

She giggled. "So—what's wrong with that? I like men. It just so happens that this is your night. Maxine told me all about it."

"You're not going to be nice to me, are you?" I asked, glancing back at her. Her small green eyes, intent on mine, were described in heavy makeup. "If you were ever real nice to me, I'd probably start thinking I was terminally ill."

Shirley lifted one of her high heels and nestled its spike against my crotch. "Just nice enough," she said. "I thought we'd go have a drink together. Everybody loves a winner, kid. Enjoy it."

Arm in arm on our way downstairs we met Walter Dzioba coming in from the street, his briefcase clutched against his chest. He stumbled and nearly fell as he rushed toward us, his usual poker face lost in excitement.

"You're in a big hurry tonight," Shirley said. "Weak kidney?"

Dzioba glanced up, moving over to make room, and Shirley studied him as we drew even on the stairs, her gaze taking him in—the unclasped briefcase full of papers, his agitated manner, a shirttail out—and it was obvious her mind was working with trip-hammer precision, calibrating the situation and leaping two or three moves ahead.

"No rest for the wicked," said Dzioba. He smiled at his partner, indicating the briefcase where her gaze had settled. "A few loose ends, that's all."

"Don't forget we've been assigned the same story," replied Shirley. In heels she was several inches taller than Dzioba, the highest point of her inflated hairdo sprayed into a fantastic red shape that defied gravity. "It's you-show-me-yours-and-I'll-show-you-mine, Walter. No more of this Lone Ranger bullshit," she said.

"I'd love to sit down with you but I'm busy right now," said Walter. Making a little half turn, he nodded in my direction. "So are you, apparently."

Shirley didn't flinch. "Joe won a Florida Press. We're going out for a little drink."

"Bully for him," Dzioba said, never once looking at me. "They say if you put enough monkeys in a room with typewriters eventually they'll produce *King Lear*." He started up toward the newsroom and then called out again to Shirley. I turned back, his small stooped figure in shadow on the landing. "Luck ain't talent. It might bear a resemblance, but it's not the same thing."

He continued up the stairs without another word and when we were outside in the thick damp air, the lights glowing from the newsroom, Shirley took my arm again and towed me to her car. "Walter wouldn't spit on you if you were dying of thirst," she said, a strange note of fondness in her voice. "You're just another hotshot with a good liver trying to steal his ink."

Shirley called the lounge at China Gardens her "corporate headquarters." It was overgrown by plastic ferns, a chilly windowless room laid out in gold brocade wallpaper. No one was at the bar; scattered across it were the leatherette menus, ponderous as holy books, illustrated with more than fifty exotic drinks. We sat on a couple of low stools and Shirley ordered mai tais.

"What's in a mai tai?" I asked.

"Three essential ingredients. Rum, a little extra rum, and then some more rum," replied Shirley.

She placed a package of cigarettes on the bar. "You're always huffing on these chick sticks. Why smoke 'lights'?" I asked.

"Because I'm kidding myself."

Shirley lit a cigarette and told me that Walter Dzioba had a similar office in a strip joint across town, Florida Teasers, where he had dinner just about every night and then three or six or eight drinks. "Instead of a living room and a family, you get this," she said.

The bartender, who had greeted Shirley on our arrival, shook up the cocktails and set them on the bar. "Dzioba not just an ass-hole," said Billy Chu. "He a *professional* ass-hole."

Shirley smiled at the thin bespectacled Chu. "That's right. But if he came in here waving hundred-dollar bills, you'd sing a different tune, wouldn't you, Billy?"

Chu shrugged. "I'm a businessman."

"That's what I like about you," Shirley said. "You know what you are."

I waited until Chu went into the kitchen and then I said, "Dzioba used to come in here?"

"For a long time we came in together," said Shirley. She took a good belt from the mai tai. "Walter and I had a thing for a while."

"You?"

Shirley laughed, blowing a stream of blue cigarette smoke at the ceiling. Her throat was freckled and taut and led the eye down to her soft full breasts. "Maxine's not the first one at the office to fuck that old buzzard. Walter gets around."

I squared myself to the bar, avoiding Shirley's eyes. "You're always saying you can't stand him."

"If you get to a certain age," said Shirley, her drink in one hand and the smoldering cigarette, red with lipstick, in the other, "and you're still on your feet, your friends and your lovers are different sets of people. Even our editor knows that."

"You don't think Maxine really likes Dzioba?"

"As far as it goes." Shirley tossed her thick red hair. "Maxine needs a service performed and Walter Dzioba is made to order: he's conveniently located, unattached, and he owns his own car. He's not gonna stick around forever. Walter thinks Maxine has something he wants and he's in there drilling for it. And for now anyway, that's what *she* wants. It's a perfect arrangement."

I must have turned pale, because Shirley said, "Look—I'm sorry. But if you're going to stay in this business, Joe, there's no sense being a fool about it. People around here fuck for information, for pull, for revenge—lots of reasons. Just like anywhere else." She nudged me with her shoe. "Don't worry. Walter loves his own career more than he likes fucking anybody on God's green earth. It won't last."

My first lover was Kathleen Quigley and sometimes after school, when no one was around, we did it up in my room or on the living room sofa and then I walked her home to the poor neighborhood where she lived. The street curved along the base of a small hill that resembled a jawbone, and the narrow houses were like teeth, some of them discolored, patched, or broken.

One gloomy winter afternoon, passing by these wrecks, I asked Kathleen why she liked me better than the other boys. "You have a nice house," she said. "I want a nice house someday."

Billy Chu came back out to the bar carrying a tray of egg rolls and chicken fingers. "Eat," said Shirley with a smirk, leaning against the bar. "You're going to need your strength."

I gulped my drink and picked up a chicken finger. It was scalding hot. "Ouch!" I said, dropping it on the floor. "Son of a bitch."

Shirley leaned forward, her breasts pushing against me, and took my scalded fingers and placed them in her drink. Her face was close enough to mine for her eyelashes to brush my cheek, and after a long numbing moment, she removed my fingers from the drink and eased her mouth over them, to the very hilt, sucking at the rum, her lipstick staining the first two knuckles.

"There," she said when she was through. "All better."

"Let's go," I said, cupping her breast. "Now."

Shirley glanced at the food and then back at me. "Now?"

"Right now." I tossed down my drink and fished out a wad of bills and threw it on the counter.

The eavesdropping Billy Chu swooped over and counted the money as we stood up to leave. "Wait," he said, smiling. "Wait for change."

"You keep it," I said. "Buy yourself a professional asshole detector."

We made it as far as the parking lot. No sooner had Shirley started the car than I was in the other door and across the front seat and had her blouse undone, straddling her, the black silky bra and then the large soft whiteness of her breasts trembling in my hands. The last of the winter rain drummed on the roof and smashed against the windows of the Buick, hiding us.

"All right, boy," said Shirley, panting. "Let me see it." She jumped in the backseat, topless now, wonderfully built, and when I started over she unzipped my jeans and tugged them open—"Very nice," murmured Shirley—making me sway to and fro like a cobra coming out of a basket. Every time I attempted to descend from my perch, she stopped massaging me and I froze there.

"I'll tell you when," said Shirley, wriggling out of her jeans. Her legs were smooth and freckled and she wore tiny black panties and had a dove tattooed on her hip. "Stay right there."

I was suspended between the front and back seats of the Buick with my pants down to my knees. It was an awkward position. Shirley stayed out of reach, tossing her hair and occasionally reaching up to squeeze her breast and point it at me. She took my shirt halfway off, pinning my arms at my sides. Smiling to herself, she leaned forward and left the red imprint of her kiss on my stomach.

"What, Joe?" asked Shirley. "Can I help you with something?"

I tore my hands loose and fell onto her, following with my body as she scuttled backward over the seat as far as she could go. Propped in the corner, her heels chafing the backs of my legs, a thumb pressed into my eye socket, Shirley made hollow sounds like a ghost at the bottom of a well.

"That's it now. That's it. That's it," she whispered, scratching me with her nails. "Come and get it, boy."

Reaching behind me, I fumbled with my wallet, took out a condom, tore it open with my teeth, and feeling its thin slick surface, rolled it on. (Surfer had given it to me recently. "Even a blind squirrel finds an acorn once in a while," he said.) Shirley's head was on the armrest, her hair in disarray, eyes closed. I kissed her and inched forward, about to enter. Moving slightly back and forth, I hesitated there, her small round plushness against me through the latex of the condom like a slice of cake wrapped in plastic. Shirley arched upward, and I drew back. She was chasing me now. I teased and evaded. "Not fair," she whimpered.

"What, Shirley?" I asked, grinning at her. "Can I, uh, help you with something?"

She laughed. "You little bastard. Quit fooling around now." I entered partway, three or four short strokes, and then stopped. "That's enough."

"Oo-oh," exclaimed Shirley, beating her fists against my chest. *"Please."*

"Tell me about Sherri Hogg. Where is she living? What did you find out?"

Shirley stopped fidgeting and opened her eyes and looked at me. "Why should I tell you anything?"

I eased into her and began moving up and down. "Oh. Oh. Oh," Shirley said. "She lives with her father on Merritt Island. Oh. Oh. T-bone beat her up. Uh. Uh. Oh. Oh. But she won't press any charges." The Buick squeaked under us. Shirley gasped, and moving faster and deeper I felt her body with its natural contour persuading me until all I knew was Shirley's faint cry in my ear and the sensation that I was asking the same question over and over, one that, for Shirley, was easy to answer. She provided it with the rolling motion of her hips and her short breathless profanity.

Footsteps approached and someone peered into the window above us for a moment, but I didn't look up and didn't stop; not even Billy Chu with a camera would have fazed me. We shifted positions and Shirley took charge again, sitting upright, her fabulous breasts swinging over me and her hair falling in a torrent across my face. "Bad boy for teasing me," she said. "Naughty boy."

Without using her hands, only her enviable balance, Shirley played a concerto on me, painted a masterpiece, illustrating her technical expertise with creative little flourishes that would have drawn raves if there had been an audience to witness them. As I was about to explode, Shirley disconnected and spun into a four-point stance on the hard upholstery of the Buick. "Finish the job," she said hoarsely.

Afterward she smoked, wearing my shirt, sprawled across the seat as casually as if we had been in a suite in some hotel. "Wow, that was weird," I said, opening the window for some air. "I feel—woozy. Maybe it's love."

Shirley wiggled for a more comfortable position, stretching her legs against mine. "Uh-uh. That might happen once or twice in a lifetime, and when it does, Joe, you're in the tall cotton," she said, and stifled a yawn. "Some people never get there."

"Did you like it?"

"You were the top, the best," said Shirley. "But it was great because we didn't do it every Saturday night for twenty years. Just once."

I watched her smoke, wondering what to do with the condom I held between my fingers like a small weighted balloon. "Do you think Sherri Hogg is ready to cave in?" I asked, swinging the condom back and forth.

"No more free advice. You'll have to ask her that yourself," said Shirley. She flicked her cigarette out the open window. "Hey—be careful. Don't spill any of your descendants on the seat."

12

Coach Van was in rare form, snapping at us like we were 0-8 instead of 8-0. Every bad kick we made or pass that hung in the air too long sent him into another tirade, standing off to one side in his faded USA jacket and that shock of white hair. Two more games and we would finish our season by playing in the state championship against the Jacksonville RFC—unless we somehow managed to lose those games, not very likely, but nevertheless an idea that must have been keeping Coach Van awake nights. Surrounded by the dark oval of trees at the fairgrounds, Van Valkenburg held us there on the chewed-up turf, and around the tight steaming circle the faces were reddened by exertion, brooding on victory, like the faces of warriors gathered on some ancient bloody plain.

"If you hold out even the slightest possibility of losing to yourself, you will lose," Van said. "You have to shut that door behind you and do whatever it takes to win. Every real winner knows that. If the other team is coming offsides, I want you to get twenty yards back and drive into them with a shoulder. Blow their kidneys out if you have to. We've worked too hard. This is our year." He raised a long arm and pointed beyond the fairgrounds to a dim row of suburban tract houses, all of them identical. "The people in those houses don't have the opportunity we have this weekend. The opportunity to stomp the living daylights out of fifteen other men and take something from them that they do not want to give up. The people in those houses don't know what it takes to get where we are. But we're different. We're rugby players. Remember this: nobody likes a winner except another winner. Whenever a teammate breaks into the open with the ball you should be like sharks who see blood in the water. Do that, every time, and three weeks from now you're gonna be the Florida State Champions."

Walking to the cars, Van Valkenburg stopped me. "You better get your game together if you want to play in that championship," he said. "You're looking pretty weak in the scrums."

Being in a scrum, particularly right in the middle at hooker where I play, is pretty dangerous. Your two props—the Argentines call them *pilars*—are supposed to hold you up. I know a guy named Malcolm who broke his neck because the referee wouldn't prevent the scrum from collapsing. Everyone said it was an accident but try telling that to Malcolm.

I stood still as Van went on and Josh passed by me, joking with Martin Campesi, and for a moment I envied his inability and the fact that he was not struggling to make the first team every week. "I'm in shape," he said to Martin. "Pear shape."

Directly from practice six of us went to a little diner on the south end of the beach. Duke Ritter and Todd sat at the counter and I shared a table with Martin Campesi, Edelstein, and Surfer. It was quiet in there, just us, and the moist smell of coffee and bacon stirred in the huge fans above the broiler.

"Ooo, me head hurts something terrible," said Martin, rolling his forehead on the cool surface of the table.

"It's your face that's killing me," I said.

Martin groaned, his voice muffled by the arm he had flung over his head. "I was out power boozing with the Duke last night."

"That's like Jew-bashing with Hitler," replied Edelstein, opening a menu. "You definitely have to be up for it."

"How's the pizza here?" asked Surfer.

"They don't serve pizza. It's a tomato cookie," said Todd. He took a napkin and covered it with ketchup, handing it to Surfer amid a gale of laughter. "That's physical comedy at its very finest," he noted.

Duke ordered only a chocolate milk shake, since his jaw was still wired shut. He looked svelte these days. The rest of us gazed at the menu, stupefied by the endless choices, the glare of incandescent lights, and our fatigue, while the waitress, a beautiful young urchin with milky skin and huge blue eyes, stationed herself beside the table with a look of boredom unto death.

"What's in a western omelet," I asked her.

She looked up from her pad. "Little cowboys."

"Just pick out the belt buckles and spurs. They hurt my teeth."

After she took our orders and disappeared out back, Edelstein said, "I love her. I'm going to stalk her for years."

"That's a fine-looking bit of stuff," Martin said. "I think the Dolan-Campesi theory of picking up women applies here."

"What's that?" Edelstein asked.

"It's a numbers game," explained Martin. "If you ask ten girls out, the odds increase that eventually one will say yes."

"In your case," I said, "the odds increase that eventually one will make an *error* and say yes."

We got to use a lot of old jokes on Martin because he was from New Zealand and had never heard them. "Ask Todd how his mother's dancing is coming along," Surfer said to him. "She's a great dancer."

Martin was hesitant. "I don't even know Todd's mother."

"Oh, go ahead. He's really proud of her."

Martin shrugged and turned around in his chair to face Todd, who sat, legs splayed on the linoleum in front of him, his rugby boots rolling in semicircles from the heels and his elbows tucked behind him like chicken wings. "Say—Todd," Martin said. "How's your mum doing on her dancing?"

"What?"

"Her dancing, mate. I dunno. I hear your mum is a great dancer or something."

We all froze, listening. Todd looked up slowly from the floor and settled his gaze on Martin. "My mother . . . has no legs. She lost them in a car accident two years ago."

There was a moment of silence, then a grin split Todd's face and our table erupted with laughter. "You bastards," said Martin, recovering from the shock. "No-good bastards."

"My mom's a lawyer, but she likes being a housewife," said Edelstein. "She's a mom who can sue you. She used to slap restraining orders on my friends."

The waitress knew what she was doing and moved gracefully from the counter to our table and back again. She appeared to be the only help besides a sullen old cook tending the broiler. She brought us a platter of soggy toast and glasses of water that we drank straight from her hand, then Duke's milk shake and two pitchers of iced tea brimming with lemons. In a minute she came back with a bowl of oatmeal she set in front of Martin and I felt her warmth and shared a moment with her that no one else noticed.

"Toss me the salt, will you, mate?" asked Martin, gesturing to Todd. The shaker flew across the little space and Martin reached up and snapped it out of the air. "With you, well threw, thank you," he said.

"Yecch," Edelstein said to Martin. "I can't believe you're eating that shit. It tastes like wallpaper paste."

Surfer chuckled, scratching at the back of his neck. "He loves it. If this was a Mexican joint, Martin would order the oatmeal enchilada."

"Keep on digging in that bowl, Campesi, and you can talk to your parents in New Zealand without that pesky dollar-a-minute charge," said Todd

"Porridge is good for you," Martin replied, between spoonfuls of the oatmeal. "It puts hair on your chest."

"Nothing will put hair on *my* chest," Surfer said, glancing down at his soiled jersey. "Not oatmeal, not tabasco, cheap whiskey, or skydiving. I can't grow a mustache either."

"Hey—that's right," I said to Todd. "You shaved your mustache off. For that All-American look."

"Looks can be deceiving," he said.

"He shaved off his moustache because he wanted to look clean cut when he met Lady Britt's parents," said the Duke. "Mr. and Mrs. Resealable Plastic Bag."

We speculated endlessly on when Todd would pop the question to Brittany Ellis, whose father was one of the richest men in Florida. Todd was an entrepreneur, very cagey. At the moment he owned a salvage company called AVAB—All Vicious Assholes and Bastards—that bought office furniture and equipment at foreclosure and sold it to secondhand stores.

Recently AVAB had purchased the contents of a warehouse lost to the creditors of a food shipping concern, and Martin Campesi made seventy-five dollars helping Todd haul away desks, chairs, office dividers, and the like, right down to the wastebaskets. When the suits from the bank weren't watching, they loaded extra stuff on the truck and rifled an entire skyscraper looking for food and booze in the desk drawers of employees who had been abruptly laid off. As it turned out, Martin found a bonanza of imported chocolate and some Tennessee sipping whiskey in one executive's closet.

I said it was poetic, postmodern man foraging through the jungle of a deserted skyscraper, pillaging the vestiges of a defunct corporate America, morally and financially bankrupt and left to the ransackers. Martin said the chocolate was stale and the whiskey, shared with Duke Ritter, gave him a massive headache.

Todd Baker had the appearance of money, if little in the bank. It was no secret he would rather be on the tennis court than working. He was in love with Brittany Ellis and the sort of life that was attached to her. Their marriage would be a shrewd investment in Ellis futures and a hedge against inflation, a real Todd Baker special, where every angle would be carefully examined and AVAB would prevail.

To the rest of us it meant nothing, except maybe a good excuse for a party—women and intrigue and a great deal of dancing and spilled drinks and joyous profanity. I pictured the wedding, Brittany's society friends and the rugby crowd, and what would happen to the champagne fountain and barrels of shrimp, the orchestra in their white tuxedos, the linen tablecloths, and the chandeliers, dense and glittering with light. There was a large number of possibilities and I was sure they would each strike the bride's family as inappropriate, like death threats at Christmas. It would be one last head-thrown-back orgy of youth.

"You can't play rugby forever," said Todd.

When Martin spoke, the oatmeal in his mouth dropped back into the bowl. "You can't?"

"At some point, I have to assume my rightful position at the West Palm Beach Country Club," Todd continued. He aimed a limp piece of toast at us and shook it for emphasis. "The Ellises have been members there since 1946."

"You have to watch out for people who had enough money to pursue leisure activities in the Forties," cautioned Surfer.

"As long as I get invited to the wedding, what do I care?" Edelstein asked.

"You guys'll be there. But not many others," said Todd. "Strictly speaking, it won't be a rugby function."

Surfer stopped the forward motion of his cheeseburger. "What do you mean?"

"Just what I said. Some of the guys don't fit the profile. I'm not going to have Steve Delong spitting on the floor. Or Josh with crumbs all over his tie. The rugby life is going to be over. *Finis.* And I'm not starting a new chapter with an apology to Hobie Ellis when one of the guys steals a suit of armor from the lounge, or the head of a kudu."

"That's pretty fucking hard, man," Surfer said. "So Delong is an asshole. Okay, don't invite him. But Josh is one of the tribe. A brother."

Todd shook his head. "Not one of the country club tribe, he ain't."

"He never misses a practice. He sticks his neck out every Saturday for the team. In my book, he qualifies," said Surfer.

"You're not making out the guest list," Todd replied.

Todd and Surfer were the two golden boys, our Mr. Inside and Mr. Outside, always on the same wavelength during rugby games and afterward. They were the first to the ball, first to hit on any available women, and the key conspirators in a long series of dares, practical jokes, bouts of drinking, and endurance contests: who could surf the longest, who could eat the most hot chicken wings, the most oysters, the most olives, win the most replays at pinball, or sink the trickiest shot at Big Beau Jeau's Putt-Putt Golf and Go-Kart. At the Christmas party, Surfer and Todd dressed themselves in the sombreros and ponchos that hung on the walls of Rancho Loco, rigged up makeshift piñatas and then, blindfolded, swung at them with pool cues while singing "Feliz Navidad."

Todd's Christmas card was a photograph from the party that showed him dancing with a huge girl wearing a pink dress. Under the photo was the caption, "Hope something big happens to you this Christmas—AVAB."

Todd leaned forward, his hands on his knees. "When I'm playing rugby, do I ever let you down? Do I ever pussy out? I give everything. And when it's finished, I'm through. I'm on to the next thing."

"Back to the wedding for a minute," said Edelstein. "Who can go, and who can't?"

"I haven't even asked her yet," Todd said, laughing.

Surfer looked off in the direction of the large plate-glass window fronting the diner. "I'll hawk one up in the caviar myself if Josh Bogannum isn't good enough for them," he said.

"Hey, Josh is all right. Fuck it, man. He'll probably go," Todd said. "Satisfied?"

But I could sense something else coming, like the crazy discordant music they play in the horror movies when bad things are about to happen. "What about Mike Melendez?" I asked.

It was plain from Todd's face that blacks were not welcome at the West Palm Beach Country Club. There wasn't much he could do about that. Except refuse to go there. Or stand up for his principles and ask Hobie Ellis if he liked to burn crosses or wear a bedsheet. But racism was a peculiar form of cowardice. Cowards perpetrated it and the rest of us watched in silence.

"Mike will probably be back in Trinidad by the time we get married," said Todd.

"Or in jail," I said. "How convenient."

The waitress came back to the table and we all looked into her lovely apple-cheeked face. Todd winked at me and called her over. He pulled a hundred-dollar bill from his wallet and waved it before her eyes, like he was demonstrating a point. "I wonder what you would do for this?" he asked.

"You must have a pretty sad life if you have to try and make waitresses demean themselves for money," said the girl. We laughed, and she turned to me, her voice hoarse and pleasant. "How is everything?"

I had often fallen in love with girls at ice cream parlors and pizza joints, young girls with shining hair and gleaming skin and snug white uniforms. "Everything's fine now that you're here," I said.

"Oh-oh. Another bullshitter," said the waitress. She twitched her nose and gave me a light playful shove.

"My name's Joe. What's yours? I'd introduce you to my friends but they all have infectious diseases and you wouldn't want to know them."

The waitress laughed. "I'll be right back. I have to get a take-out ready."

She went into the kitchen. "Smooth, Dolan, very smooth," said Martin. "You're a crackerjack with the ladies."

"What can I say? I have a magnetic personality. See—I take all the magnets off the refrigerator and put them in my pocket. Girls are just drawn to me."

"Make them laugh, get them into bed," Todd said.

"As long as they don't laugh while they're *in* bed," Edelstein said.

"Dolan's hilarious," said Surfer. "Girls are laughing so hard in there I can't sleep."

My back to the entrance, I heard the chirp of the screen door as it was unlatched, a squeak as it swung open, and then the gulping compression of the foyer when the heavy inner door gave way to a new customer. He had a misshapen face and sizable tattooed arms that hung out of his T-shirt like marbled slabs of beef. My old cellmate Jerry.

He paused for a moment at the brink of the room, not wiping the thick mud from his boots, only his eyes moving over us like an instrument for measuring danger. Jerry looked straight at me and remained impassive. Then he went to the cash register and leaned one hand on the counter, dark and filthy and menacing in the yellow glare of light. The waitress, noticing him, placed a sandwich and a cup of coffee in a bag and carried it to the end of the counter. "BLT and coffee?" she asked.

Jerry nodded. The waitress pressed some keys on the register and said, "Four-nineteen."

After sizing up the newcomer, everyone had returned to eating and drinking and talking except Surfer. He recognized Jerry from the Legion hall and, taking an occasional bite from his cheeseburger, was watching him closely. One of Jerry's hands was creeping around behind his back where the flat outline of his wallet was paired with an odd-shaped bulge that lay beneath his overhanging T-shirt and the waistband of his dungarees. The waitress, her lips apart and the deep well of her eyes filled with Jerry's image, had no inkling of what was about to occur.

I crossed to the end of the counter and held my hand out to Jerry. "How's it going? Haven't seen you for a while," I said. Just as carefully as it had gone behind his back Jerry's hand came around and took mine, dry and rough as a board, in a grip that tightened my arm to the shoulder.

"Hello, friend," he said.

The waitress sighed, jutting out her hip.

Reaching into his front pocket, Jerry removed a soiled five-dollar bill and handed it to her. "Keep the change, darlin'," he said.

The waitress thanked him and moved away. Jerry followed her a short distance with his gaze before he dropped off and made a brief though deliberate study of the linoleum, shaking his head, and then raised his flat empty eyes to meet mine.

"You are like a fucking weed," he said. "You're everywhere."

"I'm just helping you stay out of trouble."

Jerry showed me a line of pointy brown teeth. "Considering your hep is as bad as your hurt, I'll pass," he said.

It was a moment before I realized he was making a joke. Smiling again, he added, "Like Elvis. How's Elvis these days? Still up at Christmas Springs? You hepped that boy into a straitjacket."

"Nope. He's free as a bird and crazy as a loon."

"So once you got lucky. Which I'm wondering at because Elvis *should* be inside." The ex-convict reached up to scratch his neck and the muscles in his arm jumped like a tangle of snakes. "Not so lucky with what's-his-name. Your boy there."

"Mike Melendez."

"That's it. Me-len-dez. There's one nigger definitely needs hisself some in-surance. T-bone is ready to fix him," Jerry said.

"Last time I saw T-bone it was his heels and elbows," I replied.

"Only this time is different. T-bone ain't with his woman no more. He beat her up pretty bad and she split. Now there's no money angle for him, no nothing. He's drinking and laying out around town waiting on this Me-len-dez. On putting him down."

Jerry left his order untouched on the counter and made for the door. "T-bone's not going to kill anybody," I said in disbelief.

"He has to," said the ex-convict. "His woman is gone. And for a nigger. Something's got to be done."

"Why are you telling *me* this?"

Jerry pushed open the door and one shoulder slipped through, his head turned back in my direction. "I'm going up for assault, Coach. Eight years. So fuck him. He ain't my Dutch uncle." Half outside, his pulpy face mottled in the light from the diner, Jerry grinned again and said, "I'm better off. Too many fucking do-gooders around here." Then the door whanged shut, and without any hint of departing footsteps he was gone.

The waitress was at the counter beside Jerry's forgotten parcel. "What about the BLT?" she asked.

"I guess he wasn't hungry."

We were alone for that one moment, the others around us but not intruding on the pang of intimacy I felt. Her hair was dark and lovely, framing her urchin's face and large expressive blue eyes. She was looking at me without the slightest artfulness or hesitation, already past the tiresome preliminaries and well into our acquaintance. "My name's Vivian," she said. She wore a claddagh ring and on it the little golden hands were holding the heart outwards open to romance. I shook her long smooth hand. "Well, hello Viv. I'm pleased to know you."

Martin called for another pitcher of tea and telling him just a minute, Viv turned back. She eyed my bare muddy legs and dirty shorts and jersey, and made a comical face. "What's all this?" she asked.

"Rugby. You should come out some Saturday and watch us play. At the fairgrounds."

"I have to work Saturdays," said Viv. She shrugged and held one of the pitchers beneath an ice machine and pressed the lever. Ice thundered out, preventing further conversation.

The other rugby players, through eating, were stretched out chewing on toothpicks, a copy of the *Post-Gazette* divided among them. Engrossed in the sports, entertainment, and news of the day, the flow of good-natured insults had dwindled and when they spoke it was a stray word or two in soft quiet voices, the peculiar shorthand of old friends.

"The aspiring Valentino has returned," said Martin, glancing up from the lingerie advertisements.

"I'd like to bang her," Surfer said. When I gave him a dirty look, he added, "Hey, two million years of sexual stereotyping isn't *my* fault."

I sat down. Not a trace of my omelet, which had been intact, remained on my plate. "I had to," said Surfer. "It was lonely."

"So you introduced it to your cheeseburger," I said.

"Yessir."

Viv brought the iced tea to the table and Martin put down the newspaper and hailed her. "Mr. Dolan's omelet has saddled up and ridden west," he said. "Into the proverbial sunset."

"Can I get you something else, Joe?" asked Viv, collecting our plates.

"I'll have the spaghetti, please."

Surfer made a face. "Uggh. I hate spaghetti."

"I know."

In the interlude that followed, Jerry's warning, which I had considered only bluster, began to grow in my mind. The persistent image of his face, halved by darkness, betraying T-bone and his intention to stab or shoot or beat Mike Melendez to death, seemed to linger in the doorway of the brightly lit room, casting a pall over the conversation.

"Got any change?" I asked Surfer.

He reached in his pocket and handed me three dimes, shiny and musical, thin as wafers. "What's up?"

"I gotta call Mike right away."

The pay phone was in a little hallway out back that connected the bathrooms and smelled of bleach. A recorded voice said Melendez's number was out of service. Propping the phone book on my upraised knee, I dialed again and after several rings a woman answered and asked me to please wait a moment.

"Yes?" Instantly Lawyer Timmons came through the line of the telephone, hemming into the receiver, a great bridled impatience in his manner.

"Joe Dolan," I said. "Sorry to bother you, Mr. Timmons, but a good source just told me that Sherri Hogg's boyfriend is on the loose."

"Didn't we already know that?"

"Yeah, but now T-bone realizes he won't make any money or anything else from the case, so he's going to kill Mike."

In a swift firm tone, Lawyer Timmons said, "Call Mr. Melendez."

"I just did. His number's disconnected."

There was a grunt of acknowledgment and then a short silence. "T-bone beat Sherri up and he's been drinking ever since," I added.

Timmons cleared his throat. "Go to Mr. Melendez," he said.

"And tomorrow, at the latest, find Sherri Hogg and convince her to swear out a complaint against the boyfriend."

"Anything else?"

"Mr. Melendez should defend himself any way he can. Tell him I said that. The police will not go to any great lengths protecting a black man, especially one accused of rape. His death would only mean one less court appearance for them."

When I came back into the main room the bill had been paid and Martin and Edelstein, armed with forks, were nibbling at the edges of my spaghetti. "Can I borrow your car?" I asked Duke. "It's an emergency."

"Sure thing, brother," he said, tossing me the keys.

Viv was wiping tables with a damp cloth and collecting ashtrays and salt and pepper shakers. She stood on her toes to flip a switch, her hair cascading down the hollow arch of her back. Outside, over the doorway, the blue neon sign disappeared. "Leaving?" she asked.

"Yeah. I gotta go."

Turning to face me, her eyes wide and bright blue, Viv sucked in her lower lip. The strength of her gaze wavered and she said, "Come back again, I hope."

"Sure I will."

In the background, Martin was down on one knee beside the table with his arms flung out and Edelstein, sitting sideways to him, crossed his muddy legs and fluttered his eyelashes, playing hard to get. Viv glanced back at them and Martin dropped his arms and pretended to tie his shoe. I had to laugh. "They kidnapped me when I was a baby and made me join their circus," I explained.

Surfer followed me outside. I pulled up in front of him with Duke's car and leaned over and opened the door. "Get in."

It was a short drive to where Mike Melendez lived, in a studio apartment near the beach. The street was empty and a salt breeze whipped up sand and other grit that felt like needles against the skin. We stepped over a fallen trash can and entered the building. At the end of the first-floor hallway Mike's door, hung with an African mask, was ajar and the interior of his apartment smelled of paint and solvents. I tipped the door open and we went inside. Some light from the street gleamed through the uncurtained windows, setting two dim gray squares on the tiled floor and a bluish tint on the easels, palettes, blocks of clay, and other supplies crowded into the tiny space. Their shadows made a gallery of fierce tribal shapes upon the wall. Mike was sitting erect on the edge of the bed gripping a baseball bat.

"This is what it's come to," he said. "Another nigger in the dark with a baseball bat."

"Are you trying to scare us to death?" I asked.

A lamp by the bed made circles of rose-colored light on the ceiling when Mike switched it on. He was ravaged looking and his almond-shaped eyes were filmy and red. "Actually I've been wondering what the hell I'm going to do. Sherri was here a little while ago," he said.

I was leaning against a zebra skin that was tacked on the wall. Next to where the head should have been someone had scrawled: I LIKED MY OLD LIFE BETTER. "Sherri came here by herself?" I asked.

"Just to warn me," replied Mike. He picked up a bottle of wine from the mess of crumpled paint tubes and brushes on the floor and drank from it. "She had a nasty shiner, some stitches. T-bone did it to her. She came to tell me I was next."

Surfer had been gazing about the room in silence. He was standing in front of a huge dark canvas that was covered in ominous swirls, phantasmagoric shapes writhing in agony and the tiny figure of a man, cloaked in some sort of a warrior's cape, waving a broadsword that cut a yellow swath through the forces gathered against him. The canvas, resting on a great easel, was surrounded by clay studies of the warrior figure, black papier-mâché masks, details of the sword drawn in charcoal on butcher paper, and other preliminary sketches. It loomed above Surfer, dwarfing him, and he raised his arms above his head and wiggled his fingers at it. "Spooky," he said.

"I'm in my violent phase," said Melendez, holding the wine bottle in one hand and the baseball bat in the other.

"Somehow I can't see you wreaking havoc under the influence of Chablis," I said.

Mike shrugged. "You have to take your rage where you find it." Walking to the giant canvas, he regarded it closely, the bat angled over his shoulder, pausing often in his critique to refresh himself from the wine bottle. "You know, I'm more afraid of a passive acceptance of what's happening than a consumptive rage," he said. "And though I'm grateful for the support I'm getting—mostly from you two—it hasn't penetrated the chaos I feel all around me, the sense that none of this really means anything." Placing the empty wine bottle on the floor, Melendez swung the baseball bat at the center of the canvas, tearing a jagged hole in it. With a short lateral stroke, he dashed it to the floor, crumpling the easel and beheading one of the clay figures. "That's better," he said.

Surfer and I backed off in case Mike decided to trash the rest of the studio. But a little pearl of spit appeared in the corner of his mouth and he sat back down. "I got my first bill from Mr. Timmons the other day," he said, his eyes drooping in their sockets. "Eleven hundred dollars. That's the funniest part—I have to pay money for this. And right now, I have no idea where that money is going to come from."

"Never fear," said Surfer. "I talked to Roger at the Legion hall and he said if we wanted to run a party for you they would give us a third of the liquor sales for the night and anything we could get at the door. Put a band in there and I bet we could pack them in at those beer prices."

"Elvis," I said.

Surfer and Mike gave me puzzled looks.

"Elvis Lindenberg. A buddy of mine. He played at Saxophone Joe's with a few other guys last week. It sounded pretty good. I bet they would jump at a gig like that."

"I'm not sure I qualify as a worthy cause," said Mike.

"The guys will show up," I assured him. "Some of them to help you out and some because they like to get drunk. Anyway, fuck it, we'll have a good time and pay off part of your legal bill. Sherri coming over here tonight just about proves you didn't do it. This thing is over, man."

Melendez tapped the heavy end of the baseball bat gently against a tube of paint lying on the floor and it bled vermilion. "It's not over, Joe. I probably won't have to go to jail—" he lifted his head and under the taut mahogany skin I could see the bony outline of his skull "—but they won't let me go."

Surfer and I sat down on a couple of crates and took up the vigil. After a short silence I asked, "Got anything to eat?"

"Help yourself," said Mike.

I went to the paint-spattered refrigerator and found only a can of pineapple and another bottle of wine. "Slim pickings," I said.

Mike looked at me with the bat on his shoulder, rolling it and squeezing the taped handle until the veins popped out on his forearms. "It's the zeitgeist," he said.

"The what?"

"Zeitgeist. A reflection of the times."

I uncorked the wine and took out one of the pineapple rings, broke it in half, handed it to Mike, and said, "The body of the zeitgeist."

"What it is," he responded, washing the chunk of pineapple down with some wine.

Raising the other piece to eye level, I approached Surfer and he stood up. "The body of the zeitgeist," I said.

"What it is, man."

A cut on the inside of my mouth tingled when I bit into the pineapple. "The body of the reflection of the times. And what it is," I said, chasing it with the wine. The bottle went around. "If this was the sixties, you know what we'd be doing?" Surfer asked. "Some weird shit."

"Try looking at the world through my eyes for a single minute and you couldn't ask for anything weirder," Mike said. "I see a mother in the park with her children, thinking I'd like to paint them, and she assumes I'm sizing them up for a robbery and grabs the kids and hustles them off like she's just seen the devil. I'm standing on the corner minding my own business and a guy pulls up in his car, takes one look and locks his door. And these people don't even know me." He picked up the baseball bat again. "When I walk down the hallway in this building all I can hear are the dead bolts shooting across. At school, girls just about jump in the air when I come into a room and for six weeks now there hasn't been a word spoken to me that wasn't absolutely necessary. Impossible as it seems, I've been downgraded from nonperson to something even lower. Being black down here and accused of rape is punishment for the sins of generations. It must be. I should have gone to the Met. At least in New York I'd be ignored. I wouldn't be a guy with a rope around his neck just waiting for some hillbilly to get his first bright idea."

Surfer and I gazed at the scumbles of paint on the floor and said nothing. With a jab or two of the baseball bat Melendez began prowling the cramped space, in a familiar narrow route between the easels and African masks and the overturned wooden boxes. He switched off the light and the jungle shadows and the dusky smell of turpentine closed in. A strange sound escaped from him, almost like a whistle that turned into a snort. It was claustrophobic and suppressed until it grew, the muffled rattling sound of a boiler about to explode. "You have to leave," said Mike, framed against one of the tall blue windows.

He looked menacing, gaunt and bony jawed but nevertheless strung tight with muscle, the bat in his fist like a Stone Age club. He surveyed the room and all his dark fragile creations. "I have a lot of work to do," he said.

"What it is," said Surfer.

We tiptoed into the hall and then down to the street, pausing under the stars in the salty night air. "Duke must be wondering where his car is," I said. "Let's go to the house and get the motorcycle and come back."

"I'm not going back in there," replied Surfer. He looked at the entrance to the apartment building and shook his head. "Not for all the chop suey in China."

"We'll just get on the bike and ride by once or twice. Check up on things."

Surfer winced. "If you say so. But I'm not interested in having my head knocked off." In the car, he said, "What if you run into an Irish guy who's a drunk? Or a stingy Jew. Or how about a Mexican who eats tacos? I mean, really. You can't even mention it. The world's just not set up for that. You have to pretend it's not there."

The massive klieg lights the chamber of commerce had installed to reduce crime made the four lanes of the strip as bright as noonday. Only a few gas stations and the convenience stores were doing business. Just beyond Rack 'n' Ride, on a traffic island in the center of the strip, an Apollo capsule glowed in the harsh overhead light. Donated to the town by NASA, the capsule sat dented and forgotten on a strangely lunar patch of ground that was littered with beer cans and other trash. It looked like a bad neighborhood on the surface of the moon, where the astronauts stayed up late and got drunk and sang nasty songs over the radio to their colleagues back in Houston.

There was a sudden roar. Coming toward us around the capsule, bareheaded and scowling like one of the Four Horsemen of the Apocalypse, was T-bone on his vintage Norton 750, his filthy hair blowing from one rawboned shoulder to the other. He was going the speed limit, his eyes fixed on the road ahead.

"Shit," I said. "There he is."

Lined with trampled shrubs and curbstone, the island stretched for another hundred yards at least. "Wait," I said, swiveling my head around. "You can never find a fucking cop when you need one."

"Try the doughnut shop," said Surfer. I looked over at him. "I'm not kidding. Drive by the doughnut shop." Moments later we arrived at DeLite Donuts and there was a police cruiser out front. "Some call me crazy, others know me as a genius," Surfer said.

Puffy, steroid-abusing Officer Phillips was inside at the counter. His sleeves were rolled up and he wore his cap pushed back on his head like in the old black and white movies. I dashed in, nearly falling through the glass case where the doughnuts were displayed. Phillips turned when I began explaining and in a very short time his eyes narrowed, lost in the puffiness of his face, and I realized he had no idea who I was or what I was talking about.

"You been drinking, fella?" he asked, glancing at Duke's car, which was parked close to the glass doors.

"No I haven't been drinking. I've been at Mike Melendez's house. He's sitting there with a baseball bat and this other guy is on his way to kill him. The Melendez rape case. You made the arrest. The guy in the bathrobe, the screen test, remember?"

Frowning, the young cop placed his hands on his belt and thrust out his chest. "Okay. The wise guy from the newspaper. I remember."

"Look. You're supposed to serve and protect, right? So protect

Mike Melendez. This T-bone character has been telling everybody he's gonna kill Mike. I just saw him heading that way. That should be enough to go check it out."

Phillips waited for his order and then went outside to his unit and made the call. After a few bursts of static, and some confusion while I relayed the address, the dispatcher told Officer Phillips to investigate. A backup unit would also be sent. Phillips turned on his bubble lights and they swept over the parking lot, two steady revolving beams that flashed across Surfer's torso, waiting in the car beside us, and lit the underside of the dense crabbed bushes against the fence. "See you over there," I said. The policeman fastened his seat belt without a reply and, throwing the car into reverse, skidded into the empty street. Then he roared off down the strip, his siren piercing the quiet like the voice of the Old Testament God.

I jumped behind the wheel of Duke's car and followed him.

"Déjà vu. Except in high school the cops were behind us," recalled Surfer, as I struggled to keep Officer Phillips in sight. My imitation of a stock car driver sent the neon of the strip whirling by the windows and the terrain of storefronts and hotels became a blurry trail of color.

"You can really feel the soul of America on Tuesday night," Surfer said, watching the stars fly overhead and the gaudy chain restaurants unfurl like streamers.

"Yeah. It's going to hell in a handbasket," I agreed. "And we're carrying the fucking thing."

Off in the distance, throwing blades of light on the dark oily water of the intracoastal, another police car raced toward us over the bridge from the mainland. The two sirens created a weird stereo effect in the night air. I entered Mike's street and pulled up. Phillips was already inside. Surfer and I made the door of the apartment house just as the other cruiser arrived. A large cop wearing the khaki uniform of the sheriff's department chased us into the building.

"This way," called Surfer.

Soft blue light through the windows defined the studio and everything in it. Phillips, in the center of the room, talked into the radio transmitter attached to his shirt. He requested an ambulance and more backup. Mike Melendez sat expressionless on an upturned crate. The baseball bat was at his feet. T-bone lay beside it in a small glistening pool of blood. He didn't move or make a sound.

13

The studio was a shambles. Every canvas, every mask, all the clay models and figurines were broken and lying in heaps on the floor. Surfer and I paused in the entrance and surveyed the ruined paintings and equipment, then T-bone motionless in a patch of reflected light, and, beyond him, Melendez staring dumbstruck into space. The deputy sheriff lumbered along the corridor and crossed the threshold, a tall husky man, who managed to look bored and very confident at the same time. On his head was a broad-brimmed hat and around the edges his hair was gray and his jaw, square and solid, worked over a wad of chewing gum.

"Don't anybody touch anything," he said.

The deputy sheriff knelt for a moment beside T-bone and probed his neck with two thick fingers. Meeting the eyes of Officer Phillips, he shook his head and examined the wound above the dead motorcyclist's left eye. The skull had been crushed inward at the temple and the eye was open and gazing at the ceiling. Blood came from the left ear, adding to the puddle on the floor.

The deputy rose to his feet and approached Mike Melendez. "Stand up," he said. "Put your hands behind your back." He took a pair of handcuffs from his belt and applied them. "You can sit down."

Mike glanced sideways at me and said, "Call Mr. Timmons, will you please?"

The deputy went around the room and turned on all the lights without disturbing anything. He was at least sixty but narrow waisted and broad with huge red hands. "Did you call Detective

Fleischer?" he asked the young policeman. Phillips shook his head. In the same gritty voice he used to address Melendez, the deputy said, "Call him from your unit. Watch the front door and don't let anyone in or out." Phillips avoided my eyes on the way past. Ashen faced, he seemed glad to be leaving.

"Who are you fellas?" asked the deputy, eyeing our muddy shorts and jerseys.

"Friends of his," I said, nodding at Melendez. "We called the police when we heard this guy was coming after him."

"You're the one lives here?" the deputy asked Melendez.

He nodded.

"Okay. Nobody say another word until Detective Fleischer gets here. He'll ask the questions."

A neighbor appeared in the doorway. "What the hell is going on?" he asked. A middle-aged woman in curlers was at his side. "Goodness me, that nigger should be in jail," she exclaimed. "Will you just look at what he's done?"

Sweeping them into the hall, the deputy sheriff filled the door frame with his bulk. "Go back to your apartments. We'll be talking to y'all before the night's over." When they had gone, he took off his hat and scratched his short gray hair. "It's gonna be a long night, folks. Long and pretty dull."

It seemed funny that the most dramatic thing that had ever happened to T-bone would soon be so boring to the rest of us, but it was true. Dead men tell no tales, and they can't sing, dance, or juggle. Lying still is their one and only talent.

A great number of policemen and other officials began to file in. Some, like the police photographer, had specific duties and went about them in a businesslike fashion, oblivious to the commotion. He took pictures of the body from every conceivable angle, then divided the room into sections with the camera lens to record the shattered canvases and broken statuettes and the exact position of the baseball bat. The photographer appeared to notice every single detail except Mike Melendez. Not once did he so much as glance at him. When the photographer was through he exchanged greetings with the deputy and loitered for a moment by the doorway.

"You never come over," he said to the deputy. "Mary would love to see you and Louise."

"Have a party or something, and we'll stop in," replied the deputy.

"Hell. Come over and we'll call it a party."

Other officers ducked into the room for a quick look around, gave Melendez the once-over, and then went out and never returned. The chief came in for a few minutes. He was holding a cup of coffee from the doughnut shop and he signaled the deputy over to the windows and talked to him in a low voice. Once or twice he shifted his eyes to Melendez the way you would look at a pothole in the road after you had received a flat tire. Frowning into his coffee cup, the chief waited with an irritated look on his face until Detective Fleischer arrived.

"Nate, this is your baby," the chief said, a gloomy smile doing little to change his appearance.

Detective Nate Fleischer was a slender middle-aged black man of average height. He had a cropped, nearly bald head, wore a pressed shirt and striped silk tie, blue cotton slacks and coaching shoes. His expression was benign, and overall he looked quite harmless, but there was something ramrod straight about him and his quiet movements and sharp intelligent gaze suggested the military. Fleischer joined the chief and the deputy by the windows and after a brief conference, the chief shook their hands and departed.

The deputy brought Fleischer to where Surfer and I were standing and we introduced ourselves.

"Joe Dolan the reporter?" Fleischer asked.

"That's right."

His eyes were on mine. "Your Elvis article was really good. Look—we're not holding you but I was wondering if you would stick around and help us sort out what happened here tonight."

"Sure," said Surfer.

"I'm going to ask you some questions then. Before I do, is there anything you guys need?"

"I want to make a phone call," I said. "And let me tell you right now, it was self-defense."

Hands on his hips, Nate Fleischer twisted around to look at Melendez and then at T-bone lying on the floor. T-bone's eyeball was dry and filmy and a yellow translucence had crept into his skin. "Pretty effective defense," Fleischer said.

He motioned with his head and the deputy escorted me down the hall to another apartment where I was allowed to use the telephone. I reached Lawyer Timmons on the first ring and he said he would come straight over. Outside the door to Melendez's apartment I met Shirley Kimball, drenched with perfume, in a clinging V-necked jersey and red leather pants and high heels. She narrowed her eyes at me and said, "Dolan, that was quick."

"The quick and the dead."

"I was taking a bath and heard it on the scanner," said Shirley. She leaned toward me and spoke in a flat quiet voice, lower than a whisper. "I'm not wearing anything underneath and I'm still a little wet."

I looked down at my shorts. "So am I."

Shirley brushed her red fingernails against my chest and put her tongue out and wet her lips. "What have you got—is it murder?"

"No comment."

The deputy came out of the apartment and tilted his hat brim down at me. "Nate's ready for you now," he said.

"Duty calls," I said to Shirley.

"Listen, hon, this is *my* story," she said, blocking the way.

"Since you're going to be out here and the story is in there," I said, pointing to the doorway, "I guess you lost it."

Shirley's green eyes went cold. "Is Elvis in there? What about dogs—any poodles? Dalmations? Spring-haired fucking terriers? Then you're out of your depth."

No rules of chivalry applied to Shirley Kimball. Under all that perfume and makeup and hair spray was a storm trooper wearing panty hose. You had to fight dirty just to stay even. Leaning so close the ends of her hair tickled my face, I said, "If you don't stop bugging me I'll tell Maxine everything you said about her and Walter. That should get you some real nice assignments." Her mouth flattened into a taut red line. "So buzz off, Shirley."

I passed into the apartment and the deputy, solid and indifferent, filled the doorway after me. "Sorry ma'am," he told Shirley. "You can't go in."

She crossed her arms over her chest, glaring at me through the narrow space between the deputy and the door frame. After a moment, Shirley uncovered her bosom and walked out of sight, then returned. "What's going on in there?" she demanded, her eyes like two green slits. The deputy looked down like he was surprised she was still there. "Don't waste your breath," he said.

An imperious clicking of heels echoed in the hallway. Detective Fleischer, sitting beside Surfer, beckoned to me and drew up another crate. "I understand you were here earlier, to tell Mr. Melendez this man—" he gestured toward the body "—meant to do him serious harm."

"And if we hadn't, Mike would be dead and you'd be out looking for a guy on a motorcycle," I told him.

Fleischer turned to Melendez. "Is that what happened?" Melendez nodded. Then the detective settled his gaze on me again and said, "I want you to tell me what time you came here tonight, how long you stayed, and exactly what was said. I want to know why you came when you did and how you knew Mr. Melendez was in danger. And I don't want you to leave anything out." Two policemen came through the door and, after one of them asked Melendez to stand up, they escorted him from the room. "What's this?" I asked.

"They're taking him to the station and we're going to hold him in custody until bail is set tomorrow morning."

The deputy placed another officer in his stead at the entrance and approached us. "Nate, I'm going to follow them in and make my report." Fleischer nodded and the deputy's gaze strayed to the figure on the tiles and the waxy-looking dried blood. "Anything I can do for you when I'm there?" he asked Fleischer.

"Take Mr. Melendez's belt and shoelaces and have somebody watch him," said the detective. To my inquiring glance he responded, "It's a standard precaution. I don't want two investigations."

A man in a windbreaker came in and put on thin rubber gloves and made an examination of the body. He measured the wound, stuck a metal probe into the corpse's mouth, and referred several times to his watch. With a series of notations on a pad of paper, the coroner peeled back the dead man's closed eye and looked into the dull brown center like it was a crystal ball. Then he called to the officer in the doorway and two men brought in a collapsible gurney, unfolded it, zipped the corpse into a black bag, and wheeled it out.

"He was a racist and he slapped women around," I said as T-bone went past. "He liked to make threats."

Nate Fleischer's face came close to my own and his eyes were tranquil and steady. "When somebody dies—anybody," said the detective, "and it's not an accident, the very least they deserve is that someone asks what happened and why. That's all I do. I ask questions. Even if I think I already know some of the answers."

"I'm just curious. Did you get your training in the Marine

Corps?" asked Surfer.

Fleischer shook his head. "Jesuits."

I told him what I knew and the detective registered the names Jerry and Vivian and that of the diner by a mere narrowing of focus, something in his gaze that intensified for a brief moment and then passed. He didn't write anything down. Now and then he interrupted and asked for a specific detail, but mostly he was silent and gave the impression that every word I said was being aligned in his memory with the vast content of holy books. Before I finished Lawyer Timmons came to the door and was admitted.

"Where's Mr. Melendez?" he asked.

"He's being booked," said Fleischer, rising to his feet. "How are you, Al?"

"All right. Listen, Nate, this Melendez kid was in his own home and encountered a trespasser who had a grudge and malicious intent, who had made several public threats, and who had an assault record and a history with Michael Melendez that was, at best, calculating and vindictive. For me that adds up to self-defense. Let's get the kid out of a jail cell, for darn's sake."

The ex-Jesuit took a short reflective walk among the headless statuettes and broken frames. "I know about Melendez and I know his history with the victim," he said, tilting his head back for emphasis and glancing at the lawyer from head to foot. "But the facts can be argued another way, Al. Perhaps Melendez lured the victim here with the intent of silencing him on the sexual assault charge. Maybe he only meant to intimidate him and things got out of hand and instead, he killed him. That's manslaughter."

"Nonsense," said Timmons, pulling down the cuffs of his suit jacket. He followed the detective with bloodshot eyes and when Fleischer paused by the windows, Lawyer Timmons stepped over the blood congealed on the floor, joining him there. "That's not going to fly and you know it. For one thing, the telephone doesn't work. Did he lure him here by mail?"

The detective smiled briefly. "There are a number of scenarios and you can bet your ceramic watermelon, Al, that I'm going to categorize them all," Fleischer said. "Until I get the job done and make a recommendation, we're going to hold Melendez. He hasn't said a word to us yet, which was smart. Go to the station and talk to him. Meanwhile, I'll see if I can find Sherri Hogg and get a few things straight that Mr. Dolan put me on to. Sound fair?"

A faint nimbus of light appeared around the two men as they stood against the windows. They looked like two medieval saints. Lawyer Timmons, tall and dignified, brushed with gray at the temples, said, "If I get pulled over and asked one more time if it's my car I'm driving, I'll sue the city. A black man is allowed to own a German car. He can drive the streets at night. He can, if he has consent, sleep with a Caucasian woman. These are not crimes. And a black man cannot be persecuted for them as if they *were* crimes. Denying him any of these things is a violation of his civil rights. I'm not militant. Militancy bores me. But I'm getting tired of this sort of thing, Nate. As far as Michael Melendez goes, why don't they just charge him with the Lindbergh kidnapping and be done with it? Is the 'justice' system, so called, trying to hound him into criminal behavior? Believe me, I'm not going to stand by and do nothing because the police department has decided he's too dark for sunbathing and therefore belongs in jail."

The detective raised his hand. "Let me say one thing, Al: I don't govern here. I, too, am governed. I know you're frustrated. Every reasonable person should be. But in the particular, is there anyone else you would rather have conducting the investigation? It's the only possible way that race can be left out of it." Fleischer rubbed his fingertips together like there was grit between them. "I see neutral."

"I know that. If you weren't here, I'd probably be plea bargaining already," said Timmons. "And trying to make five years sound like a wonderful vacation to a kid who turned into a skeleton after a single night in jail." He touched a button on his jacket and his eyes wandered over the walls to the zebra skin. For a moment he regarded it as though he were remembering something, or listening to some far-off bugle call. "Once you lose that kind of weight you never really put it back on," he said.

"Come on. I'll walk you out," said Fleischer.

After they had gone, I circled the pool of blood where the body had lain, my hands thrust into the pockets of my rugby shorts. "What do you think?" I asked.

Surfer looked at the hard black pancake of blood. "Live by the baseball bat, die by the baseball bat," he said.

We went outside. Fleischer took our home and work telephone numbers and said we could go. I threw the keys in a long arc and Surfer caught them with a quick casual wave of his hand. "Go see Duke," I said and hurried after Detective Fleischer, catching up with him near the end of the block. "I have a lead on where Sherri Hogg is living. Why don't I go with you?"

Fleischer glanced at his watch and up at the stars, which were dim above the glow from the strip. "Suit yourself," he said. We climbed into an old rusted green Ford and I chuckled at the creaking door. "There's plenty of people laughing who aren't driving," said Fleischer. I told him I thought Sherri was staying with her father on Merritt Island. The detective turned the car onto the strip and began heading north.

"So you were a priest," I said.

"Actually, I was a seminarian at one time but I never took my final vows. I stayed there for quite some time and then finally, I left." He wore a gold wedding band and as he spoke, he clicked it against the steering wheel. The detective smiled. His teeth were small but sturdy and perfectly white and they showed up well against the deep pink of his gums. "The Jesuits are very patient but they got tired of me," he said.

"Was it a hard life?"

"Any life is a hard life. Marcus Aurelius said: 'The things of the body are as unstable as water; the things of the soul dreams and vapors; life itself a warfare or a sojourning in a strange land.' The Order is extremely contemplative. Like Marcus Aurelius, they believe that philosophy is the best escort through life. The Jesuits like to wrestle with the *idea* of sin, not necessarily its consequences. I guess my weakness was the desire to meet sin in the street and wrestle it there."

We fell into a foreign but amiable silence. Fleischer was dark skinned, much more so than Michael Melendez and even than Lawyer Timmons. When we were beyond the last of the klieg lights on the strip he seemed to fold himself into the shadows and I could barely make him out. A great distance separated us. It reminded me of a black kid I knew at Deerfield, Roy Kerr, from Yonkers. A star basketball player, Roy was also a serious student, though he wasn't in any of my classes. For an entire year, whenever we passed each other in the hallways or out on the campus, we would meet each other's eyes and nod. That was it. An understanding. Then, returning to the conversation he was occupied with or, more often, alone with his thoughts, Kerr would glide by, isolated because of his height and the scarcity of blacks at Deerfield. We never once spoke. Maybe he made a point of greeting me because we were both athletes and he recognized me from the gym, or maybe he heard about the hazing I took from Mulligan and Dubinski in the hotel room up in Canada, but I don't think so. Roy Kerr and I weren't friends. Nodding to each other was merely the first inch in the mile we needed to go. It was respect.

Detective Fleischer made a soft noise in his throat. "Did you know Batem very well?"

"I saw him tonight on his motorcycle heading toward Mike's.

The last time before that was a few weeks ago at the Legion hall on Orange Boulevard. There was almost a brawl and Batem told Mike he was going to get him somehow, maybe in his sleep."

"Were there other witnesses to that?"

"A whole roomful of war veterans. Roger the bartender could tell you who they were. Three of us from the rugby team heard it, too."

"Any other run-ins with Batem?"

I described my visit to the trailer park with Loretta and T-bone's attempt to make money from the rape charge, as well as the vicious treatment of his girlfriend and her dog. "There's not a good thing I can say about him."

"Saint Augustine would say that men are good because they are created by God," said Fleischer. "He would never allow the existence of anything completely evil among His works."

"I don't think He's handing out any merit badges for beating up girls."

We were driving through an enormous meadow of saw grass near the Rinker concrete plant and the causeway that would take us over to Merritt Island. The grass stretched to the horizon on either side, dark and swaying in the offshore breeze. Fleischer looked out his window at it and then turned back to me. "There are a lot of things about Thomas Alan Batem we will never know," he said.

"He was an ignorant bully," I said. "And I'm not too sorry about what happened."

The detective looked out again at the dim rolling ocean of grass. "'Not as man sees does God see, because man sees the appearances but the Lord looks into the heart,'" he said. He signaled a left turn onto the causeway. "The Book of Samuel."

It was midnight. On the island Detective Fleischer stopped at a convenience store to look up the address in the telephone book and I went inside to buy something to eat. "One thirty-two Highland Avenue," said Fleischer when I came back to the car.

Highland Avenue was lined with decrepit one-story buildings. They were perched on cinder blocks and so close together it would have been possible to sit in one and shake hands with the person next door. Here and there you could see a light in the windows or the blue glow of a television but mostly it was dark. A short way along the road Fleischer extinguished his headlights and pulled onto the apron of hard-packed dirt that formed the yard of 132. He reported our situation over the radio he kept hidden in the glove compartment and took out a snub-nosed revolver in a holster and his gold detective's shield and clipped them to his belt. It was odd watching a priest strap on a gun.

"Wait here until I call you," he said. Fleischer got out of the car and scanned the housefronts and the darkened alleyways before knocking on the door. After a moment he knocked again. Then he took a step down on the stairs and looked into the nearest window, one hand resting on his weapon. "Police," he said.

A shadow passed by the window. The door opened. Behind it was a man wearing a T-shirt over a huge hard round stomach. He was unshaven, a cigar stub in his teeth. The stomach was like an insult. The man went away from the door and Fleischer turned with a grim look on his face and beckoned to me.

"She's here," was all he had time to say before Sherri Hogg came to the door.

Sherri was in bad shape. In the weeks since I had last seen her, she had put on weight, her hair was long and stringy, and she had a fresh black eye. Fleischer identified himself and said he had something to discuss and could we please come in? Sherri opened the door into a shotgun hallway and we stepped inside. A strong odor of fish greeted us and I gagged.

"Thomas Batem is dead," said Fleischer in a quiet even tone. "It happened earlier tonight. Apparently he was a trespasser and was killed in a scuffle. The matter is under investigation."

Sherri dropped her chin and made a tiny grunt. "Was he shot? What?"

"No. A blow to the head killed him. From a baseball bat."

Sherri Hogg pressed a hand to her eyes and whimpered, but it was not an expression of grief. By the time her hand dropped to her side, and she had drawn and exhaled a quick breath, the mitigation of an old sorrow had begun to take root. She looked relieved. "Are you sure?" she asked.

The detective's gaze was unblinking. "Yes, I'm positive," he said. He allowed a moment to pass. "Did Batem come here tonight?"

"He was here," Sherri replied. "But I didn't let him in. He rode up and down the street on his motorcycle for a while. My father put the dog out and T-bone left. The dog didn't come back. I called him, but he didn't come."

"Did Batem give you the black eye?" Fleischer asked.

Sherri's glance darted to the next room where the television threw a changing light on the walls. "No, he didn't."

They had the wrong man in custody. Just a few feet away the cause of Mike Melendez's trouble snorted at a rerun of *Green Acres*. It was not the chain of events being investigated by the police but part of a longer chain, a history of abuse that stretched back to childhood. The overwhelming need for love had led Sherri Hogg to a jerk like T-bone in the first place, and then to a night with a debonair stranger and the fabricated rape charge.

"They want to know if T-bone went to Mike Melendez's house tonight intending to kill him," I said. "T-bone is dead. He can't hurt you anymore. Tell them the truth."

Fleischer was still. He looked like a hunter standing in the woods listening for deer. Sherri hugged herself and a mean little smile appeared on her lips. "You didn't tell me the truth that day at the trailer park, but you want the truth now. Funny."

"Look—I'm sorry about that. But I was trying to help Mike and that's what I'm doing now."

The man in the other room belched with laughter.

"T-bone was outside, yelling at me to come out and calling me a lot of names—bitch and whore and things like that," said Sherri. "He had come by earlier, just before dark, and said things about—about your friend, but this time he was really drunk and when he idled his bike down it sounded like he was crying, begging almost. I was scared."

"What did he say about Mike this time?" I asked.

Sherri pulled at a loose thread on the sweatshirt she was wearing. "T-bone kept calling him my boyfriend." Her voice dropped to where it was barely audible and her eyes wandered all over the ground near our feet. "My nigger stud boyfriend, he said. I heard him walk the motorcyle right to the foot of the stairs and cut the engine. He told me he was going to drag that nigger through the streets like they used to in the old days. That was how you killed a nigger. You dragged him."

This information seemed like enough to free Michael Melendez. But nothing changed on the detective's face and he said, "Perhaps it was just talk. Did Batem ever follow through on these sorts of threats before?"

"He shot his mouth off a lot," admitted Sherri. "But sometimes he would say just what he was gonna do and then do it, like when a guy nicked T-bone's bike while he was parking his car and he told the guy his car would make a nice barbecue. And he went to the guy's house that night and burned it."

"Was there anything else Batem said tonight that's important?" asked Fleischer.

"The motorcyle started up and I couldn't hear much else except what he said about dragging. He was driving up and down. The dog went out and T-bone left."

"In between Batem's visits you went to warn Melendez?" asked the detective.

Sherri nodded. "Only that T-bone was coming after him and was drunk and talking shit. I didn't think it would be this. A fight, is all I thought."

"When Batem came here the second time, you still thought there would only be a fight?"

"No. He was worse that time. I was too afraid to even go out looking for Toby—my dog—after that." She stammered. "I thought he might be coming back for me. I wanted to call the police but my father wouldn't let me. When I thought he was sleeping, I tried again but he came out. . . ." Her voice trailed off. "I couldn't stop shaking. I sat on the floor in the kitchen. About an hour ago that other reporter—what's her name? Shirley?—she came and said there was trouble and police over there and did I know anything. I told her I was afraid of what T-bone would do to me. She wasn't altogether sure what was going on at that apartment house but she had a good notion that T-bone wouldn't be bothering me anymore. 'You won't hear another peep out of that son of a bitch,' is what she said. I thought it meant he was in jail."

Fleischer looked into her empty frightened eyes, nodding that he understood. Extending a hand, he cupped Sherri's elbow and inclined toward her, saying, "Excuse me a minute," and went into the room where her father was slouched over his enormous stomach. Sherri walked up and down the hallway pecking at the thread on her sleeve while she tried hard to eavesdrop, but the incessant rumble of the television obscured what was being said. Only an occasional word or phrase in Detective Fleischer's patient tone slipped between the canned music and laughter.

"Will you drop the other charge against Mike now?" I asked, taking advantage of our moment alone. "There's no money to be made from it. And it's not going to prove anything."

Sherri glanced at me and turned pale, then, unable to speak, she gripped her elbows and rocked back and forth with a gush of air from her nostrils. I said, "What do you care what your father thinks? He's worse than T-bone was. Do what's right."

Her lower lip dropped and I could see the fillings in Sherri's back teeth. She wiped her nose on her sleeve. Using her fingers, Sherri combed out the tangled ends of her hair and sniffled a few times. Raising her eyes—one of them swollen nearly shut now and arrayed in purple—she mustered a froggy voice from deep in her chest. "I don't give a shit anymore. Mr. Rasterree's secretary called and said there wasn't any physical evidence and the other lawyer would say all kinds of bad things about me—why didn't I just forget about it. They don't care, so why should I? I never want to see those people again."

Sherri's voice dropped lower and her gaze went back to the floor, the wall, across my chest in little zigzags. "But I did say no that night. All to a point, and then I said no. We were on the floor and it started to hurt. And I was afraid of what T-bone would do. What he would say. I told your friend to stop." She looked at me, her eyes hooded and cold, and I felt a pang of complicity mingled with guilt. "But he didn't."

Detective Fleischer emerged from the other room wearing an expression of distaste. "It's late," he said. "I'll probably come back and talk to you tomorrow. Is there anything else you remember or anything you want to tell me?"

"Only that I'm sorry for what-all I did," said Sherri.

"Sorry for what?" Fleischer searched the woman's dejected face with his eyes. "You didn't do anything."

Sherri was gentle, but insistent. "Am I a bad person?" she asked, and before either of us could respond, she stated, "I do believe I am. Look at me. I must have done something."

The air outside was cool and pure after the close, fish-smelling interior of the house. I took several deep breaths. Detective

Fleischer made a radio call to headquarters and then started the car and we drove off. "In that house, just getting out of bed every morning must be like climbing a mountain," he said.

A small dark shape appeared on the side of the road. We were almost beyond it. "Pull over," I said. Fleischer looked at me with mild surprise. "Stop the car."

The dog lay in the gutter in a shaggy heap. He was dead. All of the short black hair and some of the flesh from his brisket had been worn away and his entire flank was torn up and bloody, abraded to the consistency of hamburger and stuccoed over with sand and pebbles and bits of glass. An extension cord was wrapped around his neck and the broken end of it trailed off into the weeds.

"I can't believe nobody heard this. This poor animal must have been howling in pain," said Fleischer, aiming a flashlight. He ran the beam along the pavement, which for several feet was glossy and wet, and then back to the carcass. "It would have been impossible not to hear."

I rolled the dog over with my foot and we squatted down to examine the throat and the wound made by the extension cord. On the thin gray skin under the jaw I pointed out a double line of surgical stitches. "This dog was mute. He couldn't make a sound," I said. "He was barking all right, but nobody *could* hear it."

The detective kept the beam fixed on the dog's throat for a long moment and the light seeped upward through his fingers, making them glow and casting a reddish tint on the smooth black complexion of his face. He looked like a shaman squatting over a pile of burning embers, about to perform some mystical rite. But he only stared at the dead dog and after a while, switched off the beam, plunging us in darkness again.

"Life itself a warfare or a sojourning in a strange land," he said.

Fleischer radioed for the animal control officer to come out and get the dog and put it on ice until the county vet could be summoned. He wanted to be certain the cause of death was being dragged from a motorcyle.

"Are you starting to get the picture?" I asked.

Fleischer backed the car up, his arm flung across the seat, looking over his shoulder. "I work real slow," he said, "because I make fewer mistakes that way."

He left me there and approached the house again. Sherri answered this time, and in the rush of light from the open door I saw the detective motion up the street and Sherri listening to him. Then she said something and went back inside. Fleischer returned and drove to our earlier location to wait for the animal control officer.

The crisp sound of a car door being closed somewhere in the neighborhood thudded against the housefronts. Beside me, Detective Fleischer was still clean and pressed after all the hours he had put in. He studied Toby's carcass in the headlights. "You must learn a lot about people at the newspaper, Joe," he said. "That's what I love about my job. People. The things they say break your heart almost every time, if you listen. I told Sherri about her dog. She said it didn't matter. Every time the dog went out, she didn't expect him to come back."

Then a car came slowly toward us, a low-slung convertible with four white teenagers in it. Music was blasting from a huge set of rear speakers, somber and filled with bass, pounding in my lungs like a funeral march. Fleischer turned his head to meet the eyes of the driver. "Sherri's father was just the opposite—he figures the world owes him a living," he said, watching the car continue past. The music reverberated among the cottages. "You should have heard this guy. His daughter is a no-good little tramp, he says, and if she hadn't slept with a colored boy—no offense—she wouldn't have broken up with this Batem and come crawling back home. When I told him Batem was dead, he didn't even blink. More trouble comes from between a girl's legs, he said, than from hell itself.

I asked him about Sherri's black eye and he said that was family business. If she was going to live there on his charity, he was going to make the rules. He acted like I was out of line to even ask."

We sat there for half an hour. Finally a van pulled up behind us and was waved on and then parked a short distance from the dog. Fleischer and I got out. The animal control officer, a chubby black woman dressed in a police uniform without the hat, gun, and handcuffs, came toward us with a plastic bag and wide-bladed shovel. "Hello there, Meryl," said Fleischer. "Sorry to call you out at this hour."

Meryl smiled, showing us the gold in her teeth, and laughed in a husky voice that tore into the silence. "Well, there's nothing so romantic as Nate Fleischer and a roadkill by moonlight. I went runnin' for my shovel and my rubber gloves soon's I heard De-tec-tive Fleischer was wanting *me* after dark." She laughed mightily and her flesh jiggled under the uniform. Then her eyes cut in my direction. "We don't need no chaperone, neither. Just the two of us will do. Nate Fleischer, you might be something of a small man, least'n compared to me, but anyhow it ain't the size of the weapon matters most, it's the fury of the attack."

Fleischer looked sheepish. "Come on now, Meryl," he said.

The woman donned her gloves and went about her work. "C'mon now nothing. I'm jes' givin' you the first alarum. Watch out around me. I might shovel you into the van and that's the last your wife ever saw you." She slipped the blade of the shovel under Toby's bloody flank and heaved him onto the plastic bag she had spread upon the ground. The dog nearly came apart and Meryl scraped the head and brisket into the bag. She fluttered the edges of the plastic from under the dog's weight and then scooped up what remained, a bright red hamburger, adding it to the carcass. "Can't forget the giblets," she said.

I was nearly sick. The specter of T-bone and his dented skull joined suddenly with the wet pavement, the smell of bloody entrails, and the scraping noise of the shovel. Big Meryl, wheezing with effort, maintained her relentless good humor in the midst of the stench coming from the bag.

"*Phew.* No dog, dead or alive, ever smelled like a rose," she said, "and this one ain't starting no trend."

"Will the vet be able to tell anything with the carcass like that?" Fleischer asked.

"It ain't rocket science. Even I don't need no degree to tell you this one's been strangled and drug around on that cord. Doc Piedmont could figure on that in his sleep."

I went back and sat on the bumper of the Ford. "He looks like he seen a ghost," said Meryl, leaning on the shovel. "If'n that is, that ghost won't do nothing worse than knock over your trash and then eat it."

"It's been a long night," explained Fleischer.

"Long or short, the sight of a dead dog puts your dinner in a spin, you want another line of work." She called to me. "You a cop?"

"No. A reporter."

Meryl hoisted the bag into the van with a short pendulum motion, the shovel clattering in afterward. "Catch some, fetch some, bag some, and burn some. Report on that," she said. "Dogs, cats, goats, rats, snakes, ducks, and sheep. Wear gloves and take a long shower afterwards. The world's full of 'em."

Fleischer walked around to the driver's side of the van after Meryl climbed in. "Thanks for your help," he said. "Tell Doc Piedmont I'll call him."

"I'll be telling Doc Piedmont a lot of things," came Meryl's voice from within the van as it shifted into gear, "and some things I'll be keeping to myself."

The tidal basin was soft and damp around us on the trip over the causeway and I felt like an ordeal was finally over. Detective

Fleischer felt it, too; he hummed in little snatches, tapping his ring against the steering wheel. The moon gleamed on his bald head. For the first time I understood the benefit of how methodical he was. And his own reward for being that way: it allowed him to sleep at night. Suddenly I was curious about Nathaniel Fleischer and his home and who lived there with him.

"Does your wife worry?" I asked.

Fleischer smiled. "A lot of the stuff is routine, but she doesn't like me near the bodies. I don't help matters much. Every time we go past a cemetery I point to it and say, 'The people in there can't hurt you, it's the live ones you have to worry about.' Drives her crazy. We've been married for eight years, Sophie and I. Got two kids now. Two little boys."

I saw the kindness in his face and just the way he said *two little boys* I could picture their smooth shiny heads, the clean overalls and little striped jerseys they were dressed in. Behind them was Sophie, small and pretty and just as good natured as Meryl, only quieter. Outside of work I imagined Nate Fleischer spent most of his time at home or on family outings, pushing a stroller through the Space Center and taking day trips to St. Augustine and Vero Beach. Just like the excursions I made with my own family, the car seats sticky in the heat, smelling of plastic—then breaking through a cool dark ring of trees to see the sun flashing on the lake, mirror smooth, the bathers' voices purling up from the shoreline.

"Did you quit the seminary to get married?" I asked.

"No, I met Sophie afterward. I knew I didn't belong in the seminary, but I gave it a fair shot. I needed a wife. And of course my boys, Ezra and Isaac. If I had missed out on them, I would've missed too much. When I pray, Joe, that's who I pray for. My kids and everybody else's. I see my boys and they're *happy.* Of course, life's going to get a lot harder for them, but there's no hurry. Sophie and I are always trying to surprise them, educate them. We sit around dreaming up fun things for them to do. Right now they don't even know they're black. They'll find out later. But it will be a point of pride, like it should be, if they know we love them and they grow up loving themselves."

The strip was deserted and most of the streetlights had been turned out. Fleischer asked me where I lived, and then: "You married?"

"Nope."

"When you meet the future Mrs. Dolan you'll know exactly what I'm talking about," said the detective.

The trick was finding her. A nineteen-year-old exotic dancer seemed out of the question. But an intelligent witty girl, with a flat stomach and perfect round breasts, strong, gentle, sleepy eyed at night, dedicated to some passion but not very serious, having white teeth and wearing little makeup: was that too much to ask? Apparently so.

"When I meet the future Mrs. Dolan I'll probably be playing bingo," I said, "with my teeth out."

"You have to be ready for it," advised Fleischer. "Something like that, it could be around the next corner. Or an hour away. You never know. Life happens fast."

I made a gesture and he stopped the car in front of the house and shook my hand. "I'm sure I'll be seeing you in the loop," he said. "I appreciate your cooperation on this one. Tonight and tomorrow I'll sift through everything and then the chief will decide what we're going to do. I'll say this, you're a true friend to Michael Melendez."

"I don't even really know him."

"But you're trying," said the detective. "And that's something."

14

Late Friday afternoon, waiting for Surfer to come back from the store, I sat at the kitchen table and made a list of all the women I had ever slept with:

Kathleen Quigley
Cindy D'Orio*
Gael O'Connell
Nancy Demarais
Diane Simcoe (Simco?)
Tammi
Fried Chicken Girl
Tammi's Friend
Diane?
Alice Cousios
Peg O'Connell
Girl from Scotland
Diane #3
Marie Iannacelli
Tracey Contarino
Suntan Lotion Girl
Tina
Loretta Sweet*
Shirley Kimball

Looking for trends, I noticed an affinity for girls named Diane, although I didn't have much luck remembering their last names and never went out with any of them longer than two months. The longest I ever went out with anyone, the luscious and lovely Cindy D'Orio, was a year, from my sixteenth to my seventeenth birthday. Eight one-night stands were on the list. The most memorable was the suntan lotion girl from Daytona Beach, who insisted on making love on the pool deck of her hotel after we had coated a tarpaulin in aloe vera and slid back and forth on it, lubricating ourselves. There on the deck in the solid black hours of the morning, under a steady tropical wind, an otherwise normal, wholesome-looking blond girl put herself and me through some slippery gyrations that would have amazed an anthropologist. Immediately afterward she disappeared. I went back to the pool on four consecutive days and never saw her again; that sort of passion was embarrassing.

The O'Connell sisters were the closest I ever got to a ménage à trois, which wasn't very close since I went out with them three years apart. But the summer after I graduated high school, when I was seeing Gael, fifteen-year-old Peg would run to answer the door. If we stayed up late watching movies together, Peg would join us on the couch and in the darkness under the quilt she would wriggle behind me, sliding her knee between my legs, touching me with her small white hands. At the same time Gael pressed against me from the front, shifting and murmuring in the play of light from the television, my nose buried in her shiny brown hair. It was a pleasant way to spend a summer evening.

Alice Cousios was the first girl to talk dirty to me during sex and I found I liked it a lot. She was a big outdoorsy Greek girl, with the hint of a mustache and very large breasts decorated in purple nipples the size of my fist. She was quiet, almost sullen, hardly saying a word all day skiing or trout fishing on the Swift River where her family had a camp. Then, at night, as soon as we climbed into her old down sleeping bag and I began kneading those huge breasts, feeling the milk roll under my hands, silent Alice would let out a string of marvelous curse words, imprecations so commanding and perverse they would have made a convicted pornographer blush. Sometimes Alice would tape our sessions on a miniature cassette recorder but she never played the tapes for me. I have no idea what she did with them. Other than an occasional *uggh* or *wow* I didn't say much. And from those months onward, whenever I smelled wood smoke I thought of dark foul-mouthed Alice Cousios and wondered what had happened to her.

I'll never forget the first time I saw Cindy D'Orio. She was on a date with a friend of mine, Geoff Finn, at the youth center. Cindy was a small, almost frail girl, shapely but built on a tiny scale with a face like a porcelain doll. She had an incredible mop of thick brown hair that made her skin look creamy and set off her huge brown eyes. The jukebox was playing "Cinnamon Girl" and I had just descended the stairs into the church basement, made stiff legged by a two dollar bottle of wine. There she was across the dance floor, Geoff's hand caught in her belt while he leaned over the jukebox to select another song. *I could be happy the rest of my life with a cinnamon girl.* Cindy was wearing Navy jeans and a white midriff jersey, her doe eyes blinking at the confused scene. Although Geoff had a firm grip on her, you could tell she was untrained and wild, ready to leap. "You're looking good," I said, angling for the men's room.

"You're not bad yourself," said Cindy.

She gave Geoff the slip at eleven when the center closed and we walked along the bowered cinder paths of the church grounds, beneath the unlit windows of the rectory and the tall marble statues of Christ and the saints, their hands raised in blessing, and through a dense thicket and then down a fire road to the low stone bridge that spanned the river. The water was black and silent, except for a small noise at the edges of the current that was like the sound of paper tearing. It was a holy place and I was in awe of the holiness I felt just being close to another human being. In near total darkness Cindy and I dangled our legs over the river and talked for hours, but in memory the conversation lasted only a few moments and the bridge and moving water and the fire road were illuminated by a persistent golden light that seemed like the light of heaven. Each word that we spoke drew itself out in tangible form and was inscribed on the air surrounding us like it had been etched upon a slate.

Love, as a word or even a feeling, had little to do with it. I can only say that the golden light saturated everything I did for months afterward and trailed after me no matter where I went; it was as much a substance as it was a quality of light, a fine glittering golden dust, and I was constantly inhaling and exhaling it until it filled my lungs, was processed through me like grist through a mill, and lined every corner of my life.

Cindy and I went to movies and hockey games and parties, had little arguments and then made up, and talked on the telephone until the early hours of the morning. We would dial, let it ring once, and then hang up if it was late—our signal that we were home and wanted to talk. I jumped out of bed in the morning and swaggered to school, knowing that a fine creature like Cindy D'Orio loved me. I had already slept with Kathleen Quigley and Cindy wasn't a virgin so when we did it, about a month after we began dating, we knew the basic moves, and yet there was enough mystery and excitement to make the blood shake in my ears. Handling her naked body—the small breasts with their perfect brown nipples, the taut stomach, smooth round flank, her legs like silk, and that triangle of glossy black hair—was the luckiest sensation I had ever known, like receiving a gift from the emperor, a windfall you could retire on. One weekend Cindy's parents went away and for the first time in my life I had the chance to sleep all night in a real bed with a beautiful girl.

On my way to the football stadium in the morning the entire town was scented with her perfume. Leaves were piled in golden heaps on the lawns, strewn like party favors on the pavement and in the gutters. Although the perfume was on my hands, embedded in my clothing, it seemed to fume up like incense from the chimneys and the piles of burning leaves, rising until it met the violet morning sky.

Then it ended. Maybe I was too cocky, taking Cindy for granted, or maybe it just wore itself out. Another old girlfriend of mine said love was like a feast: one person usually finished first and started clearing away the plates while the other was still eating. With Cindy D'Orio, I was ordering the appetizer and—boom—the check came. I walked into the youth center one Friday night and she was in a corner making out with Geoff Finn. I saw them, my eyes swept across the room in an arc, and when I looked back all that golden dust had turned to poison, a caustic brown grit that stopped my heart, scalding me from the inside and burning my face and the ends of my fingers with its peculiar dry fire.

Cindy wasn't mine anymore. The next few nights I'd dial her number, let it ring once, and then hang up, but my phone never rang afterward. It was like trying to call Mars. My birthday was that week and one morning, on my way to school, I ran into Geoff Finn. "Sorry, Joe," he said. "Nobody planned it that way." I didn't say anything, just kept going, and behind me, he added: "Anyhow, happy birthday, man."

The rusty brown grit evaporated from my system and left me in a prolonged and nasty withdrawal, drying my system out, hardening more than just my arteries. Falling in love with Cindy D'Orio was a real thrill, the most dangerous thing I had ever experienced, bright like the grave might be, and as black as the sun on the clearest day in summer. It never really happened again. Sometimes, not often, the dust was in the air, but I was very careful about how much of it I breathed in.

Like with Loretta. Since Elvis had been released from the hospital he had been living in a cabana on the beach, washing dishes at Saxophone Joe's and performing when they needed someone to fill in. One day I stopped to visit, and Elvis took two beers from the refrigerator and then put on some music. The sun was going down, sending a breeze through the open window. Something about the time of day, the stillness, and the pink wash spreading on the horizon affected me and I mentioned Loretta's name in a wistful tone.

Catching myself, I glanced over at Elvis and said, "I don't know why I'm so freaked out. She's just a chick."

Elvis was wearing one of those cabled sweaters he favored and he reached up and scratched the back of his head. "Sure she is. That's what I said about Priscilla."

I just shrugged. Count Basie was on the stereo and he turned it down to ask me something. "What's this little honey's name again?"

"Loretta Sweet."

"Just the way you're saying it is the whole story right there," Elvis replied. "Do what you want, Joe, but I think you should be out working on that problem."

"She's long gone," I said, turning up the stereo. I reached for my beer. Elvis said something else, his lip curled up and his face calm and serious, but I couldn't hear him anymore.

Of the nineteen girls on my list, six were of Irish descent, three were Italian, two Jewish, one Greek, one Scottish, one French, and one said she was Danish and Iroquois. The rest were unknown. The youngest, Cindy D'Orio, was just fifteen; the oldest, Shirley Kimball, on the other side of forty. Tina, the barmaid at Saxophone Joe's, enjoyed being handcuffed. Maria Iannacelli whistled in bed, reaching notes that only dogs could hear during her frequent orgasms. Modeling underwear in high heels was Nancy Demarais's favorite method of foreplay. Sometimes she would parade several sets of lacy bras and V-cut panties by the end of the bed before finally peeling them off, glancing over her shoulder to make sure I was paying close attention. I was. One of the Dianes insisted on doing it standing up, which was murder on the legs. Some liked ropes, tarpaulins, rough sex; a few came equipped with oils and lotions, peanut butter, cucumbers, vibrators, and masks. Two or three preferred to stay partly dressed. The majority wanted it dark. And some were turned on by lies, others by the truth.

"Joe—do you love me?" Gael O'Connell asked me once, just before we started. Her body was tanned and sinewy against the white of the sheets and already tiny drops of sweat, like jewels, shone on her torso.

"No," I said. "Not really."

Gael attached herself to me, running her tongue along my neck and into my ear. "Good," she murmured. "That would screw things up royally."

As a teenager I would spend hours talking about girls and how to get them. I remember breasts falling into my hands like warm fruit, and what it was like to get drunk in the woods for the first time and to spend hours marveling at the loss of coordination and ordinary speech while thoughts and observations and feelings that had seemed somehow locked permanently in my heart materialized at once and spilled into the thin wintry air. From inside the cold darkened interior of someone's station wagon or family sedan, borrowed for the evening, frost performed delicate arabesques across the windshield. As my breath went in and out, carbon dioxide gathered and condensed on the glass, and the frost shifted, creating little characters that changed positions and faded away only to be replaced by hundreds more. All my childhood friends were with me and it was an experience so significant and irrevocable and so holy that their faces became carved into my clearest memories as if they were carved in the stone that would be placed above my grave.

Surfer banged through the front door and into the kitchen with two bags of groceries, setting them on the counter. One sagged and then fell over, spilling oranges that rumbled along the counter like bowling balls down an alley. "I went to buy some new groceries because the old ones were no good any more," Surfer said, catching the oranges as they cascaded toward the floor. "I ran into Edelstein at the gas station. He's gonna swing by here in a few minutes. You ready?"

I reached under the table with my foot and slid a black nylon kit bag, packed with rugby gear and a change of clothes, out where he could see it. "Always," I said.

Surfer sat down and dug his thumb into an orange, releasing its sweet scent into the air. "Whatcha doing?" he asked.

"Minding my own business. You should try it some time."

His boyish face bent over the table, chewing on a section of orange, Surfer took one look at my romantic history and gave me a quick peppery smile. "Part of the American dream," he said, the list reflected in the mild blue of his eyes, "is having sex with more people than your parents did." He scrutinized the names while I busied myself putting away the groceries. "Is there an order?" he asked.

"Strictly chronological."

Surfer nodded. "I couldn't understand why Tina would be down so low, even if you deducted points for the hairdo and the handcuffs." He ate some more of the orange and was quiet for a few moments, then he said, "What if, when you die, nobody cares how many girls you slept with? Like, I mean Saint Peter tells you they no more counted the number of times you had sex than the number of times you shook hands."

"So?"

"So there's nothing wrong with it. It's totally natural—totally human. We should have been doing it as much as possible. But we didn't, because of all those sexual hang-ups and taboos that are just a lot of leftover Puritanism, forced on us by a bunch of limp-dick Englishmen who couldn't get any pussy and decided none of us should have any. What a bunch of hypocrites. They were all running around trying to fuck Pocahontas, and then going to church on Sundays."

I was pulling out a series of weird items that always came back from the store when Surfer did the shopping: baby clams, lentils, artichoke hearts in oil, pickled onions, macadamia nuts, tamales, and foil packages of imported cheese. It was like dinner by ordeal on the nights Surfer created the menu. Serving these foods in combination took months, even years off your life.

"Many of your ideas are unsound," I said.

"Ha. They laughed at Leonardo da Vinci. At Galileo. Louis Pasteur. All the great visionaries," he said. "And who's laughing now?"

"None of those guys. They're all dead. It's just me now. Me laughing at you."

Surfer flicked the piece of paper with his finger. "A man with a list like this has nothing to laugh about," he said.

"Fuck you, da Vinci. Go doodle the head of a poodle."

The sound of a horn came from outside. Grabbing my kit bag, I busied myself shutting windows and locking doors. Surfer fetched his things from the other room and we went out through the garage. In the moment before we stepped outside, in the cool dark of the garage away from the bravado we shared with the other rugby players, memories of old girlfriends—the way they smelled, their long soft hair and clean limbs, and the fact they had been utterly and irretrievably lost—filled the shadows around us.

"How many girls are on *your* list?" I asked Surfer.

"I dunno. More than a hundred, I guess," he said, pressing the button that sent the garage door climbing its mechanical track. Light seeped in beneath it, moving in a steady line over the oily concrete slab we were standing on.

"Ever in love with any of them?" I said.

"One," he replied, squinting at the bright sunlight and the van full of rugby players while we waited for the door to go all the way up. "A girl named Maria. It was a long time ago, I remember, and I've been auditioning replacements ever since."

Edelstein stuck his head out of the driver's-side window. "This is your captain speaking. Flight 69 to Miami will be departing momentarily," he said. "Please put your tray and seat back in the full upright position."

Surfer and I were considered part of the lunatic fringe and shunted to the back of the van. It smelled like dried grass and wintergreen chewing tobacco and different varieties of analgesic balm. We scrambled over kit bags to some open seats. Duke and Sporadic Violence Bob and Martin and Special Ed all spoke up, directing insults at us. Riding in front, Josh waved a dull green ax out the window and roared, "Let's get some beer. The Green demands beer."

Edelstein put the van in reverse. He was barefoot and wore a pair of rugby shorts and an old cutoff football jersey and sunglasses. "We'll get the beer out on Orange Boulevard," he said.

Josh let out a war whoop, brandishing his axe. "The Green is pleased."

Sitting on the hard vinyl benches around me were schoolteachers, accountants, salesmen, air force officers, landscapers, and college students who were already beginning to act like paroled convicts and we hadn't even reached the city limits. Our game against Miami was usually a laugher and going in everybody was relaxed, not a tooth grinding anywhere. Kickoff was scheduled for noon the next day and it might have been next year as far as anyone seemed to care.

"Where's Iain and Sean?" Surfer asked.

"They're busy this weekend," said Edelstein over his shoulder. "Iain's building a house."

Duke looked up with skepticism from where he had stretched

out on top of our kit bags. "Iain's not building any house," he said, refusing the literal interpretation of Edelstein's remark.

"No big deal," I said to Surfer. "We won't need 'em this weekend."

Surfer folded his arms across his chest. "If this was golf, I wouldn't be worried."

Traffic was light going over the intracoastal, the afternoon softening into early evening. Players took out pieces of gum or chaws of tobacco and gazed out the windows at the tranquil blue sky. The day rested for a moment. The summer I turned eighteen I came home on such an evening to an empty house, nothing but quiet in every room, and the telephone rang once and then was silent. My heart started up like a lawn mower: Cindy D'Orio. Then the telephone rang again, and a residue of golden dust broke loose inside of me and it was like that first rush a junkie feels when he plunges the spike into his arm. The room still bright from the low startling ring of the telephone, I turned myself around and left the house.

Some emergency vehicles and two utility trucks went by us in the other direction and Duke sat up and watched them go past. "I used to work for the gas company so I feel guilty whenever there's an explosion," he said.

At a convenience store on Orange Boulevard we met the rest of the team in the other van. I got out first and Steve Delong yelled, "Where's your boyfriend, Surfer?"

"Where's your blow-up doll, Whizzer?" I shot back.

Most of the players went in to buy beer and snacks for the road and then Steve Delong and Whizzer crept around behind our van and began writing on it with sticks of white shoe polish: JUST MARRIED, KKK TOUR BUS, DECADENT BEER SLOBS RULE, MARIJUANA ON BOARD, and FAIRY BOAT TO MIAMI. The shoe polish dried almost instantly and was hard to rub off. Delong raced around the van, guffawing at his accomplice and spitting streams of tobacco juice onto the paint job. A moment later Todd Baker cornered into the parking lot in his shiny black Corvette, stopping several feet away to join me in watching the van become covered in graffiti.

"Dipshits," he said, hopping out of his car. He stood with his hands behind his head and looked on. As our teammates came out of the store, shouting in protest, Todd sauntered by them with a grin of retribution on his face and went inside.

The store was nearly empty. Over by the dairy case, Josh and Martin Campesi were doing whippets—inhaling the nitrous oxide at the top of each cannister of whipped cream. They suppressed their laughter and ran through a dozen or more cans, glancing over the shelves at the clerk. "Campesi is the shortest grown man I've ever seen," said Todd, passing by. "He poses for trophies, if you can get him to stand still long enough."

Then Todd cut up and down the aisles with mechanical precision, selecting a loaf of bread, tuna fish and a jar of mayonaise, and two small cans of cat food. He paid for the items and began constructing sandwiches, first with the tuna and mayo, then with the smelly red cat food.

"You're not," I said in disbelief.

"Oh, yes I am, Joe," said Todd, stacking the sandwiches together. "Most definitely I am."

Outside, Special Ed was trying to wipe off the graffiti and Delong and Whizzer were leaning against the storefront hooting like morons. "Listen carefully, Joe," Todd said to me. "The other shoe is about to drop."

He eased over next to Delong and spread the plastic bread bag on the hood of the van, weighing it down with the sandwiches. The top one was tuna and the next four were cat food. "Hands off," Todd said to Delong. "Those are mine." Then he bit into the first sandwich and walked toward his car like he had forgotten something. Delong glanced at the sandwiches, looked to make sure Todd's back was turned and then eyed the sandwiches again.

"I wouldn't do that if I were you," I said. "Those are Todd's."

"Fuck him," said Delong, grabbing two of the sandwiches. He folded one in half and stuffed it in his mouth. He chewed vigorously, then more slowly, and finally the motion of his jaw stopped altogether and Delong's face grew pinched and white. "Phllaaagh!" he said, spitting it out. "That's cat food!"

I ducked behind the grille to avoid the spray, and bent double with laughter, staggered around the van to where Todd sat in his Corvette, racing the engine.

"That was just fucking perfect," I said. Delong and Whizzer were livid, scraping off the bits of cat food. "They're ready to play now, that's for sure."

Todd gazed up at the sky. "The enemy of my enemy is my friend," he said.

"Does that mean the friend of my friend is my enemy?"

"No, it means my next-door neighbor's cousin is my sister-in-law," said Todd. He grinned at me. "See you in Miami, Joe," he added, departing behind a trail of smoking black rubber.

Edelstein herded his passengers together and we hit the road. As the sun dropped low in the sky, I faded in and out of the conversations going on around me, thinking about my list back on the kitchen table (which was a sword that cut both ways—one old girlfriend, who said she had slept with more than fifty men, told me I was definitely in the top five, maybe even the top three). Then the other van, with Delong at the wheel, swerved too close, the horn blaring, and Josh leaned out and waved his ax at them in short choppy strokes. "The Green is very upset," he hollered.

Before the last light was gone, a curious thing began to happen. Drivers and passengers in the other cars were gesturing at us or more often fixing us with dead-eyed stares. And the guys around me who weren't busy talking or drinking were giving it right back to them. Josh even flourished the Green once or twice. Apparently they had all forgotten what was written on the sides of the van. The people driving by were reading those messages and we weren't doing a single thing to change their minds about what idiots we were.

Surfer looked out at a sedan with Michigan plates that contained two elderly white couples, the men riding together up front, all four tourists watching us pass with fear and contempt in their eyes. "See that?" asked Surfer. "They hate us."

"They're just looking at the outside," I said.

"Like we're a bunch of child molesters or something," said Surfer.

"'Not as man sees does God see, because man sees the appearances but the Lord looks into the heart,'" I said.

"Huh?"

"Nothing. Just something I heard."

It was after eleven when, half drunk and cramped from the ride, we pulled into the Thunderbird Motel on the shabby art deco end of Miami Beach. U-shaped, with a single diseased palm tree and a swimming pool filled with green water, the Thunderbird rented by the day and week and was home to jockeys and exercise boys, liquor store clerks, pickpockets, street performers, and other transients. The rooms had veneer furniture and battered indoor-outdoor carpeting and old boxy televisions with loose knobs and chained-down cable selectors. On our semiannual visits we hardly ever saw any real tourists at the T-bird, just a decrepit security guard passed out in the lobby with a huge revolver strapped to his side and the nocturnal migrations of the rumpled, sad-eyed losers who lived there.

"I love to stay at the Ritz," said Duke with a yawn, stretching beside the van.

A lightbulb over each of the blue doors showed us the way to numbers 10 through 13, eight players to a room. Within minutes we discovered we were sharing the motel with a group of middle-aged men from Brooklyn who wore flannel shirts with the sleeves cut off and called themselves "the Gardenias." We were taking turns in the bathroom and flipping channels on the television when Sal Gardenia wandered in carrying a bottle of rum.

"I come over to see if any of youse wanted a drink," he said.

Duke took the bottle from him and said, "Not usually, but it would be impolite to say no."

"Youse some kind of softball team or something?" asked Sal, popping open the beer that Surfer handed him.

"Rugby," said Edelstein. "We hate softball and softball players. We would rather lose at rugby than win at softball."

"Hell—whatever," Sal said. "Come out to the pool and meet the rest of the boys."

Josh and Martin were already poolside, drinking beer and talking to a group of hairy Italians wearing the trademark flannel shirts. Their arms from the shoulders down and their noses and bald patches were streaked red with sunburn, and the rest of their skin was the unhealthy pallor found in social clubs and pool halls. Sal introduced us to Joe and Tony and Vic and Leo—who each said "hey" or "yo"—and we shook hands all around.

"Ritter," Tony said to Duke. "You ain't any relation to King Ritter, are you?"

"My father," Duke said.

The Gardenias perked up. "King Ritter the ballplayer?" asked Leo. "I knew your old man. I saw him play. What a fireball."

Duke sat there, his nose blazing, broad shouldered and trim now at the waist from having his jaw wired shut, a bottle of rum in one hand and a beer in the other. They saw the resemblance, and in an informal moment of silence, drinking or just rubbing their tattoos, the Gardenias paid homage to a hero of their youth.

"I saw your old man play in '39 against Jim Thorpe at the Polo

Grounds," said Tony. "I was just a kid myself but I remember King Ritter scored three touchdowns that day."

Joe Gardenia threw up his hands. "Thorpe was an old man then. He must have been fifty. He was just hanging on."

"A great ath-a-lete, Jim Thorpe," said Tony, "but a real whoremaster. I remember this one broad—"

Sal stopped him. "You dumb bunny. This is King Ritter's boy, these are his friends, and you're flapping on about Jim Thorpe. Have some respect. Fuck Jim Thorpe. This is the son of King Ritter and you're sitting there like a bump on a goddamn log, with no sense of hospitality. Where's your sense of hospitality?"

"No, you're right," Tony said. With his gaze he searched the night air for an appropriate gesture, and then the dusty reaches of the pool deck and up the bent gray spine of the palm tree. His muddy brown eyes lit up. "Here," he said, pulling a paper bag from underneath his chair. "Have your own bottle of rum."

"Oh boy," I said. "Just what he needs."

"These boys have a game tomorrow," explained Sal. "They're in training."

Josh took the rum bottle. "On behalf of the entire Ritter family, I accept," he said.

"What are you guys doing in Miami Beach?" Duke asked, sidestepping all the attention.

"We come down for a week each year, to get away from the city," said Leo. "Then we get here and it's hot and dirty and we never leave the hotel. What a vacation, huh? It's Brooklyn with one fucking palm tree."

"We was sitting out here today when they came to empty the Dumpster," Tony said. "They put the fork under it, it start to come up, and out pops this guy and he beats it across the parking lot. The homeless fifty-yard dash this guy's running, and we're all pissing ourselves laughing. See it here, see it there, no fucken difference."

"Only here nobody's buggin' us," added Sal. "It ain't the wife, it ain't the kids, it's just the Gardenias. Like the old days on the corner, right, boys?"

"Fucking right," they said.

I said good night and went back to the room. Most of the players were already in bed, sleeping or watching television. Josh and Martin stayed with the Gardenias and I could hear their voices above the street traffic and the sounds of World War II coming from the late movie. The room smelled like a hay field. Loretta usually slept at my house on Friday nights, massaging my neck and shoulders and the backs of my legs until I was relaxed enough to get to sleep. In the room now snores mingled with an artillery barrage and I tossed and turned on my half of the box spring, unable to get comfortable. Without ever feeling like I had been asleep I saw the pearl gray light of morning come up behind the curtain and the procession to the bathroom started and I was on my feet, exhausted but awake.

We couldn't find a decent place to have breakfast and then for an hour we couldn't find the field, driving up and down the battered streets near Jackson Memorial Hospital until by chance we saw Todd idling at a stoplight. "Hey, you geniuses," he called out. "The field is back that way." We swung around and both vans followed him into the parking lot of an abandoned building. "I've been looking for you guys all morning," said Todd. "Where the hell have you been?"

"Driving around," Edelstein said.

"That's about as practical as an eighty-yard football field," said Todd. He hooked his thumbs in the waistband of his shorts and walked bowlegged to his car. "Well, mount up, men. The Indians are waiting."

Five minutes later we were putting on our cleats while an impatient referee and our opposition glared at us from a hard dusty field that was too short and too narrow, stubbled with rocks and shards of broken glass that glittered in the sun. "This is practical. Artificial turf," said Duke.

Van Valkenburg hadn't appeared and as captain Delong brought us together to announce the lineup the coach had selected. Edelstein, Surfer, Todd, Duke, and the others walked onto the field as their names were read and I was taking a step toward them when Whizzer was called in my place. He smirked at Delong and ran on to the field to warm up. My heart tumbled in my chest. I stood there frozen with my foot still raised and Surfer came back and slapped me on the ass and said, "Van's just trying to fire you up for the championship. This game don't mean shit. You'll be out there against Jacksonville."

"Fucking right," said Edelstein, who had also jogged over. "We *need* you out there."

Then the referee blew his whistle and they started the game. I looked around the sidelines at who was left. Josh wore a sombrero, his eyes red from being up all night. Sporadic Violence Bob was sleeping among the kit bags with a towel spread over his face. Off by himself, Special Ed was going through his weird stretching ritual and almost religious meditations. "He's trying to move the ball with the power of his mind," said Josh.

"Yeah, he's rugby's answer to Rasputin," I said. But it was embarrassing to be left out, especially when Sal and Leo Gardenia walked up.

"Did we miss anything?" asked Sal, a camera dangling from a strap around his neck. In the rising midday heat the Gardenias wore dress shoes and socks with bermuda shorts and the same flannel shirts they'd had on the night before.

"The game's just starting," I said.

"Where's King Ritter's boy?" Leo said. "There he is. Number 8."

Duke caught the kickoff and was swerving between the defenders. Leo Gardenia dropped into a crouch and moved his arms like a locomotive, inching down the sideline. "Go, Ritter. Go. Go. Go," he said. "Amazing. He looks just like his old man out there."

Sal nudged me. "What are you, hurt or something?"

"No. I didn't get picked today."

"We'll help you keep the bench warm, then," Leo said, and they both clomped after me in their shiny black shoes.

Things went wrong from the start. We were disorganized and lackadaisical and Miami scored right away, sending a cheer up from the spectators on the far sideline, which further galvanized the home team. A minute later they intercepted one of our passes and raced eighty yards for another try. The kick after was good and we were twelve points down, more than we had allowed in weeks. Their sideline was going nuts.

"I told you we shoulda gone to a strip joint," said Sal Gardenia.

"Shuddup, I'm watching the game," replied Leo.

Sal winked at me and said, "Remember, even baby Jesus was born naked."

"But He wasn't wearing spike heels," Leo said, stomping away.

On the ensuing kickoff we maintained possession and began grinding into them with short bruising runs, our characteristic style of attack. Then disaster struck. Changing speed and direction in an instant, Duke snatched the ball from Edelstein and dodged a tackler, stiff-armed another, and, running left, flipped a pass behind his back to Todd Baker scissoring against the grain. Todd tried to make a move on the hard ground, there was a loud *snap* and he fell over like he had been shot. The game stopped and we edged out from the sideline. Surfer was kneeling beside him with a scared look on his face. Somehow the kneecap had detached itself and floated around to the side of Todd's leg. Players from both teams stood staring at it. The referee walked over and immediately yelled for an ambulance. Todd moaned and clutched his knee and we all walked away.

"If he was a horse, you'd have to shoot him," Sal Gardenia said.

It took half an hour for the paramedics to get Todd off the field and the game under way again. Martin came on as a replacement in the backline and our luck continued as Miami scored on another long break. At halftime we all gathered under the goalposts and the players took water and Delong ranted a little bit, trying to motivate them, but it wasn't the same without Coach Van. I stood for a moment between Duke and Surfer. "What's wrong?"

"We suck," replied Duke.

"It's like a nightmare," said Surfer, "where your legs don't move right and your hands don't work and the ball takes funny little bounces. It's right there in front of me and I can't catch the fucking thing."

The Gardenias met me again on the sideline. "I don't know squat about this game," Sal said, "but it sure looks like your boys are taking the gas pipe."

In the second half Duke and Edelstein made some courageous runs that gave us a little hope, and Surfer's tackling and the impossible spinning height of Steve Delong's kicks had us walking up and down the sideline with clenched fists, screaming encouragement. But then the ball would take another bad bounce, or somebody would make a boneheaded play, and the opposition stuffed us. All we could manage was two penalty kicks and the game ended with Miami on top, 16-6.

They went berserk at the final whistle, jumping all over each other like they had just won the World Series. Our players came off the field in the wavering heat and dropped like stroke victims, falling in the dust without a word. Duke had a huge raspberry on his hip. It bled down the side of his leg, causing him to limp. "I don't know why the fuck I do this, when I could be sitting in a nice dark bar somewhere," he said.

A while later we formed up our second team and trotted out there. The heat quickly took its toll and less than ten minutes into the game, running after a loose ball, I happened to glance over my shoulder and saw three players sitting in the middle of the field and more than half a dozen walking in the general direction of the play. It looked like geriatric football. Sporadic Violence Bob punched somebody and then just seemed to lose interest. Under the goalposts Josh was vomiting and one of their players had neglected to take his sunglasses off and was scurrying around like some sort of spastic movie star. Both teams tried their level best not to score, handing the ball back and forth, and the game took on the ferocity of lawn bowling.

Special Ed gathered us together at halftime for an inspirational talk. Some players gulped at the water jugs and the rest lay down in the stiff grass with their arms across their faces to block out the sun.

"They put their pants on one leg at a time, just like we do," said Special Ed, unfazed by the heat. "Winning isn't everything, it's the only thing. And the only thing we have to fear is fear itself. Remember boys—we've forgotten more rugby than they'll ever know."

Josh looked up from the ground. "Shut up, Ed. You're using my air."

"But we're getting lambasted out there," cried Special Ed, pronouncing it wrong.

"It's *lambasted,*" I said. "A lamb bastard is a poor little goat who never had a father."

Nothing much happened in the second half. We pushed against them and ran in circles and they did the same. The final score was 0-0. "I should have tried that dropkick," said Special Ed, frowning as we came off the field. "The vector was perfect."

Surfer walked over and handed me some water. "What the hell

was Special Ed doing out there?" he said. "He puts the ball up, and there's nobody around. He looks like he's throwing it to the ghost."

"He has top secret clearance," I said. "So everything he does is shrouded in mystery."

One of our vans, loaded with most of the players from the first game, left for the motel. Sal and Leo walked by on their way to the parking lot and when he saw me, Leo held his nose. "Phew. You guys stunk," he said.

Sal enlightened him. "They're just the scrubs, whaddaya expect?"

After they left, I spotted Todd on the far side of the field, sitting by himself with a canvas brace wrapped around his bad knee. On the ground beside him was a pair of crutches. "I need major surgery on my ACL," he said when I got over to him. "And the sooner the better." Todd shaded his eyes and looked over the deserted rugby field, each blade of grass glowing in the afternoon sun. "The next time you see this good old boy, he'll be wearing a tuxedo."

I helped him up and handed the crutches to him. "I'll tell you something else for nothing, Joe," he said. "Know that broad Sherri Hogg? I had her out to my place for a little cattle drive the night before Mike Melendez nailed her. She tore her back up on the carpet. I woke up in the morning and gave myself a pretty good fright."

"You gotta tell Mike's lawyer about that," I said.

Todd spit between his teeth. "Not a chance," he said. "I'm getting married pretty soon and they could make me swear on a warehouse of remaindered Bibles and I wouldn't tell anybody what I just told you."

Before he limped off to his car, Todd took a final look over his shoulder at the two sets of goalposts and the empty field. "I've never been more alive than when I was out there. Never been happier," he said. "I loved it. I really did."

Back at the Thunderbird everyone was in a foul mood. Our

undefeated streak had been broken and the maids who cleaned our rooms had stolen some cash here and there and a gold chain that belonged to Tony Gardenia. I took a shower and changed my clothes. When I came out to the pool, they were doing some heavy drinking, and the faces arranged around the fetid green water were grim and blanched from the heat. No one seemed interested in food until Edelstein and Surfer emerged from the room and the three of us wandered down the strip for some tacos. When we returned it was getting dark.

"That fucking referee cost us the game," said Delong, putting down beers and spitting tobacco juice into the pool. "He's got something coming and it ain't another birthday."

"Quit your whining," said Surfer. "We lost, and that's it."

Delong squinted up at him for a moment. "Some of us lost the game. Those who ain't got no balls."

One of the maids, a young black girl, crossed the parking lot to the office. "There she is," said Whizzer. "There's the little nigger stole six dollars from me."

"I want my chain back," said Tony Gardenia.

The grumbling spread. I leaned against the fence, staring over the dirty pool deck, and watched something take hold of the group and distill it into a mob of would-be vigilantes. Duke Ritter had to stand up, weary on his feet, and with Edelstein beside him like his sergeant-at-arms and then Surfer and Martin and me up there, we disarmed the situation. "She didn't do anything, you bunch of drunks," Duke said. "She's just a kid. Whizzer—you probably spent that money last night and don't remember. So shut the fuck up and drink your beer."

The crowd settled back down. Surfer and I went inside to watch the news and then came back out. Mischief was in the air. "I hate that palm tree," said Josh, eyeing the only one on the lot. "Me too," said Tony Gardenia. "I hate 'em all."

Josh went to his room to get the Green and Tony Gardenia crept over to the office to make sure the security guard was passed out in his usual spot. Josh got to work hacking at the base of the palm tree, making little progress since the Green was as sharp as a pair of nail clippers.

"Bring it down," said Delong in a hoarse whisper. "Cut that fucker right down."

Leo Gardenia wanted to help so he climbed the scaly trunk of the palm tree in his flannel shirt and bermudas and began swinging back and forth in a pendulum motion, weakening the trunk. The fall of the ax resounded in the silent night air and Leo swayed against a sky filled with stars. After a fair amount of Josh's hacking and Leo's swinging the tree gave way with a loud crack, sending Leo twenty or thirty feet through the air, with the startled Gardenia and the palm tree landing in the pool. Leo swam to the edge and pulled himself out, dripping with slime. The palm tree stood upside down like a stalk of celery in a giant green drink.

"Florida's overrated," said Sal Gardenia, settling back down with his cocktail. "There's really nothing here except assholes and oranges."

15

Maxine invited me to lunch and we met at a new outdoor café on the beach called Hero's. Taking a table beneath one of the huge red umbrellas, I perused a menu filled with avocado quiche and other airy dishes that make me want to go out for pizza afterward. Maxine removed a small mirror from her bag and applied fresh lipstick. She was wearing a raw silk suit that picked up the violet in her eyes and her auburn hair, tied with a ribbon, fell in a thick shiny ream across the nape of her neck. Maxine smiled at me as she closed her compact, crossed her clean bare legs, and then looked off at the tumbling surf.

"I'm leaving the paper," she said.

I raised the menu and pretended to study it. "Great. When do we quit this hellhole?"

"You're not going anywhere. I'm the one that's leaving."

A waiter came and stood beside the table. "Gin and tonic," I said, handing him the menu. I placed my hands about a foot apart. "Big one." Maxine ordered an iced tea. When the waiter departed, my cool indifference lasted about twenty seconds before I dropped to my knees in front of Maxine's chair and bawled into her lap. "Don't go. Don't leave me here all alone."

Maxine giggled, pushing me away, while her glance darted among the nearby tables. "Dolan—cut that out. Get up."

Rising halfway to my feet, I came level with Maxine's narrowed eyes—her arms folded, smirking at my antics—and then I grabbed a spoon from the place setting and held it against her throat. "Ha-ha-ha. If I can't have you, nobody will! Do you hear me? I won't be made a fool of like this. Your only mistake was taking me lightly. You'll soon see that, my dear!"

Maxine lowered her chin and stared at me. "Joe," she said in her editor's voice, "sit down."

I went back to my seat. Around us, mouths hung open, forks of pâté and bean salad were suspended in midair, and the general clatter and conversation of the lunch hour had evaporated. "Rehearsal," I announced, waving them back to their food. "We're in a bad play."

Maxine was composed and lovely. "I'm going to kill you," she said through her teeth.

"Kill me? Why bother."

The waiter brought our drinks. Talk resumed at the other tables and Maxine reached over and clasped me by the wrist. "I'm going back to New York," she said. "My ex-sister-in-law is going to lease me some space uptown and I'm starting my own literary magazine. That's what I set out to do and I'm not waiting any longer. I'm doing it."

"You're quitting the newspaper business, just like that," I said.

Maxine leaned back in her chair, stirring the ice in her glass with a long paper straw. "Joe, the hardest kind of respect to earn," she said, "is respect for what you *might* do. I've always wanted to be a real editor—discovering new writers, shaping their talent, publishing the kind of work that stands up over time. Not something that lasts for a day—but something that will be read for generations. I'm not going to line any more birdcages."

"Tweet-tweet," I said.

She looked out to sea. In the distance, tiny sails glided across a smooth blue plain. "When I was first married, I thought my husband was God—" she smiled to herself "—and now I'm an atheist. I'm not waiting for someone to save me anymore, Joe. The truth is, most of these magazines end up dead in two, three years. Can I do it? I think I can. And if not, so what? I just woke up one day and said, what do I really have to lose?"

"Me, for instance."

"You're on your own now. I think you realize that already," said Maxine. "Limited time, limited energy—that's life. No apprenticeship is going to last forever."

In high school I had a hockey coach named Mr. Parker, very fast on his skates, who said, "Excel at *something*. Mediocrity really irritates me, and if you're going anywhere, it should irritate you, too." He never wore pads skating with us—just his skates, gloves, and a stick—and he didn't need to. Nobody could touch him. He floated over the ice, went left or right, backward and sideways on a cushion of air. It was the first time I had ever seen ability like that coupled with the will to make the most of it. Now I was seeing it again.

Maxine smiled at me. "I'm going to miss you, Joe. You always made me laugh."

"Oh, so I amuse you. You find me laughable. My efforts are somehow humorous in your eyes."

Our food came to the table: gazpacho for Maxine and a tiny plate of linguine with pesto sauce. "Anything else?" the waiter asked. His hair was permed and he wore a pair of tortoiseshell eyeglasses.

"Yeah. Another linguini," I said.

The waiter smiled and went away. "Queer as a football bat," I said.

"You know, someone else in the newsroom thinks your work is pretty good," said Maxine. "Guess who?"

"The kid who empties the wastebaskets."

Maxine's ponytail swung back and forth. "Walter Dzioba."

"A dipshit from the word go," I said. "Go!"

"Walter was at my house on the morning your story about Elvis came out and it was the first thing he looked at. 'That kid is going to be a top-notch observational journalist,' he said. 'A Hemingway or Michael Herr. All he needs is a kick in the ass.' I almost fell out of bed."

"Spare me the details," I replied. "I don't need to hear about Dzioba burning holes in your sheets with his cigar."

"That's very high minded coming from a guy who did Shirley Kimball," said Maxine. She laughed out loud. "In the parking lot of a Chinese restaurant, no less."

"How did—who told you that?"

Maxine smirked. "I have my sources."

Again I heard Shirley's breathless gasps in my ear, the whispered profanity, and then someone was looking in at us through the window. Shirley's feet pounded against the upholstery and kicked at the ceiling and I glanced up a second time at the retreating figure, his hair oiled, cigar smoke swirling in his wake. Dzioba.

"Are you taking good old Wally to New York with you?" I asked.

"No. He's staying here. As editor."

I threw my napkin in the air. "You're kidding."

"It's only temporary," Maxine said. "As soon as he wins the Pulitzer, he'll be gone to Washington or Miami. Until then, you might learn something."

"Like what?"

"Straight reporting. Walter's very good at it. Let's be honest: yours isn't so hot."

"You can teach me what I need to know."

Maxine shook her head. Her eyes grew wide and, for a moment, blurred with tears. "Not anymore, Joe. I'm not tough enough on you. That's what happens when you love someone."

We avoided each other's gaze. An old brown poison flew through my system and I wanted to get up and dash between the tables and umbrellas over the whitened strip of beach and into the ocean. Maxine was gone, disappeared into the gaping darkness that had swallowed up everyone else I had ever loved or cared about. I had an uncle who used to pray for the souls of old movie actors: Cowboy Bob Steele, Adolphe Menjou, Lillian Gish. He would doze off in front of the late show, saying Hail Marys for people he had never met, black and white images that had flickered across his early life and then vanished. Why not pray for them, he would say, we're all gonna end up like that.

"Take this one piece of advice from me, Joe. Never settle for less than what you really want," said Maxine, holding my gaze with her soft gray eyes. "Don't ever compromise for second best in life."

A minor commotion erupted on the far side of the dining area when Elvis, in a terry-cloth beach jacket and nubbled swimsuit, came swiveling between the tables. He was with Tina, the barmaid from Saxophone Joe's. She had on a black gauze skirt, slit to the hip, and a strapless bikini top made of black leather. Her hair was arranged in a wild jungle of glistening black curls. Heads were turning everywhere, a water glass was upset—someone cursed—and murmuring followed the couple to where we were sitting.

"Joe, how's it going?" Elvis asked. We shook hands and he peeked over his sunglasses at Maxine. "Howdy, ma'am."

I stood up. "Maxine, this is my friend Elvis. And this is Tina."

Maxine extended her hand. "It's nice to finally meet you," she said, beaming at Elvis. He grasped the tips of her fingers and they looked into each other's eyes. "Same here, little lady," he replied.

"I'm hungry," Tina said. She pouted, swinging a tiny beaded handbag, one leg tanned and naked to the hip. Sleeping with her seemed like something I had read once in a book, not something I had actually done. In his beach jacket and shades, the lock of hair dangling on his forehead, Elvis looked like a movie still, frozen and perfect. Maxine was lost in schoolgirl fantasies with a rock 'n' roll backbeat, grinning at her teen idol sprung to life. Under the blazing sun the three of them were trapped at an intersection of present and past, evaporating and dried into memory. If I swung a hammer at it, the whole picture would have shattered into a million pieces.

"I said: *I'm hungry,"* repeated Tina.

Elvis straightened up and rubbed his washboard stomach. "Of course you are, honey. I could eat a horse myself and by the looks of this-here place, I probably will. Wonder if they got any fried chicken? Chicken and gravy and mashed potatoes." He hugged Tina against his side. "There's a place in Mississippi you can buy yourself a bucket of bones for a dollar—a pile of chicken bones stripped once for sandwiches. We'd sit around with beer and the jukebox playing, gnaw the skin and the little pieces of meat, and have a regular ol' party."

"I think we can get a bucket of filet mignon bones for about thirty bucks," I said. "We can sit around with some domestic champagne and a string quartet, chew them bones, and have us a regular ol' heartburn."

Maxine laughed. Elvis slapped me on the shoulder and said, "We still on for the weekend? Me and my band are all set."

"What band?" I asked.

"We call ourselves the Aspiring Valentinos," said Elvis.

Maxine looked at me funny. "We're trying to raise some money for Mike Melendez's legal fund," I said.

"I'm taking the night off work to go," said Tina. She danced a few steps between the tables. "A lot of my girlfriends are going. It'll be a real hoot."

"A hoot," I said to Maxine.

"Joe—I think you're gonna have a good-size crowd there Sat-urday night," said Elvis, leaning toward me. "We been putting up handbills and announcing it every night at Saxophone Joe's—two-dollar cover charge and a buck a beer." He flipped his hair into place. "This boy's gonna make you enough money to pay a whole truckload of law-yers."

A table opened up on the other side and Tina hailed the maître d', started in that direction, and then turned back to us, one hip thrown out, her curls scattered on her lean brown shoulders. "Elvis," she declared. "I'm about to *die* if I don't get something to eat."

"Be there in a minute, darlin'," he said.

Tina made a loud sigh, turned on her heel and went toward the maître d' who smiled with his top teeth and held out a chair for her. Several male diners tracked the agreeable motion of her rear end. For a moment no one spoke, and it was quiet except for the rattle of plates and the waves slipping onto the beach.

"I never met a pretty girl had a lick of patience, bar none," Elvis said to us. "They're used to having what they want right away, and that takes half the fun out of life, now don't it?"

"Not to mention half the money out of your wallet," I said, and Elvis laughed.

"Lunch is gonna be on Tina, matter of fact," he said. "All I'm making these days is music."

Maxine touched me on the arm. "Joe—" she said, with a quick shift of her eyes.

Hulic Rasterree had arrived and taken a table not far from us. He was accompanied by a bald man in a pin-striped suit who wore a diamond ring the size of a golf ball and an expression that said he didn't want to hear what he was being made to listen to. Rasterree was bent forward over the table, his yellow eyebrows knit together, talking in a low voice and searching the other man's face for a sign of agreement or sympathy.

"That's Bob Rosenthal he's with," said Maxine. "The state attorney general."

Elvis looked over. "Hey, ain't that blond feller the one sent me to the hospital? I'm gonna go over and tell him everything's worked out all right," he said, and before I could speak Elvis was standing beside Rasterree's chair, grinning at him. The district attorney checked himself and turned to acknowledge the intrusion. "What can I do for you?" he asked in a tight voice.

"Nothing you ain't done already," said Elvis. In his swimsuit and sunglasses, framed against a panoramic blue sky, he was larger than life—a walking, talking bit of Americana. "You put me in the hospital a while back, remember? The doctors there thought I was a car salesman or something. Turns out they were wrong. I'm a damned singer! Joe there—" he pointed to me, gushing "—Joe rode out on the hood of this other feller's Cadillac and suddenly it came to me who I was and what I'm supposed to be doing. Nothing can stop me after what Joe did and I just wanted to thank you for trying to help me and all."

Still grinning, Elvis loomed above the two pencil pushers. Rosenthal was mystified. His mouth was open, displaying two even rows of capped teeth. Worry lines began on his forehead and ran to the peak of his bald head, turning crimson in the afternoon sun. He stared at Elvis—tall, lean, and outrageously familiar—and over at Rasterree and then back again at Elvis.

"Maybe you should do something," Maxine said to me.

I kept my eyes on Elvis. "Let him talk," I said. "He's doing fine."

"I'm playing a gig Saturday night. If y'all are free, come by the American Legion around eight," continued Elvis. "We're gonna help Mike Melendez with his legal bills on that rape charge. Joe told me you dropped it to keep things out of the paper. That was pretty smart thinking. The way I hear it, Mike didn't rape anybody."

Rasterree struggled to contain himself. "Can't you see we're having a private conversation?" he asked, gripping the edge of the table. His index finger shook when he pointed at Rosenthal with it. "This is the attorney general for the state of Florida."

Elvis pivoted and stuck out his hand and Rosenthal shook it. The attorney general looked stunned. "The top dog," said Elvis.

He leaned toward Rosenthal, still grasping his hand. "I'm beholden to you and your man here for burying that criminal trespass charge against me. Joe said y'all had enough bad publicity lately to last a lifetime."

"Get out of here," Rasterree said in a furious whisper.

"Do you have a camera with you?" I asked Maxine. She rummaged in her pocketbook and handed me an old .35 millimeter loaded with black and white film. "Photo opportunity coming up," I said.

Rosenthal was now gazing at Elvis with keen interest. "Son—did you say Mr. Rasterree has been dropping or altering charges in agreements made outside the courtroom?" he asked. "That he made deals, or at least offered deals, to the newspaper?"

"As sure as I'm standing here," replied Elvis. "Ain't that the damnedest thing you ever heard? I'm obliged to him."

Rosenthal rose to his feet. "Thank you, son," he said. Then he spoke to Rasterree. "This lunch is over. There's not a thing I can or will do for you, Hulic. You can simply forget all about reelection. You'll be lucky to stay out of prison. Very lucky."

"You're going to believe this—this psychotic hillbilly?" blustered Rasterree. "He just came back from the goddamned funny farm. Nothing he says is ever going to be admissable."

"You're forgetting something. I went to the University of Tennessee," said Rosenthal. He tugged at his lapels to straighten his jacket and had difficulty concealing a smile. "They love ol' Elvis in Tennessee."

Rasterree, twisted around in his chair, watched the attorney general make his way toward the parking lot. He righted himself after a moment and drooped over the table. The expression on a man's face as his life drops its last stitch and comes unraveled isn't easy to look at, even when it's a prick like Rasterree. Elvis noticed and said, "Hey, come on, man. Things ain't so bad. At least you won't have to wear a suit every day."

A shriek erupted in the district attorney's throat and he leapt at Elvis, swinging his fist. At that very moment I raised the camera and began clicking the shutter as they wrestled between the tables, plates crashing to the ground. Women began squealing; the whole restaurant was in an uproar. For a second I thought I saw Pedro Sanchez in the viewfinder, his pale smiling face at one of the tables, saluting me with a shrimp fork. I took a few more pictures of the action, and when I swung around again, he was gone.

"Maybe you should break it up," Maxine said.

"Not yet," I said. "Elvis is getting some real good shots in."

The maître d', our waiter, and some of the other diners grabbed Rasterree and threw him aside. Then they pulled Elvis to his feet and dusted him off. "Nobody minds watching a lawyer get beat up," someone said.

"I think we got a page one right there," I said, giving the camera back to Maxine. She strung her arm through mine. "I'm going to miss working with you, Joe. If there's no news to report, you just make some."

Early Saturday night, under a fair sky, Elvis drove up to the Legion hall in a van with the Aspiring Valentinos. Decked out in his leather jumpsuit, which had been cleaned and refringed for the occasion, he stood looking at the soft evening light spreading itself beyond the tree line. Elvis leaned back, grasping his hips, and took in a great draught of air scented with pine needles and brine.

"Here I am," he declared. "Ready to rock."

While we were unloading the gear Elvis told me he didn't want to press any charges against Hulic Rasterree. "I'm a peace-loving man," he explained, struggling through the door of the Legion hall with his guitar and a snare drum. "Ol' Tina sure was impressed, though. We had ourselves a grand time until she lost the keys to the handcuffs. Couldn't get those damned things off to save my ownsef."

It was six o'clock and Roger was behind the bar filling his coolers with beer, cracking rolls of quarters and dimes into the cash register, and slicing fruit. He smiled at me and said, "It's gonna be a great night, Joe."

The entire room had been washed with oil soap and all the tables and chairs were stacked up, making a big dance floor. Up on stage, the Aspiring Valentinos uncoiled wires and plugged in amplifiers, twanging their guitars. I recognized the drummer and bass player from one of the bands that played at Saxophone Joe's. They were good. Together with Elvis they would form a genuine rock 'n' roll band.

At the front door, Josh was setting up a table and cash box. He was wearing a bright yellow African dashiki that fit him like a tent.

"Toss out anyone who gets unruly," I said to him. "Including yourself."

Josh tried to look mean. "I kill people for money," he said in a slow accented voice. "But you—you are my best friend. I kill you for free."

Surfer ran up, carrying something made of wood and plastic in a big box. "Joe! Joe! Look, Joe. I bought an ant farm," he said. "They're carpenter ants! And carpenters make thirty dollars an hour. They can build us a new porch." I was standing there glassy-eyed and Surfer said, "There's two thousand of them, and I just let them all loose so they can get up in the rafters and practice."

"An ant farm?" I asked.

"Shut up," Surfer said. He took the contraption out of the box and set it on Josh's table. "What an idiot. It's not an ant farm. This is much more practical. It's a Beer Blaster."

The device had a series of chambers and tubes that allowed you to fill it with beer and drink huge amounts in one swallow by releasing the pressure with a valve. Josh grabbed two bottles of beer from Roger at the bar and loaded one into the Beer Blaster for a demonstration. The golden liquid wound through the chambers and tubes, then Josh took the clear plastic hose and held it between his teeth. He loosened the valve and twelve ounces of beer disappeared into his stomach with only a tiny hissing sound.

"That's about as useful as a giraffe with a short neck," I said. "Where did you get that ridiculous thing?"

"Invented it myself," replied Surfer. "The faster people drink—and the more they drink—the more money we make tonight. Greed is the mother of invention. I wasn't about to let my engineering degree go to waste."

"He's a genius," Josh said, when he had caught his breath. "I'm putting myself in charge of marketing. If necessary, I will travel around the country giving seminars on the Beer Blaster. I *know* we can sell it on late-night tee vee."

"Wanna try it?" Surfer asked me.

"No thanks. I haven't finished saving up for my liver transplant."

Martin and Edelstein came in, and Iain and Sean Caffrey and their families. Lila Caffrey gave her son Bobby a five-dollar bill and watched in amazement as he sauntered over and said hello to Roger at the bar, made change, bought a soda, and crossed the empty dance floor to the pinball machine.

"A chip off the old block," Iain said.

Lila wrinkled her sunburnt nose at him. "In your dreams," she said. "That boy is never going to play rugby and he's not going to spend half his life in bars."

"What's wrong with playing rugby?" Iain asked.

As if on cue, an unshaven Duke Ritter stepped through the door, in a wrinkled polo shirt and sporting a black eye. "Howdy," he said. Lila glared triumphantly at us and drew her sister-in-law and the other three kids toward the stage to look at the musical instruments.

"I get that reaction a lot," said Duke.

"You may not be the perfect role model as far as Lila is concerned, but we all want to be like you," I said. "You're an inspiration."

"And the poster boy for a number of fine rehabilitation facilities," said Edelstein.

Martin Campesi spoke up. "Todd's getting married. He and Brittany were sailing on her father's boat and the question just popped out."

I covered my eyes. "And he said yes?"

"Wrong answer," said Surfer.

"His life is over," Iain said. He nudged his brother and called to Roger behind the bar with two fingers held up. "Todd has just condemned himself to a life of house arrest."

Sean Caffrey agreed. "First you have to suffer the indignity of getting married in front of everybody like that, and then they start beating you at cards," he said. "It's downright humiliating."

Duke and Martin followed them to the bar and ordered drinks. Edelstein came up beside me and said, "I talked to Mike this morning. He's too embarrassed to come by but he wanted y'all to know he appreciates the help. He owes his lawyer a lot of money."

"How much?"

"Almost three grand. Since the charges have been dropped, he just wants to pay up and get out of here. He's going back to Trinidad next Saturday."

"He's gonna miss the championship," I said.

Edelstein pursed his lips. "Mike doesn't give a rat's ass about that," he said. "Can you blame him?"

By eight o'clock a lot of the rugby crowd, including Coach Van, had arrived. Elvis signalled that the band was almost ready. At the door, Lawyer and Mrs. Timmons and then Nate Fleischer and his small pretty wife were talking with Josh and exchanging money. The appearance of the two black couples attracted several awkward stares and some whispering along the far wall and at the bar.

I rushed over to greet them. "Hey—thanks for coming," I said, shaking hands with Nate Fleischer.

He grinned, and introduced his wife, Sophie. She was the color of India ink and just as small-boned and neat as her husband. "I'm thrilled," said Sophie. Her hand was cool to the touch. "He never takes me anywhere."

"Not true—I take you to all my bowling nights," joked Fleischer, throwing his arm around her shoulder. "And we went to the Keys for our anniversary."

"Four years ago," said Sophie, smiling at her husband and then looking at me. "Big deal."

Lawyer Timmons shook my hand and Mrs. Timmons bent and kissed me on the cheek. "I think it's wonderful you and your friends helping Michael like this," she said. "Isn't that right, Aloysius?"

"Since it's my fee we're talking about, I thought I'd at least come down and buy a few drinks," said Timmons, herding us to the bar.

"Light beer for me," Fleischer called after him. He touched my elbow. "No charges at all against Mike Melendez in the Batem case. We ruled it self-defense. He's innocent."

As the house began to fill up, Elvis became more energetic and animated. He warbled little pieces of songs and jumped on and off the stage adjusting the amplifiers and his guitar. "I'm as nervous as a whore in church," he said to me. "But it's nice to see a good crowd coming in."

Tina and her friends were at the door paying Josh and then giggling as he demonstrated the Beer Blaster. "Here's some of the women we need," said Elvis.

"I like women," Surfer said, "and glasses of beer."

"You're gonna see plenty tonight," Elvis assured him.

"Good, 'cause lately I couldn't get the dog to play with me if I tied a pork chop around my neck," Surfer said. "Somebody must've got me with the ugly dust when I wasn't looking."

Tina and her friends, in sheer dresses and with their hair teased and sprayed into marvelous wild shapes, made a beeline for Elvis. "Maybe I should take up the guitar," said Surfer.

The music started and out came that deep resonant voice: Elvis was singing "Town without Pity" and he owned the room. Nate Fleischer held his beer like a microphone, tapping his foot. At the pinball machine, Bobby Caffrey lost track of the ball in play, staring with his mouth open. Conversations tapered off and the women gazed at the King in action, the lock of hair dangling on his forehead, belting one out. More people crowded through the door. I took a long drink, finishing the beer Lawyer Timmons had given me, and Surfer leaned over and said, "That's pure fucking magic."

I wanted another beer. To handle the expected crowd, Roger had the woman with the enormous breasts and dyed blond hair behind the bar with him. "Hey, sweetie. You were in here with that crazy salesman, weren't you?" she asked.

"Pedro Sanchez," I said.

She opened a bottle with a quick snap of the wrist and presented it to me, shaking her head. "It's too bad," she said. "I kinda liked him."

"Why—what happened?" I asked, although suddenly I knew.

"He died a few days ago. Heart attack." The barmaid imitated a tree falling with the motion of her arm. "Dead before he hit the ground."

"Sanchez is dead?"

"Dead as all get-out," the barmaid said. "They buried him in that cemetery out near the air force base. Some undertaker friend of his took care of the whole thing, which is unusual. Those guys wouldn't bury their own mothers for free."

The sound in the room all passed away. Then I could hear the bubbles sizzling in my glass. Pedro Sanchez wasn't airborne any more. He was locked in a wooden box under six feet of sand. Screaming into the big blue empty. But he had departed owing the federal government a hundred and sixty-nine thousand dollars in back taxes and his friend Rollo the price of a headstone, plot, and funeral. Now I understood what he meant about the pyramids of tomato puree. They weren't important. Dying was just another way for Sanchez to illustrate that.

The band struck up and Elvis leaned into the microphone and sang the opening lines of "Not Fade Away." Everything—the dance floor, the rugby players, the smell of oil soap and beer, and the electric guitars—came roaring back.

"You're cute," the huge barmaid said. "I like you." She bent over, showing me half of her massive bosom, a dark line of cleavage that looked like the entrance to a mine. "Think about me," she said.

"Huh?"

She stared into my eyes, heaving her breasts. "Just think about me."

I was trying not to. Turning from the bar, I nearly collided with Loretta, who stood holding a glass of beer. "Hi, Joe," she said. "How are you?"

"What are you doing here?"

Loretta gestured toward the other side of the room. "I came with some people from work," she said. "To help the cause." Her green eyes were fixed on mine and she smiled and tossed her hair.

"I miss you," I said, touching her cheek with my fingertips.

"Too late," said Loretta.

"Let me tell you anyway. I miss you like—like when you're a kid and it's June and school just got out and it's a beautiful warm breezy day and you're walking along enjoying it all and wishing you had enough money for an ice cream, the first of the season, and suddenly you find a dollar bill on the sidewalk—which is enough for two ice creams—and you go running to your best friend's house to share your absolutely incredible ice cream joy. That's how I miss you."

Loretta pressed my arm and laughed, exposing her throat and all her pretty white teeth. "Dolan," she said. "You're such a bull-shitter."

"This time, though, it's like when the boy cried 'wolf' and it was really there," I said, trying to look angelic and seductive at the same time.

Loretta gazed at me for a long moment. "I wonder what kind of women you're going out with now—who they all are," she said. "They're probably dumb as stumps and have nothing to say. There's not many out there like me. But there's not many out there like you, either."

"Like what?"

"First of all, your body. Your Irish movie star face. Then there's your creativity. Not many men have that side, the creative side."

"Neat," I said. "Who were we talking about again?"

We were standing on the edge of the dance floor, facing the stage, and while Elvis crooned and his fans stamped their feet and whistled, I felt the warm familiar curve of Loretta's body against mine. Falling in love with her after she was gone wasn't the smartest thing I had ever done, like charging into a dark room, but there were some sharp glittering moments in our relationship. Like Sanchez said, what more is life, really, than a collection of moments: some you remember and some you'd rather forget.

I made a noise in my throat. "What?" asked Loretta, glancing at me.

"Remember that time on the living room floor you started crying?"

Loretta looked into my eyes. "I just realized you didn't love me.

I wanted to keep you close and I knew I never could."

The music vibrated along the dance floor, coming up through the soles of my sneakers. Tina and her friends were gyrating in front of the stage and Surfer and Edelstein and some of the other rugby players were dancing among them, carrying bottles of beer. Lawyer Timmons was talking to Van Valkenburg and, on the other side of the room, Nate Fleischer played pinball with Bobby Caffrey while the women—Mrs. Timmons, Sophie Fleischer, and Lila Caffrey —stood immersed in conversation.

"Are you sticking around for a while?" I asked.

"Not much longer," said Loretta. "I have a date."

"With who?"

Loretta made a face and glanced away. "Rob Jackson."

"Dr. Jackson—the asshole? You're kidding."

"Rob is nice to me," said Loretta. "He takes me places."

"I took you to rugby games. Out for oysters. To all the bean suppers Saint Michael's ever had. I can't believe this. Isn't there like a warranty period, six months or something, where you have to check with me before you go out with anyone? Rob Jackson is a violation. I'm going to have to veto that one, and you'll have to pay a hefty fine."

Loretta smiled and kissed me on the cheek. "You're nuts," she said. "Take care of yourself, Joe."

I said "Adios" as Loretta slipped through the crowd and it also meant farewell to her soft beauty and the unique qualities of forbearance and concentrated interest she brought to everything I ever said, everything I did, all I wanted to be. She was a friend in the abolute sense, a *compañero,* and that, of course, had changed.

Surfer came up, drenched with sweat, and he pounded on the bar and sent perspiration flying from the ends of his hair. He glanced over his shoulder at Loretta. "Let's have a sex reunion and all swap. Once, when Van was taping me up, he touched my testicles and that's not right in an organized program. Want some firewater? I'm getting drunk." He ordered some bourbon and turned his back to the bar, leaning on his elbows. "That little blond with Tina is driving me crazy," he said, indicating the spot on the dance floor where a girl about nineteen was spinning in a circle while she made flapping motions with her arms. Other men and most of the women were glancing at her bountiful chest as it leaped beneath her tube top. We watched this going on and I said, "A lot of girls are concerned about the size of their breasts."

"Then again, so am I," said Surfer.

He took the glasses of bourbon from Roger and handed one to me. "I've gone from the pork chop to wearing the whole pig," Surfer said. "Sex is out of the question at this point. I told the blond that all she had to do is shake it a few times. It won't take very long."

"My advice is to let her come to you," I said. "You can't chase them."

Martin Campesi leaned over from a separate conversation and said, "That strategy has led to a lot of lonely nights of masturbation for me."

Surfer drained the bourbon and plunged back onto the dance floor, catching the little blond in his arms and flailing his legs in every direction.

At the end of the bar, Van Valkenburg, solid and menacing with that torch of white hair, jerked his head sideways at a remark made by Martin Campesi. "Yeah, I'm a fanatic," he said, jabbing at Martin with his index finger. "But if there weren't any fanatics—in sport, in government, in business—a lot of other people would *never* reach their potential."

"Rugby's just a bloody game, Van," insisted Martin.

Van Valkenburg stared down at the other man's face and nodded his head. "Life is a game," he said. "Work is a game. Politics is a game. You're born playing and you die playing." He moved away from the bar. "Rugby is the model for all games. You should know that. You're a fucking kiwi, aren't you?"

Martin looked after the big man. "There's something wrong with him," he said. "I was just telling my psychiatrist that the other day."

I went to the door to check on Josh and the profits. Special Ed was helping him, dressed in a black flight suit and aviator sunglasses. "How're we doing?" I asked.

Josh waved the cash box in the air. "At this rate, Mike can knock over a liquor store and gun down a couple of old ladies and we might have enough to cover it," he said.

"Tell me when we hit aggravated assault or kidnapping," I said. "Then we'll really be doing well."

Hands clasped behind his back, Special Ed scanned the crowd for security risks and then directed the blank green orbs of his sunglasses toward me. "I need to make a piss call," he said.

"Go ahead. We'll mind the store," I said.

Special Ed hustled to the men's room and Josh got up and made sure he was out of sight. "I'll be at the bar," he said.

Up on stage, Iain Caffrey was playing the piano for an old Jerry Lee Lewis number. The music pounded and the dancers writhed and clung to each other, undulating furiously. Almost everyone was dancing. Scattered among the crowd, rugby players were leaping and spinning and crashing into each other, careless about style, their eyes bright, hollering nonsense.

The front door opened and a gust of warm salty air came in. Behind it was Viv, the waitress from the diner. Her long dark hair arranged over her shoulder, blue eyed, glowing with a smile, she said, "Well, I'm here."

"About time," I said.

Special Ed came back and I excused myself and led Viv on to the dance floor. The Aspiring Valentinos launched into "Sea of Love" and Viv melted into my arms, our blue jeans rubbing together at the knees.

"I'm not much of a dancer," said Viv.

"Oh, don't worry—I'm a great dancer. I was with the ballet at one time. Then there were many, many happy years on Broadway. I've hoofed it across every big room in America."

Viv looked down at the floor and then back into my eyes and I went on. "I'm very light on my feet."

"You can't dance to save your life," said Viv.

"At least a good fraud has pride in his work. What's your excuse?" We laughed and continued shuffling in a tiny arc, one song after the next, talking and then whispering and sometimes nearly shouting as the music rose and fell.

Vivian Fontaine was from a town near Pittsburgh, of an abusive, addicted family—her mother awash in tranquilizers and booze, a father who screamed and broke things and then ran off when she was nine, a brother dead of gunshot wounds. "I moved to Florida for a new start," she said. "Everybody deserves a chance. Why not me? Why shouldn't I be happy?"

Surfer heard that and tried to cut in. "I can't think of a reason," he said, winking at me. His blond hair fell in sweaty ringlets to his shoulders and his face, shiny from dancing, radiated confidence mingled with the air of a pirhana. He smiled at Viv and I held my breath as the bluest eyes south of the Mason-Dixon Line met those of the biggest bullshitter east of the Mississippi.

"You look beautiful tonight. It's great to see you again," Surfer said. He extended his arm. "May I have this dance?"

"No thanks," said Viv, clinging to my side. We moved off while Surfer stood dumbfounded. He held up his hands and stared at them. "Nothing," he said. "It's gone."

"What's with him?" Viv whispered in my ear.

"He's doubting his appeal. It's very traumatic for him."

Viv glanced back at Surfer, frozen on the edge of the dance floor. "Maybe he should try a little sincerity," she said.

We danced close. There was something strange and wondrous in this experience, a palpable quality of merriment that came over the darkened Legion hall. I grasped Viv by the upper back and began kissing her. "Uh-uh. No mashing on the dance floor," she said, giggling at me.

Viv excused herself to go to the ladies' room. The whirling and stomping of those on the dance floor pushed me to the sidelines, close to the lit window of the bar where Roger was opening bottles of beer as fast as he could get them from the cooler. The hefty barmaid caught my eye and again mouthed the words, "Think about me."

I spotted Nate Fleischer and his wife near the exit and hurried over to them. "Fantastic. We had a ball," the detective said. His brown eyes swam a little and he rocked back and forth on his heels, grinning at me. "If I have one more beer, I might do something really embarrassing," he said.

Josh called him over, flourishing the Beer Blaster. With a brief wave, shaking his head, Fleischer refused the invitation. "Not on a bet," he said.

"You're the life of the party," I assured him.

"Nowhere in Scripture does it say you can't have a couple of drinks once in a while," said Fleischer. "God has a sense of humor. Didn't you see me dancing? That proves it."

Lawyer Timmons appeared, holding his wife's coat and guiding her by the elbow though the crowd. "Very enjoyable," he said. "I prefer classical music but that fellow has a lot of enthusiasm."

"Apparently enough to make you sing along with 'The House of the Rising Sun,'" said Mrs. Timmons.

Special Ed ushered them out. On the way back from the ladies' room, Viv was intercepted by Surfer and I watched as he touched her arm and beamed, gesturing toward a quiet corner. Their eyes met and from Surfer's body language and a long history of observing him in action, I knew he was putting out his best lines for the lovely young waitress. They exchanged words, Viv smiled and shook her head, and continued toward me over the oiled parquet floor. Surfer shrugged and cursed under his breath, turning his attention back to Tina and her friends. In that instant I realized that my old roommate and I, for all our similarities and the depth of our friendship, wanted different things out of life. For Surfer, the conquest was what mattered most. He had good looks and enough personality to raise womanizing to an art form. And I was just as afraid as he was of commitment, of rejection, and loss; always wanting to be in control and never too attached to anyone. But I couldn't picture myself going through the motions ten or fifteen years from now, out for a chase I no longer had the speed or desire to engage in. More than that, glimpsing the trust and the promise of real friendship in Viv's eyes, I believed that some things might be worth the risk. Maybe not now, maybe not even with her, but somehow, someday.

We danced another song and Viv had to leave, after promising to stop by the rugby game on her break the following Saturday. Elvis warbled and hummed and snarled, delirious with energy, and the night rattled to its conclusion. Surfer disappeared with the blond from Tina's crowd. The lights came up and Josh handed me the cash box. Then, starting for the exit with an inebriated rumble, wrestling with each other and shouting, most of the rugby players filtered out.

To avoid the provocative stares of the barmaid, I helped Elvis and the band put away their equipment. "We had our mojo working tonight," said Elvis, rolling up the wires to his microphone. He was subdued now, drenched with sweat, and he took a towel from the bar to wipe his face and neck. "It was crazy. We went straight in the air and took the whole place with us."

I rolled a bulky amplifier out to the van and came back inside. Roger gave me seven hundred dollars, a third of his liquor sales for the evening, and I counted out two hundred and handed it to Elvis.

"No way, man," he said. "The gig was free."

"That's okay. Use it for the band."

Elvis took the wad of bills and stuffed it in his pocket. "It'll buy us some gas. We're going on the road. There's a slew of bars prob'ly use a good band." He flipped his hair into place, cocking his chin, the success of the show glowing all around him. "I just want to play my music, man. That's all."

Outside, under the dark curving trunks of the palm trees, Elvis and I stood in silence for a moment, breathing in the warm marshy air and listening to the cars rushing by on Orange Boulevard. "Nothing to do now but hit the road," said Elvis. "Thanks, man. I owe you."

"Get yourself a gold lamé jacket and do it right," I said.

A half smile crept across the singer's lips and he made a sound with his teeth, a tiny note of regret, and then turned with his hands flung out in salute. "So long, Joe," he said.

The thing that bothered me the most, as Elvis walked off to join the Aspiring Valentinos with his guitar slung over his back, was that my life had grown so much and then compartmentalized. With my mother and father dead, there was no one to make sense of it, nobody to really tell it to; and my past—who I had been as a young boy and what I had done—was filling up with darkness.

Beneath the klieg lights on the strip, there was someone in the doorway of the Apollo capsule, his elbow on his knee, supporting his head with one hand. It was Surfer. I parked Duke's car and ran across the lanes to where he squatted in the dust, holding a can of beer, a pink bra strewn between his feet.

"What's going on?" I asked.

Surfer looked into his beer can and then up at me, squinting in the light. "Nothing much," he said. "I was just thinking."

"About what?"

Again he turned his chiseled tanned face up to the light, his gaze clear and blue and calm. Surfer drank some beer and then he said, "I was thinking that I always wanted to be an astronaut. A boom jockey. Ever since I was a little kid." His face was down now, away from me, as he placed the beer can on the ground. "And I never will be."

The brassiere, which I couldn't resist picking up, was silky and light and spread to an imposing size. "A man has to know his limitations," I said.

"That's right," Surfer said. "I've learned to stick to what I do best."

16

The morning of the championship I was up before six, my stomach fluttering as I prowled through the house, into kitchen cabinets and closets staring at nothing, out on the lawn for the newspaper and four or five times to the bathroom, where I stood looking down at the garish blue water in the toilet but couldn't go.

Surfer was asleep across his bed, feet tangled in a blanket, arms thrown up like a man winning a footrace. Tina was beside him wearing his jersey with the number 9 on the back. A sigh escaped from her and she flopped on her stomach, hugging one of the pillows, her dark hair scattered over the sheets. They both remained sleeping, quiet as children, their breaths coming directly after one another in a quick shortened rhythm like toy trains.

With Elvis on the road and probably gone for good, Tina was back in circulation. "Catching the same fish twice is better than having your line go limp," Surfer said.

It was still early when a faint knocking brought me out to the front door. Opening it, I was met by a dissipated Michael Melendez, his gaze cold and sad, moving to the empty space around me and as far along the hallway as he could see. Melendez wore a blue blazer and slacks that hung loosely over his frame. Behind him in the driveway there was a taxi with the engine running.

"I brought you a going-away present," Melendez said, the stench of mothballs clinging to his jacket. He was the one going away, not me. In his hand was the small clay statue of a warrior brandishing a sword. Using a sculptor's knife, Melendez had made abstract cuts that created a fierce but terrified expression, and with his cape furled back and sword raised, the warrior appeared to be fighting for his life.

"He's a Quixote. Like you," explained Melendez, continuing to look at me without any hint of warmth or appreciation.

"But we won," I said.

"Do I look like a winner to you?" asked Melendez. His fatigue was obvious, and he turned his head to look at the neighboring houses before returning to me. "They showed me a way out and I'm running for it. That's the game they always play with us. Scare the nigger. As soon as I bought a white girl a drink, danced with her, kissed her, I was no better than an animal and would be punished like one—by being put in a cage. I should have known, the way everyone was staring at me that night. Waitresses, bartenders, townies—even the rugby players. Even you, man. But it's not your fault." For a moment the veil of hostility dropped from his eyes and we acknowledged each other. "Around here there's a few old, old rules and I broke some of them."

The statuette was light in my hands and I could tell any amount of pressure would snap off the head or the sword. "I'm a racist," I said, surprised at myself. "I guess most people are, to some degree. But that doesn't mean you shouldn't try to be good."

"That's you," replied Melendez. "A lot of other people hate blacks, hate Jews, hate Puerto Ricans and wouldn't have it any other way. Like T-bone. It was a full-time job with him. A smack on the head with a baseball bat was the only way to curb his enthusiasm."

"T-bone was an asshole. Nobody—and I mean nobody—wanted to listen to that shit."

Melendez smiled, and it was cold and humorless. "What about Steve Delong? I heard the things he said about me. Nigger this, nigger that. And I played right beside him." I started to interrupt but Melendez wasn't finished. "Delong says what he says, and just about everyone looks the other way. But what can I do about it? I can't go around assassinating everyone who thinks it's his moral right to treat black-skinned people like they're not really human. Not that I wouldn't enjoy it. After what they did to me, I'd gladly take a baseball bat to every last one of those bastards."

That afternoon our success would depend on Steve Delong's ability to catch the high ball in traffic and on his strong right leg. In my gut I was already praying for him. Because even though Delong was a narrow-minded, tobacco-chewing, racist son of a bitch, he was going to help me get something I wanted. I had no plans to sit out the game. So in a way I was tolerating it, just as society had endorsed every other kind of evil that had crawled in on its belly. We were all acquainted with racists, liars, philanderers, and thieves, hid them in our families, worked and vacationed with them, even loved some of them; otherwise, most of us would be pretty lonely.

"When T-bone went down and didn't get up, it was like finishing a great piece of work," Melendez said. "I felt like I had accomplished something."

There was movement in the house, it sounded like Surfer on his way to the bathroom, and Melendez glanced at his watch and took a step backward. "Well," he said. "I have a flight.

"Could you give this to Mr. Timmons?" he added, handing me a cashier's check. "It's the money I owe him."

Melendez turned and dropped off the stoop, hollow cheeked in profile, with his long yellow wrists dangling from the cuffs of his blazer. "I'm not ever coming back here," he said, and his flat disinterested gaze swept across the modest homes and attached garages and toolsheds like they had been incinerated and were now smoldering in ruins. "It wasn't the America I dreamed about."

Then he left, no good-bye, no nothing, down the walk and into the waiting taxi and gone. His eyes were straight ahead as he sailed by the house. The taxi turned the corner and Melendez disappeared, buried in the past, no more tangible than Douglas Fairbanks Sr. and Myrna Loy and the other movie stars my uncle used to pray for. I pulled the little sword out of the warrior's hand and rolled the check up and stuck it in there.

In the kitchen, Tina was lounging at the counter immersed in the horoscopes printed on the last page of the newspaper. Already the smell of coffee was beginning to circulate and Surfer rattled pots and pans and threw together a vast collection of cartons, jars, measuring spoons, and boxes. He cracked six eggs into a mixing bowl, splashed in some milk, and added salt and pepper. "It's important to start every day with a good breakfast," Surfer said. "Especially those days when you intend to kick some ass."

"If you say so, professor," I replied.

Tina watched Surfer almost ruin the eggs over a flame that was too high. She had relinquished his jersey and was dressed in a cotton sweater and shorts, her hair tousled about her shoulders. "What's with you guys?" she asked, watching me join Surfer in whipping up omelets and homefries and a mountain of toast, arranging them on platters. The activity carried us away and we hustled around the kitchen like two short-order nitwits.

"Do you want any of this?" Surfer asked me. "I'm just making it to stay busy."

"Hell, no," I said. "I can't eat. My stomach is jumping all over the place."

Surfer said "ehh" and continued piling up the food.

"You're acting weird," said Tina. "Nobody's gonna eat all that."

"We're making it for nobody," I agreed, "because nobody's hungry."

Surfer attacked a wad of pancake batter with a wooden spoon. "It takes my mind off the game," he said.

"What game?" asked Tina.

We both stopped and looked at her. "The championship," Surfer said. "It's today."

"Oh, *that,*" Tina said. Her hand went out from the newspaper and she nibbled on a damp wedge of toast. "It's not the Super Series, or whatever. It's just a rugby game. Nobody is gonna be there."

"Well, after nobody has a nice breakfast, nobody can see our game," I said.

Tina was baffled. "You guys are never gonna grow up," she said. The toast drooped in her fingers. "You should get a freaking car. Buy yourselves some new clothes. A decent stereo. There's more to life than rugby, you know."

Surfer and I reacted with horror. "Rugby *is* life," I said.

But Tina was being obstinate, maybe even ready to move on to nasty, and I could tell Surfer's romantic interlude was coming to an end. "You don't make a cent playing rugby," Tina said. "It's just an excuse to get drunk and chase girls. Look at Duke Ritter. Look at the Caffreys. They're practically bums. And so is Van Valkenburg. A forty-year-old man and all I ever see him do is drink beer and talk about rugby. It's ridiculous."

"Come down from your high horse for just a minute," said Surfer. "You're a cocktail waitress. That's not exactly discovering a cure for cancer."

"Take it easy, champ," I said under my breath.

On her feet now, circling the counter, Tina poked Surfer in the chest with the newspaper. "I work hard for my money," she said. "I have a car and my own condo and anything else I want. You're the one who's supposed to be an engineer. Well, you dress like one—a sanitation engineer. Only I'd be surprised if NASA let you take out their garbage."

"I'm sure they let you perform brain surgery at Saxophone Joe's," said Surfer, "after you finish Jell-O wrestling and competing in the wet T-shirt contest."

Tina stormed from the kitchen cursing and muttering, got her things, went past us again and out the front door. At the stove, Surfer ate a handful of fried potatoes. "All she ever talked about was Elvis anyway." He made a snorting sound. "Elvis never played rugby. Not with that hairdo he's got."

We still had a long morning ahead of us. Duke came by to watch *The Three Stooges* and I borrowed his car. "Urgent errand," I said. "I'll be right back."

Winter cast a pall over things at the beach, dimming colors, putting a grit in the air. I drove to the strip and waited my turn to enter Rack 'n' Ride. The long-haired attendant appeared and I ordered a quart of orange juice and a good cigar. "What happened to your Cadillac?" the attendant asked.

"Traded it in," I said. Then I crossed the intracoastal, the water glittering below, dotted with sailboats and other pleasure craft.

After twenty minutes, tooling south on A1A with hardly any traffic, I drove through the gates of the cemetery beside Patrick Air Force Base. The cemetery occupied a slight rise that dropped off a few hundred yards from the roadside, exposing an immense panorama of sea and sky.

Pedro Sanchez was buried in the last row, under a patch of fresh sod that would soon wither in the sandy soil it was laid over. His headstone had two huge polished orbs balanced on top. They were a strange metallic brown and must have weighed several hundred pounds each. It looked like the final resting place of a professional bowler, but with the insignia of the 82nd Airborne and the epitaph: INHALE/EXHALE.

I parked on the narrow white road and got out, my thumb over the top of the orange juice to keep it from spilling. "Fuck the pyramids of tomato puree," I said.

Entombed under six feet of sand, Sanchez was busy yodeling into the big blue empty. Still, he was such an all-out confident son of a bitch, I had to believe he had prevailed in spite of his circumstances. Somewhere, somehow, Pedro Aurelio Garnera Sanchez was kicked back drinking highballs in his rumpled suit, telling profane stories and tales of his bawdiest feats—the most outrageous and modern of the dead.

Beyond the edge of the cemetery I heard the whine of a jet engine, and then a military cargo plane took off and roared overhead. The smell of burning fuel drifted down to me, the afterburn glittering in the sun like gold dust. I waved the quart of orange juice and leapt in the air, bounding over the grass, my shouts obliterated by the echoes of the jet. I felt like the member of a tribe who would slit the throats of another tribe just to get away with their women and a slew of buffalo carcasses. Then, with a pressing urgency in my bladder, I unbuttoned my shorts and watered the bright green sod on Pedro's grave, just like I promised.

From the cemetery I picked up Duke and Surfer and we drove to the fairgrounds. Horses were being exercised on the track and a trainer was rubbing one down in front of the stables. Lila Caffrey and her children stood against the fence watching as the horse, shivering in the cold sunlight, dropped a huge load of manure that spattered the trainer's boots.

"Look, Mom," said one of the kids. "He's pooping."

Surfer vaulted a turnstile that separated the paddock area from the grandstand. "Little masters of the obvious," he said.

Climbing over the fence was like stepping into the ring for a championship fight. Most of the team was assembled beneath the live oaks in the infield, and brooding off to one side was Van Valkenburg. In his faded sweat suit and white hair he looked like a doomed Confederate general. We stopped to lace up our cleats and jogged over: Duke ambling along with a slight limp, grunting at the effort, and Surfer beside him, his jersey looped around his neck like a sweater. The air was glowing, particulated with iridescent specks that might have been specks of souls or souls themselves. Running across that long expanse of grass was like being a kid again, never bored, never tired, in a shower of golden light from a sun that always seemed directly overhead.

Coach Van named the starting team. "Put your jerseys on," he said. Special Ed and Josh and the other substitutes edged away from us and Van Valkenburg spoke as if they weren't even there. "You are going to win or lose on the strength of this talent," he said. "Look around. It might be a good memory and it might not, but you'll remember who you played with."

Jacksonville had arrived in their red and white jerseys and were warming up at the other end of the fairgrounds. They looked big. We spread ourselves out and Steve Delong took us through a series of exercises: high stepping, crossovers, backward running, push-ups and sit-ups and then a good long stretch. Van Valkenburg weaved in and out of the circle we had formed on the thick grass, towering over us like a colossus while we worked our hamstrings loose, evoking that unique combination of hate and love and deep unwarranted fear that good coaches always do.

"Watch for the breakdown point. Stay low and burst onto the ball," said Van. No one else had uttered a word for nearly an hour. "Don't loaf when you think the ball is going the other way. Get it in your heads right now: there won't be any goof-off time. So don't expect any."

Grim faced and sweating, players tied the drawstrings of their shorts, adjusted their jockstraps, and put their mouthpieces in. I remembered the cigar in my pocket and threw it on the ground. "Sometimes a cigar is just a cigar," I said to Surfer.

Soon the referee was blowing his whistle from the middle of the field and the captains ran out there for the coin toss. The rest of us went to the sidelines for some water. During the warm-up, a steady flow of cars had arrived at the fairgrounds and now a good-size crowd lined the field and were scattered across the grandstand. They hollered and whistled and one man waved the Confederate flag. Ross Donleavey shouted something and then came over to the railing with his notebook. "I thought I'd dash off a piece for tomorrow's paper. Something light and funny." He licked his pencil. "Now: do you expect to beat them handily?"

"We expect to beat them like a redheaded stepchild. We want to beat them handily and footily. But in a light, funny way—at the same time depriving them of their manhood and all they hold sacred."

Donleavey looked up with mild alarm. "Oh. Ha-ha. You're joking." He turned over the page of his notebook. "I'm impressed. Rugby is a very physical game. What does your team do to prepare?"

"We bite the heads off live chickens. Then we drink the blood and call on the gods of rugby to help us achieve victory. If that doesn't work, we go down to the strip and throw rocks at late model cars. It's a primitive ritual, but effective."

"No, seriously," said Donleavey. "Does your team have a strategy?'

I leaned forward. "Stomp their guts out. Ride in a swirling rage of death until not one fucking cavalryman is left. Piss on their graves."

The sportswriter looked at me with a pained expression. "Maybe I should talk to someone else," he said.

"You need a real expert," I said, scanning the crowd. I pointed to Josh, who wore a pair of antlers on his head and, re-creating some moment particular to wildlife, gestured to a group of young women. "Try Josh. You don't see many of his elk these days."

Donleavey closed his notebook. "I need a clear explanation of the game," he said. "That's all." I motioned to Josh and he came over. The sportswriter asked, "Can you answer a few questions about rugby?"

Antlers swaying, Josh said, "Hi Mom," speaking into Donleavey's pencil as if it was a microphone.

There was a slight delay when the referee asked for a new ball and Special Ed had to run to his car to get a good one. Surfer wandered over to me. We stood side by side, hands on hips, surveying the opposition. In a tight pack under the goalposts, Jacksonville stared back at us like zombies in a trance. They were a mangy bunch, some of them balding, missing teeth, chopping at the ground with knee-raising steps.

"They look like their genetic pool is only a foot deep," Surfer said.

I studied one of their players for a moment and said, "Jesus Christ, it's Mitch." Lined up twenty yards away was Mitch from the Orlando club, the dirtiest player in the league, bowed legs and cauliflowered ears and the torso of an old-fashioned Hercules. The jersey was unfamiliar but there was no mistaking the blank look on his face. I turned toward Duke, but he had already noticed.

"I see him," Duke said. He spit in the grass. "What a nice surprise."

A new ball came out from the sidelines and it rolled to Mitch's feet and he bent over and picked it up. For a moment he stared at it and then tossed it to the referee who was waiting at midfield.

"It's a rugby ball, Mitch," I said.

"He looks like a caveman discovering fire," Surfer replied. "Not sure what it is, but getting the idea it might be important."

Steve Delong took three quick steps and kicked off, the ball rising in a steep arc. It hovered for a moment, black against the sun. Then gravity started it tumbling downward, Duke and I and the Caffreys and the other forwards charging beneath it, clods of dirt flying, wild eyed with panic like we were all escaping from a fire.

Mitch waved off his teammates and called for the ball. Just as it arrived, dropping into his arms like a bomb, Iain Caffrey and Duke slammed into him, the ground shuddering beneath the impact. My momentum took me past them, leaning hard, digging in my cleats, and as I swung back in their direction Mitch and Duke exploded with punches, rolling on the turf, the ball lying there like a huge egg abandoned in the grass. The referee blew the whistle and retrieved the ball, ignoring them.

"Save it, lads," he said, twisting his heel into the turf to mark the spot where a scrum would restart play. Blood dripped down the side of Mitch's face and Duke's nose looked broken. The referee only shrugged and drew both teams up to the mark he had made. He was an old Irishman with a piece missing from his ear and plenty of scars. "That's the way the game is played, gentlemen," he said. "It's not cricket, now is it?"

"Ready. Ready. *Now!*" came the call, and the scrum collided with the thump of bone on bone. Grunts and hoarse breathing echoed in my ears. In a deep crouch, poised on one leg, and beset by fifteen large men who were all heaving and pushing, my job was to sweep the ball backward with my foot. But the Jacksonville forwards had me in a bad position: my ribs were caving in from the pressure and I could barely move. Then Surfer slid the ball into the tunnel between the two packs and Mitch hooked it away from us. A snicker came from somewhere among the other team.

Play began again at a frantic pace, and immediately I was in oxygen debt, my heart pounding, the field and the blue sky and goalposts whirling in a chaotic stream of colors, mixed with the distorted unintelligible sounds coming from the sidelines. The entire scene whipped by at an incredible speed, blurry and foreign. Then my perception sharpened to a fine razor point, and I could hear something their fullback was saying over thirty yards away, or the ball would float by and MADE IN ENGLAND would be legible on the side even though the print was tiny.

Breathing became a focal point of the game, in and out, my body somehow reduced to a pair of lungs and the tunnel of vision that widened and narrowed with each new segment of the action, each new breath.

It was bloodthirsty. Runners came into tackles with their elbows and knees high, and punches were thrown whenever the referee's back was turned. We managed to break through their first line of defense a couple of times, but not very far, and before we could link up with each other and spin the ball out for the second phase of the attack, a near melee would break out.

"A very unpleasant bunch of lads," said the referee, breaking up a scuffle between Steve Delong and two of their players.

I got hit in the temple by somebody's knee, and everything went black for an instant. The ref asked me my name and where I was, and then let me continue. At the center of my vision things decelerated into dreamy waves. Images on the periphery were ruffled into points and I found myself drifting above the field at times. Then Mitch punched me in the face when I was on the ground, my adrenaline went soaring, and I played the best rugby of my life. I won all my scrums, all my throw-ins, stomped on arms and legs, and ran fifty yards to save a try by sliding on a loose ball.

There was no score at halftime. Josh brought water to us and Van Valkenburg stalked out to midfield like an angry God, the white-haired Messiah of rugby.

"This is bullshit," he said. "Don't spend the rest of your life regretting what you didn't do for forty minutes." Beyond the fairgrounds was a row of houses, with only a few shrubs or a metal toolshed to distinguish them. "There's people on the other side of that fence who would cut off their right arm to win a championship. They're out in the garage right now painting birdhouses. Or watching golf on tee vee. They're not willing to make the sacrifice. That's why you're here—" he pointed toward the row of tract houses "—and those guys are out there."

"We've got to pick it up," said Delong. He was lean and dirty and pacing like a tiger. "No guts, no glory."

"All out," said Iain Caffrey, shaking his fist.

I glanced over at the sidelines and Viv was there, dressed in tight blue jeans, an oversize leather jacket, and tiny boots, her hair in a shiny cascade over her shoulder. She waved and Surfer caught my arm. "Save it, lover boy," he said.

Shortly after halftime, Steve Delong made a fifty yard penalty kick to give us the lead, 3-0. Jacksonville came right back, camping near our goal line for several agonizing minutes. The tackling was vicious and there were four scrums in a row. Before the last one, with my heart hammering and my lungs on fire, I said, "Come on, fellas. We love this shit."

I stepped through the knot of players and slung my arms over the props' shoulders. The two packs slammed together, jarring my vision, and then the ball came skittering into the tunnel and I struck with my right foot, heeling it toward the back of our scrum. I could smell the grass at my feet; it was like manure. Edelstein pounced on the ball when it shot out of the scrum, tossed it to Delong, and he booted it downfield.

Racing after the kick, I could sense Vivian in the crowd, somehow glowing in my mind's eye. The ball skipped on the turf and I grabbed it. With a feint toward the inside, legs churning, I swung behind a moving wall of players, then burst forward again and made a behind-the-back pass—it was at this instant that I seemed to hear Viv call out "Nice one, Joe"—and Steve Delong caught the pass and darted in for the score. I was flying, I was soaring, over the hardpan of the field without an ounce of effort, my mind almost ashamed of what my body had just done. Arms outstretched, I ran toward the middle of the park, never more in love with the world and the things and people in it than I was at that instant. I was airborne.

Delong's kick was good and we went ahead, 9-0. For the next few minutes Jacksonville played like berserkers, their rugby deteriorating into madness. They arrived at every breakdown point with their cleats high, fists crashing all around. Since I never could throw much of a punch, I use the thirty-pound hammer of bone attached to the end of my neck. Diving into the red and white jerseys I rammed Mitch with my head, clipping him above the left eye. Momentum drove him over the pile and landed me on top. "I'll fix you up good," he warned, cocking a finger at me.

Supercharged by adrenaline I laughed in his face, looming over him with my most lethal weapon, the human skull. "You're not going to fix anyone up," I said, my eyes boring into his. "You're finished." I rang another head butt off the side of his noggin and he started punching me.

The referee awarded us a penalty and we broke through their lagging defense. Flooding the gap we had created, in sync from hours of practice together, the ball was flicked on from man to man until there was nothing left but open field and Surfer took it the last twenty yards. Fists in the air, we leapt and shouted and ran in every direction over the plush green grass. Steve Delong jumped into my arms and we fell to the ground.

"We did it, motherfucker," he cried. "We're the champs, baby. We're the fucking champs."

Another try before the final whistle made it 21-0. The sideline erupted with cheers, and, passing by me, the referee leaned close and said, "You did a yeoman's work out there today, son."

My teammates were jumping around and screaming and hugging each other. Josh shook up cans of beer and sprayed them on us, tears coming to his eyes. "I kill you all for free," he said.

Surfer and Edelstein and Duke Ritter and Martin. The Caffreys, like two friendly giants, and Special Ed and Delong and Sporadic Violence Bob. During those few moments I saw the best in them, youth and charm and optimism, the expression of every single thing they had ever wanted to celebrate. If you bottled it, you could last through any mundane future that might lie ahead. The horror of nonexistence meant nothing when you were dancing under the Florida sun.